TOKIO
WHIP

TOKIO WHIP

a novel by
ARTURO SILVA

Stone Bridge Press • *Berkeley, California*

Published by
Stone Bridge Press
P. O. Box 8208, Berkeley, CA 94707
TEL 510-524-8732 • sbp@stonebridge.com • www.stonebridge.com

"Tokio Whip: Warp 'n' Woof," a helpful appendix to this book and a guide to its creation and understanding, is available at the publisher's website, www.stonebridge.com.

Front cover photograph courtesy of Yoshiichi Hara.

Printed in the United States of America.

p-ISBN: 978-1-61172-033-4
e-ISBN: 978-1-61172-922-1

CONTENTS

Lang hadn't wanted to come to Tokyo; but once he got here – well.

Roberta was already here, you know; she'd lived in America, had done Europe, she and Lang, they were going nowhere standing still and falling – he couldn't see it – she needed a change – there was a job available – here – maybe: and so she came.

Lang never wanted to come here; he had a passing, a professional interest in Japan, but winters get pretty gray in Vienna, or so I'm told, and the few letters from Roberta only added to things being that much more up in the air, too far for his comfort and he couldn't abide that couldn't abide being the vague-gray Lang at a loose end, and so he had to find out, to settle all one way or another – and so he came.

Roberta'd been here six months; she was feeling comfortable here, feeling herself, making her own way; as for Lang's imminent arrival she was ambivalent, curious and felt I suppose she didn't really have a choice but to "welcome" him, put him up for a while, see what developed – and so he got the little living room – until he up and left.

Lang didn't even pay attention to Tokyo at first, he wanted something from Roberta but it wasn't coming; and then he simply didn't like her life here, didn't like where she was living, somewhere between Shinjuku and Nakano and Yoyogi, "honcho" no less, he called it "nondescript" and she said yes, yes she thought it was wonderful for having no character, and one simply doesn't say something like that to Lang, no way, and anyway, after all, he'd brought all his Euro-baggage and had no idea what he was getting into and she already into it, she was settled, the woman was moving she was becoming a real Tokyoite – and then besides, he didn't like her friends. Oh, and the party.

It wasn't easy but eventually Roberta had to ask Lang to leave and he was glad to, glad to get out, glad to get away from her for a while at least, at least to clear the air; so he found himself a place in Kichijoji, which he didn't like either, all those foreigners, the discomfort of the easy living of it all, he thought (at first), at first he thought he'd be west of everything she or at least her Tokyo represented, but eventually, soon enough really, he came to like it, came to praise the place's "charms" as he said – god he can be so condescending! – he came to see something of what all she'd been telling him: ha!, Lang came to like Tokyo – Tokyo was alright.

So there was Lang in Kichijoji, and enjoying it; it wasn't Roberta's Tokyo and so it felt like a kind of truce; she had no interest in the west, and so Lang could feel like a pioneer, he'd made his discovery – and then she made her move – it wasn't against him so much as it was for herself, she'd found a place she could finally call "home" – she moved to the low city, you know, the old city – nothing could have surprised Lang more, but Roberta was happy really, happy, she loved her new/old Tokyo – Roberta'd made her last move.

CHAPTER 8. TAKADANOBABA–MEJIRO 199

Lang came to love Kichijoji, but it was only his own, he felt only more distant from Roberta, isolated, and after all he'd come here for her for them to see how or what they were, what they were going to do and there she was an hour's train ride away and she happy rarely leaving her home her neighborhood – and so he became jealous of it all, jealous of the city for what it had done to her – had done to him.

CHAPTER 9. IKEBUKURO–OTSUKA 231

Roberta's Tokyo – they'd meet once or twice a week, she chose the places, the classical café in Nakano, tempura at the Hilltop Hotel – you know, the writer's hotel – they carefully avoided anything further West and … and eventually they extended their borders, began to explore Nishi-Ogikubo, Kokubunji – and he began to explore the city more, both directions, came to be intrigued as she'd known he would and hoped he would, the Lang she knew, the Lang she suspected – Lang, liking almost all of Tokyo, her Tokyo, hers his.

CHAPTER 10. SUGAMO–KOMAGOME 258

Lang was changing, it was clear to us all, and Roberta liked it, liked this Lang, a Lang she'd always suspected; and Lang liked her: she was an unsuspected Roberta, a neglected Roberta, and a Roberta she too acknowledged she had neglected … a Lang and a Roberta they both needed to know, to acknowledge, and more – a Roberta he'd long refused to see and one he now had no choice but – but for now they stay united on separate sides of the city – they have no choice but.

CHAPTER 11. NISHI-NIPPORI–NIPPORI 291

And then Lang had to return to Vienna for a few months, there was no choice, an unfinished job, a previous commitment, I forget what but there was no choice – we all felt sorry about it, not knowing what would develop – Roberta seemed to take it alright, and I emphasize the "seem" –

apparently they wrote and spoke regularly ... but she was never sure if he'd return – and then she surprised us all, she visited him, they got away and were together – wherever they were .

Roberta returned to Tokyo; Lang finished his work – there it is – here they are!

NOTE

Many Japanese names occur in the course of this novel. Most are either people or place names, or the names of things such as food items or pieces of clothing. The reader really need not worry about their pronunciation or meaning – some will be familiar, some are explained in passing, others are not. However, two do require some orientation. *Yamanote*, commonly called "The High City," is that westward area arcing around Shinjuku, and traditionally the wealthier and more modern side of the city. *Shitamachi*, or The Low City, is the older, more plebian and traditional side of the city, arcing east around the Imperial Palace and extending as far as and beyond the Sumida River. In this book they are also often opposed as the East and West sides of the city – but even those distinctions are questioned, as the reader will see. Yamanote is also the name of the train line that makes a loop around most of the central wards of the city (though not the entire city) – embracing both *yamanote* and *shitamachi*, twenty-nine stations in all, but here reduced to twenty-four. This Yamanote is what is referred to by the titles of the chapters that comprise Parts One A and B of the book.

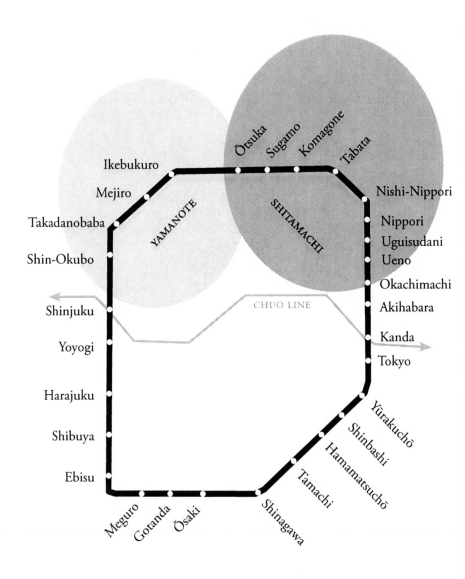

The Yamanote Line makes a loop through downtown Tokyo, traversing the High City (Yamanote) and Low City (Shitamchi).

TOKIO WHIP

Tokyo is a city where one learns to gaze only at the immediate prospect, blotting out what lies beyond.

— Edward G. Seidensticker

Outside and inside abolished, talk can now begin: at last, at last the dialogue.

— Julio Cortázar

Our language can be seen as an ancient city: a maze of little streets and squares, of old and new houses, and of houses with additions from various periods; and this surrounded by a multitude of new boroughs with straight regular streets and uniform houses.

— Ludwig Wittgenstein, *Philosophical Investigations*, I, 18

We drink coffee with cream while suspended over the abyss.

— Andrei Bely

It's funny how some things make you think of other things.

— Carole Lombard

PART ONE (A)

THE YAMANOTE

Chapter 1

KANDA–TOKYO

Lang hadn't wanted to come to Tokyo; but once he got here – well.

we began walking somewhere around sunset

– Hey! This building wasn't here yesterday.

across the city

– Say it again: the two most beautiful words: sunset, –

to Shinjuku and Roberta's party around Midnight

– Better lost in Tokyo than found in any other city.

and then further west, talking our way

into the

Sun-

r
i
s
e
!

* * *

Rich and strange, strange and rich, Marianne muses, and once more rich and strange. Oh, Tokyo, damn you! Where am I? Here, yes, and one more step – there. Now I'm here, now there. Rich and strange you are, Marianne, a here and there myself. Bless you, Tokyo. Walking in step like a waking dream. A girl in her dreams talking to herself.

* * *

- Oh, comeon, it's not modern at all, all this brick, that wood. And look at those dives right under the tracks, that *yakuza*-type over there eyeing me – what a racket!
- Still, if we can stay steady –
- As she goes!
- On yer feet!
- Aye aye, Sir!
- Tokyo Station should be just ahead.

But Hiromi does not "stay steady," thinks a detour will help, and though the tracks are generally still in sight, she and her friends have lost their way. She stares in the window of a shop selling medical equipment – all of it made of glass.

- Orange Card, IO card, and why "SF Metro" card? – this isn't San Francisco.
- And mine's all run out, now it really looks like we have to walk.
- Well, try to enjoy yourself, Dear.
- Eh?
- That's what my Granny used to tell me every morning when I left for school.
- Let's see, she says, as she finds the page in her compact Tokyo map-book. This must be that real old bridge; homeless people sleeping there now around all these banks. My city!
- And mine!
- Mine too!

* * *

Tanizaki's Dream: Orderly thoroughfares, shining, newly-paved streets, a flood of cars, blocks of flats rising floor upon floor, level on level in geometric beauty, and threading through the city elevated lines, subways, street cars. (But see also Tanizaki on Asakusa: "Its constant and peerless richness preserved even as it furiously changes in nature and in its ingredients, swelling and clashing in confusion and then fusing into harmony.")

* * *

Van Zandt is himself, that is, as he is now, though in the dream he is back in high school in Amsterdam, where he sees a classmate, Jenny, blonde and thin, whom he wishes he were not too shy to approach. (VZ often has this dream, and it is the one he hates most, because it reminds him of that long period that no one would ever guess now when he was shy and inarticulate, and rarely spoke to a female.) He sees the school auditorium; it is the night of the senior prom (and this scene looks as if it were taken from an American teenage genre film ((VZ in fact never attended any such dance; in fact, had never even known of the thing till he saw *Carrie*.))) The prom goes on, people dancing, and Van Zandt feels lonely. Then all the girls are told to get on stage. It's time for "boy's choice," instead of the usual "ladies' choice." VZ asks Jenny to dance. They walk away (however much one would think the occasion demanded a dance). She takes his hand. They walk out of the auditorium and in the dark alley she stops and kisses him. He is surprised. They are walking through Akitsu, in Kiyose, in northeastern Tokyo, just there at the border with Saitama Prefecture. There are white box houses with pink motorcycles for Mom and that always mean the suburbs. The suburbs, a Frankenstein for the 1990s, with the rent of a 4LDK two-thirds of a 1LDK just west of the Yamanote. On a wall someone has spray painted the title of a favorite song "*kimi ni mune kyun kyun*" by YMO. There is much greenery, a clear stream – he sees fish in it as he peers from Maebara Bridge. And then in the dream where he sees the long rows of houses that look like military barracks (did he live in one once, see them in a home movie? ((these are private plots))), he sees a map made of books, and in a park public art the likes of which one does not usually see in Tokio: a "Peace Monument" (Showa 49), abstract, steps, two monoliths almost meeting as if hands closed in prayer. VZ and Jenny go to the house of some friends. They are no longer in high-school, but as they are now – or as he is and she as how he dreams of a girl whom he hasn't seen in fifteen years. Jenny takes him into a corner and kisses him, forcefully, deeply. Her hand reaches down and grabs his crotch. Then Van Zandt is walking swiftly, muttering to himself, "How could this happen? How could my trip be so suddenly cancelled?" It is another city, another time. He walks into his home; the entire family is there, but everyone is busy and so they ignore him. (Throughout this last scene his siblings are as they are now, and all scurrying about the room.) VZ's mother appears. Her hair is cut very short (like Falconetti's, but that's where any resemblance ends). She rushes up to her son, sobbing, "Why do they all say I'm guilty? What have I done? I'm not guilty. I swear. You believe me, don't you?" And then VZ awakes.

In the background of VZ's dream, as in the following dream, he hears the black death lyrics of Howlin' Wolf: "Smokestack Lightnin' shines like gold / I found my baby layin' on the cooling board // Don't you hear me talkin' Pretty Mama // Don't the hearse look lonesome rollin' 'fore your door / She's gone – oowhoo – won't be back no more."

In Kazuo's dream he is walking in Akitsu, turns, and there is a valley, and a river below. A group of people are happily swimming, gamboling. They are all strong swimmers, and the image is an almost ideal one of human physical grace. There are some steps, a large rock, a bridge down-river. It is a short, idyllic dream. And then Kazuo wakes.

* * *

Kazuyoshi Miura: Murder in the Media

With very few exceptions – most notably the Abe Sada story of 1936, known to most people through Nagisa Oshima's film *In the Realm of the Senses* (1976), and the Imperial Bank Robbery of 1948 – murder in Twentieth Century Tokyo has been an unexciting affair. In recent years there have been the usual sushi-knife slashings, the occasional dismembered body parts (in one case, in thirty-four separate bags just around the corner from the author's home), and the fortunately more rare true horror story (infanticide, cannibalism). One pop star ("idol") did throw herself off of a building – to include suicide for a moment – after being jilted by another singer; that may have been "romantic" of her, but the jilter himself was so uninteresting, so predictably "cute," hardly worth the adolescent gesture. Even with the brief wave of copycats, that story too soon lost public interest. A much more talented singer, Yutaka Ozaki, took a few pills too many one night mixed with too much alcohol and was found in the street next day near his home – no, contemporary murder has little glamour and less imagination these days in Tokyo.

Perhaps the most interesting modern murder was that of Kazumi Miura, a murder that was allegedly set up by her husband Kazuyoshi.

While having some interesting complications, the case is especially compelling for the huge role the media played in it – or roles, for it has doted on Kazuyoshi Miura as much as he has courted it; it has also been attacked by him in court; and eventually it was the media – or one of its representatives – that cracked the case open. The story of Kazuyoshi Miura is a particularly relevant tale for our times.

Los Angeles, November 18, 1981. The clothes importer Kazuyoshi Miura, age 34, and his wife of two years, Kazumi, 28, are on their "second honeymoon" in Los Angeles. (The Miura's have a young daughter.) While taking photos in a parking lot – Miura will claim he just happened to spot a possible advertising location – Kazumi is robbed and shot in the head, and her husband in the leg. Kazumi falls into a permanent coma, and two months later returns to Japan. Within a year of the shooting she dies. Despite some suspicions, the Los Angeles Police Department is helpless – no evidence, no suspects.

On March 31, 1994, Miura, by now 46, is sentenced to life imprisonment for conspiring to murder his wife. He is so judged on circumstantial evidence, the judge saying that it is "logical to assume" that Miura was the mastermind behind the death of Kazumi. The judge describes Miura as being "selfish and cold-blooded," a man who has shown no signs of remorse over the death of his wife.

The murder plot was simple enough; Miura is said to have hired an employee to do the job, including shooting Miura himself. Miura's testimony however was shot through with holes (if we may be pardoned the expression). To take only one important example: Miura claimed that the assailants fled in a green car; witnesses of the scene – though not of the murder – saw only a white van. The suspected assailant had hired a white van the day before the murder.

Miura is also believed to have made two other attempts on Kazumi's life before his final success. Three months earlier in Los Angeles, Miura had asked a former mistress and porno actress to kill Kazumi in Tokyo in August 1981 by bludgeoning her with a hammer. The actress did so, but Kazumi recovered. He is also supposed to have asked two former employees to kill Kazumi.

With Kazumi's death, Miura collected one hundred-fifty million yen in insurance money.

Apart from the details, Kazumi Miura, sadly, is lost in the story. The murder was one thing; the "follow-up" was another.

Crimes involving Japanese abroad are big news in Japan. While still in Los Angeles, Miura was holding interviews with the press from his hospital bed. He was an immediate media favorite and national hero for the fortitude with which he bore his pain and loss. Like a good Japanese, he even sent letters to President Ronald Reagan, the Governor of California, the Mayor of Los Angeles and the U. S. Ambassador to Japan decrying the violence of the American way of life. He even had photos of his daughter distributed, bearing the caption, "Give Me My Mommy Back!".

For two years Miura was off scot-free (and rich). In the autumn of 1983, thanks to a tip concerning the insurance payment, a team of reporters from the weekly magazine *Shukan Bunshun* began to investigate him. The following January it ran a series of articles detailing Miura's past, which included: three marriages; seven years in prison for more than one hundred petty robberies; assorted other crimes (arson, assault, possession of a sword); and the story of a former employee and lover who had suddenly "disappeared" after having received 4.3 million yen in a divorce settlement. (The money had been taken out of her account shortly after she had "left the job" in March 1979; her body was later found in May 1979 in Los Angeles).

The police reopened the case.

The articles were called "Bullets of Suspicion." Miura responded with a book called "Bullets of Information." From then on there was no let up. Articles and interviews flowed back and forth. Miura courted as much as he evaded the media. It was a mutual affair. He was said to have charged anywhere from five to fifty million yen per interview. He signed an exclusive contract with one television network to film his latest marriage – he was engaged within six months of Kazumi's death – in Bali in April 1985. He even played himself in a movie. As one Los Angeles detective remarked, Miura was "pouring gasoline on the fire."

Finally in September 1985 Miura and the porno actress/would-be murderess were arrested for the August 1981 murder attempt. The arrest was broadcast live on television. (As many arrests are in Japan, the police tipping the media off shortly before.) The woman confessed. (She received two-and-one-half years.) In May 1987 Miura was finally sentenced to six years. In October 1988, after further investigations by the LAPD, Miura was charged in Tokyo with the murder of Kazumi. (So too was his accomplice, the man in the white van who did the actual shooting. He was eventually acquitted for insufficient evidence.) Now the Miura-media tug-of-war grew in fury. He began to sue newspapers and magazines for libel. And not only did he defend himself, he usually won. He even sued one paper for writing that he sued too often! By summer 1994 he was involved in 230 different suits. Of the first hundred cases, of which he won seventy, he was awarded more than thirty-three million yen in damages.

Unrepentant and litigious to the end, Miura blames all his misfortunes on the very media whose willing darling for a time he was.

* * *

Yes, I believe it's perfectly alright if he loves the city as he says he does. Who am I to doubt him, or to deny him? No love can be judged. I can't agree with Roberta, for example, who simply calls him "mad." But then perhaps she is intending a pun. I don't know, but in this case I do doubt. No, I only wonder what the nature of his love is (again, without in any way judging it). It can, after all, be as rough a city as it can be a tender one. And we know that while he usually treats us all rather fairly – I really have few complaints, and most of those small – he can, well, have his moods. But can his love match the city, then? Can his love be strong, consistent over the years and adapt to the changes that must inevitably occur? Is he a faithful partner? (He does say this has been his most successful relationship – his relationship with the city, that is.) Is he capable, by my standards, of loving the city lightly, softly? It does seem to me sometimes that he is a bit too aggressive in his declarations of love, as if he were afraid of any doubt making itself known. Perhaps even an unconscious doubt. He seems occasionally to press his love, to forward his suit, to crush the city to his heart. Well, we shall see. In the meantime, too, the evidence of his love lies all about us. – So the kindly Kazuo.

* * *

Hiromi and friends had begun somewhere around sunset, somewhere east of Kanda, on the way to Roberta's. They finally made it to Tokyo Station without too much discomfort. Then to Marunouchi where she sometimes worked at the Palace Hotel.

- Ohh, give me the huddled homeless 'stead of all these three-piecers.
- So, this is where they all come from, eh?
- All those banks we just walked past, rich Japan – ecch!
- Bricks for brains.
- Yeah, but some of 'em are gold-bricks.
- No way!
- Sure, why do you think they call us rich?
- Whadda'ya' mean, call us rich? I ain't rich, you ain't rich.

- I mean we Japanese.
- We Japanese?
- Ok, the country.
- But the station is kinda' nice, you can take a bath after watching a porno movie. And it's made out of brick. Kind of Euro-looking.
- Gee, just think of it too, the old man – just over there – asleep for a thousand years –
- No, that's that monk guy on Koya-san.
- Whatever, still the Emperor …
- ???
- … asleep, I tell you, for a thousand years. Strange family.
- Yeah, and all that money.
- And he can't spend it! It's all locked up somewhere.
- Him too – locked up at home.
- Hey, Michiko-san!
- Yeah, Michiko-san, wanna play tennis with us?
- Hey, Michiko? Comeon out and play!
- Oh, why doesn't she answer?
- Who's that knocking?
- Go away! Go away!
- We'll blow your door down!
- Michiko!
- Michiko-o-o-!
- Think of it, guys, we're just walking around here, lighting cigarettes, making stupid talk, and Michiko's over there all alone –
- – trying on her hats.
- One after the other.
- Hat after hat.
- All of 'em the same.
- But to her, don't ya' think, they're all different?
- Could be.
- Do you think she knows how to rumba?
- Michiko-o-o-o-o-!

* * *

Jeez (VZ thinks to himself), they just pee all over the place. There's this lady in my neighborhood, everyday, the same time she takes her dog out for a walk. They always stop at the same spot, she lays some tissue down on the sidewalk, the dog shits on it, she wraps it up, puts it in a plastic bag, puts that back in her purse, and walks the dog home. Really,

I've seen it. I also saw a woman jack her dog off once. And you've heard about how mothers relieve their sons when they're tense about their exams? A-fucking-mazing. Jeez.

* * *

The Way

clouds are torn
a skirt is worn
sentences form

live near the sea;
sleep before sunrise

* * *

"What is this shit? This movie isn't moving!"

And thus Roberta created the great wall in her relation with Van Zandt. For two or three years they'd talked at least three or four times a week about his Tokyo film. She'd seen him overcome every financial and linguistic disadvantage that the city could offer; seen him hire his small staff (the photographer's assistant who took the lead, and whom he never touched); helped him choose the twelve select sites; had even provided him with his title. And tonight he was finally showing the film. He'd chosen a small gallery in Yanaka, wanted to be near the River and away from the uptown artsy crowd. Many friends had come, plus the few art and film people he respected in Tokyo. And then her shout, exactly thirty-six minutes into the 144-minute film. He shut the projector off, mumbled an angry apology-cum-explanation ("The point is that the excitement of the city is in the stillness of the images, the man, the woman and their location in the various sites are both a praise and a critique of the city") – and made his exit. Roberta and Van Zandt didn't speak again for a month. No one could intercede. She felt horrible, of course, but stood her ground – "The film really was not interesting. I only wanted to excite him, to make him go further; really, he could have done so much more. That wasn't a city he'd filmed, it was two machines – three if you include the city," she explained herself too late. When they did meet again, he smiled her apology away. They didn't speak of the film again, or what new project he might be working on.

And work on he did. Stealthy, alone. (The photographer's assistant stayed enlisted, however. She was beautiful in that early 80s Tokyo sort of way, that slow, smooth walk; that curt pout that belied a real friendliness; that readiness to help on any experiment.) He remade the film, all of it, new locations, new setups; it was the same film as before but different, new. It premiered in Amsterdam, and then made the circuit of competitions and festivals. He figured she'd come across an article about it someday, and then the regrets would flow – and the pride, and friendship, restored. And so it came to be. (And she did see it when it played six weeks at Euro-Space.)

He called it

Guys and Dolls
A VZ Film

It's shot in black and white on color stock. It's stark, radiant (bright blue and gold aureoles around some images), sometimes bursting into flames at frames' edges, the film falling apart as it reassembles itself, with briefly caught glimpses of texts and maps in the background. The story may be about a woman trying to find a man in some buildings; or a conversation among friends (the only dialogue in the film, and in color); or maybe it's about sexual (re)union; or even possibly irreparable separation and the impossibility of union and conversation. Or maybe it's just about two people walking around the city, looking at this or that building. But it is Tokyo –VZ's Tokyo – Tokyo as film.

The "story" is simple enough. As is the structure: twelve scenes, each twelve shots and minutes, preceded by a brief prologue, and with an interlude between scenes Six and Seven. But this structure is not so very strict, as there seem to be some "miscellania," unaccountable items scattered about that at first mislead the viewer, but are in fact a somewhat charming chaos that alleviates the order.

PROLOGUE

We see the feet and hands of people on a not very crowded train at about two in the afternoon; glimpses of magazines, of dozing heads at shoulders; print advertisements all about, flapping in the train's aisle; the soundtrack is the regular rhythm of a Tokyo train, like the sound of any Ozu train. A station name is called; the train comes to a halt. We see the torso of a man (somehow we recognize that he is a foreigner) suddenly jerk awake, he quickly gets off the train, leaves the frame, and we see in his now abandoned seat, a large, black portfolio. Cut to a Japanese woman, slightly tall (by Japanese standards), dressed in a black Commes des Garçons suit with white blouse; short, bobbed hair; a round face, big cheeks. an almost childish face but for her eyes that speak experience. Her movements are lithe and determined. About 27 years old, she has had some experience of Europe, and is not wary of foreigners. She quickly reaches for the portfolio and then calls to the man ("Excuse me!", we see her lips say), but too late, the doors have closed. She opens the B-4 size portfolio, leafs through the black and white photographs quickly – twelve photographs of twelve different buildings, or Tokyo "sites" – notices there is no address or further identification, but seems to recognize most of the places, and then – close-up – makes a determined face: she will find her man!

The camera slowly zooms in on the first photograph.

SCENE ONE: RIKUGIEN GARDEN

The Woman enters the garden, after losing her way somewhat. Left or right? It is obviously one of those gardens that requires a certain knowledge of the Chinese classics. With its wayward paths, its "empty center," hills and valleys, and its ease and immediacy, it is like a miniature and metaphor of Tokyo: if the city were a garden, she thinks, it would be Rikugien. It offers refuge – a bench; transport – some stepping stones; memory – elderly couples; plus an occasional sight of the buildings and madness just outside. She crosses the thin stream of legend, reads the old poem ("wakasekogakubekiyoinarisasaga ..."), sheds a wistful tear (she has a grasp of the classics) – and knows that she is alone. It's closing time; the attendant tells her that a "tall, foreign gentleman" has just left.

* * *

And then I thought to myself of those many unexpected signs – a chance meeting, an appointment cancelled, a woman's rejection in so few words – and time is given, restored, a surprise and display of something quick and solid; the path redirected, honest now – I never expected the meeting, was unprepared for the appointment, didn't really want the woman – and for a moment joy, an opportunity, as if I have been promised something more now, and the path is that much more – just a bit, but oh so much! – opened. And I stop and wonder to myself, am I equal?

* * *

The costs of confusion notwithstanding, Arlene thinks, where did I read that? Someone complained that the city seemed to be built like a cow's wandering path. Hey, that isn't unnatural. Don't all our footsteps trace the pattern of the universe or spell the name of god or something? I'll take the cow's path anytime. I know my way around. The city milks me.

* * *

All she knew. She knew he loved her, she loved him, and love was strong. Wasn't it?

Hiroko tells him, "My head is not a hatstand."

A new alliance, the trembling widow. Her wing, her heart, her hair.

* * *

Where oh where oh? And with whom and when oh? So deeply ponders Hiro. How long – that's the easy part. I had to fight for the extra three days. Fight? Hey, I surrendered; that many more hours come October. Well, it'll be worth it. Bye-bye Tokyo. But where? One of the islands? Guam or Okinawa, Thailand, Bali. I guess they're pretty used to Japanese tourists, so I shouldn't have too many problems. The beaches, the bungalows. And those enormous Germans and Australians. People wonder how *sumo* wrestlers do it – they should ask how *two* sumo wrestlers do it, that's what those couples look like. Australia, that's an idea. Maybe a whole week on a beach, no matter how much sex. Besides, the islands aren't known for their clothes boutiques. Hmm, maybe Australia. Nice cities and beaches, I hear. But Australian women, I don't know. Pretty big women; noisy too. And all that hair, like Americans. They might think me small. Of course, some older women like young guys. Fifty-fifty. No, when you come down to it, our own *yamato-nadeshiko* really are the best, the true Japanese girl. Neat hair, nice clothes, and they don't mind serving a guy no matter how unruly he is. And those huge cans of beer. Maybe another time, when I have a girl to go with and who speaks English. "Gu'dai!" Maybe better, Hawaii. It's half Japanese anyway, and then I wouldn't have to worry about speaking English. I'd better think about that too, otherwise I'm never gonna get anywhere in this company, no matter who my father is. Hawaii, sure. Beaches, girls, good shopping: Japanese!

* * *

- Hmmm ...
- ... mmm ...
- They really are nice ...
- Yes, yes they are.
- Ohhh ...
- Hm?
- Oh, it would be so nice if they could stay together.
- Hmm ...
- Wouldn't it?
- Yes, of course.
- If *they* could – then who could ever be apart?
- Hm?
- If they could, who could ever be apart?
- You mean –?
- Hm, I just mean that, well, I wish they could stay together, and then I'd feel better about ...
- About?
- Oh, you know – any one of us ...
- Us?
- Mm!
- And if they don't, or can't?
- Hm. Well, we all try all the harder then.
- All?
- Of course.
- Then let's hope ...
- That's what I've been saying –
- Oh.
- But, I mean it – really hope – for all of us. After all ...
- After all?
- We're all a part of it; after all, they, Roberta and Lang, love us – and we love them.
- Us?
- Oh, Kazuo! We can't abandon them. Nor we one another.
- You mean ...?
- No, I don't – you should see what I mean.
- Sorry ... You're right.
- ?
- But I don't.
- It doesn't matter. The important thing is that no one abandons any-

one in this. We are together; I see it now – radiantly – even if no one else does. And that's all I have to say.
- That's all?
- Well, not quite. I must speak with Marianne – oh, she is so odd! – but lucid in her way. She's told me so much already. For example, did you know this?
- What?
- *Lang hadn't wanted to come to Tokyo; but once he got here – well.*
- No, really?
- Yes. Marianne told me. Roberta and Van Zandt have also, sort of, said similar things.
- Yes, he certainly behaves it sometimes.
- Yes, but he did come here – for her sake, or at least that of their relationship – he did come here, let's not forget that.
- Yes.
- Yes – we have a lot of work to do.
- Oh?
- Yes – the work we have to do, Kazuo, if successful, should bring and keep us all together. *My sweet embraceable* ... In the meantime ...
- Yes? No, I know: to work! Oh, what an odd couple!
- Kazu – I thought you were fond of them?
- I'm referring to ourselves, Kazuko.
- But –
- Oh, here you talk of the foreigners' shenanigans, and ... What did Van Zandt tell me once? That Americans have to be reminded every twelve hours that they are loved; and we Japanese say it once and it's supposed to last forever.
- And you can't stand that? Well, my man, as even Arlene would say, you're going to have to take it like a man. Ohh, what ever's happened to my speech? No, I don't mean that, of course. If it weren't for my foreign friends I feel sometimes I'd leave next time for good – back to Kyoto – or to Lang's Vienna.
- Ah, Kazuko, your "always elegant speech is only enlivened by the occasional slip into the vernacular."
- ?
- It is one of your "charm points."
- I hope you don't expect me to say naughty things in bed!
- No, Dear, I do not. Another drink?
- You have one. I'll have a coffee.
- So what shall we do?
- What do you mean? I just decided to have another drink, and you

a coffee.

- No, silly, I'm referring to your plan to fix the universe in a permanent state of love.
- Oh, stop it now. ... Well, we just, uhn, we ... why, we ... establish ourselves in a state of benign benevolence! And, uhm ...
- Ohh, it sounds very easy, very clear, my General. Our divine love sets an example for all to emulate. Our divine, platonic love, I might add. Ha!, our example would lead the human race to extinction.
- Kazuo! Living with my aunt is not conducive to ...
- Kazuko: the city provides means.
- Means that I do not, uhn, that I ...uhn ...
- Too high-bred, eh? Well, what if I rented a tea ceremony room?
- Oh, Kazu, stop it. I'm sorry. And stop that high-bred talk, please. You know that I'm not, and that that's not the reason.
- But you are, and yes, I am sorry. I just wish we had more time – time alone, I mean.
- Oh, Dear, we have time, will have ...
- I know. Anyway, back to our benevolent society.
- Yes. Well ... uhm, well, why we just – oh, you know what to do! We talk, we take walks. Oh, maybe I am being unrealistic, "as unrealistic as Shakespeare," as Marianne might say, but I believe that, that ...
- That our love for each other and our love for them shall lead them into loving one another again.
- Well, I'd hardly put it into a formula, but yes, something like that.
- Easily done. Perhaps we should start by taking advantage of the city's provisions.
- Ka – ... perhaps that wouldn't hurt –
- And perhaps it might.
- Kazuo! I mean that it might help.
- It certainly shall. Finish up.
- I already have. I've been waiting for you.
- Kazuko?!

* * *

Fifty, sixty, seventy years old, the red and white ribbons get larger, the magnifying glasses and rulers more useful, he's the third man to thank everyone for taking time out from their busy schedules, to congratulate the happy couple, the graduate, the new president, the budding author, the elected official; the waiters bustling around now, refilling glasses, must be the last speech, getting ready for the toast. Hiroko lights cigarettes, makes polite conversation, giggles when it seems appropriate to do so. Three or four nights a week like this, six to nine, gives her her spending money, though she still hasn't yet mastered her kimono or her hair style. The hotel provides old women to help her get dressed. (The women help young girls too on mornings after so that they'll look just the way they did when they left home when they return home.) She glances across the room, notices Hiromi accepting a namecard; "no wonder she has twice as much money as I do!," Hiroko pouts. Maybe two hours more to go, a quiet night. When she wonders at how smoothly these parties go – a few broken glasses at the most, a foreigner acting silly – they never realize how silly they really are – the whole point is to be polite, to see that nothing goes wrong; it's certainly not to have a good time, to party as a verb – she happily recalls the day when Roberta had called her to help her organize a party she was going to give Lang and VZ. Her husband – was that right? – had been staying with her awhile, and was now going to stay in Japan longer, but on his own; and then there was something about making peace with VZ; she never got that right either. They were passing acquaintances, parts of overlapping circles, she figured Roberta'd noticed her with Van Zandt, knew nothing of her hotel and hostessing job, but called her nonetheless. She said something about getting to know her better, knew she'd grown up in *shitamachi*. Those few days were pleasant, but the subsequent events of the party itself had sort of put a halt – over now, it seemed – to any further friendship. There'd been a lot of coordinating to do, especially of schedules, messages going back and forth, maps – Roberta had made an excellent one, simple, and fun what with the *tofu* and *soba* shops marked – and last-minute phonecalls. She and Roberta together had made the food; the neighborhood liquor store brought over the beer, wine, and *saké*. That certainly didn't help matters, too much too soon, and then another phonecall just before closing time. The day itself was wonderful, uncommonly warm, the windows open and Roberta singing to herself. A mood all too brief.

* * *

Never felt so weak and alone. Went shopping.

"It's hard to fight after a Lubitsch film."

City only feels a bit crowded at rush-hour.

* * *

Ah, this city, Kaoru pauses, thinks to himself, well, you put up with the commute, get to work early and leave late. Thank the gods for the drinking afterwards. Come home, the rice and dinner ready – and the wife, what's-her-name. An occasional screw, for whatever that's worth. Sleep and back to work. Good kids. It's just a city. Have to remember O-Bon.

* * *

- Eyes getting weak – want to see you.
- Damn you.
- Brain getting soft – have to talk.
- Damn.
- The soul freezes over – need to kiss you.
- You.
- Roberta.
- Damn you, Lang.

* * *

R'n'L!

What did my brother say? That in a hundred years if all the numbers continue the same as now, a tenth of the world's population will be Elvis imitators? So the world will become a better place, after all.

Ach, I want to close my eyes and count to twelve and when I re-open 'em all the platform shoes in the world will have disappeared. Be warned: By their shoes shall ye know them.

Yippie! I have found a way to unite the world. Or at least the quotable world. Start with a song, say: "Ashes to ashes, and dust to dust / show me a woman a man can trust / she's gone but I don't worry / 'cos I'm sitting on top of the world." Which leads, of course, to James Cagney in *White Heat*, "Top'a the world, Ma!," which in turn takes us to Dylan, "It's Alright, Ma." Get it? And on and on and on. Wanna play? Anyway, it might cure me of all this constant quoting and name-dropping. But then what happens to all the quotes left out? Do they form a kind of "anti-system," one that cannot be controlled or fit anywhere, all the loose miscellania? (Sounds great.) Does it all ultimately derive from my boyhood reading of Superman?

Anyway, hope your August is as you like it – me, I like it hot as hell.

And my dreams: First there's an hysterical nurse, explaining she's only so 'cos of her recent divorce, and why should everyone blame her? Then the school caretaker – a sort of sad guy whom I always remember; maybe he had a lowly job, but he was getting his daughter a good education – anyway, he comes in and starts shouting, "Goddam Catholics! They say they'll leave but they never really do, the Catholics keep coming back, there's no getting rid of them!" Why now, why back in school, now, just when I thought I was becoming an adult?

Some people want to read all of Dostoevski. I want to see all of Carole Lombard's films. Speaking of CL, you know that great Walker Evans photo – well, I finally found a reference to the film; it sounds ok, but the title apparently has zilch to do with the story.

So, whadda'ya' think – is it a pink city or a gray city? A pink and gray city? A light yellow city (like Baudelaire's gloves – he also had pink ones) or a sky blue city? A pastel city, to be sure. Blue roofs and vegetables. Serious supermarkets playing raggae for BGM. Pink and yellow supermarkets. I stopped wearing green and brown years ago, hate natural colors. Hey, my fave coffee shop – Ada and Eve, you know the one in Jimbocho I call the lesbian café – well, it's gray! And all the gray boutiques in Parco that is a rainbow. The trains might be color-coded but they're all green, like rivers. And kill the freeways that killed the real rivers sez I.

"I Confess" Dept. I have come to think that Tommy James and the Shondells' "Mony Mony" is one of the great jams. "I Need to Know" Dept. What the hell's a "Shondell", anyway?

I gotta show you my fave public phone someday.

I bought a pair of nail clippers today at the cheap Chinese shop on the Spanish Steps. Pink and black and with a green dragon on it.

Met an air-head today. She denied she was one. Isn't that cute?

A thousand cities claim to be my birth-place! Ten thousand women die with my name on their lips!

* * *

ARS AMATORIA / ARS POETICA

For Vicente Aleixandre

1. Being Spanish
   we cross the Bridge of Dreams;
   Japanese,
   we die for we do not.

2. I've read myself blind.
   Aleixandre is dead.
   An unknown woman
   pours too much *saké*.

3. Calderón recites *waka* –
   turns away;
   rice-skinned women
   in red and black.

4. Civil wars persist.
   I take three trains a day,
   a moment of peace – noon –
   an empty café.

* * *

Downtown Hiromi is in her uptown element, Shibuya.

- Here we go.
- Ohh god all the way up this stupid hill just for some cheap Chinese food on ittty bitty plates. And the love hotels over there, "for after the movie" that jerkoff told me. No, for after the Nepalese restaurant – maybe, I told him.
- You mean what's's-name?
- So many accessories for a sexy young girl to buy! I can't seem to can't get enough – of accessories or boys.
- But how little Hiroko spends – one CD and one new accessory a

month? How's a girl gonna get by on so little? I thought she believed in shopping.

– One each a week for me. And the cheaper, at Dai-Chu. Why are Chinese things so cheap? I thought China was a big country.

– Beats me.

– I wonder why Shibuya's so hilly. Is it supposed to be a charm point? If so, it's lost on me. Why don't they just flatten it all out, it'd make the shopping go faster.

– Oh those tanned boys, all tanned so.

– You mean those ones?

– When I used to come here in high-school … well, I guess it was the same. Sort of. All those boys trying to pick us up, and all we could do was giggle. Silly girls we were. Till we gave in! You sort of graduate from shop to shop, from Marui to Parco's basement, then to the upper floors, and then if you're a real lady – guess that count's me out – to Tokyu. But you graduate in price too, count me out, two. It's like a *ramen* bowl. Yup, I'd flatten it all.

– Would you?

– Poor little Hachiko; what did VZ say? – that the story is all made-up, that he wasn't really waiting for his master, poor dead man, poor dog, but that he was really just an unwanted pet looking for some affection, and everyone really hated him. How terrible! Well, then maybe he was better off dead.

* * *

Gangsters in the early morning build the Third New World.

The only intelligent cabbie yet: "Never heard of the place. Let's go."

"Don't cry, please. Here, have a cigarette."

* * *

We may not find happiness, but we have a right to live.
   – Sylvia Sydney, *You Only Live Once* (Fritz Lang, 1937)

* * *

Triumphant, tripartite Tokio, we are one. – Lang to himself.

Chapter 2

YURAKUCHO–SHIMBASHI

Roberta was already here, you know; she'd lived in America, had done Europe, she and Lang, they were going nowhere standing still and falling – he couldn't see it– she needed a change – there was a job available – here – maybe: and so she came.

Cafferty'd spent the morning at the German bakery in Ningyōchō, stocking up on breads and cakes. The *pot au feu* simmered the afternoon; it would be easy later to prepare the *daikon* steak, as well as his favorite, steamed, young eggplant smothered with purple Osaka *miso*. He had a quick sandwich – salmon and tuna, double lettuce, no mayonnaise – and espresso at Doutor, then stopped to pick up some "traditional Japanese ice cream." Home, he cleaned house, an easy job as he was such a neat man, always picking up after himself – and no, the moral irony was never lost on him. He had four wines, two white, two red, and a few beers available in case his guest preferred that. Candles? Why not? At ten minutes to eight he remembered the *genkan*; he hurriedly cleared the area of his shoes and slippers, straightened the umbrellas, made the pile of old newspapers into a neat stack, and just as he was about to place a "fresh" flower (amazingly real-seeming) in the bamboo holder, the bell rang. He froze, could feel the sweat begin, froze again, and then relaxed because he knew it was all a signal that all was well, the old flame held, and it'd be a fine evening after all. He was ready to be witty, sympathetic, obscene, whatever his old friend needed, wanted. As he opened the door he briefly recalled Roberta telling him about her famous party, how she'd just finished dressing but hadn't quite finished her hair – and wouldn't have a chance the night long – when her doorbell rang, and how that nagged at her all evening and only got worse as the party got worse. He remembered her telling him so sadly, "Oh, Cafferty, I knew that if only my hair had been right, the way I wanted it, it would have been an entirely different evening. It should have been such a nice party, Lang and I should have been so happy – but ohh!"

* * *

The nun carries a Prada bag.
Melmoth-Lang roars Tokyo.

* * *

The costs of confusion notwithstanding, Roberta has never really felt confused here – maps make sense – bus maps a bit confusing – but hey, what confusion? – feels like home – a system, maybe – I've made my own.

* * *

SIR WILLIAM RUTLAND, MATCHMAKER

As most Asians, the Japanese are known for having an especial respect and fondness for their elders, whether they be ancestors, wise men, or teachers. An English teacher or an ecologist, a military strategist or an instructor of Western table manners – whomever – if they share with the Japanese something of their special knowledge and skills, they are never forgotten. Examples abound in Japan: Dr. William S. Clark who encouraged the young men of Meiji, "Boys, Be Ambitious!" (his statue can be found in Sapporo); W. E. Deming, the creator of "Quality Control," which method revolutionized Japanese industry and proved no small contribution to the Japanese "economic miracle" (and who, it needs be said, died a near-forgotten man in the West, while in Japan he was universally mourned when he passed away in 1993). The list could easily go on.

Another such gentleman was Sir William Rutland of Great Britain who was there at the beginning of Japan's – and the world's – electronic revolution, that is, the invention of the transistor. He was a dear "friend of Japan," and after having made his crucial contributions to the nation was always received carte blanche whenever he visited his much beloved second home. (The reader might think here of Nixon's later visits to China.)

A serious and dedicated businessman – whose later life was spent representing a major cosmetics firm – Sir William – we'll call him "Rutland" from here – was also something of a wit, a bon vivant, and an incurable romantic. (He shaved before showering.) His more than readable memoirs tell us less about his scientific researches than the amusing episodes and events of his much-blessed life. Among his many visits to Japan, he recounts one particularly memorable event: that time when he was inadvertently forced to spend a week as a boarder in the home of a resident foreigner, and was cast in the unexpected role of matchmaker – and almost instigated an international incident.

It was October, 1964, only a few days before the Tokyo Olympics were to begin – that event that Japan took such great pride in, symbolizing as it did the nation's post-war recovery (and the symbol of the symbol of which became the Shinkansen). Rutland's reservation at the Hotel Okura was for opening day; it hadn't occurred to him that the city would be over-filled with visitors. In a word, the ever-accommodating hotel was reluctantly forced to inform him that they were fully booked: there was no room at the inn. Checking at the British Embassy (where he was rudely interviewed by the Second Secretary of Protocol, who did not recognize Sir William until after the bad impression had been made), he chanced upon a notice board advertising a room to let. The room in which the apartment was located was being rented by a Christine Easton, a young woman working for a local firm. Rutland drove over immediately, announced himself, charmed his way in, and before Miss Easton knew it – she had a roommate. At 6,800 yen a week. (A comparably-sized apartment would cost six or seven times that amount three decades later.) If the attractive and charming Miss Easton could be said to have had one fault it was her being overly fussy and precise. She informed Rutland that she would shower from 7:15 to 7:20; that would be followed by breakfast; at 7:32 she would then brush her teeth for two minutes; and then the bathroom would be his; but from 7:42 to 7:54, she would need it again to put on her make-up and do her hair. Complications reminiscent of a Mack Sennett comedy ensued the following morning.

The next day (keeping to the memoir, we revert to the present) is filled with the usual business appointments and conferences; in passing we are informed that Rutland was working on remote control devices. Leaving his host (most likely Sony), Rutland observes a young man taking photographs of the corporate headquarters. This is Steve Davis, an American architect, who is accompanied by a Russian friend Yuri (recall, this is during the Cold War). And here again we have prophecy in that Davis seems to be keenly aware of what would become that other – and far more valuable – Japanese "miracle," its great architectural achievements of the 1960s and 1970s. Davis is, as it also happens, an Olympic athlete. Rutland takes a liking to the young man. He writes, "He reminded me of myself quite a few years ago, only I was much taller." Moreover, they have something else in common: Davis, having arrived early in order to look at the city's architecture, is without a room.

Accordingly, Rutland rents half of his apartment to Davis, unbeknownst to Miss Easton (who, incidentally, had an inclination to end sentences with prepositions, for example: "you don't have half to sublet a half of"). She is also a bit nervous over sharing her rooms with two men, who soon discover that she is engaged to no one less than the proper Julius D. Haversack – the smug, officious and obnoxious Second Secretary who'd earlier offended Rutland.

Rutland obviously sees Miss Easton as being rather repressed (that tight schedule) – and that she will only become moreso if she goes ahead with her plans for marriage to Mr. Haversack. He also sees what she cannot: her own real, and physical, attraction to Davis. (At their first breakfast together, Davis stares intently at her. Taken aback and uncomfortable, she asks, "What are you gawking at?" His answer is simple, American: "You. You look nice." Flustered, she can only respond with a weak, "Oh.") And so he decides to play matchmaker.

However, things go wrong when the two men return home drunk one evening and, like two nasty schoolboys, they spot Miss Easton's diary and Rutland begins to read it, while also speculating on her sexual experience. She overhears them; hurt and offended, she asks them to leave the next morning. The next afternoon, Miss Easton returns home to find Rutland already gone and Davis packing. He hands her a present from Rutland – a prototype of a new moving-image viewing device. It is accompanied by a note from Rutland, explaining that the fault is entirely his, and that Steve had nothing to do with the nastiness. "How do I know he wrote it?" "You don't," Steve answers. "Well, if he wrote it, how do I know it's the truth?" Davis's elegant answer: "You don't – only it's the truth." She is genuinely touched, and knowing that without a room – the Olympic Village hasn't opened yet – Davis might very well be sleeping in Shinjuku Gyoen – she offers him his old room for the night.

He gladly accepts, and goes so far as to ask her out that evening. "But what about Mr. Haversack?," she faithfully wonders. On their way home, he makes affectionate overtures, a caress here, a stolen kiss there. She wonders about the women in his life: "Who was next?" "Jane Alice Peters." "What was wrong with her?" Nothing, except ..." "Except what?" "She wanted to get married." "Well, what happened?" "She got married." Meanwhile, unbeknownst to either of them, Rutland has re-introduced himself to Haversack, and is pretending great interest in *his* Japan memoirs. Haversack takes the bait. Meanwhile how- and more-over, the ever-vigilant KGB have seen Yuri and Steve with their small tape recorder and cameras; the agent Dimitri takes Yuri, and informs the Japanese police, and suddenly Steve and Miss Easton – as his land-lady – are up before a judge. Some phonecalls are made, and Rutland, accompanied by Haversack (rambling on – "I would think it devastat-ingly paradoxical if I opened chapter five with my arrival in Japan!") – who discovers that his fiancée has a handsome roommate – testifies to everyone's good character. However, Haversack also smells scandal, and – after more complications – it turns out that the only way out is for Steve to sign a waiver, and to marry Miss Easton. Steve meanwhile has disappeared in preparation for his Olympic event the next morning: the fifty-kilometer walk.

And walk he does. But how to avoid the ensuing scandal? Steve must sign the papers. But he'll be walking for hours! Rutland is inspired. He gets into a cab, locates Davis on his long route, undresses, and joins him in the race – in his white boxer shorts! (Steve comes in tenth place.)

Exhausted, Steve and Chris marry. Haversack thanks him, and shares a glass of champagne with Rutland, who leads him away to hear more of his memoirs, and then just leaves him – and Steve and Chris – and his life in the movies.

Oh, why continue this charade? No doubt, the reader who has not fallen asleep or turned to the next section long ago guessed that no Sir William Rutland ever existed, no such memoirs were ever written, and *certainly* no such silly story ever transpired. What I have done, however – and here I offer no apology – is given a précis of a mediocre film called *Walk, Don't Run*, a film which is set during the 1964 Tokyo Olympics (though it was not released until 1966), and whose only real distinction lies in its being the seventy-second and final film of Cary Grant.

Walk, Don't Run was directed by Charles Walters (?), and costars Samantha Eggar and Jim Hutton, two small blips on the 1960's screen. Besides being Grant's last film, *Walk, Don't Run* is also a remake of the far superior *The More the Merrier*, directed by George Stevens in 1943, and starring Jean Arthur and Joel McCrea (no blips they!), and with Charles Coburn in the Cary Grant role, and who won that year's Academy Award for Best Supporting Actor. *Walk, Don't Run* tries to be funny – it is mildly amusing – while it also takes the best bits from the original (that lovely seduction scene, Jean Arthur all nervous and innocently sexy, for example) but never surpasses them. (The movie's trailer even boasts of "The Land of the Rising Fun"! There are a few good things in the film: it's nice to see the actual locations, while the set – at 2-35 Osaka Road!? – tries hard to be real; good fun is made with the presence of two children as Rutland's shadows; Rutland takes a deep breath and coughs from the pollution.)

It does, however, try to make something of its being Grant's sayonara song. There are allusions to his earlier films: for example, twice he whistles the popular theme from *Charade*; in another scene he sings of a "love affair," and even mention marriage "in name only" (regrettably, the only film he made with Carole Lombard). In yet another, Hutton comes across as trying to imitate James Stewart (with whom Grant was paired of course in *The Philadelphia Story*): "Hey now, wait just a minute you" – complete with typical Stewart gesture. More important is the end, Cary's departure. He says goodbye to Steve and Haversack; he gives Christine a glass of champagne and kisses her hand. He leaves the apartment. He glances down the stairwell – and all we see is his shadow. That would have been a perfect and poignant moment to end the film. Instead, Walters distastefully plows on and has Rutland get into his car – where his driver offers him a sayonara present: a statue of the god of fertility.

* * *

– Hiromi says the Pam-Pam girls used to give the GIs blow-jobs for a quarter here.
– What? Where, here – *outside*? Under the tracks?
– Here? These tracks?
– VZ calls it "yakitori-dori," good food, cheap.
– That's a dumb joke, a foreigner's joke.
– It's funny how you get all these run-down joints and those old geezers hauling those wooden crates collecting paper like they were attached to their backs, and just next to it all, these big, expensive department stores and restaurants –
– Right, and all those bars where the salary-guys pay ¥10,000 for a bottle of beer.
– Really?
– Yeah, of course.
– Right, and that's a cheap one.
– Cheaper blow-job.
– I heard of two guys once who had three bottles of beer – normal

bottles, you know – and they had to pay ¥50,000.
- No way!
- It's true.
- Yeah, but then it must've been a yakuza-run place.
- Well, I don't know about that, all I know is that I heard it.
- So, you just trust everything you hear?
- Well, I trust my friends.
- Anyway, ya' know, Lang's always bragging about how short the walk is, he says he often strolls from Nihonbashi to Yurakucho, but that sounds crazy to me – it's like four or five stations!
- No, this place just isn't your type, Hiroko, my pal.
- The girls are too nice for me –
- And the guys are nice, too, but ... well, it's just like at work.
- ?
- Smile and keep your makeup on close.
- And then it all ends at Shimbashi, lickety split, it's like another world once you go under the bridge. Ginza so p. e. and then things get funky again
- But the same more suits.
- Hey, who's this Prometheus guy?
- Who?
- Really, what a weird statue.
- Isn't he in the *Heike Monogatari*?
- *Noli Me Tangere*?

* * *

Rich and strange, Arlene thinks, that the changes I need to effect are coming to me naturally, here. And when they come into clearer focus, it will be time to leave. Roberta and Lang are right, I shall be more free in Europe, more the self they see me as than I yet see. But I will nestle this city inside me. Wherever I shall be.

* * *

Before you leave, don't forget to pass on the cartoon: cock at desk, "up betimes and crowed."

I was a child then, naked. Came to Tokio. It clothed me, made a woman out of me.

* * *

R'n'L!!

Dig this: on my little, 12-minute walk home from the station, there are four dry cleaners, five convenience stores, and three hair-dressers.

So whadda'ya' think – did Priscilla do it with the Colonel?

The day a star was named after me.

Ya' know, I've always wanted to finish a smoke by just throwing it on the floor, just like in the movies. But one thing I don't get is how whenever someone hangs up on another, the hung-up-on one starts clicking that phone thing, like being hung up on is temporary.

Cleaning house, I came across this in an old notebook: "Finish Whip fast; spend next five years writing only two short stories, and studying ancient Greek." Small ambitions, eh?

"Wish I'd Said That/Quote of the Week" Dept. "It was such a beautiful day that I decided to stay in bed." Courtesy W. S. Maugham.

And then I loved LC's description of her work: "A transitory witness to the changing conditions of light."

The other day someone asked me if I'd been raised in an apartment. What a great compliment!

Did I ever tell you that the climax of *North by Northwest*, ie, the Mt. Rushmore sequence, occurs on my very own birthday?! No kidding; there's a shot in the movie of a newspaper – you know, "Diplomat Slain at U. N." – and you can read the date and then figure out the rest. (But did you know the dates are all wrong in *Walk, Don't Run*?)

Looks like I have to reread Nerval. His name's popped up in three conversations in the past two weeks.

Just saw *Angel* for the first time. Lubitsch, Dietrich. So this guy goes nuts over Marlene, woos her, takes her to dinner. End of meal, she says, "You must be quite a success with women." He asks why, and she answers, "Any man who can order a meal like that must be." Ah, a line worthy of Wilde!

God, this new camera, what am I gonna do with it? Got one idea: two "portraits" of you guys; but not yer faces necessarily, more your "worlds." You know, those fave things around you, souvenirs picked up in yer travels, the pictures on your walls, a favorite pen or coffee cup, that sort of thing. All together it would end up giving the viewer an idea, uhn, I mean picture, of youze. And in between the two people portraits there'd be a third "project" as my artist friends would call it. I'd take photos of all my fave and the most interesting places in Kichijoji, including the bad ones, like those patches of lawn and concrete they dare to call "parks" here; the village idiot; the mother who's always walking with her two daughters (I think I saw the husband once); the fat lady at the dry cleaners, etc. Write some captions on the margins of the photos. In the end it should be a portrait of Kichijoji and indirectly of me. Whadda'ya' think?

* * *

- I can't quit 'ya, Roberta, but I gotta go.
- Lang, you can be such a fool.
- Should I repeat myself?
- You will, Lang, regardless of what I say.
- Why these Americanisms?
- Why all this violence?
- I love you, Roberta.
- As I said, to repeat myself.
- The violence?
- The love, Lang.

* * *

City of my sins.
– Spanish phrase

* * *

Other friends could tell other stories.
– LZ

Whose are these young, these innocent faces? And why do I mistrust them?

                                    * * *

                                    ABC

–   It was a shell, a spiral, an unfolding screen, Cafferty was explaining
    to Roberta and Arlene – a two-dimensional plan/accident perhaps
    that divided into the low and the high cities, but more the shell-
    spiral, a labyrinth that let the traveler out in Ome, Tama, across
    the Edo River, on some happy tropical islands. This "empty center"
    business has gotten much too out of hand; I prefer to see other
    pictures.
–   Bric-a-brac, Arlene responded; a crossword puzzle on top of a poin-
    tillist painting on top of a digital photograph.
–   Too easy, Roberta pointed out. I think of it as a Mika Yoshizawa
    drawing: a circle bisected on the right by another circle bisected
    by yet another: the city, the Yamanote, the Palace. Like some giant
    Mickey Mouse eye.
–   And what of the river, Roberta?, Cafferty asked.
–   Arteries, of course!
–   And have you thought of this: abstract the circle of the Yamanote,
    square it and then bisect it horizontally by the Chuo: the sun; bi-
    sected again by the Sobu: the eye. That is a pretty standard picture.
    What we have now as a result of all that 80s overbuilding – overbit-
    ing? – is the Bay bisected by the Rainbow Bridge: in other words,
    the city, the sun-eye not only doubled, but enlarged.
–   Land and water!
–   Yes, Arlene, and more, it's tripled: the Bay has become the reposi-
    tory of the low city's riverine past, while the life of the low city has
    moved west; it's climbed over the Yamanote, completely passed it
    by – which in its snobbery didn't even notice – and made its new
    home West, say from Ogikubo on. You see this historically too, how
    so many institutions have been displaced or removed to the safer,
    newer west.
–   Ogikubo?
–   Okagami.
–   What?
–   The Great Mirror, Roberta explained. The city doubles and even
    triples itself, and we only read ourselves into it. I see a Yoshizawa
    drawing ...
–   And Lang sees the face of James Joyce.
–   How's that?, asks Cafferty.

44   TOKIO WHIP

- That odd shape of the Yamanote being Joyce's scrawny head; the Chuo and Palace being the eyepatch; and that area near Hatchobori where so many train lines meet make a huge ear. Joyce resting his head listening to the language of the river ...
- Ingenious ...
- Or silly.
- Yes, so many pictures. Look at the actual thing, with all the mountains and rivers ....
- A corn cob ...
- *Wasabi* ...
- A grotesque, an old man's penis in some *ukiyo-e* ...
- In the mouth of the Bay.
- Thank you, Roberta.

* * *

Well, while they're all arguing back and forth with him about Tokyo, I'm out there enjoying myself in it. What would they have to say to that? I mean, it is just a city. Sure it's big and the capitol and all, but hey, you have the same work and play in Nagoya or Osaka. Same difference. What's the big deal? Ok, maybe a few differences in food or clothes, but anyone would expect that. Girls still come with two legs all over Japan, so who's complaining? – So remarks that minor annoyance Hiro, from whom we do not expect much in the way of thought.

* * *

They got married, placed their faith between his legs.

The ashtray slides its way across the tabletop, and having slid ...
The new kid in town asks around: "So, what gives with this burg?"

* * *

Hiroko and company got off their bus a stop or two too early. As they – and so many before them – passed the Fuji Latex building, they all immediately wondered.

- Does that look like what I think it looks like?
- I think it does.
- Is it supposed to?

-   I'm not so sure. Maybe it's supposed to be something else.
-   Well, it is that.
-   ?
-   Something else!
-   What the hell building is it, anyway?
-   Let's see.

[They step back to read the name and logo.]

[Followed by universal laughter.]

-   No wonder it looks like a condom!
-   Uh-oh.
-   What?
-   Are you wondering what I'm wondering?
-   I'm not wondering anything.
-   Me neither, I'm just still amazed that we got this giant condom in the middle of the city.
-   Not only that, the Palace is just over there, too.
-   Oh m'god, you're right.
-   Do you think they ever drive past it?
-   Do you think anyone ever says anything when they do?
-   No way.
-   Oh, so, what were you wondering?
-   Do you think there's a corresponding building somewhere else, you know, a building that looks like a –
-   Ha! I hope so!
-   Yeah, get this country a sex life!

Then suddenly they were almost trampled over by a crowd of high-school girls who'd just been released from school. Stopped to stare at the joggers circling the moat, runningly asphyxiating themselves.

-   So, whadda'ya' wonder the Crown Prince is having for lunch?
-   I really wouldn't care to know – I'm sure I couldn't stomach it myself.
-   Hey, anyone know what's in the Science Museum?
-   Does Japan have any science?
-   Sure, you know, all that bullshit about our enzymes.
-   And our brains programmed for kanji.
-   And our weird architecture!
-   Hey, but remember Hiraga Gennai?

- Oh right, we had to read about him.
- Yeah, cool dude – in a way, I guess.
- What's that way?
- Yasukuni-dori.
- Look, you can look up and down – the other side of the river.
- Those *torii* are massive!
- They better be, you know who's there, don't you?
- Oh, right, the war dead!
- VZ told me once that there's some sort of fascist architecture around here.
- Do you really think Roberta's place is just straight ahead?

* * *

Tough, tender Tokyo, we do understand each other, don't we?, Marianne queries.

* * *

- Thanks, let me get the next one.
- Ok.
- It's delicious. How did you know this place?
- Well, actually, Kazuko introduced me to it some years ago, before she went to the United States. And while I was gone, I continued to come here. They soon got to know me. I keep a bottle here, bring friends. It's one of my regular places now. But it's funny, I've never come back here with her.
- Why not?
- Oh, I don't know. Maybe because it reminded me of an "earlier Kazuko"; I suppose it had something to do with that split in time. When she returned, her style had changed. She stopped wearing the Tokyo style of clothes – you know, all that black that made Tokyo look like a city in permanent mourning.
- Kazuko used to dress like that – like me?
- Oh yes, when she first moved up here from Kyoto she fell completely into the city's ways. You should have seen her then.
- Oh, I'd love to see some pictures!
- I can show you some sometime. You'd never recognize her.
- Oh, I'm sure. My elegant Kazuko from Kyoto, a Comme des Garçons vamp. It'd be fun to tease her about it. You oughta' marry that girl, Kazuo – she's the most sensible person I've ever met – totally

romantic – I mean, she dresses fabulously now, very fashionable – but I gave up on European clothes long ago. And I only dressed like an American when I was a teenager.

– That's true, I've never seen you in jeans.

– Actually, just recently I bought a pair of black levis. I do have a sentimental fondness for black denim.

– I've noticed your black denim coat.

– Have you, Kazuo? I'm flattered. It's by Yohji.

– Of course.

– Do you like fashion?

– Oh, I guess I have a small interest. I enjoy Kazuko's interest, and enjoy looking at her ...

– That's important ...

– But essentially I just like something functional; you know, something that will last, always look good.

– Like a personal uniform?

– Oh no, I wouldn't go that far. I do like some variety. But I wouldn't call myself as rigid as some salarymen, or as severe as Lang.

– Ah, you've noticed. Well, who wouldn't? Ohh, fifteen years ago it must've been, we were already in Vienna then, he told me then of his idea of a private uniform. Hence all those black smocks, black pants – never denim, of course, the man is Viennese, after all – and all the different socks, they're the only variation he allows. And, he is *very* particular about his shirts. He once told he couldn't respect a man who would wear a shirt without a collar. I thought he was kidding. But boy, did I find out he wasn't when I sent him an Issey shirt for his birthday a year ago! A few months later I was back for a brief visit, and there was a big dinner of family and friends. And there was a friend of his wearing the shirt! I'm sure he meant it as an indirect but mild reproach. That would be his way, of course – almost Japanese – a polite, and unspoken anger. Anyway, none of it matters. He always does look good, there's no denying it.

– And you and he look good together.

– Now, Kazuo ... touchy, touchy.

– How is he, by the way? I haven't seen him in a couple of weeks.

– Oh, alright, I suppose. He spends a lot of time with Van Zandt, you know. Always talking books and music and the city. Oh, those two can talk forever. I have much the same interests – don't we all – don't we all enjoy books and music, the place we live? – but I try not to go overboard. As Susan Hayward said, "I want to live." I like to read a short article or story at night, savor it. I can listen to the same album

for a month before I switch to something else.
- Kazuko's like that too.
- Oh?
- Oh yes. She says that when she visits me she gets exasperated with the many records I'm forever changing. She says she often doesn't know if she's supposed to feel like she's down on a ranch outside of Nashville, some smokey jazz joint in New York, or a research lab somewhere in Germany.
- That's cute. I can also relate to it. I must say though that I have learned enough about music and film through Lang to last me a lifetime – I've even learned quite a bit from Van Zandt, and his tastes are even more eclectic.
- Van Zandt – VZ.
- Yes, as we call him. We've been friends – or should I say "had been"? – for so very long. I don't know if the "Van" has any deeper significance ... some Americans would probably resent it; I don't mind – don't mind being an American either, sometimes. There was once an ad that said something like, "America has had 34 presidents, and only one king" – and there was a picture of Elvis Presley. Maybe you've seen it on Arlene's kitchen wall.
- Yes, I think I have. So Arlene likes Presley?
- Oh yes, our darling, practical Arlene is a believer.
- Hmm, I might have to revise my opinion of Arlene.
- Why Kazuo, you're less straight than I've thought you.
- Oh, I'm only joking, Roberta.
- You know, Lang's jealous of her for having a copy of that ad. She also has a copy of that Thai Airlines ad with Cary Grant in the crop-duster sequence. Hers is from a magazine. Well, he tried to out-do her – he went to the ad agency that made the ad, and asked them for a copy, but they wouldn't, or couldn't, give him one. He's still jealous of Arlene.
- That sounds very much like him. Lang.
- Yes.
- If I may, Roberta, how are you and he doing?
- A rather bold question, Kazuo. I am only slightly surprised.
- Forgive me. But I do ask out of a genuine concern.
- I know. And I appreciate – and like – your asking. How are Lang and I? Why the same as we've been – madly in love, madly hating one another, staying, leaving, breaking up, down, in, through – nothing, nothing new, and yes, thanks, I will have another.
- Leaving, staying?

   –   Oh, I came here because I wanted to. Lang had always known that someday I would fulfill my dream of coming to Japan. I always had a great interest in Japan. You know, that typical Western thing, the "mysterious, elegant Orient." But I caught on quickly, and that was good. I'm simply not much of a romantic. Maybe that saved me, being here. That and the fact that I very quickly fell in step here. Lang had to accept my going – *I was already here, you know, in a way: I'd lived in America, had done Europe, Lang and I were going nowhere – standing still, falling – he couldn't see it – one way or another – I needed a change – there was a job available maybe: and so I came.* But then, well, then I didn't so much fall in love with the place – I just ... found a home. And that infuriated him. That I really could feel – feel well ... feel myself whole here without him. So I stayed, and I stayed. Three months, six, more; I "lingered," as he calls it. Now Lang, you have to understand, is Viennese. He hates and loves his city. Oh, he's traveled a lot, and lived in a couple of cities – he stayed with me in San Francisco for a couple of years until it became too provincial for both of us – except, I should say, for the film culture, the lack of which here drives us both up the wall. Anyway, though he has lived elsewhere – outside of Vienna, that is – he is very stubborn in his Viennese ways. Though, by the way, I'd say, he's really Spanish at heart, baroque. He could not believe that I would choose Tokyo. I chose it *for* myself; it was never a choice *against* him. Oh, where I live now isn't even Tokyo to most people, *shitamachi's* just some 50s backwater, another take on the national Disneyland hysteria. Sure it's the old city, the low city – traditional wood houses, craftspeople, people think it quaint, old-fashioned, they condescend to it. The same who think that Roppongi and Shibuya and the other *suteki/saiko* areas, all that metal-neon, are the "real" Tokyo. Oh, but I love my neighborhood. And I do not want to leave it – not now, not for a while, really.

   –   Oh, stay, Roberta – you add so much to the city!

   –   That's sweet, Kazuo – and insincere. No, that's not it – I do not add to the city – I'm not even sure it adds to me. But I do feel it as the home I've always lacked or longed for – even as much as I like Lang's Vienna, or VZ's Amsterdam, or Marianne's Paris. Anyway, I'm in Tokyo now, and I'm staying a while. Am I a Tokyoite? The question's never even occurred to me – it would, immediately, to Lang, of course. And so, to return to our sad little story – here I was; and Lang finally had to accept that I was not hightailing it back to the old country. And so *he* determined that it was time we were together again – which I could not argue with, I never wanted us to not be together – I didn't see my coming and staying as our breaking up – it was just a break, you know, I was only taking one, for some undetermined time – and then it began to feel like home – why couldn't he see that? – see that the world is not Vienna or Europe or our mutually beloved Paris alone? – not that he does, certainly, but when those Viennese are away from home, it becomes the sole world – till they return – I always wanted him to come here – to experience Tokyo – not just my Tokyo, but his too – *his* Tokyo, the one I knew he'd make – the city makes you make your own version of her – no two Tokyo's alike – isn't that marvelous? – Yes, one more, why not? ... Anyway, Lang determined – and decided he would come here and "rescue" me.

–   *Rescue* you?
–   Thanks. Oh yes, our Lang, who never had the slightest interest in Japan – he once said that if there were a museum of the Orient, Japan would be in a rear gallery of precious, decorative, and decidedly useless objets d'art. Anyway, so here came our boy – and what happened? – he fell in love with the place! – he never wanted to come here, you know, but once he did, well! – but I'm getting ahead of myself.
–   But isn't that good? That he likes Tokyo, good, I mean, for the two of you?
–   No, it's not good at all, Kazuo. You see, he *loves* the city. I just live in it. I know almost nothing about what happened here before the war. Oh, I know a little history, but all that Edo/Tokyo lore – that's Lang's material, not mine. I know my grocer, I know my ladies at the *soba* shop. Isn't that enough? Lang, on the other hand, devours the city – just as he did with Cortázar and Duke Ellington – I'm content with the *Blow-up* stories, and *Such Sweet Thunder* – He's been everywhere, and he's getting to know what seems the history of every block of the city. He's jealous that I live in *shitamachi* – he even berates me – gently, gently – for not knowing my neighborhood's history – oh, I know it's fascinating – he's taken me on his tour – but like I said, I'm content with the *soba* ladies and my grocer. So now we're in a situation where I am in a place I like, and Lang is in a city that he *loves*. I only fear that his love for the city will overtake his love for me. Oh, I'm sorry, Kazuo, it's been such a nice evening, and here I've gone on with my problems. But, you asked.
–   No, Roberta, forgive me.
–   No.

- Ok, yes I did ask, and I thank you for your openness. I should say that I asked out of my concern for the both of you – I, we, Kazuko and I, like you both very much.
- Thanks. Yes, I feel that, and if I didn't like you too – or you two – with a "w"– I would never have been so open.
- I'm glad you like us, me.
- Oh yes! It's nice talking with you, Kazuo. I like Kazuko very much, and have, I suppose, hoped to make some contact with you, but I guess I was never sure how to do so. It was "objective chance" that had us run into one another tonight.
- Uhn?
- Oh, it's a Surrealist phrase. And no, I did not learn it from Lang. I do my own research sometimes too. Anyway, it has been good to make this connection. I thank you, Kazuo. And I feel even better for Kazuko.
- Thanks. But, if I may ....
- Yes?
- Well, is there anything I can do, anything Kazuko and I can do for you, for you and Lang?
- Oh, Kazuo, that's sweet of you. But no, oh, I don't know. Because I don't know exactly what needs to be done. I want to stay here a while longer; Lang seems to want to stay forever. Maybe he'll get over that when it comes time for me to leave – if I leave – and then where to? Me return to his Vienna? That'd be a great irony. No – I don't know, Kazuo – just remain friends with both of us, both of you – talk with us, walk with us. And you and I should have dinner together again. I like you, and you know that though I don't go into the city very often, when I do I like to go to good restaurants – Kazuko's told me about your knowing some very good places – after tonight it looks like I could have no better guide than you.
- Fine, it's a deal, Roberta. Let me get this.
- – and you should be my guest sometime.
- With pleasure. And for that next time I'm already thinking of a small "ethnic" place in Omotesando ...

* * *

I love the Ogata Ken beer commercials – caught in the rain, diving on to a couch, a big swallow and bigger smile, a wonderful actor.

Say it, Arlene: take a little walk with me – just two or three big steps – the quality of our love: say it, Arlene: the city in a moment, a word, a neighborhood.

* * *

SCENE TWO: DEPARTMENT STORE

The second scene finds the Woman in the basement floors of Seibu Ikebukuro, once the largest department store in the world, now second (or is it third?) to Sogo of Yokohama. How to find her Man amongst all the pickles and vegetables, beef, pork and chicken, lunch boxes, Chinese foods, brown beans in pink rice cakes, liqueurs, beers and wines, and all that *saké* (including local *sakés*, such as Richard's from Ogawamachi)? She stops for some *shumai*, and then a "health" drink. It's closing time, and the store is closed the next day, so the shouting of the foodsellers increases. Voices rise as prices fall. Bargain time, and the housewives are at their most violent. Pity the children in tow, pity the foreigner trying to ask politely what that delicious-looking lumpy orange thing is. As she's sipping her strawberry with ice, she notices some pin-striped cuffs. She throws her drink down, and rushes to the elevators. Too late! To console herself, she orders a freshly squeezed combination kiwi and orange juice.

* * *

Ah, this city, Kazuo contemplates, Tokyo, Capitol, home of my family for how many generations? Yes, I will be true to you. I have my calendar of festivals. Would Kazuko be interested? Maybe not, she is from Kyoto, after all. But maybe. So I'll go. And bring her a present – a paper balloon, a spinning top, a dragonfly.

* * *

ABC 2

I've just got a couple of maps at home, says Roberta. The TIC one is just Lang was showing me his map collection the other day, Arlene began. It's one dimensional, it's two dimensional, it's three, it's four. I was hasty fine. Then a couple of guide books, but those are mostly for visitors. I Maps from the Edo Period, all military or festive. That great panoramic of course to call it two. It's all your pictures and mine, a Great Mirror,

think you pick up the train system pretty quickly – the stations them-
photo, a city all black, flat, except for the fire towers. The map from the
yes, Roberta, as well as two facing mirrors, receding mirrors, Chinese
selves are the hard parts sometimes. I remember it took what seemed
earthquake, where the fires were, where people were lost – or assassinated.
mirror-lined boxes. Pictures on top of one another yes, perhaps, Arlene,
months before I felt confident making my way around Shibuya, and
The JTB overhead photos of the entire city, every seven years, trace the
pictures that obscure any seeing, but pictures that are all transparent too.
now I rarely go there. Then there are stations like Akasaka and Hibiya
rise and fall, what stood three years ago on this plot of land, for example.
Like Borges's perfect labyrinth that is a straight line, Tokyo is a great thick
where you can walk for miles, a real underground city. But no I have
The Yohan map, the TIC map, the Kodansha map, they each show a
volume of page after page of pictures that are all transparent. Perhaps the
really only one map: my neighborhood. I copied the basic plan out of
different city. And the bus maps! The train and subway maps; you know,
whole is empty, and the center, what? An empty emptiness? No matter.
Yanasen magazine, and now as I wander I fill in the shops and places I
you almost never see them together, it would be so convenient. I like the
The three regalia thrown into the sea at the end of the Heike Monoga-
like. There's the handmade ice cream place, as well as the "traditional"
maps in the subway stations – why don't they issue those? And the pock-
tari. Regalia that probably never existed, and therefore perfect. Shinto.
ice cream place which used to be in an attractive old building and is
et maps wallet size, the whole city the size of a credit card! The 3D map
But I like to think of it as being like those medical textbooks, you know
now in what looks like a clinic – ha, an ice cream clinic – "I'm going
of Ginza, the Pia maps and the BT maps. The "My Way" map: all white,
what I'm referring to, textbooks with those plastic sheets that you unfold
to the clinic for a check-up, Mom!" There are at least five tofu shops,
fill in according to need. Those real estate maps, every single detail, each
one after another: the sheet of skin, the sheet of muscles, the sheet of
four or five noodles shops, there's Hobos, where the woman sits at the
little house and shop, how do they do it? Those funny metal maps you
bones, the sheet of viscera. In my body-city we'd have the sheets of res-
spindle weaving. The kamameishi restaurant with the Klimt posters,
find every few streets – and people complain about no street signs; it's an
taurants, of cinemas, of bookstores. The sheet of memories, and the sheet
and Hantei of course – you know, the Pond used to extend so far. The
easy city to find your way around in – or get lost in, but that can also be

of desires. The sheet of crime and assassination. The jizo sheets, and the
New Year's walk of the lucky gods. That photo shop with the window
fun. Sort of. And the handmade maps, the type Barthes liked so much.
Yoshiwara sheets. The work sheets, dress well sheets, and the date sheets.
where he changes the display every three weeks. There's always a callig-
Scraps of paper, matchbox covers if anyone ever uses them anymore,
The sheet of foreigners who got it wrong, and the sheet of those who just
raphy scroll, a small rock garden, a seasonal flower arrangement. I visit
chopstick wrappers, meishi, cutesey stationery, a variety of surfaces and
accepted it. The Cafferty sheet: half a dozen homes, as many loves and
once a month and take a picture. Oh, and there's usually an insect, too.
scripts, each a map a kanji itself – what a jigsaw puzzle they could a make!
losses. And back to the spiral city, the book's cover, the winding sheet.

* * *

–   On occasion Hiroko simply likes to wander. She closes her eyes, lets
    her finger fall on the map, takes a train to the closest station, and
    from there hops on a bus. The custom comes from her childhood,
    when her grandparents were still alive; they'd take little Hiroko-
    chan on tour busses outside of Tokyo every few months. These days,
    she doesn't really like to go into the country, so she maintains the
    tradition by exploring areas of Tokyo unknown to her, and most
    likely areas never known by her beloved grandparents either. Today
    her finger fell on Yoga Station (Shin-Tamagawa Line), and that's
    where she got on a bus, having declined the Hanzomon Line, and
    so having willingly screwed up by taking a couple or triple of bus-
    ses from Shibuya (the Toei 6), she first found herself in Shimouma,
    went back to Shinjuku and got on the 91. It all seemed so fresh and
    clean (and expensive, she was sure). She traveled farther afield. Baji
    Park to see the horses; an old man taking photographs from be-
    hind people. So many apartment buildings (on the bus trip back she
    looked up and saw the old man now shooting from his balcony).
    Back at the station she had some spareribs at Kenny Roger's restau-
    rant. Good, but a bit messy.
–   Is that so?
–   Yeah. Ya' know her grandfather designed T-shirts. Taisho period.
    People were very fussy then.

* * *

Lang keeps telling me, "you must read Bernhard, Kazuko," and I keep telling him to read Schnitzler. But he does seem pretty well-adjusted – to Tokyo, I mean. Oh, I'd love to be back in Vienna. When was it, three years ago? The Graben, the Belvedere, the Esperanto Museum. You go round and round, just like the Ring, the "girdle." Walking, looking, shopping, stopping at a café; then you do it again; and then once more. The coffee might be a glass of wine, but the cycle remains true. What is it? "Situation desperate, but not serious." We Tokyoites could learn a lot from the Viennese. *That's* the city we should have a sister relationship with. But no, maybe we're more alike than not, with our sentiments and silliness, our baby-talk and finger-food. Spoiled brats. The old and the new worlds meet and go crash, boom! Will I *ever* get out of here and back home? Will I ever see Vienna again? Maybe Lang is right, and I do find something of myself in the two cities. Shadows I'd never suspected before.

Oh, be careful, Kazuko.

And Joan Fontaine was oh so pretty!

* * *

Kazuo is in the San Francisco apartment of a friend. Or, rather, he is in a dream-combination of familiar apartments, rooms that he or friends have inhabited, both in San Francisco and even a few rooms from back in Japan, rooms he's seen in films perhaps, and that have obviously made a deep impression. Three women are cooking in the kitchen; in one corner a man and a woman are breaking up, laughing hysterically one moment, silent or sobbing the next. Kazuo takes the stairs that lead from the kitchen down through a bedroom, where the woman who was just breaking up is now sleeping peacefully. He descends finally into a large living room dominated by a grand piano in one corner and a bar in another; a party is going on. Country music is playing in the background: Roseanne, Iris, Dwight, Lucinda. There are no arguments here as to what constitutes this music. (Do people tap their feet in dreams?) He is not dressed for the occasion, and his embarrassment shows immediately. He tries to move to a corner where he will not be noticed, but an American (whom he does not know) comes up to him and begins asking Kazuo about "the market." Kazuo detests this type of person: smug, successful, superior – superficial. Always speaking in initials ("Read DR in the JT today?"), or reciting statistics ("53 out of 89, I tell you, no less than 53 out of 89!"). But he can laugh to himself because the Yuppie is rapidly losing his hair, and growing stupider with each day. The woman who had broken up and then slept it off now comes over to Kazuo. She takes his arm and leads him away, saying, "I could see you weren't comfortable. Let's go over here and talk." They walk off into the small garden of a *danchi* where a barbecue is taking place. They are in Funado, Itabashi Ward. Kazuo is drinking champagne, enjoying talking with the woman. He compliments her on her Japanese, but then learns that she is in fact half-Japanese. She tells him that she knows Kazuko, and knows what she is doing right now.

In Hiromi's dream she opens the door of a large auditorium, where she sees people milling about, drinking, small-talking. A band is on stage playing Country music (Dwight, Roseanne ...). Later in the evening there is to be an awards ceremony. Hiromi has no idea why she is here. She walks around and around the auditorium. Sometimes she takes an exit, but that too just leads around and around, from one snack bar to another. There are conventioneers sporting happy-face name-tags; sports fans with megaphones and pennants; kids dressed for a Rock concert, like in the magazine cover-story on London she once read. All she can do is continue looking for an exit. Finally one appears; she takes it. Funado, Itabashi Ward, another area of Tokio that the economic miracle passed by. If Nakano is the 50s, Funado is the 60s. Makeshift houses all falling apart now; factories with tall chimney stacks; rag-and-bone men. The nation's Self-Defense Forces has a large dormitory here; so too are there numerous schools for the mentally and physically handicapped. And *danchi* after *danchi*: those long, multi-building apartment blocks; 2 or 3LDKs, with whole families in them, everything falling apart, and no funds to fix any of it. Hiromi is aghast; Funado is not the Roppongi and Shibuya she hangs out in. When did she ever visit here? What's it doing in her dreams? Why can't she wake and get out of here? And besides, she doesn't even like Country music!

* * *

Everything changes. What's the rest of the line?

The escalator of the Edo-Tokyo Museum is out of order. She climbs the hundreds of steps, and wonders, "What did people do before escalators? Maybe the world really was flat."

* * *

I'd found a new way around the moat one early winter evening and decided to try it – there was so much I needed to mull over – to walk it over to Hibiya where Arlene was working late. (I used to love coming into San Francisco across the Bay Bridge. The slope, the ascent, the towering pillars and then the cityscape and skyline the ocean beyond and above and between and below it all the setting sun. But it was all anticipation and no fulfillment. It made no sense as to what a city might be; I knew the people too well.) Tonight, however, circling the moat counterclockwise (without a sunset, happening in some other city perhaps) and thinking about all the changes that were to come in all of our relationships – the storm ready to burst, the chill to follow – I was suddenly lifted and briefly felt blissfully light, empty even: it did not matter what became of us here – what was this sudden glimpse of the city? – a corner turned a shot of light and we all forgotten against that silver wall – it wasn't the sun and it wasn't the moon, merely an effect of light, Tokyo light – that others too may discover going round the moat.

Or exiting a station, kissing goodnight, asking the operator for a phone number, a stranger for a light.

* * *

I have seen the traces of the city, Lang drunkenly boasts to himself, have traced the outlines of its stories and legends and multiple names. I have followed the rivers, eaten and slept in the black, long, low houses of the powerless, and bathed and made love in the mansions of the powerful; have seen Utamaro with hands bound, and seen him watch the naked pearl divers; have seen Taisho Tokio, mingled with Modern Girls and Marx Boys and ridden the trams of Ginza, and seen Sakae Osugi carted off to his terrible death. Can any other man say the same?

* * *

I can't afford to hate anybody. I'm only a photographer.
– Miss Imbrie, *The Philadelphia Story* (George Cukor, 1940)

* * *

the poet
alone with his word
in the crowd unknown

you take the train with your last goodnight
I wait for the cab by the station side.

Chapter 3

HAMAMATSUCHO– SHINAGAWA

Lang never wanted to come here; he had a passing, a professional interest in Japan, but winters get pretty gray in Vienna, or so I'm told, and the few letters from Roberta only added to things being that much more up in the air, too far for his comfort and he couldn't abide that couldn't abide being the vague-gray Lang at a loose end, and so he had to find out, to settle all one way or the other – and so he came.

What bell, Bashō, was it, Shibuya?, Shinjuku?

Dutifully, she burst into tears.

* * *

A certain superficiality of expression in order to reveal the nature of the void hidden beneath.

– Toyo Ito

* * *

- Lang, you said you loved me.
- I did I do love you.
- Lang, love is strong, isn't it?
- Isn't it?
- Why did you come to Japan, Lang?

–   I hadn't wanted to come, Roberta.

* * *

Coming out of the World Trade Center, where they've bought some art books at the annual sale, Cafferty and friends decide to visit one of his favorite galleries – Gatodo; spacious, separate, and tasteful, it reminds him of those in New York – and then to avoid at least some of the noise and traffic by strolling through the Hama Gardens.

–   So few people visit here, one of them remarks, but no one bothers to pursue the question and wonder why.
–   Let's –
–   – walk along the Bay –
–   – see how the construction's going.
–   Why not?
–   It's going to be an all new city.
–   Once again.
–   Kids are going to grow up knowing less and less of what came before. My wharves gone for bad or plain mediocre restaurants that'll thrive for six months and then the whole shebang'll be as shabby as, well, as shabby as my wharves are now. Damn the 80s, and all that money.
–   Horrible buildings.
–   I give 'em twenty years. It'll serve 'em right.
–   That Satoh kid's photos hit the right note – the glare of a city being raped –
–   Our typical Tokio attraction-repulsion effect, eh?

They decide not to avail themselves of the Keio University library; pass the Shibaura offices of *The Japan Times* where they run into Donald Richie, a passing acquaintance, and who's come to deliver an article. And further on.

–   Trudge on, you old Cafferty.
–   Donald was looking perky.
–   Yes, I was glad to see that; heard he'd been ill recently.
–   Well, I for one am beginning to feel the walk now. Are we really going as far as Shinagawa?
–   Look – pilgrims on their way to Sengakuji.
–   Well, 47 *ronin* or not, this pilgrim's of another sort – taxi!

* * *

Hiromi is in an automobile. A Western woman unknown to her is driving. They are passing through Shinozaki-cho, heading east and about to cross the Edo River, and thence across the border. This area, so deep a part of Tokyo's past now represents its future: warehouses, bed towns, convenience shops; total, pristine anonymity, with dilapidated postwar housing still hanging around, forgotten (and looking like munitions warehouses); this Tokyo is a combination of *Blade Runner* and *Alphaville*. Van Zandt too is in the car, is in the rear, speaking to Hiromi. But the radio is too loud for her to hear what he is telling her. (It is playing a frenzied Clara Ward, live, moving up higher and higher yet.) She keeps trying to turn it down but it won't go; she keeps trying to point the driver's attention to this, but she seems to be totally incognizant of Hiromi's presence.

Arlene is dreaming of a woman who wants to sleep with her, but Arlene is not ready yet. She is at the woman's apartment; she looks out briefly as the view is so uninteresting, Shinozaki. Now Arlene is sleeping; she is in bed with two other women whom the first woman has chosen for Arlene to sleep with. The woman is watching, disinterestedly, not quite voyeuristically. Later, Arlene walks around Shinozaki, and revises her earlier opinion, having found some small interesting shops, an attractive office block, small children on tricycles. It is Sunday morning, and softly, the radio plays some Gospel, arousing, caressing.

* * *

The costs of confusion notwithstanding, Kaoru refuses to be confused, no costs, no confusion. Everything in order. Office-home-office-club-home. Business is done. How old are the boys now?

* * *

Passed the Chinese restaurant, you know, the one that caters to the theater crowd and the hostess always wears a different hat. It smelled like cotton candy.

He notices a passing woman and immediately starts thinking of how to seduce her when he almost as immediately sees a building and starts to film it – and loses the woman.

* * *

The Lady of Musashino (*Musashino fujin*, 1951)

The past and the present and by obvious implication the future, the east and the west sides of Tokyo are one, Mizoguchi seems to be telling us in that final shot, a masterful pan that begins with the tall *susuki* reeds of the ancient Musashino Plain, and concludes with a view – the very first in the film – of the city itself. Morally, it is as if Mizoguchi is saying that the young hero of the film, Tsutomu, will choose the city and its excitement and relative freedoms over the insidiousness of rural family life. Moreso, Mizoguchi is making a reversal here: one usually views the city from East (good, tradition) to West (bad, novelty and expansion). In making this reversal, he is deepening the argument of union, a view with which this author is in complete agreement; after all, he lives in Kichijoji, where once those reeds and marshes flourished (they are still to be found in pockets here and there), and which was founded as an extension of an east-side temple.

We see the Plain; the deaths of the parents; the distant air-raids; the discovery of a skull. Michiko is played by the "enjoyably plump and radiant" Kinuyo Tanaka. Her cousin Tsutomu (Akihiko Katayama) has returned from the war, from Burma. Young, restless, and *good*, Michiko allows him to look after her estate.

Complications arise: her cousin Ono (So Yamamura), who lives nearby, has lost his fortune, for which his wife Tomiko (Yukiko Todoroki) is ready to abandon him for Michiko's husband, the unimaginative Stendahl scholar Tadao (Masayuki Mori), for whom, as Mizoguchi's biographer says, "adultery signifies stimulus." Worse, Tomiko spreads the terrible rumor that Michiko and Tsutomu are having an affair. How absurd! They may certainly be fond of one another, but they could never even imagine such a thing. (Tsutomu's modest aspirations are for a young fellow student whom he visits either at her home or at "La Vie est Belle" café in the city.)

Things get worse. Michiko and Tsutomu go for a long walk. A thunder-storm erupts; they must spend the night together at an inn. Chastely, certainly. (There is a tremendous long shot of them walking in the fields as the daylight sky is lit up by lightning. One must wonder how long Mizoguchi sat there waiting to get that shot. If for no other reason, the film must be seen for this and the final shot. ((Of course, the author does not dismiss the film as readily as the biographer does.

Perhaps it is not a major film, but it is certainly worth seeing.)) Anyway, back to the story.)

And worse. Akiyama and Tomiko steal away with the deed to Michiko's property. Tomiko obviously has no real interest in the weakling. Dejected, our Stendahlian returns home only to discover that – distraught over the *rumor*, Michiko has suicided!

And then Tsutomu takes that long walk east.

* * *

project myself into you
projector
seed city
bloom town

looking at ads rather than you
choosing a shirt in place of a word

* * *

- Oh it's a nondescript area enough, I suppose, but I'm sure Roberta would have been charmed by it here.
- Well, tell her, next time you see her, do.
- Yes, I must.
- But if she'd seen Kagurazaka first, would she ever have found her Yanaka?
- Mmm, not likely.
- And, she'd have lived in so many times: the past, the Roppongi of the 50s; the present, the science students –
- The French students –
- The British English students.
- And the future: Yotsuya and all that *that* means just ahead –
- The Palace and Marunouchi, and all that *they* mean back over there.
- You think they're part of the future? Let's *hope* they're a thing of the past!
- No, Kagurazaka would have been too much, not to her liking at all.
- But to yours, Cafferty? – who knew it when!
- I really must at least introduce her to it; she'd love the Meiji house, you know that *saké* restaurant where you get your own room.
- Doesn't that Hakushu architect have his office in a Meiji building around here, too?

- Oh, right, we have to visit him some day.
- But look – what's this?
- "Zonar" – a coffeeshop?
- "Zonar"?
- Sounds like a *manga*.
- How would it go? ... "When the planet Zonar was threatened by aliens from the planet Nozar ..."
- Oh no – I'm sure Roberta would insist Zonar is a woman!
- "When Zonar's lover Nozar revealed himself to be the interplanetary master criminal Rozan ..."

* * *

Ah, this city, Hiro "thinks," a bit bigger maybe, but no different from home, or even Takasaki, same shops, bars, girls. More or less. But I gotta make it here. No more years in the provinces. Those flat-feeted women. No, here. And I will if it kills me. Ha!, the old samurai spirit.

* * *

It was only nine o'clock and already Van Zandt was feeling the alcohol. The Chinese had iron rice bowls, and the Japanese iron stomachs. Though a strong drinker, his stomach had still not gotten the trick of mixing large quantities of whiskey, beer, *saké*, perhaps wine, and worse *shochu*. It's that *shochu* that does it all the time, tips the tipsy scale, he thought coherently for the last time that night, as he grabbed an Ebisu beer. Fortunately, given his good physical condition, VZ would remain in a slightly-over-tipsy state most of the evening through, and still not return home till after two. The next morning he would recall that everyone had been so *nice*, it had been such a *decent* party, the conversation so *level*. What's wrong with that?, he wondered to himself. Didn't he deserve a nice time once in a while? After all, he could be well-behaved and polite when called upon to be so. His reputation for rowdiness was certainly ill-deserved , he defended himself to no one in particular. Yes, people were pleasant, some girls were really nice, what's wrong with making light conversation? (Roberta's party had started that way, he recalled; he remembered a good conversation with Kazuo about Shinohara's Ukiyo-e Museum in Nagano, and the early houses.) Yes, Maybe he ought to try it a bit more, mingle in a politer society. He knew people, he could make his way. Wasn't there an art to keeping conversation at a certain level, not low certainly, but not too rarefied either – light, tripping (was that

British English?) – smooth ... small, white breasts, a young girl surprised at her behavior. Yes, there was another angle to discover.

* * *

Ivy covers the tall smokestack. (Inokashira line)

The way you watch a newscast in English as if it were a messenger from the real world the forgotten tongue and you question again if you are kidding yourself your existence here.

* * *

Cafferty told me once in conversation that when he first set foot down here he'd felt his testicles fall to the earth, had felt himself for the first time a part of the real living world, had felt free to find out who he was or might be, felt that "he" was a no man who might be any man or any other being or thing, and wasn't that enough or more than might be expected to have or to feel at least one's testicles feel that – the testicles, the earth, you know. I thought of this tonight as I thought at home alone of how long I've been here and would, yes, call it "home," but wondered how that had ever come about.

* * *

Lang didn't know if he was gaining or losing.
Roberta? The city?
This strange language.

She didn't want an orgasm, said it'd make her fall in love with him.

* * *

Hmm. Yes, to love. To love the city. All the varieties of something so singularly unvaried. A mother for her child. A man for his money. A musician for his art. Me for ... well. And he for the city. What does it mean "to love a city"? Many people "love" their city for its history or its beauty or its convenience or any number of other reasons. But basically, I would say that they *appreciate* the place they live in. How does he "love" Tokyo? I can say for myself that I do not mind the place, and sometimes I really do enjoy being here, and at others I can find it exciting; but I must also admit that I always look forward to those times I can go back for a visit to Kyoto. Only twice last year, and one of those for the funeral. But even our funerals are different. It's nice if he is happy loving the city, but I have to wonder if that love is the reason he is not married? We must be careful with our love, knowing where and when to give it, and not allowing it to go astray. Thus the gracious Kazuko.

* * *

The girl who's in the "radical *manga*" group – she was born in 1963, the city was beginning to boom, and her friends called her "transistor glamour" because she was light, quick and had a brilliant future. It's true, I've seen the photos, Marianne recalls.

* * *

- No, no, Kazuko, this is mine – and so are those to follow.
- Lang ...
- No argument. The evening is ours, the cost is mine. Your coat.
- Thank you, Lang.
- And how is Kazuo these days?
- Well, besides working ...
- He's got a nice job, hasn't he? With a publisher, is it?
- Yes.
- A publisher of what?
- Oh, one of those big publishing companies – factories, I should say. They do everything from Western classics, to Japanese classics, from weekly magazines to comics, and even from bestselling blockbusters from anywhere to pornography.
- So I've heard. Sounds exciting, fun.
- Well, he is intelligent enough to have covered most of the field in just the few years he's been there. Now he's an assistant manager in one division, but he may be transferred once again soon.
- Porno?
- Sorry, Lang, no.
- Oh, too bad, I thought I might have gotten some introductions.
- Well, I'm sure he could do that for you if you're really interested.
- Kazuko, I'm interested in everything. Have to be.
- Well, I can ask
- No, no need to push now. I like the man, but hardly know him well enough to ask for a porno introduction. But that aside, I really

would like to get to know him better. He seems a very intelligent man, and he knows his Tokyo.

- Well, I'm sure he knows it better than you or I.
- Better than me?
- Uhn, sorry.
- No, I'm sorry. I just take a certain pride in how well I do know the city ... but not being a Tokioite, I suppose I have to give pride of place to Kazuo. For now, that is.
- Yes, perhaps. Anyway, as I was saying, yes, Kazuo is often busy with work, but he does not allow that to interfere with, or should I say, take over his life.
- And that's why you like him, eh?
- Well, yes ... that and other things.
- Such as?
- Lang! ... I suppose I'm still not used to such direct questions. Well, Kazuo is very intelligent, as you mention, and sensitive – he's been abroad you know, and though he's not from Kyoto – oops, there I go, I didn't mean that
- Yes you did.
- Well, perhaps, yes, and no, I really didn't – I think. ... Anyway, may I go on?
- By all means. You were saying that even though your boyfriend is not an aristocrat ...
- Lang!
- Sorry, Kazuko. Just teasing.
- Alright. Kazuo is, well, he's *alive*: he listens to people, he listens to himself.
- He likes listening to Jazz.
- Yes; and he listens to me. And to you, I might add.
- He listens to me?
- Yes, certainly.
- And what does he hear, might I ask?
- And might I answer?
- Go for it, as Van Zandt would say.
- Van Zandt! Alright. He's talked to me about you. He says that you are in pain, that you are confused, that you have a conflict regarding ...
- Does he listen to me or talk about me? What's this about a conflict? And pain – what pain? Or which?
- Yes, between you and Tokyo and Roberta.
- I like the man even more. Not too bad an analysis. What does he

charge an hour?
- Lang.
- I'm sorry. But I can be stubborn, you know.
- Oh, I know, I've seen.
- So, Kazuo's analysis?
- Well, he sees you here, your great enthusiasm for the city. He wonders why you ever came here, especially when you hadn't wanted to at first. He understands that you came here for Roberta's sake, or rather for the sake of your relationship.
- Oh?
- But it couldn't have been for her sake really, because she's been doing fine here. And, if I may ...
- Please.
- Well, he feels that your being here has only upset Roberta.
- The man is astute. And what do you see and say, Kazuko?
- Well ...
- Yes?
- Well, I see things pretty much the same as Kazuo.
- I see.
- But are we wrong? Oh, forgive me for saying all this.
- It's perfectly alright, really ... no, you're neither entirely wrong.
- ?
- It's alright. And it's good to speak with you. Believe me, I do appreciate your honesty.
- And concern. Lang – our real concern.
- And concern, Kazuko. Thank you; you are sweet; the both of you. As I said, I like Kazuo, and I like you, and I like the two of you, and I might add, I like Roberta and me – however it turns out.
- Yes?
- Well, Kazuo's not too off the mark. Yes these are tough times, indeed. It's true. *I never wanted to come here; I had a passing, a professional interest in Japan, but winters get pretty gray in Vienna, as I'm sure you've heard, and the few letters from Roberta only added to things being that much more up in the air, too far for my comfort and I couldn't abide that couldn't abide being vague, gray, afloat. And so, to find out, to settle it all one way or the other – I came.* I came to Tokio. I can't deny I came here for her, to get her out of here and back with me in Europe. But I can't deny Cafferty's thesis either –
- That, uhm, the ...
- Yes, that the, uhn, anyway, she'd settled here – good for her – I wasn't resident. But now it's all changed, the conflict Kazuo speaks

of: the woman or the city? I am settling in in my own way, and I want the complete elaboration, to take the city in and the city to take me in, splendor and darkness, eye and anus, I am drunk on the city in a way I have never felt, or rather, only felt once and that was when I first met Roberta, and I know that she does not feel the same way about Tokio as I do – so be it – but for now I have to recover the city and so discover myself, and then perhaps rediscover Roberta, Roberta and I, and too –

- Lang. Stop You're not talking like a human being. Are you really saying that a mere city is more important to you than your love for Roberta and hers for you?
- Oh, Kazuko, maybe I am. And maybe you're right, maybe it's not human. How can I know? I'm so wrapped up in this – so … human – place.
- Lang, if you really loved Roberta, your arms would be around her right now.
- But I do love her. I don't deny that I have gotten a bit lost in all this. I came to take her away, and now I can't myself.
- Lang?
- Yes?
- Can't you reconcile this somehow?
- Oh, believe me, Kazuko, I wish I could; I am aware of the dilemma – no, it's more than that. Believe me, I want Roberta; I also happen to want much else – or rather, only Tokio.
- And where does that leave her?
- Well, first it leaves her here in Tokio. And that's a place that I wouldn't mind being in. But too, our Tokios are so very different.
- A place you "wouldn't mind being in." In other words, living with her?
- Well, that wasn't what I meant; but yes, yes. I was referring to the contentment she's found; and it so small.
- We Japanese don't seem to mind.
- Yes. In any event, the point is that I have to find a reconciliation of my current obsession with the city, and my – believe me, Kazuko – my real love for Roberta.
- Yes. To any normal person it would all be very simple.
- Yes. But why this interest, Kazuko, why the petty problems of a European and an American in Japan?
- Lang, you really do surprise me.
- Eh?
- Lang, Kazuo and I have known Roberta some time now, and you

some few months less.
- Yes, true.
- Oh, you're exasperating! What would Marianne say? "Don't you get it, man?" Lang, we like you both, we like you, we like Roberta, we, you, both. We see a lot of confusion, and we'd like to help in whatever way we can. Is that so extraordinary?
- Like friends, eh?
- Lang!
- Ok, I'm sorry. I appreciate it, I do, really. But what is to be done, what can be done?
- Well, I'm not sure, really, but let's all calm down. Let's take a walk, talk a bit.
- Sounds –
- Sounds good, basic, Lang. There is *her* Tokyo to discover, to take part in. Perhaps for her too there is yours. As long as – what do you say? – as long as you don't "hit her over the head with it." What a terrible phrase.
- Let me remind you that your own language has some pretty ugly phrases too.
- Please, don't. Anyway, there is also my Tokyo, and there's Kazuo's; all those restaurants! You should know more than anyone – there being so many Tokyos. Tokyo's to share.
- Very true. But it begins to sound too much like a plan, a strategy to win her back. Not that she's left; maybe I have. And then I wonder, would she go for it?
- No, Lang, that's not it at all. I am not proposing any kind of plan to keep you two together – that will sort itself out in its own way. All I am proposing is, well, a means, a means for us all to be friends, friends in the city, as you, no doubt, would see it.
- No doubt at all. I thank you, Kazuko. It sounds wonderful.
- No thanks required, Lang. Oh, haven't you ever felt that in a friendship? Two people like one another, and one of them has to make the first move, has to say something, something personal or private, make some opening, some invitation or overture, whether mutual or no, but to open something, some path – to the open?
- Yes, yes, of course you're right, Kazuko.
- Even a self-opening?
- Yes?
- To say that I find you a strange man, Lang – and that I like you.
- Thank you, Kazuko. I like you, too, I always have; I've long wondered who the hell you are. No more mysteries. Or maybe more

indeed! ... No, no, let me get this. I am indebted. And tell Kazuo
– no, let me tell him –
–   Tell him what?
–   Why, how lucky he is!
–   Oh, Lang, we're all lucky!

* * *

Rich and strange it is, Roberta reflects, I hardly ever reflect on the
city – thought about it occasionally – the first few weeks – but had
already naturally fallen into step – so there goes Lang's testicle theory
– why must he beat the city so to death and call it love? – is that what
he does, to resurrect, what, himself, me, the city? – to make it his own
– Lang the conqueroo. Oh, but I should've been named Miranda – yes,
that'd've been nice too. Oh, Miranda! You *are* here beside me, *aren't* you?

* * *

–   "*Ginbura*" – wandering, wending, fucking in Ginza. Do the hicks
    get it, or the sopshisticato cockatoos?
–   Who knows, Cafferty?
–   They discovered a piece of the old "red bricktown" recently. Don't
    tell a soul about it! The city fathers – or whatever relation they are,
    more like very hungry ghosts – will manage to get rid of even more
    history if however some of the charms remain.
–   I'm sure.
–   Twilight: mothers and daughters going home after the theater, cake
    – or *kay-kee* – a bit of shopping. Office and department store work-
    ers leaving too. Thankfully, Ginza just doesn't have that youth ap-
    peal. And then twilight, it begins – you smell it first, the women in
    kimonos or equally exquisite dresses, silk, brocade, crêpe de Chine;
    they emerge from the subway stations like Kyoka demonesses, per-
    fumed, the hair done just so – that lovely swirl, can't recall the name
    of it. Shimada?
–   Could be.
–   First they go for a short visit to their favorite cakeshops – a bit of
    gossip, final touches to their makeup – and then to work! How
    many hundreds of bars are there here really? Does anyone have any
    near accurate idea?
–   Not I.
–   And then, suddenly – they're gone, they disappear! That cool Ginza

quiet: the hum of the icemen, the so few ricksha now with their so few geisha – you only see one every few months these days, probably more back in Kagurazaka – the Mama-sans seeing clients off, a few couples at the few good restaurants – the triple pasta behind the police-box, the sushi restaurant that caters to the family restaurant, and ... and then it's midnight ...: all the girls out now, cheeks rosey, the hair a bit loose, the makeup worn, the step unsteady. The streets filled with limousines for the big executives who've been coddled in ways no self-respecting wife would do, and most of them only coddled, a quick feel at the most unless the man's ready to make a life investment. The girls wave them away, they stagger, and they weave their ways into the night.

* * *

You tear-stained, teenaged Tokio, I know you better than you think I do, Arlene declares. Oh yes I do.

* * *

ANTOKU AND ROKUDAI

We die early and late
ashore a-cradle

cast before the lie
our voices abate

in cradles we lie
with out shores of hate

our voices await
the cradle of fate

* * *

Tokyo is like flypaper; the more you struggle to get out, the more stuck you are.

– Anon.

The press reports that the Princess will be taught how to shop.

* * *

SCENE THREE: OLD/NEW BAR, IKEBUKURO

Coming out of the department store, overloaded with vegetables and fruits and some firm, good-looking tofu, the Woman saunters over to Old/New, the bar with its Isamu Wakabayashi iron patinaed walls. It provides her a respite from the hordes of kids and their countryish parents (though never together, of course). It is very cool, gray, indifferent, very 80s, she feels comfortable here, very cool and mysterious herself. She orders one too many near-frozen *sakés* – in fact the second sets her off – and she recalls evenings at other Old/News (she always called it "Old and New," however): in Kichijoji, with a Dutch friend, and where when business was sinking by the early 90s they'd sell off half the space to make way for a *karaoke* room; then there is the Old/New branch in Shibuya, with its Natsuyuki Nakanishi murals, purples and silvers à la some Japanese Klimt Nouveau, and where her American friend had insisted they go to a less "piss elegant" place for a drink; the one in Roppongi with its Noriyuki Haraguchi walls, also iron, but even more cool, severe (was the fish restaurant just across the street?, she can't recall), and where her Swiss friend had forgotten her umbrella – it was still there a month later. In her inebriation she thinks the waiter – so long in coming – is her man. Would he like to see her home? She fucks him like crazy, says goodnight, and can't recall a thing the next morning.

* * *

The aim of art is to prepare a person for death, to plough and harrow his soul, rendering it capable of turning to good.
                                                            – Andrei Tarkovsky

Three miracles: my dream of a religious convention; the dream of a dragon-fly and being saved; and the one where they are fucking in the rice field and she has crooked teeth.

* * *

R'n'L!!!

So Calvin opens his skull and his brains drop out. He goes to his mother and says, "I let my mind wander and it didn't come back." She's lying on the couch reading and says, "I thought you lost your mind years ago." But the best is where he plays Godzilla and destroys Tokyo!

"Nothing special, just talk, and suddenly just to talk with you." Someone in Wenders' *Wrong Move*. Japanese Noir – gotta find out more.

I love that thing that Dwight Yoakum said, and that he said he was sayin' it even if it sounded like white trash talkin', that if Elvis had married Ann Margaret he'd be alive today.

I made a huge salad with everything in it. Want some?

I need a new pocket knife. Do you think I need to have a license to carry one here?

Now let us take the word "lettuce." Give each letter the numerical value of its order in the alphabet. A=1, ... Z=26. So, we get, T=20; U=21; L+E+E+22; and T+C=23. A neat order, transposed, TUVW. – Uhn, no, I don't do this all the time. Hey, some people count license plates.

And anyway, just remember, "Love laughs at locksmiths." (Ok, ok: it's Houdini via Buster.)

Did you ever hear that Bill Anderson song, "He Died of Love at 3AM"? Me neither. Dylan mentions it in *Don't Look Back*. Must be easily available; I should put it on the list and look for it. Oh, lazy-busy me.

Another movie title. *History is Made at Night.*

The major headache in my life right now – besides love, money, work, and your absence – is my clothes-dryer. Why am I telling you this? (Can either of you fix clothes-dryers?)

Thursday I had no coffee at all. Friday I caught a cold. There is a connection, a lesson here, isn't there?

Forget that Zen stuff about the face you had before you were born. Can SV even remember the original color of her hair!

* * *

I hate the country – two hours between trains, an hour between busses, and no record stores. It's such a nuisance.

– *Street of Shame* (Kenji Mizoguchi-Silva, 1956)

* * *

Seventy-two hours and counting. What's the "X" in LAX for, anyway? Hiromi, you've got three credit cards, a week's worth of tight pants, four days of pent up sexual energy, a box of condoms because you never know about American guys, and a heart of ... well, we'll just leave the heart home this time. I don't know why it's taken me so long to get to Los Angeles. Just because Hawaii was closer. A dumb one, Hiromi-chan. I mean, it wasn't bad, that's for sure, but it wasn't LA either. The cars the freeways the boys. The first Disneyland – I hope it's as good as ours, might be pretty run down though. Is there crime in Disneyland, too? Must be, it's American, isn't it? (Oh, I have to be careful, careful, careful. What if I was robbed? God, what would I do? Oh, please, don't let it happen. I'm near the end of my savings. I couldn't possibly come home empty-handed. Oh, what if I shopped – and *then* was robbed? What if I'm robbed on my first day there, what would I do? Will there be some sort of secret place where I can keep my money safe? Isn't the country supposed to provide for people like me? Can't I just call up Sumitomo Bank and get an advance or something?) Universal pictures. Rodeo Drive. Is that a branch of the Daikanyama shop? Let's see: shop wisely (no problem, I'm from Tokyo, I was born to it); light lunches, and let the guys take care of dinner; drink moderately; look hot. Those American boys are suckers for Japanese women. Oh am I going to have a *great* time! But why isn't Jurassic Park in my guidebook?

Chapter 4

GOTANDA–MEGURO

Roberta'd been here six months; she was feeling comfortable here, feeling herself, making her own way; as for Lang's imminent arrival she was ambivalent, curious and felt I suppose she didn't really have a choice but to "welcome" him, put him up for a while, see what developed – and so he got the little living room – until he up and left.

* * *

Love means acknowledging the dangerousness of the way and feeling the incomprehensibility of the coincidence with another.

– Robert Musil

What did I say, overhear? *Lang meditates to himself.* And what the price I have paid for it now? Tried my best to be a man – the one you want? – a woman and child, tried to love, friends, family – and you, Roberta. All that sunless steel, concrete boys with cars and curtain walls, wanting only facts and not their feelings, blinding me to the facts of the feelings of it all, of what we were in fact doing or not to one another – the loved, the non-loved, the not-yet loved, all these Names of Love, strangers all, the frail flesh in frail breasts. And what have we – I – come up with? – faith lost. Betrayed from within. How, why did I go on for so long in that contempt, that negativity that threw me over in time, refused to get me through. Sick finally of all of us, fathers and daughters, mothers and sons, the natural antagonisms.

We know, dammit, what we know. And then we forget it all.

It's not supposed to be this way. What the hell've I been doing all this while, Lang?, *the silver-haired, 35-year-old boy/man asked himself as the sun set– in Tokyo in Lang in this his long moment of self-candor.*

Boy, indeed. Hadn't Roberta once asked him to "Cheer me up, Lang," and he'd quoted Bernhard, "Man is wretched and only death is certain," and she laughed and asked him to "Say something nice now, Lang, something about men," and he came back with, "They're all boys at heart," and she tried again, and he hesitated a moment and then added, "A few of them might grow up and become men, and a few of them might become more," and she called him an angel and he told her he had been, "Since the day I was born, Roberta," and she loved him all the more, all the more despite the familiar and too truthful sting of those words of his that would remain with her long after she'd decided to leave him for however long necessary, remain while she was making her way in Tokyo.

Whadda'ya' hear, whadda'ya' say? Love is there – in the window, at the door, in yer arms, m'boy, yer thin, thin arms. And look where it's gotten you anyway. What did I do? Spoke to her. Listened. Doubt the love in hand? The name of a woman. Never enough there to dive into, but ever thinking there is more ahead: overthrow, dissolution, some further union down the line. (Say it simply, the heart of the matter, the responsibilities of memory. In this sea, this maelstrom some call the heart's desire. Runes upon – walls is it? – Poe's gates of ice.)

No, to achieve some newer music with the frail material allotted us? Something new, free of contempt, no malice aforethought. (The way Marianne years ago seemed to fly across the room into my arms.) Something blue …

A dozen years, two or three cities, one woman (who refuses to be one ((Who refuses? Who too many? Who more or less than enough?))) And now, this place, city – who are these people – this distant love – that I walk among, listen to?

Oh Roberta. This impossible city and you of all people in it and me of all … My comeuppance. If I go, you'll stay. If I stay – (Where would we go? But no –you've already left.) Oh, Blaise. I should've stayed home. Maybe I have; it's where the heart is, they say.

No – I'm a dead man's ghost.

No – I can change, I swear. I'm not yet the man I want to be, but soon enough the man you want … just a few weeks more – won't you?

Ten thousand ways to love. A bird of thought. A palm perhaps, a kiss, a greatness deferred for some other occasion. "Waiting for someone … to come out of somewhere." No, don't kiss me yet, soon already I'll be yours, kiss you too much.

What the city? Who the woman?

I never wanted to come here. She's set up now in the Low City, needs to be alone, demands it. Accepted. I make my way then. And what is this place, this Kichijoji? A lot of foreigners, grocery stores and restaurants, even a Parco – you get off the train and the whole world looks fifteen years old.

Who the city? What the woman?

No, that's not, dammit, what I need to say. Recall all. (Everything fixed in memory. Somewhere in the brain they say, it's stored, and apparently can all come out. I remember standing before the *Rokeby Venus* and thinking it would be quite a while before I saw it again and so I determined then and there to fix every inch in my memory-eye. (The flesh, contours and folds, like the Master's lace.) But is it all retrieved only on the deathbed? Do I start babbling like the Dutchman?) Hell, what *do* I want to say? No, no, let's not get sentimental, boy. Say your beads. "Swift, Musil, Joyce; Swift, Musil, Joyce."

No new language, no new truths, and none eternal, either. Me, myself and I. And Roberta? Yes, all the while, Roberta and her times. An end to pain. Pun intended? Leave it to the reader. No, take that back; we know and love the reader too well, we know what he'll do to it. Leave it to … well, any or all of us; who's a reader, anyway? Shit, enough of that sort of talk, all we say, half-digested, and who's competing anyway?

I have forgotten so very much.

And I? Now new or the same again?

"Not find happiness? A right to live?" Who said it to whom? You know, I fell, I think now, less for what you said than for the voice you said it in. Falling for a voice, then the eyes and smile, the mind and humor in the hips.

And me – it's been too long since I worked on my Buddy Holly imitation.

Now it seems or never for Lang.
"What profiteth it a man, Lang?"
(From whence these phrases and images?)
"If I pull the skin back for a closer look at the frail scrotum ..."
(What did she say?)
"Oh, you're only another part of another love story."
(You'll never get out of these blues alive, Lang.)
"Ahi mi! My splendors and miseries lay about me!" Palm out, hand to brow, I fall back on to a sofa, and whisper in tears, "why all this violence?" – and expire.
(Lang, wake up, Lang!)

A stolen kiss and a broken word and now look at all the damage transpired. The way you left her then, walked out of the room and she knew you'd come back. The way she left you now, walked out of the city and you now so unsure. Then the short note, and a couple of weeks later a call from Tokio. Love – all of it – had been offered me – *(To me, to be so blessed, of all my sex, center of all beauty!)* – and I held back. You refused: remember: a promise, loyalty, wholeness, time. Freely refused, and freely condemned. Not God's will, yours, Lang. And now you are in Tokio where madness seems a form of an unknown love and she is asking you to leave her herself her city.

And only some few women some few men willing to try again. (What movie was that?). He walked into his own labyrinth, and never saw the sun again. Damn, Lang, can you finally halt what you like to refer to as your desire and refuse to acknowledge as resentment and recall her to you now and give her back what she saw in you once – not faith, but maybe its possibility?

I saw her figure on the street, a Klein blue bag, a string of hair that refused to stay in place, a swimmer's legs, and ... in her smile was my peace, in her eyes my Paradise. All those Robertas to discover! Our life and times, the unions and separations of those first months together – who left whom then? And why? Not so much indecision as only that when the decision came it would be irrevocable, permanent, the first day and last.

The will to serve.

And then the years, the innurral and renewal, and then again until you brought it to its inevitable end, pushed her to it, nothing she desired, never anticipated: that you you turned into. And what disappointment

– coming just when you seemed, she thought, so ready! Resentment was hers then, rightfully. And she so ready, "I can only give you everything," and it really was oh so true and you could not see it for the life of the city you needed to embody – a city you had no concrete idea of, no Tokio of the mind yet. But if this too be a man, what is indeed to be said or done? That is what you recognize now too late to make amends. "Amends"? As if there were *repairs* that could be made. Not towards her, not now, no longer. In yourself, in prospect. To be a man, woman, child. Finally, at this stage, you must or never be a man.

Oh, live up to your name now, Lang, now or never!

Ah, Roberta, Tokio … all the time before me. You, Roberta, new? Changing-changeless. Isn't that what they say of Tokio? Ah, now, Carole Lombard, she would have understood.

"I opened my heart to the whole …" – well, to the city – "and I found it was loving."

Lang sits in his darkened room, the eyes focussed in thought, the mind hovering above the city he is only recently, slowly, coming to recognize. How does one become a city? What do we mean when we say we fulfill ourselves, our nature, only in the city? That we are only wholly human and moreso in the city, and wholly cities in you, Tokyo?

(Tokyo, I gave everything to you– body and soul, I'm all for you – absolve me, release me now with grace ascending so that I might live again, and rely on the expectation of a peaceful death. If I am not all yours, not a true Tokyoite, then I am unworthy, a reprobate, and I will get the death I deserve.)

There is light inside the tunnel, too. With faith, belief, whatever it takes me now. Friendship, toughness, tenderness. "Without which nothing": Godard's beautiful ending. "Love or destruction": Aleixandre's beautiful beginning. "Brothers in mourning, sisters cradled in sisters' arms": Bergman's beautiful memory. Roberta and Lang, together in Tokio – in our lifetime, Lord? And *Gertrud*. To be able to say at the end: *I have loved.* In the city, in the woman, in me, Lang, the man women love to – women love to what? Might I only know it in this city, this woman?

"Banal" van Zandt called the people. Or what is the difference after all between fucking and talking? ("To fuck and be fucked. 'Oh, by Jaysus, but I am be-fucked.' A love by any other name." – *Oh, Lang, get a hold of yourself!*) Ok: to live one's time, place, at most, no less than that; this: to describe a mood, to describe an arc – a style, a geometry. No more nor less. (Christ, why all this now?, where from, what gash, now of all places and with all that's transpired (("loose usage" – so regarded by whom? – that too, where from?)) with all that's transpired between Roberta and me? From whence this gush?

Years together in our fashions and it still was new. Roberta as the USA: red hair, blue eyes, her milky white skin –tight dresses and lipstick. Northern Roberta, black eyes and a blue dress; Spanish Roberta, black hair and a red dress. The angular Roberta, the reclining Roberta, Roberta at her desk – Roberta, your body changing according to your moods, your "circumstances." Your small breasts became large those months and then small again. Looked Chinese once, and now once more so American. And now again changing – a sort-of Japanese look. Ah, but throw any bolt of cloth at you and any way it falls it looks made for you. And that voice still. (And speaking what variety of languages.) The monotone, the rush, the strung together phrases, the leaps across thought and grammar, the resistance, the edge, the profundo and the moderato. Within, between and above them all, the One and the Many, unique, you, alone, the multiple capital ARE.

People are good. I have seen and known a few good people.
(The mother's skull in a dream of death for the newborn babe and I see you whole.)

But that's not what I wanted to say either. Or is it? You wanted to say something that speaks like children with as much control over their bodies as … that speaks of some however small tenuous or inappropriate connection with – with what?, where? – Beijing? … that speaks to a woman who's asked you to leave and with whom you want to stay.

(But what am I to do with this Tokio? Roberta's not going to play guide and hostess. Better call van Zandt tonight … "Everybody's tryin' to be my …." To be my what? Never met so many one-conversation bastards. Well, folks, you've come to monologue's end, your telephone cards have run out. What happened to the ear that listens, the two-way street? What was that line about hangers-on, friends and virtue? And every artiste here seems to have a tale of despair and final triumph against the philistines – but they're the system. Leave 'em all behind, Lang – I've got work to do. So, JG, write a novel when yer 25, and then leave, tend yer garden and seek wisdom. And if you do have children, remember Voltaire's advice: kill 'em before they begin to think of heaven.)

Whose were those young, innocent faces I passed today? Young couples holding hands. Skirts swinging, leather bags, comic books, laughter and silence. A remembrance, a view from a bus window, a young couple's first kiss. To compassionate. "Running with instinct," and what remains, eh? "Young Couple on the Run: An Essay in Aesthetics." I wonder if I still have a copy of that somewhere. To recreate myself, or better – to cleanse myself of years of one-liners, of my own embellished tales told too many times, hardly a mythology, only silly in the end. (Perhaps destructive. "Believe Christ and His Apostles ...") That's maybe one biography; look for the other one, the faces, voices I've so neglected and that were there with me all the while, there in the shadows, in the corners and backgrounds, on the verandahs and stairs, too unassuming to come forward. (My Noir set as redone by Minnelli. ((Or Phil and Tina: "It's those little things that mean so much, so very much.")))

Or Zen, Blaise, we ought to try some sitting. Take Roberta's advice, visit the temple, live like that.

Love. Purely. Do not think.
No, no, think, man. You are leaving her – you've been asked.
("Leaving? Who's leaving? Who said anything about leaving?")
No, Lang.
The times are very different. Indeed.

Lang ... Lang ...
Sorry, Blaise, but nothing happens to you when you're standing still. Not to me at least. I don't have that kind of Zen. You've got to move.

I need to re-enter the world.

This is it, for our exhausted hero, as he summarizes the end of a near-year-long meditation, a meditation that had begun with the Chinese silencing.

A sudden screech, a wing glimpsed, a woman's opened speechless mouth – The city is a skull where all the voices resound in words and notes repeated forever in each friend and lover's specific articulations, and all their images flash in instants fixed forever in single takes; it is here I encounter myself my destiny alone – and where I meet it hand in hand *with Roberta* both of us with eyes wide open, all pain forgotten, disappointed love forgiven, where my friends are forever present, conversing, we walk through backstreets or across boulevards, meet simply to wander, or linger in cafés and bars, we recommend books and records, participate in the quotidian, glory in it all, and at night when the bars have closed, the lovers returned to one another's arms, the children's terrible dreams undone with a parent's unseen kiss, we each in our own ways return home to dream, reminisce, make a late night phonecall – or write a few notes.

My room, skull, city is bare – perhaps a print or postcard on a wall: Bernini's Teresa, Fischer von Erlach's Karlskirche, something by Sesshu or Lee U-Fan, something perfect, hard and yet all emotion; no more than one shelf of books, a few pens and paper; the gray tabletop stripped but for the keyboard and monitor ... the drama of lovers – *Roberta and I* – and others too, friends, the family drama – all played out – an inner struggle of gestures, journeys that end either in death or go nowhere at all, pleas that no one listens to, murderous loves that are endured ... for what? ... sisters and brothers all of us understood finally in our tragic fullness that turns too late to grace and splendor – they become one, friends, couples, more – finally, union, the misremembered dream of life.

The body is restored and the soul rediscovered – sea and sky! – the mind is as fast as the hand as immediate as the writing – here: desk, skull, city – Tokio, *Roberta and I*, where all these wanderings end.

What more can I say, Roberta? – *Lang now out of his delirious access, letting go the weight of doubt the burden of questions, the spirit and flesh raised, standing once more prepared to speak with the sun behind and the moon above – sunrise and sunset reconciled!* – Roberta? With Aretha then, "I love you. And I love you! And I love you too!" A world of you inside me – and I failed us both. (And you love me too!) Union, yes – but not now, not just yet. No second chances for fools like me. Go your way in this city that belongs to you. If there is a Tokio to be mine too I'll find it. In time, I pray, for us to rediscover one another. You leave me, stay where you are. And I'll stay with you – by going. And as far as you are I shall be near.

Inside.

Lang then in a moment of self-candor that was so much like the May-June events in China, 1989. A decade and more of frustration, inaction, the gathering finally, discussions with some few friends, forays into action, and then the gush, the relentless holding on, the demand to be heard, the flood, and in it finding oneself again among friends, thousands, hundreds of thousands and more, across generations and places, classes, the great criss-cross, the multiple antagonisms for a moment swept over by something even more essential, permanent, valuable, and no violence. An insistence on love – what's so funny? – the voice, its place. For a week (for his and Roberta's many years) the most exciting place in the world – until the fist.

But this time no sullen disillusion; this time his body shook, reawakened with a sobriety he had almost forgotten himself capable of. No mere "clarity," but a shimmering of the flesh, a trembling of the spirit, a determination body and soul that things this time could be accomplished, the defeats accepted, retreats regained, the landscapes reworked, and earth, all of it, this one, Tokyo – he, Roberta – won.

Lang's Meditation then, a wish for union, his usual wish for his life, despite the theme of separation, a life where finally all would be one: beauty and sadness, body and soul, memory and desire, poetry and the city, China and China, in a word, Roberta and Lang.

And so began Lang's long meditation – it continues in its way – as he walked the city in that long stride of his, down his lost highway, following whichever alley in the old part of the city, or cycling around Shinjuku, or trying to avoid the too many foreigners in Aoyama, or straight-arrowing his way through Shibuya towards a cinema, or even a humble walk through Inokashira Park, near home, or the long walk across Zempukuji, these thoughts would come to him, memories, dreams, trying as ever to comprehend his life, where he and Roberta had gone wrong and why he had not stopped it, knowing all too well that the fault lay in him, that she was all love and its readiness, the whole giving believing thing, while he held on to his infuriating and often terrifying, impossible dreams, memories – and meditations.

But we fear, fear there is so much more to his fear, and so fear for ourselves.

But for now, alas, an end, an end to Lang's longish meditation.

* * *

A moldy fig, a hard fart, a cool piss in the grass.

* * *

- Sony-dori should've been the lowest loop of the Yamanote, VZ declares. I mean, what do you get instead – Osaki? Has anyone ever gotten off there? I've seen 'em get on, but off – no way, man.
- What's down there, anyway – some of the old canals?
- Maybe.
- A mall, or something like one.
- Sony spillover probably, a perfect set for William Gibson.
- And Gotanda's mini sex street –
- But oh what those tall thin buildings hold! – the tales they could tell! – at least from the looks of all the posters.
- Ya' know, I never did make it to the, what was it, the Emperor love hotel? – *the* hotel of the 80s, eh?
- Right next door to the hundreds of Buddhas.
- Lots of old money around here – the Teien and the Hara mansions, but sprawling houses too. Second homes maybe a hundred years ago, like in that doctor novel, a second home in Shibuya, you can imagine it once was "far," almost countryside.
- Right, and now your family home comes three-generations after you.
- The three-generation mortgage!
- Do you even live long enough to see it?
- "Here's your graduation present, son."
- "Gee, thanks, Dad."

* * *

To haunt the great city and by this habit to penetrate it, imaginatively, in as many places as possible – *that* was to pull wires, *that* was to open doors, *that* positively was to groan at times under the weight of one's accumulations.

– Henry James

* * *

Ha! He says he loves it *all* – even Sanya? Dream Island? Edogawa Ward? Keep me away from there, Master, and I'll do my best by you. And, please, let me roam the few places I really enjoy. Shibuya, Jiyugaoka, you know. And those few nights when I can go out with you-know-who for an expensive meal in Aoyama or even Kojimachi. And a real hotel afterwards. I don't mind. A man with skin like a woman's. Maybe Hiroko is right and I should have taken some business classes. I could talk with him more then about his work, and then maybe I could see him more often. But do I really want to see anyone regularly? Keep 'em on a string and your profits run higher. That's all I know about business. Ah, but now I have to get that fancy watch repaired, and it's too late to ask him to do it for me. I'll have to pay for it myself. I guess that means I am taking a loss. Is that called a debit? But hey, why did the watch screw up like that? ... No, he wouldn't give me a fake, even something Korean as a gift, would he? The food's not fake, the hotel's the real thing, so why should a present not be? Or would it be? Well, anyway, it is a good-looking watch, and if it is a fake, then it's certainly done a good job of fooling a lot of people. No, he's not fooling me – at least, no more than I'm fooling him. But isn't everyone trying to fool everyone else almost all of the time? Gee, it gets a little confusing sometimes. My parents never fooled me. And I know I can trust Hiroko. I'd better call home one of these days soon. What if he told me he loved me on April Fool's Day? Then we'd really have to stay in a hotel so I could hear him say it again the next morning. Hmm ... Let's see: Get the watch fixed. Call home. Pick up the dry cleaning. What else was there? Something about the city. Well, later.

(Uhn, well, that *is* Hiromi, she too a Tokyoite.)

* * *

Oh, you tantalizing, transparent Tokyo, I could just kiss you!, Roberta exclaims.

* * *

The eclectic and uninhibited Yoshiwara way seems the genuine Tokyo way.

– Edward G. Seidensticker

* * *

THE TEIGIN INCIDENT

You can pass today by the little corner in Nagasaki, Toshima Ward (a photographer friend lives nearby) and never suspect that it is the site of the most infamous of postwar Japanese crimes. Everyone is implicated, and only hosts of questions (and rumors, scandals!) remain. And they reverberate still.

Just as most of our "Stories and Legends of Tokyo and Edo" are simple enough – summarized in a few sentences – their meanings speak the proverbial volumes.

A man dressed as a doctor enters a bank at closing time; he tells the staff that the neighborhood water supply is polluted with dysentery, and they should take the serum he has brought. They willingly oblige – and within two minutes twelve people are dead, the bank is robbed of ¥160,000 (with another ¥350,000 inexplicably neglected). The police gather disparate files, desperate evidence (two previous similar incidents; a search for a name-card; a U.S. Occupying Forces jeep mysteriously parked nearby), and seven months later they have their man: a painter of some small reputation who'd lost the name-card he'd been given months earlier by the doctor whose name was used in the crime. The suspect had also long before been affected by the fantasy-inducing Karsakoff's psychosis, a condition that can sometimes lead its sufferers to agree to anything. He signs a dubious confession, and in no short time is sentenced to death. Justice is served. (On the strength of a lost name-card! Fortunately, this was the last case in Japan in which circumstantial evidence was sufficient to convict a man.)

But the sentence is never carried out. Articles and books are printed; appeals filed; petitions served. The suspect dies at the age of 95, joking about being freed and marrying a girl of 25.

Japanese justice. Rumors, scandals – such is the norm here. Name the last ten Prime Ministers. Name the last five who served more than six months. Name the death row prisoners who have been released – after serving a decade or more time – their so-called "confessions" now admitted by the police as having been forced upon them. Name the political and financial scandals of the past quarter-century – the scandals that make the front page of the morning newspapers such a bore to read. And name the names of the rich and powerful who have served time – the shortest list of all.

The Teigin Incident (the name is an abbreviation for *tei*koku, "imperial," and *gin*ko, "bank") has deep, unresolved implications. The principle thesis has it that the perpetrator – an expert in poisons and chemicals – was a decommissioned officer of the infamous Unit 731, the chemical warfare division of the Japanese Imperial Army, which was located in Manchuria, and which devised the worst imaginable inhuman experiments. It is said that the Unit's staff was given their freedom by the Occupying Forces in exchange for information.

There are two points.

1. Corruption and complicity up and down. Recall the best scene in Visconti's *Götterdämmerung*: Dirk Bogarde lies in Ingrid Thulin's arms, whispering, "Complicity grows, complicity grows"– now translate it into Japanese.)

2. Gullibility. I mean, 16 people (four survived) just accepting the word of a guy in a white coat? A hundred million accepting another who says he's a god and telling them all to die for him? Could you or I go into a bank in Toshima Ward today, wearing some sort of uniform and tell everyone to lie down, take off their pants and, well, whatever? I hesitate to answer.

* * *

Rich?, strange?, Kaoru queries, no, steady. Twenty-seven now and everything going according to plan. Yes, rich someday, but strange, no, according to plan. Out of the Magazine Division soon enough, and then Books, preferably Classics and Bestsellers. And then I will astound them. My blurbs. Flaubert in three sentences! Balzac in two!

* * *

The waiter's vest slides across the waitress's breasts.

* * *

Fellini's *Satyricon*; Mizoguchi's whores pouring too much *saké*, pouting but in the end always putting out; a Butoh dance, dark, insane, the body ripped open; Marianne's laugh, the sudden shout that is a form of dance; those kids down the street always shouting, taunting their mothers to no end but they too in the end always rushing home to the tit; the cash registers in Seiyu: it's gotta be the noisiest city in the world. Well, one of the noisiest. What'd Richie write once, that "Nikko was a monument to the megalomania of the Tokugawa?" Whores, monks in gaudy makeup. One party, every party, yours ends where mine begins. Is everyone only talking to himself? "Talk to me, Roberta, goddamit! Say something nice! Lie to me!" What's everyone so afraid of saying? Don't be so nervous. Why should I want to make you feel uncomfortable? "Goddamit, Roberta! Here, have a cigarette. Oh, you quit?" Oh was I horrible that night of Roberta's party; just a few words and you could feel everyone tense up; by the end, I merely had to make as if to speak and you'd see their bodies stiffen up. And then VZ and Arlene trying to make everyone ease up – not their particular skill when also drunk. But what's curious is that everyone's conversation was dislocated, that night we all had a certain edge, a shrill stridency. We were all defensive, aggressive. But my mood prevailed – and look where it's got me.

* * *

Merchants – the way they kowtow still – what a legacy! Like in Mizoguchi.

* * *

- It was the crazy lady's birthday today.
- The "translator's"?
- No, the other crazy lady – the one at the Indian restaurant. There were flowers all over the place; three bunches arrived just during my lunch.
- Sounds like the crazy lady is loved. Why, by the way, are there so many Indian restaurants in Tokyo?

* * *

What did all that flesh mean then? Her thin legs, long neck, small breasts? A glimpse of what? What train line?

* * *

THE ARTICULATION OF A NEED / THE DESIRE TO DESIRE

– Quick – my bow!
– Which?
– Of burning gold!

It begins with those moments of moral cowardice and continues with social and artistic posturing, rank arrogance in the face of others' genuine modesty, and more and on, but, moral cowardice above all – these have left us wrecks, wrecks aesthetic, human and otherwise – had it not been for some few friends and the mutual recognition that our destinies, yours, mine, those of these friends, are all somehow conjuncted, and even and only as we acknowledge them – alone, together – might we ever see them through – plus the notion, foolish perhaps but there, of our charting of some new moral, aesthetic and amorous territory – and that this awaits us all – is this what attracts us all one to another, Marianne?

Rouze up, O Young Men and Women of the New Tokyo Age!

Set yourselves against the hirelings of advertising, of entertainment, of so-called urban and social pleasures, for these would forever prolong your spiritual and corporeal sufferings. Suffer not fashionable fools to depress your powers by the prices they pretend to pay for your would-be joys and sorrows. Believe the Buddha and his many avatars that some people are born only to destroy – while you are born to create and to live in a city of your own sublime Imaginations divine!

A chance to articulate a need that has been so long hidden and unsaid; and given our mutual and individual histories, dreams, and conversations, erotic, philosophic, cinematographic, and all the other arts at our disposal (conversations made too often of broken sentences, long silences of unheard speech) – these will see us through, fully forward, incorporating all within a single body, shining and unbreakable, a mutual, commingling and consubstantial body of gratified memory, need and desire (everything vertical!) — Marianne: is it possible?

So rouze up, you Men and Women of the New Tokyo Age!

Walk as you talk, the two one and the same, and each of you your own. You, Kazuko, who have made the journey from the western capital to the new, a history from which we can learn as we observe your calm steady walk, and so your talk. And you, her partner, Kazuo, with a not dissimilar ambulance and speech – rouze!, for the two of you form a prophecy. Young Hiro: stop that foolish walk of yours – this is no showroom, you are no whore; put bite into your speech: perhaps you do not possess any depths, but nonetheless ... Likewise you, Hiromi, you are no twin to your friend Hiroko; focus: a concentrated stride, and likewise that frivolous speech of yours; the city expands around you and yet you see only your shoes' brand name. And Kaoru – one more effort, please! We understand your despair, but again, the city opens up before you, offering a second life, Spite, maliciousness, and an uncaring walk need to be abandoned, let go: remake yourself now before it is too late and even the city despairs of you. And finally, gamine, Hiroko! Cute, silly, frivolous, superficial, immature ... it's all true ... and yet ... and yet ... in your case these negatives are indeed positives as we see you transforming them into more than 'charm points' – superficial depths indeed. You are a true Edokko, and thus your success assured. Oh Hiroko ... rouze!

> – Quick – my arrows!
> – Which?
> – Of Desire!

* * *

I saw a child in a crowded ceramics shop, Arlene recalls, something dropped, a cup or vase or some such object. The shop owner came up to the mother and apologized to her for having been so foolish as to have put a delicate piece in the way of a child. He then gave the kid a piece of candy. The mother slightly scolded her child. Now you *know* you would never see that happen in any other country.

* * *

–   Zonar – is that what Cafferty told us to look out for?
–   Sounds like a porno star – the snake-lady – no, that was Zora –
–   Whoosh!, through the glass you replicant.
–   But what is this place?
–   God-awful. The groves of the nation's future leaders. Typical Tokyo campus: fast food, *pachinko*, Mom and Pop shops. You go down Kagurazaka – hey, I had a dream about a "Number 14-Slope" recently! – and Miracle Queen, an ice cream and perfume shop, does it still flourish? – so ... you go down past the SDF
–   If you can – you're getting a little shakey there, VZ.
–   Had a bit too much?
–   Me?
–   You thought you could make it to Roberta's from Kagurazaka, huh?
–   Wait, now where was I? Oh yeah: ya' know, Mishima's last meal was

in Shimbashi, he did himself in ... no, it wasn't here – look, from the bottom of one bowl to – look! – that light on the river and those trees: the city disappears! – like in Ochanomizu – and past that apartment building with a swimming pool, no less! – there's the bottom of the other bowl.

 – Man, what's he talking about?
 – Beats me. Memories, I guess.
 – Half made up, it sounds to me.
 – Nah, not VZ, he's got a lot of shit we ain't half aware of.
 – Ichigaya, the Spanish bookstore – did the Italian one move from Jimbocho, or just close? – up a bowl and down – voilá – Yotsuya!
 – Like I said, a lot of shit.

* * *

Why did they take that cruise round the world? Couldn't they just have taken a walk across the city?

* * *

Arlene is in grade-school. Puberty. The classroom is large. For twelve- and thirteen year-olds, these kids seem to be adult-sized. The boys are either extra-shy, or they are crudely attempting to raise the girls' skirts. Typical classroom chaos. Arlene sits at her desk, observing the teacher who has no control whatsoever over his students. Arlene's glance goes from one boy to another; in between, she focuses on a couple of the older girl students. No one talks to her. She is curious, and not unhappy as she rubs herself. A glance out the window shows her shopping arcades, pachinko parlors, people dressed as film actors; in between the public announcements exhorting shoppers she catches snatches of the voice of Billie Holiday accompanied by Lester Young.

That evening, Van Zandt had gotten drunk on tequila at a gallery reception for an exhibition of drawings by Mika Yoshizawa. In the background Billie Holiday records were playing. The reception had been held in Kamata, the former Hollywood of Japan. Lang had once "explained" Yoshizawa's work to VZ. In his dream, VZ is still at the reception where so many young Japanese women seem to be walking in circles around him as he tries to cut a path across them in order to talk with one in particular who is talking with Lang about Yoshizawa. The work, like eyes and breasts and machine parts or instruments to be employed in sacred and/or sexual rituals whirl around VZ. The Kamata associations don't help. As he sleeps he is aware that he is drunk, and he is happy about it, except for the gnawing frustration he feels at his inability to reach the woman whom he feels genuinely attracted to. When he wakes up he thinks that a Yoshizawa drawing of a circle whose right half is taken up by a circle whose right half is taken up by a circle could also resemble Tokyo whose right half is taken up by the Yamanote loop whose right half is taken up by the Palace. Tokyo then as an eye, a breast, a Mika Yoshizawa drawing.

* * *

brown walls
behind blue curtains

fragile world
fragile woman

blown walls
beneath blue tiles

* * *

Of all the shops she loved, she loved this one best.

* * *

R'n'L!!!!

There are more than 2,000 magazines titles published in Tokyo. Isn't that a happy thought? And then their titles!

I've ordered my new computer but it doesn't arrive for a few weeks, and I am almost paranoid to do anything on this one on its last legs. Ya know, my favorite button used to be "delete," but now it's "Yes to all."

Ya' know, the other day I realized that in the last couple of years I have attended one funeral (Ikuko), two weddings, and half a dozen couple friends have had kids. Not too bad for the Life Goes On [or Doesn't] Dept.

Song of the Week: "Bossa Nova Baby" (1963), with these immortal lyrics:

> I said, Hey Little Mama, let's sit down, have a drink and dig the band.
> She said, Drink, drink, drink, oh fiddleydink, I can dance with a drink in my hand.
> She said, Hey Bossa Nova Baby, keep on workin,' 'cos I ain't got time to drink.
> She said, Hey Bossa Nova Baby, keep on dancin,' 'cos I ain't got time to think.

Oh, Ann Margaret, we love you!

A style to accommodate chaos – that's what we want here.

Parentheses, like vaginas (and both, like the city), are a matter of lips opening and closing, quivering if you like, all the meanwhile maintaining their delicate order within the frenzy of all they are expressing. I limit myself to three on either side (Roussel's five!) and then work my way back in. Anyway, but how do you explain this to anyone? "Hey, Roberta, Lang, what's new?" "Oh, we were just talking about parentheses, vaginas and quoting songs in letters." "Oh, I see, heh-heh." Vaginally then, like some etymology, I unfold myself to you.

Cary and Carole together in one great movie! The missing link to human happiness.

Ok, how's this for a photo project. I was talking with Junko about the three portraits idea and it suddenly occurred to me: "What about all my other friends?" So I thought about taking photos of 'em all when we go to our fave bars, and calling the thing *Tokyo Twists and Hardons*, "twist" of course being gangster slang for a broad, uhn, I mean a dame, uhn, I mean a chick, uhn I mean a girl, uhn – hell, what do I mean, anyway?, and "hardon" being the same for a prick, uhn I mean a guy, uhn, I mean ...

Which reminds me: years ago when I got my first 8mm camera, this camera store had a kind of amateur night. (Very) amateur models would prance around and the equally amateur photogs [ugh, I mean, I hate that word, but I equally hate typing out the whole thing – maybe

I can make a macro out of it, anyway:] would shoot 'em. Anyway, I attended, and shot. Then I shot a lot of cranes around the city – and you know how I love cranes. Then I tried ever so ineptly to edit it all together in a quasi-structuralist manner. And what did I call it? Why *Guys and Dolls*, of course.

Am beginning to think that *My Darling Clementine* is my all-time fave Western; and besides, Fonda – "with a portrait as beautiful as his who wants true?" – surely has the most beautiful walk (among men) in the movies.

February is the cruellest month. Why?, you ask. Because *Movieline* doesn't come out then. I think it's my fave mag, along with *October*.

Crime of M. Lange tonight. Wanna see it with me?

* * *

Why was I so graced?, I ask myself. An eighty-year old man spoke with me on the train home about his collection of Chinese ceramics, "nothing later than Ming, of course." Why so graced to forget you for thirty minutes? Such grace – all? – so short.

* * *

They make porno films on bridges and crosswalks; the buxom woman crosses Sukiyabashi on the diagonal; three takes just to get it right. Bouncey bouncey.

* * *

The costs of confusion notwithstanding, Kazuo thinks to himself, to think one's way through Tokyo is not unlike mastering any of the finer arts. I remember my first lessons in calligraphy. My parents, bless them, had insisted that I remain left-handed. And so, it was like a new language. My arm just swept across the sheet. And I am forever grateful to my teacher for starting me on *sho* instead of *kai*, to let me be fluid, never being sure what I was writing, but writing it well. Did those calligraphy lessons free me to understand the Tokyo system better? Perhaps.

* * *

How many more years raping his life?

* * *

SCENE FOUR: SHINJUKU STATION

Refreshed and disoriented, she is in Shinjuku Station. She feels like a newcomer to Tokyo. Takes twenty minutes to find an exit, climbs some stairs, and gazes on a three-story high television screen. Some Pop star is advertising "Godzilla Condoms." She walks back down, takes another exit, and for a moment thinks herself in a Post-Modern Paris. She gazes on the towers of Notre Dame, the new Tokyo City Hall, and reminds herself that she has to get tickets to *Les Miserables*, and will have to go alone because all of her friends think it's tacky. Musicals are a developed taste. "Hugo? Who's Hugo?," she wonders, a rambunctious boy, a hunchbank, a clothes designer. She walks back down, takes another exit and faces a porno cinema. She enters. The familiar scum and cum. A man in the third row wears a gray felt hat. Why has he thrown his jacket over himself? Oh, yes, of course. She goes up to him. "Excuse me?" He looks at her – comes – asks, awkwardly, how he can help her. She mumbles some excuse to get away as fast as possible. Definitely not her man.

* * *

The dreams are fulfilled. Feel no pressure. You are beautiful in the city standing on my open palm. The palm is a map – its' name is Tokyo. The face is yours.

* * *

–   Recovered?
–   From what?
–   Oh comeon, the party, the girls, Lang.
–   By drinking again? Hardly.
–   Well, it was an interesting evening, you have to admit. Those girls are absolute ditzes. But Hiroko seems to have some potential.
–   ?
–   For adulthood, I mean. She seems to listen, takes things in, notices – until Hiromi butts in and it all evaporates –
–   Into cuteness.
–   Have you –?

- Noticed? In passing.
- Cute?
- Delicious. Hey, they're available, they make themselves so. Arlene, they're *eager*.
- Yes, I know. That's your business; I have nothing to say.
- Jealous?
- !?
- Comeon, Arlene; I can see it in your eyes. The curiosity. It's alright, you know.
- That's my business, Van Zandt; I have nothing to say.
- Alright, alright. Anyway, it's funny, you know, the happier drunk Roberta becomes, the gloomier Lang becomes.
- I don't think it's funny at all.
- Curious, not ha-ha. Roberta really is curious. So intelligent, and so quiet about all she knows. What does she do with it? Is she writing something? No, she's not a writer; not an artist, or not in the usual egocentric terms. Is she a craftswoman then? Heavens no, better an artist, which in the non-usual sense I suppose she is, the living sense. I don't know; maybe she's just happy to be intelligent, quietly, to use her mind, but for no end, no necessary end, that is. To live quietly as she does.
- That doesn't sound so bad.
- Oh, I'm not criticizing her at all, believe me. I suppose, when all is said and done, I admire her, actually. She seems so content.
- Well, you and I both know that hasn't always been the case. It took her some time. Remember how lost she seemed when she first arrived? Not just the usual foreigner in shock over Tokyo; but also the dilemma of what it all meant and would mean for her, her leaving Lang like that – what was she going to do here, would she stay, would she go, go back to him? She certainly never expected him to come here.
- Yes, to "rescue" her. The man's impossible. So grounded in reality, he thinks, and yet all these grandiose ideas.
- But he seemed to me to be more frustrated than angry. He can't get over the fact that Roberta really is content to stay at home, do her small rewriting jobs. Isn't she doing Zen?
- I'm not sure. I know she has a pillow, but she's never said anything to me about it. There are certainly a number of temples nearby. But no, I don't know. And what of it? She may sit, but I'd doubt if she'd expect anything from it.
- But isn't that the point?

- I suppose so. So let's say she sits ...
- ... in her fashion.
- Can you imagine Lang doing Zen?
- Ha! Yes – once. And then unwrapping his legs, and ...
- ... and then?
- Why, then instructing others, of course.
- Right. The Master, of the Urban Scene. But not the Master of Roberta. Can he stand it, do you think?
- Oh, he's alright; he can bend; it just takes him time, sometimes a long time. And besides, I don't think he has any choice but to in Roberta's case, in this case this time.
- No, I suppose not. You're right, she has come a long way.
- And in so short a time. I mean, she really did get over her romantic illusions about Japan real quick. Remember: *She'd been here six months; she was feeling comfortable here, feeling herself making her own way; and as for Lang's imminent arrival she was ambivalent, curious, and I suppose she felt she didn't really have a choice but to "welcome" him, put him up for a while, see what developed – and so he got the little living room – until he up and left.*
- Yes, yes, I do remember it all. I'd never seen her so anxious. She certainly did not want to be rescued – had no need of it, really – but she was nervous about what exactly his plans here entailed. Fortunately, she was grounded by the time he arrived to withstand him.
- Yes, but not grounded enough. That time she put him up was no easy job.
- For either of them. But it also made it easy for us to give her support. As for him, well, I've never seen him so helpless.
- Which he'd deny now.
- I'm not so sure. I suspect he'd take it as a point of pride now; how he "overcame and conquered," or something like that. That is, if he ever allowed us to speak of that time.
- Very delicate.
- Oh, "very, very."
- ...
- ...
- Oh, there were parties then!
- If "party" here means war.
- Like Roberta's that night?
- Skirmishes. I think they are becoming friendly once again. Or as far as I can tell.
- ...

- I wish I'd known them in Vienna.
- Oh, they were a wonderful couple! They were everywhere, doing everything, knew everyone. But then I suppose it was all Lang's game. She shone – and Vienna can be very dark – but not always with her own light. But then to say they were "doing everything" in Vienna is not really to say a hell of a lot. It's certainly less provincial than Roberta's San Francisco, but Vienna is no great metropolis. Films and books yes, and a great place to talk. In that sense, Tokyo is exactly what Lang has needed. Not so much café talk, as this sort, walking around the city. Though of course, again, he wouldn't admit it. The city has been preparing itself for him, preening, awaiting his arrival. I've always felt he'd find his real element here. I can't see the Japanese committing suicide in the winter.
- ?
- Winter in Vienna is ghastly; gray. You don't see the sun for weeks.
- Oh. Anyway, I don't really know if they're making any progress –
- You mean towards getting back together permanently?
- Yes. Unless we call progress the fact that the battle lines are clearly drawn. Roberta loves her quiet life here, and she loves Lang. Lang meanwhile seems to be falling headlong in love with the whole maddening city.
- You're right.
- And he loves her.
- And the city.
- Yes, and he loves her. But he's let himself get so caught up here. Yes, he loves both – but doesn't seem to be able to see how easy complete reconciliation can be. Where do they go from here? And too, while it may be ours, is it their wish to get back together? Who are we to say?
- Oh, comeon, Arlene! Don't you think they do?
- Oh, I suppose so, but I really can not say, wouldn't dare to. Roberta's so quiet about it all. Doesn't say one way or another. She just waits.
- Sits.
- In her fashion.
- And we, what do we do? Sit?
- No, of course not. We walk, we talk, with each other, with them. The way friends are supposed to do.
- Do you hike?
- What do you mean?
- Lang, the Austrian.
- Oh. Yes, I can hike. Do you?

- This Amsterdamer? Of course! I also sit – in my fashion.
- Back to the girls, eh?
- Not tonight; they said something about waking up early for a sale.
- What spangles will we see them in tomorrow evening then?
- Are you going too?
- Oh, Hiromi said she'd call.
- Ah, Mona.
- Oh, she is cute, you can't deny that. But I am still trying to locate evidence of terrestrial intelligence there.
- Well, don't be disappointed if you don't.
- Oh, never! I too sit in my fashion.
- Sit *on it* sometime, Arlene.
- Really, stop it, Van Zandt!
- Alright, sorry. But what about now?
- What about it?
- For recovery's sake –
- For recovery's sake.

* * *

Pure and licentious in the Absolute.

— Robert Desnos

* * *

- A thousand dives and I knows 'em all: Shakespeare, Old and New 1, 2, 3, Raison d'Etre, Infinity, even got tipsy on beer at Zonar, D Ray, Copa's ("Step into another world," indeed), Sometime, Eau de Vie, Somewhere ("Watch your steps"), the FLW, that Old World place in the basement of the *shabu-shabu* restaurant, D Grace, the Irish bars, the German joint with all those kids singing drinking songs, Mu Ichi Mon, Golden Dust, Gargantua, Sans Soleil, the *saké* and kushiyaki place by the Scientology office, Big Pal, Shot Bar ("Est. 1984," Japanese absinthe), B (and Plan B), all the grappa we drank at Cucina, the Tobu Hotel and the other hotel bar in Shinagawa, the FLW – no, I said that ... Jeez, am I gonna make it home in one piece?
- Steady, VZ, steady.

* * *

Ah, this city, Kazuko reflects, five, seven years here now? No matter. It has given me much. Might I return it? How? To be myself, to become the woman I want to be. To be both the Kyotoite I was born, and to be the Tokyoite – though never an Edokko – heavens forbid! Yes, to be myself, whomever, wherever I am.

* * *

I've been here just a few years and it's still a surprise to me. You take an innocent girl from across the river and put her in the big city. Hiroko-chan, you've still got some growing up to do. Even after how many hundreds of times there, I still get lost in Shibuya station. It's those first floor Tokyu doors; do they face different directions? And I still haven't gotten the way right to that Italian restaurant in Jiyugaoka. What is it? Right, right, right, ramen shop, left. Uhn, that doesn't sound quite right. Ooh la la as Maxine would say. And I'm still looking up at six-story buildings. What did van Zandt say about it being a street-level city? Well, maybe when you're as tall as he is. But it's an ok city – sure it's crowded and noisy, but you learn to live with it. It is clean, and it's safe too. You take the good with the bad. That's life. Isn't it? Then I don't really know any other place. Maybe I don't know much about life either. I've been to Sendai once; that was nice, very pretty, and a good size, too. But this is the place where I was born, so I guess I'd better try to appreciate it, maybe even make my small contribution someday, who knows. Yes, that'd be nice. I wonder how Kazuko can stand it though. It must be such a contrast for her. Such a nice girl, but that's how they make them in Kyoto. Can prostitutes also be ladies? "An innocent girl from across the river." Sounds like a title. But I really do have to do something about that innocence. I don't want that story to be written about me.

* * *

Oh, if only you could have recognized what was always yours, could have loved what was never lost.
– Joan Fontaine (b. Tokyo), *Letter from an Unknown Woman*
(Max Ophuls, 1948)

* * *

Arlene? She likes hotel lounges, poolsides, pink or turquoise cocktails served with umbrellas.

Chapter 5

EBISU–SHIBUYA

Lang didn't even pay attention to Tokyo at first, he wanted something from Roberta but it wasn't coming; and then he simply didn't like her life here, didn't like where she was living then, somewhere between Shinjuku and Nakano and Yoyogi, "honcho" no less, he called it "nondescript" and she said yes, yes she thought it was wonderful for having no character… and one simply doesn't say something like that to Lang, no way, and anyway, after all, he'd brought all his Euro-baggage and had no idea what he was getting into and she already into it, she was settled the woman was moving – she was becoming a real Tokyoite – and then besides, he didn't like her friends. Oh, and the party.

* * *

cellular
dragonfly pinhole
molecular
microchip
mosaic

* * *

The poor and fatherless, suffering the quiet punishments of despair, may see themselves as permanently damned for crimes they can't remember having committed.

– Ross MacDonald

* * *

3AM and she needed a record store.
3:30AM and she had a record store.

* * *

Lang wakes up somewhere in the Ogasawara Islands. It is h-o-t.
He has island-hopped his way here via Okinawa and the Mariannas and
has further hopped from island to island here – here too a Mukojima,
a Mamma Island and a Pappa Island, Sis and Bubba Islands too, and
of course the infamous Iwojima. Here too Japan – Tokyo in this case
– reaches as far east and south as it will, these the borders of the city,
the borders of consciousness. He gets out of bed and is in the street
with Roberta. They walk along a stream in search of a decent café. They
pass what they think is either the remains of an ancient Roman capitol
or a French Gothic church (all architectural knowledge suddenly having slipped them by). It is a building whose interior has been blasted
out, the lining of the gut alone remaining, not unlike the memorial in
Hiroshima. They cross the stream-now-become-a-river and enter a café.
Lang's mother is there. She asks the waiter for a "frou-la-la, you know,
like they have in Amsterdam." The waiter is flustered, he's never heard
of such a thing. The mother becomes flustered. The drink arrives. Lang
becomes angry after his mother now complains that the frou-la-la costs
2.75. Outside the café now, Lang is with Roberta again and now too her
French friend Yolande. They are in a public square where a "Folk Music
Festival" is going on. There's Bill Monroe and Nathan Abshire, Amedée
Ardoin and Bob Wills, as well as Mrs. Williams' son Hiriam. Country
Heaven. Monroe is wailing, ever so high and lonesome, "I'll waive my
time here on earth, love, and come to you when I die." Then the group
tries to cross the street but only gets half way; they are stranded on a
grassy pathway that divides the road. A jeep-load of soldiers stops them,
asks for their passports. Five men get out of the jeep. They surround
Yolande and Roberta, feeling them up for their passports. What kind of
soldiers are these, what are they doing here?, this isn't Okinawa, Lang
wonders, this is Tokio!

Hiro is a young boy; he is on vacation for five days in the Oga-
sawaras with his mother. ("Take photographs, not plants. Leave foot-
prints, not garbage.") He is annoyed by the American music, all fiddles,
accordions, yodeling – he's seen Japanese dressed up in Cowboy outfits,

but seeing the real thing now is a bit disconcerting. (Real in the dream, that is, after all, these are the tropics.) In two days they will return to Tokyo; the following day he will have an important exam. For the last three evenings before falling asleep she has fellated him. She allows him to kiss her breasts, but no more. He's never seen her fully naked, and so his daydreams are filled with her in variously different costumes – his Mother in high-school uniform; in a bikini, but only the top half, and revealing a very dense bush; severe and black in Yohji Yamamoto; in Alpine dirndl (breasts exposed); in a "smoking" and mules, with a girlfriend at her side; in classic Chanel, deep blue; and finally, in Japanese military uniform.

* * *

– Oh, it's lovely! A glass of *saké* with a flake of goldleaf in it. I've never seen such a thing, really. But isn't it expensive?
– Not really that much more. Anyway, one glass, ok, Arlene?
– Sure. But what's the occasion?
– Oh, a small bonus from a friend.
– Good for you; I wish I had such friends.
– But you can, Arlene.
– Uhn, no thanks. Anyway, it is nice to see you alone, Hiromi.
– Thank you for coming. And please call me Mona.
– Oh, ok, Mona. But why the name change, why Mona?
– Because Hiroko got Maxine first. But don't you think everyone should have an artistic name?
– An "artistic" name? Oh, you mean an artist name. Well, I've never really given it much thought. I know that Kabuki actors and writers do – but does everyone?
– No, only we artists.
– Oh. I'm sorry, Hiro – , I mean Mona, but exactly what art do you practice? No, let me see ... I suppose your calligraphy is exquisite.
– Terrible, to tell the truth. My father's always correcting my strokes; and I can't remember any complicated *kanji*. Do you know *kanji*? The stroke order? I can teach you some, uhn, strokes.
– Perhaps some other time, Mona. But really, what art do you practice? Traditional dance?
– No, silly, the "contemporary arts" – you know, make-up, fashionable dressing –
– Ah! So you're a *Non-Non* girl.
– No, and I don't read *An-An* either. I'm an independent. There are

lots of us.
- Ah, I see. Of course, silly of me to think otherwise.
- I'm happy. You know, Arlene, I've known quite a few Americans –
- Boys?
- Yes.
- Van Zandt?
- Yes.
- Ok, go on.
- And, if I may be so bold – is that phrase ok? – and if I can ask you something personal … would you be called "square" back in the States?
- Well, Mona, because you've offered me this *saké* with goldleaf, I won't take offense, and I will answer you honestly. Yes, I suppose some people would consider me square. But mind you, a lot of people would consider me perfectly normal.
- Oh.
- Why, Mona, that's really not so bad.
- No, I suppose not. Here it's the desired thing, of course.
- And not only here, let me remind you.
- Well, no offense. In fact, I like you square, Arlene. It's so different.
- Thank you – I think.
- Why "think"?
- Oh, it's just a phrase.
- Oh, I see. Do you think I have a nice body, Arlene?
- Mona? Uhn, yes, I suppose one would have to say that by most standards you have a nice body. I'm sure most men would find it attractive.
- And not only men, Arlene.
- Not only men, I'm sure. Anyway, do you have anything against normal people?
- No, I was just wondering because your friends are so far out.
- Oh, you mean van Zandt.
- Not only. Lang and Roberta too. And that old guy, that Cafferty.
- Cafferty is a wonderful man, and so strange and curious, Mona, that he is perfectly normal.
- Really? Well, I hardly know him. He seems to have no interest in me at all, and that does not strike me as being normal in a man.
- Anyway, do you find Roberta and Lang so odd, so abnormal?
- No, I just wonder what kind of couple they are. I mean, I understand that she left him – just like that [snaps fingers] – and then he came after her – and now they're having all these problems.

- You've been talking to VZ too much.
- Oh no, we never talk.
- I'm sure.
- No, occasionally I see things, you know.
- No, I didn't.
- Yes. I mean, if I was Roberta – or should I say, "If I were Roberta"?
  – I could never leave a man like Lang. He's so ...
- So ...?
- Well ...
- Yes, I understand. Go on.
- Well, I don't get it! That's all.
- Look, Hi–, Mona. Remember when Lang first arrived here? You know, he never really wanted to come to Tokyo in the first place. But then he arrived, and boy! *He didn't even pay attention to Tokyo at first. He wanted something from Roberta but it wasn't coming; and then he simply didn't like her life here, didn't like where she was living then, oh where was it?, somewhere between Shinjuku and Nakano and Yoyogi, "honcho" no less. He called it "nondescript" and she agreed, said yes it was, she thought it was wonderful for having no character ... and one simply doesn't say something like that to Lang, not at all, and after all, he'd brought all his Euro-baggage and had no idea – no idea! – of what he was getting into, and she already so into it, she was settled. Oh, Roberta was moving – she was becoming a real Tokyoite. And then besides, he didn't like her friends. And, oh yes, there was, uhm, the party.*
- Didn't like me?
- No, he didn't like anyone. I'm sure he liked you, in his way. Anyway, he stood it for a while, and then he up and left.
- But I thought her friends were wonderful.
- So did they. That was the trouble for the both of them. She needed that boisterousness for a while, it lifted her, especially in the wake of her suddenly up and leaving Lang and going for something she wasn't really sure of herself –
- Not sure of?
- Not sure where or really exactly why – only something that she must do.
- Must?
- Going on instinct.
- Feelings!
- She and Lang had come to an impasse. They'd been so good together for so long, and then that, that *stasis*.
- Impasse. Stasis.

- Yes. It was against Lang to some extent; but also to some against herself. But more for.
- But she needed her quiet far more. It was not coming from them, and it was definitely not coming from Lang either.
- I can't stand quiet. But then, she's so much older than me. What kind of quiet did she need?
- Oh, Mona – don't you see? Haven't you ever been in love, I mean for a long time? No, I suppose not, you're too young.
- Three months?
- Too short, Dear. I'm talking of permanency.
- You're right. Too young.
- Thank you, I see we agree.
- I can be agreeable, Arlene.
- I'm sure. Anyway, no, it just simply wasn't working for them together at her old place. They needed another break. Maybe that way they could come back together.
- And if not?
- Well, let's not think of that right now. In the meantime, we should all try and be good friends. You know, talk, talk freely, caringly, take a walk together sometimes.
- And if they don't, will Lang be free?
- I suppose, but I wouldn't get my hopes up, Dear. I don't think you're his type.
- Not too young?
- No, just not too ... well, it doesn't matter. Content yourself with van Zandt.
- Ok!
- So, as I was saying, they needed that other break. But then that sort of backfired.
- Ah, Lang the Edokko!
- Ah, there is something upstairs!
- ?
- Yes, Lang the Edokko. But that's another chapter. Tell me, Mona, what are you going to do tonight? After I go home?
- You mean ...?
- Yes, Dear, I want to go home.
- Why do you call me "Dear"?
- Oh, well, it's an endearment. That is, we say it when we are fond of someone.
- "Fond"? Does that mean like?
- Yes, but not in the way you think.

- Or not in the way you'd like perhaps to think, Arlene?
- Really, Hiromi. Between you and van Zandt –
- Yes, between us?
- I mean, well, I mean, look, you are cute, yes, but I don't know if I ... that is ...
- Don't worry. Another chapter, as you say. We have lots of time ...
- Yes, but I wonder if I can turn that page.
- It's not for us to say. Dear.
- Oh, D–

* * *

Gotta get to Kamakura, there's a bell I wanna see.

* * *

Rich and strange, Kazuo regards Kazuko's friends Lang and Roberta. They are rather superficial, really, in spite of all that earnestness. I suppose they say the same about us, but in reverse. Ah, but we are all – what? Rich, open to change. Strange, alike. Ah, but Kazuko's parents?

* * *

"Hagiwara [Sakutaro] himself explained his especial liking for beer as permitting long arguments about poetry as one proceeded slowly toward incoherence."

* * *

Just so, relax, hang out. Talk, laugh, smoke, drink, eat, in any order – and no speeches, thank you, no beribboned magnifying glasses. "Hi, my name's Marianne, and I want to fuck your son's brains out." "Hi, my name's Marianne, and I think your article was shit." "Hi, my name's Marianne, and I saw your scumbag husband with a high-school girl yesterday." "Hi, my name's Marianne, and your wife just went down on me." "Hi, my name's Marianne, and guess what? You're Korean." Oh god, here comes that horrible art critic. She smiles politely, and turns quickly to the man at her side, a scruffy looking, photographer whose work she likes: people-less black and whites, just the massive jumble of Tokyo. The most honest photos of the city we have, she feels. They begin to talk about music; his taste runs to Iggy Pop and the Clash, hard Blues,

Otis Rush and the Wolf. He's never heard Monk, never heard of Hawk – which reminds her of how things really started to go wrong at Roberta's party, how Roberta wanted to play Monk, solos, clear enough, tasteful certainly, who could possibly argue? But Lang had other ideas, suddenly insisted on hearing Hawk, the European stuff with Benny Carter, which Roberta didn't even have, and Lang was sure he'd seen it in her collection, couldn't find it, of course, which only pissed him off more, so he yanked the Monk off, and put on – in a complete switch in direction – Dwight Yoakum real loud, which really annoyed everyone, and then what was it, the Mississippi Sheiks, which only made things stranger, not exactly party music. Oh, Roberta was fuming, and she knew she was powerless to do anything about this husband of hers that had such a gift of being an asshole at the worst moments – at least she knew she would be powerless for only a little while yet.

*　*　*

Fiction a verb, an improvisation. "Ask Lester Young," a song.

*　*　*

R'n'L!!!!!

Wireless, wireless! Whatever happened to coils and cables, springs and connecting rods – the stuff automata's dreams are made on? Bah! "My Last Sony."

Randolph and Cary, Cary and LSD, Cary as a wife-beater ... jeez.

Isn't it terrible what happened to Veronica Lake? And then to wind up waiting tables? I mean is fate cruel or what? Why didn't someone know beforehand, why didn't someone go to her? I know I would have, and I know you would have too, and I know that that's one of a zillion reasons we're friends. Ohh, Veronica!

And whatever became of Teresa Wright? Ya' know she had this great contract that went, "The aforementioned Teresa Wright shall not be required to pose for photographs in a bathing suit unless she is in the water. Neither may she be photographed on the beach with her hair flying in the wind. Nor may she pose in any of the following situations: In shorts, playing with a cocker spaniel; digging in a garden; whipping up a meal; attired in firecrackers and holding skyrockets for the Fourth of July; looking insinuatingly at a turkey for Thanksgiving; wearing a bunny cap with long ears for Easter; twinkling on prop snow in a skiing outfit while a fan blows her scarf; assuming an athletic stance while pretending to hit something with a bow and arrow." Anyway, whatever became of her? But would we have wanted to see her "mature"? This is the question. Perhaps the studio was wise and said to itself (assuming for the moment that a studio has 1) the ability to talk; and ((even more grandly metaphysical (((if we can apply the term to anything that came out of Hollywood – and we can))))) 2) the ability to converse and interlocute ((if we can put it that way)) with itself; and ((here we really go, we're talkin' stratospheric (((if the stratosphere ((whatever that may be)) is part of the metaphysical, of course))) now)) 3), the ability to carry out the results of that self-dialog into action), "No, this kid's just too good; give her a couple of superb roles, create that effect, that age, that just-in-betweenness of innocence about to see the other side – and then, in the nicest way, of course, get rid of her." By the latter I mean like did she become a nun, or return to Nebraska and finish college and become a pharmacist or something good, or meet and fall in love with a nice guy who really was a nice guy and rich to boot and he did his business while she did her charitable work? E-nough! Phew, I don't know where all that came from. Like VM, I even drive myself crazy sometimes.

My list of places I most want to visit: Graceland, Monument Valley, Gettysburg, Vaux le Vicomte. Wanna come?

I have a red soap, a yellow soap, a pink soap, and a purple soap.

Further Inquiries into the Laws of Gravity Dept. Why every so often do I find a couple of pubic hairs on the ceiling of my bathroom?

Do you think dental assistants make good kissers?

What did Manu say as we crossed a red light? "It's more of a hint than an order." And then she mentioned her "trail of debts." God, could I mention mine. (Better not.)

Question of the week: what's Campari made of?

Reading Levinas. God, I wish I could talk with you about Minnelli!

Oh yeah, and my shampoo's blue.

* * *

She started moaning much too high, unnaturally. I told I her I never confused sex with seriousness.

* * *

- If it weren't for the record shops, Euro-Space, and the Nepalese restaurant, could I kiss Shibuya goodbye?
- Youth!
- Money!
- Swagger!
- Don't forget the cigar shop below the dog, and the used bookshop.
- And the best: Tokyu Hands.
- Best non-clothes shop on the globe!
- Hard to say. There are a few friends with offices here, too.
- Oh, and Yagura, great *miso*, and Egg Gallery.
- But Ebisu? Screw the Garden, a monument to the megalomania of money.
- Bad taste – what the city excels in.
- No Ebisu is for me only one thought, Yoko's office.
- Two: that snowy day –
- – the nice lunch restaurant –
- and that guy –
- – screwy guy –
- – nice guy – and screwy –
- – yeah, funny guy –
- – bringing in snow-covered branches for all the women in the party.
- Going out –
- coming back in –
- – out and in –
- Flowers in winter.
- Snow-flowers.
- Nice guy.

* * *

The costs of confusion notwithstanding, Hiro quickly thinks, well, what do you need to know? I can always find my way in a Tokyo house.

Not that anything corresponds, but just the fact that the piano is in the kitchen and the dish cabinet in the living room makes me feel comfortable, at home, she likes that, that I settle myself in, make the bath and bed for her. Too natural.

* * *

I couldn't see their faces anymore – but I could feel they were all men.
    – Julie London. *Man of the West* (Anthony Mann, 1958)

* * *

Mmm, I'm not so sure. No, I prefer to "love" parts of the place. The whole things seems a bit too much; and frankly, it sounds both a little crazy and impossible. Unreal. No offense. Hmm, that soba shop in Kanda that Grandma took me to. That quiet tempura restaurant in the middle of Kabukicho that Father took me to that afternoon we saw *Sorekara*. The stationery shop in Kunitachi with that nice old man. Ah, then I suppose people like certain areas. But are shops places, sites? Do they qualify? Am I supposed to mean parks, or the air or mood of an area? The quiet of some temples, the buzz in Ameyokocho, which I don't really care for, but just to use it as an example. But they're all shops or parks in their own ways, aren't they? I remember a chair in a café, it was mass-produced. Can't I love that too as a "Tokyo place"? I don't care what Hiromi says, I still think Ginza is wonderful, and I hope that after I'm married I'll still be going to Kabuki and Fugetsudo for a snack afterwards. Ah, but tonight we go out, maybe run into those American guys again. Hmph, and if not them, some other Americans; there are lots to go around. The whole city? No, just the combination of places I call my home. Hiroko, has outdone herself.

* * *

HAZUKO'S HOAX

The immediate postwar years were traumatic ones for the Japanese people – the Tokyo air-raids, Hiroshima, the Emperor no longer a deity: complete loss, utter devastation, a nation and a people in ruins.

It was also a time of mass hysteria, a time when people were gullible for any sign of hope and promise. "New religions" abounded, the worst crimes easily perpetrated (as we have seen). Tokyo was a city ready to be taken in.

Hazuko Hata was nineteen years old in 1948. Her father had been a radical labor organizer in Tokyo, and in order to avoid imprisonment, in the mid-1930s, had taken his family to a village outside of Sendai where he quietly worked on a farm. Hazuko grew up resenting the government, and longing to see the capitol. In 1946 she saw how she could make her move. Health scares were numerous, and many of them real. With her doctor (and lover) she invented an incurable illness – "radium poisoning eating her bones," said to derive from malnutrition and the noxious air-raid fumes that had spread over Sendai – and with the aid of another lover, a newspaper man, she saw to it that notice of her fatal disease was placed in a Tokyo newspaper, where – again, as she'd planned – an "enterprising" editor (who was also in on the hoax; and yes, he too became her lover) saw the chance for a sensational and melodramatic story. He invited "brave, little Hazuko, who'd never seen Ginza, the Imperial Palace, or the brave, little people of the capitol struggling their way back up from the piles of ash," to come and see just those fabled sites and more in her final, miserable, pain-wracked days.

And so she came. She was given a suite in the Imperial Hotel and immediately became the pitiful toast of the town. She refused any expert medical attention, proclaiming, "If you can't trust your own hometown doctor, who can you trust?" Her suffering visage was to be seen on magazine covers and billboards ("Hazu-chan, May merciful Kannon [the Buddha of Compassion] grant you a painless death, and Miroku [the Buddha of the Future] embrace you in eternity"). Interviews appeared in newspapers ("I'm only sorry to put everyone to so much trouble; but soon they will no longer have to put up with me"). And there were radio appearances ("Tonight, a special composition, "Sendai Drapes Itself in White for Hazuko" [white being the Buddhist color of mourning]). Meanwhile too, the newspaper editor saw to it that she had one last chance to "live it up". Besides an audience in Parliament, she went dancing at the Ginza Gazebo, took a tour of Toho studios, posing with the famous film stars (including the young Mifune, with whom more than glances were exchanged), and walked among her devoted "little-but-really-oh-so-big people."

And in between and throughout there took place the infamous sexual escapades.

No one knows how she did it. Could there have been a Hazuko double? Experts estimate (how?) that no single person could have performed all the *documented* acts that Hazuko – the "human heatwave" to those in the know –performed in her two short weeks in the capitol before she "departed," as her dwindling believers still call it, to the "other city." (Hazuko's defenders scoff at the 'experts' and their estimates; they claim that time has no measurement when the spirit is in its ecstasies.)

A brief list includes the following. For convenience's sake, they follow the order of the authorities. Of course, anyone versed in the combinatorial arts -- they can sometimes resemble a perverse marriage between the arts of Busby Berkeley and Raymond Queneau -- would have more than a holiday in devising other systems for them.

GROUP 1: "NORMAL" (THE AUTHORITIES COMMENT THAT THE FOLLOWING ACTS MIGHT BE EXPECTED BY MOST SEXUALLY WELL-ADJUSTED PEOPLE. THOUGH TOO, THEY ADMIT, THE NUMBERS AND OTHER DETAILS MAKE EVEN THIS CATEGORY SUSPECT.)

– There are twenty-one files for the daily – and separate – servicing of her doctor-lover, her reporter-lover, and her editor-lover.
– Many files show her in tandem with groups of men and women, and occasionally, boys and girls dressed in an array of costumes: school children, kamikaze pilot, farmers from Sendai.
– One file contains photographs of her with two or three men, being penetrated wherever possible. (Interestingly, many of the police files contain thick envelopes filled with photographs; visual documentation seeming to have been another of her predilections. In fact, many of the photographs contain mirrors in which we can even see Hazuko taking the photo while simultaneously being gratified.)
– A moderately sized file contains documentation of her providing her pleasure herself – manually.

GROUP 2: MECHANICAL (SELF-EXPLANATORY)

– Another group of files represents acts in which a range of objects are employed to achieve carnal satisfaction. These include marmalades (black market?), *wasabi* and other cylindrical edibles (*daikon*, etc.), as well as esoteric religious implements. In many of these, depending upon the object employed, an appropriate costume is donned.
– In another, during a reception with representatives of the nurse's union, she was apparently servicing herself under the tablecloth with a dildo made in the likeness of the long-nosed god Tengu; the apparent moans of satisfaction were naively reported as the result of pre-death-throe visions.

GROUP 3: ANIMAL. ANOTHER THREE PERCENT ENTAIL ACTIONS IN WHICH ANIMALS (NON-HUMAN, THAT IS) ARE INCLUDED. AGAIN, WE OFFER ONLY A BRIEF SELECTION.

– At Ueno Zoo, in front of the tiger cage and dressed in a tiger costume, and what looks like her howling (or so we assume from her contorted mouth); we see her being serviced by a man similarly dressed, the long and mighty member clearly visible. Apparently, for three days afterwards, the tigers kept the neighborhood awake with their anxious growls. They eventually had to be shot, and their meat was then given to the appropriate official agency where it was mixed with the local available fare (already questionable) and distributed to the needy.

– The next file, shows her after the tiger incident, grabbing a monkey and being serviced by him. (However, as a result of the intensity of their mutual pleasure, she broke the animal's intercostal clavicle, this last seeming to be the only act she ever regretted in her life). (This event occurred apparently on her third night in Tokyo, for newspaper photographs from the fourth day on always show her accompanied by a small tiger monkey. This type of monkey's thin pink penis was to become the principal amulet of those who later joined the Hazuko cult.)

GROUP 4: PUBLIC

– A small number of files show her under the Yurakucho girders servicing GHQ personnel. (The aptly named Yuraku – "where pleasure can be had.") In this, she showed herself to be a real "woman of the people" – though, for obvious reasons, she was unable to identify herself (one naturally wonders what would have happened had she been recognized and exposed – joining in with the Pam-Pam girls and their famous blow-jobs for a quarter ((or stockings, or cigarettes, Luckies or Chesterfield being favored by all.))) Apparently too, this is where she gained her pungent lingo (oh those GIs!), her favorite remark to anyone being, "kiss my ass."

GROUP 5: SACRED

– On one occasion she spent the night at a Buddhist temple in Kamakura. (Driven in an ambulance? There seems to be no record of this journey.) While there, she asked the head monk how she might best please the infinitely merciful Kannon-sama. He told her that she could consider fellating him (the priest, that is). She duly obliged the wizened old man who achieved a state of spiritual transport more sweet, he later remarked, than even *satori*. Upon recovering from his ecstasy, he is said to have asked Hazuko if she experienced the same sweet delight that he had, and she answered – "Kiss my ass!" (which, we might add, being poor in English, he took as a "yes.")

- The next evening she was back, but this time in the dormitory. (She had had, incidentally, her entire body painted in goldleaf and robed in gossamer – no explanation is given: was she posing as a Buddhist statue?) Finding her man – or boy, really – she thrust her ungilded pudendum upon the mouth of the youngest and most studious acolyte (asleep at the time), thrust her arm back to grab his erect member, and as he was initiated in the art of cunnilingus (he seems to have been a fast learner), she held him fast until the two, the semi-divine couple, simultaneously reached climax.

- That young man, upon receiving the tonsure, removed himself from the world to the shores of Shimoda. There he erected – it is the only word – a solid steel phallic image, so solid that the rushing, salt-sea waves are unable even to this day to wear it away. To this day too, pilgrims come to visit the image of the erect Avalokiteshvara – pilgrims, that is, who have problems with premature ejaculation. It is further said that from this acolyte's experience comes the contemporary practice of mother's masturbating or fellating their sons during the anxiety-filled time of their university entrance examinations.

GROUP 6: DISGUSTING. A FULL TWELVE PERCENT OF THE FILES DE-PICT FOUL ACTS THAT INCLUDE THE GROSSEST USE OF THE FULL RANGE OF BODILY FLUIDS AND SOLIDS. IN RESPECT OF HUMAN DECENCY, ONLY TWO – TAME, COMPARED TO THOSE NOT DESCRIBED – ARE PRESENTED HERE.

- A photograph shows her urinating on a lover as he reaches climax.
- In another she is suspended mid-air and showering upon a unit of rope-bound soldiers (privates), while from above another unit (officers) is masturbating over her.

GROUP 7: MISCELLANEOUS

- Another file tells of the time Hazuko was walking along the shores of the Sumida River. Spying a snake, she immediately grabbed it and thrust up inside herself. Not knowing where he was, the startled thing scurried about for cover. Equally surprised, Hazuko was at first quite happy, and then worried: she certainly didn't want to die of something so common as snakebite! Given her excellent muscle control, however, she managed to expel it from within herself. A curio peddler, chancing by, picked up the reptile, and some time later took it to a taxidermist who was able to preserve it. The two, amazed at what they'd gotten, were, within a few years able to sell the skin at the then astounding price of ¥150,000 to a collector in Hong Kong. Why amazed? Because the snake had died with what believers claim is nothing less than a smile on its face! (The awe in which such objects are held reminds us of the early Meiji Period murderess Takahashi Oden, the "she-devil" subject of a Kabuki play, and whose sexual organs were preserved in the crime laboratory of the Tokyo Metorpolitan Police, as she was believed "to have been possessed of an extraordinary sexual drive.")

— In a private visit to a tattooist in Fukugawa, Hazuko had these emblems engraved on her body: a red penis on her inner right thigh; another, this time the palest blue, just below her lower lip; and, in an intense yellow dye, a sun burst around her anus (almost lending a sacral air to her favorite riposte); and finally – and – again, we cannot help noticing – the sacral note: weaving across, encircling all, labia majora and minora, the *Nembutsu*.

— Numerous files show her body bound in ropes or wire or chains, suspended from ceilings, bound to trees, sunk into abysses (snake pits?). In a manner of speaking, these are the least interesting files of all, the national press showing greater creativity everyday in its regular pages of bound nudes.

The files continue, 288 in all.

The mystery of Hazuko Hata does not, however. In time – it was after all inevitable – the reporter, the editor, and the doctor discovered that they too – like the entire doleful metropolis – had been taken in. That is, they had each been played against the other. (What did the fools expect?!) After duly accusing one another of having "souls of eels, and brains of tarantulas" or being "foul botches of nature," they made their way to Hazuko's hotel suite. There they found her surrounded by a circle of nuns and monks burning incense and reciting sutras. There was no way through this gathering. So, they devised their own publicity stunt, and arranged for a special international group of physicians – Doctors Emil Maximilian J. Egelhofer of Vienna, Dr. Oswald Wunsch of Prague, Dr. Felix Marachuffsky of Moscow, and Dr. Friedrich Kirchinweisser of Berlin – to give Hazuko one last examination, "so as to bequeath our sorrow-filled knowledge of her pain-wracked, thin, but-oh-so-very-brave body to the other suffering creatures of the world." How could she refuse? A quick glance and Hazuko knew the game was up.

But she had one more card up her fertile sleeve. She had herself pronounced dead. (The Herr Doktors had been duly serviced, of course.) What could the newspapers do but print the story? The Japanese public bought the morning and then the afternoon souvenir editions, and then they mourned their "little country saint who'd only wanted a glimpse of the city lights." Through the assistance of her ship's captain-lover, Hazuko made her way across the Pacific and the Atlantic oceans. After some further exploits, she finally arrived in the City of Light, Paris.

(Those exploits, by the way, do not form a part of the Japanese files. Local authorities seem to have been more than amused by her. As for the Japanese authorities, they figured that well, no real or serious crime had been committed – putting one over on the public ... hell, what had that damned war been anything but? – and too, Hazuko had provided the public a sentimental diversion in their time of strife. And then, they had all those photographs! Too, for all the pleasures she had indulged in, so that many were shared. She had shed a certain gay light when all was said and done. And, as mentioned at the beginning of this tale, it was a time of hysteria and fear and mass manias. Within a few months the "brave, little, country girl" was forgotten, and replaced with someone new, another victim, another actress or religious fanatic who could shoulder the nation's burdens.)

Yes, Hazuko Hata, had gotten what she'd wanted. And like many another Japanese woman who causes a scandal, she knew she could not live long in Japan where she would only become a comic figure. But in Paris things could be otherwise! There she opened a bar, "The Lair of the Lustful Monkey," and entertained customers with *saké* and good cheer for four more decades – until she passed away, embracing her simian, and dressed in goldleaf and gossamer.

* * *

Coincidence is an extraordinary thing only because it is natural.
  – *The Earrings of Mme. D. ...* (Max Ophuls, 1953)

* * *

Ah, this city, kilometers of area to cover. Let's see. I like the boys in Aoyama, certainly. Nice clothes – that boy stuff, Batsu, Melrose, Lautréamont – of course they can't afford the more masculine Commes des Garçons and Ys – but then neither can I – and, oh, I'm tired of thinking,

Hiromi admits, I have to get dressed, go out – what to wear? Sadistic Mika or Hysteric Glamor?

* * *

Why has no one wondered what happened to Virgil after he could go no further? What did he do?, feel – write? Did he really make it back, and was he able even to tell the others? I'd like to write a Borgesian piece, "Virgil: Author of the Divine Comedy."

* * *

- You know, few people ever notice or much less remark on the real charms of the Yotsuya, and Shinjuku 3-chome areas.
- Yes, Lang?
- Well, look, the Park is unfairly associated with Prime Ministerial garden parties, 3-chome with the "gay area." But Inez used to go to the park all the time with her kid, and I know straight men and women who feel perfectly comfortable in 3-chome's bars, as if it should matter.
- But feeling comfortable does matter.
- No, I meant as if one's sex should matter.
- Oh.
- There's delight too in the long broad streets, the clean sightlines evenly blended with the usual mazes, and some decent bars and restaurants.
- Such as?
- Well, Bé, for one; that second floor Jazz place with the long windows; that restaurant that charges whatever the day's yen rate is. And then, just to know that you're on the edge of Shinjuku, that you can see it beckoning, just over there – look!
- Roberta!
- Soon!
- And the choice is yours!
- Choice of what? – bar?, sex?
- Those too!
- What time to go home tonight?
- Or wherever.
- Whatever home.
- Whenever.
- Whichever clock.

* * *

She was conceived in Kyoto, but born in Tokyo. He the reverse.

* * *

- As Brian said, "let's drink to the good and the evil."
- Hurt me now, get it over.
- Later.
- As Minnie Pearl said of Hank Williams, "the most haunting and haunted eyes I'd ever looked into."

* * *

SPANISH JOYS

Lyrics that seem to lie
flat on the page
unfurl and float legs
that curve and beckon
skeins of language.

(and)

JAPANESE SORROWS

The thick black line
describes an arc
a woman's mouth curves
and from out emerge –
the serpent.

* * *

Toes shine in cowboy belts.

* * *

I saw this, a child lost in the Asakusa festival – what's the name of it?, Roberta remembers, and a hundred people converged around her – to console her, to find her parents, as if she were their own child – and in a way I guess she was. (I saw too, in Beijing, a child who had been naughty or disobedient in a way I had not seen. The father walked up behind the kid, and in one move, a single instant, tore its' toy out of its' hand, and smashed it on the sidewalk. The child immediately got into line.) The Asakusa mother finally turned up, mother and child reunited, the crowd dispersed, chuckling. All one happy family.

* * *

That endless, lolling boat ride out of Shanghai and across the open sea, then the long train ride up from Yokohama – and then, well, admit it, old boy, this half-dilapidated town, then confusing as anything but Alighieri's hell (but isn't that all order, in fact?), a horrid mess, really, all that sheer naked poverty, and yet the eyes were so alive, so bright – and I was home free. Sweet home Tokyo. Cafferty, old man, your bones will become ash here, become a part of the soil at last. A long long way from – from where? Like Orson Welles, I was conceived in one city, named in another, and born in a third. Young parents on the run. From? Towards? Only further into themselves. And I became a young kid on the run. Rejecting the hot-rods of the Midwest for Los Angeles and a bit of script doctoring, small bundles of cash, never even any sense of waste or disillusionment; call it Hollywood, call it New York, that other coast, the glamor mags, captions, copy, filligree, a manufactured poetry at most. So much for the homeland. Europe was a pleasant base for a time, but I needed to rid myself even of that, the "old world," if I were to wholly reinvent myself. I needed something even more unknown, strange, welcome, whatever age, new and yet seeming ancient. Desperate, expectant, I was coming close to arrival. It was the hottest day of my life, never been another. The haze, the humidity, the sun so low you could almost reach out for it, such exhaustion after that boat ride, wondering why the hell I'd ever bothered to come to this country I'd never had any real interest in, and had only a head full of clichés. Never really wanted to come to Japan; oh, but once I got here, well. And I landed, sank to the balls. I once was lost, and then was found, ready now to discover whomever I might be – so here I am, and here I have.

* * *

It's a story of a story being taken over by another story. You move West, bringing the East with you, making the old West the new East.

* * *

- How much? How many again?
- 502 pages, seven chapters, thirty-nine sections and areas, four four-stars (Kabuki-za, Sensōji, the National Museum, and Meiji Jingu), 24 three, 43 two, 53 one, and three with question marks, and 527 years. I've read it two and a half times now, and made my way through – visited the sites, that is – more than half of it, it's become my "bible."
- What's it called again?
- *Tokyo Now & Then, An Explorer's Guide.* Paul Waley. But then I have to wonder about tourism in Tokyo. I've read a couple of proper guide books – Waley – yes, he's a relation – is too deep, too brief even, to qualify; Judith Connor's first edition is wonderful, but of so precise a time; the others – what do they amount to? On one hand they all admit that there isn't really much to see in Tokyo, the sites being so new; and those worth seeing are all in the old part of the city, and old in Tokyo equates with boring, so skip those, for the "real" Japan you'll be going to Kyoto anyway. I mean just look at the four-stars: Kabuki is hours and hours long, so skip it; Sensōji is just a temple, which means better Kyoto; the National Museum is old and musty and in the city's only proper park, but in *shitamachi*, so skip it; and Meiji Jingu will also be bettered by Kyoto. There is no Ryoanji or Golden Pavilion or great stroll garden here. So, what's left? Ginza, but it's glorious name has long faded. Shinjuku, but with all the new skyscrapers, it resembles New York or any other anonymous big city. Where's that leave us? All the neon, I suppose. And the Shinkansen, but it too will soon be dated as other countries have their own versions. (Of course I'm leaving out students here, of architecture, for one, or people who come here for a specific purpose, a conference or a business deal.) So, in a word, there's nothing to see here, and there go the tourists.
- Strange idea, Lang.
- On the other hand, there is everything to do. And so any decent Tokyo tour-guide would skip all the normal front-section stuff, all those sites, and only keep to the back-section stuff: where to stay, how to get around, what to eat, and especially where to shop, hell, even where to get laid, or where to take your partner to make love, even where to get drunk, and where next to get drunker, and where to take a bath, and where to whatever.
- Maybe not so weird.

* * *

"I can't believe I'm still wearing long-sleeve shirts." That's the only phrase I remember now from that evening before the scandal broke and I quit her. She and I had walked home in a rather quiet rain a Friday night wondering just when summer would arrive. The rainy season had gone on as far as the end of July, the longest in 55 years; the sun had not been seen in Tokyo in 18 days; and over the weekend there were scores of earthquake tremors centered around Izu, and quite palpable in the city. When we awoke Saturday, summer had arrived. Hot, bright, clear, hot. Summer in Tokyo. I had to wander Ginza that day, paying some bills, picking up a Tokihiro Satoh photo, one of his rare color views of all the hideous building projects that were going on in Tokyo Bay, and getting a few books for her. She'd chosen to stay home and listen to the Japanese Punk stuff that didn't really interest me. That Saturday was also the night of the annual fireworks display on the river and we hoped to see them. By early afternoon my shirt and jacket were sweat-soaked. I finally finished my errands and, in the heavy heat decided to head home, far too west of the river. As much as I would have enjoyed myself alone at the fireworks, for this occasion, I wanted to be with her, to see them with that child of the city I was then just discovering and letting go, as I am now discovering it all anew and all alone. The reduced amount of clothing, the constant secretions, the general abandon: the feeling that your body had abandoned you, that it really was not your own reminded me of E. G. S.'s phrase: "The eroticism of summer nights in the great city." (And what's that other phrase: "Lost his collection of erotica, and so, they say, came the eccentricities of old age.") I thought I should be alone because I wanted to go over the argument I'd had earlier that week with Cafferty about nostalgia for the city. He defended it; I said it was antithetical to the nature of the city. He said that if we consider ourselves a living part of the living thing, well then, what is memory about? I had to finally concede that he was right. (And now I was beginning to have a sense of the past, too. Just look at me and my own nostalgia for the Eighties, hardly one of the more exciting or creative of the city's decades.) Not only did I want to review the talk, I was already bolstering his arguments like any new convert. I had told her that I had learned so much from him about how to write about the city and she took me to mean a manual. "Well, you begin with the seasons and with what has been lost; don't forget the legends and place-names; the women, the fashions ..." What could I say? Perhaps she was right; perhaps it all does read like a manual. But before such thoughts could develop any further, the heat had come in full force, though it did not dissipate those late rains.

Nor has her heat and rain left my bones. She was as much an early morning surprise as a typhoon that I was not prepared for except in my best moments, moments that are leaving me by now as I find myself moving ever deeper and willingly so into the past, the city's heat – wet, lingering, exhausting: and purifying: if you are prepared to surrender yourself to her.

* * *

> Dolls without hair
> cracked fingers
> faded brocades
>
> their lonely eyes
>
> blessed
> ablaze!

* * *

Roberta and Lang: arm in arm, hand in hand, eye to eye, mouth to mouth.

* * *

SCENE FIVE: A HOME

She is in Kichijoji, just outside a typical family home: stucco, blue roof tiles, shutters on some windows, the others *shoji*. No doubt, a "Western room" (chairs) and a "Japanese room" (tatami), appliances and comic books piled high, some cheap gee-gaws here and there (Edo courtesan in glass box; Roccoco ceramic copy, young woman at piano, lap-dog, suitor). She'll be greeted, be persuaded to stay, served tea and *sembei*, and all the while lose the scent. But enter she must. Suddenly, it is vast, palatial, huge! – she'd never expected to find such a place in Tokyo. Has she confused outside and in, did she judge the building's size right? Is this a dream, a movie, a drug experience? Endless rooms, like Lubitsch, Busby Berkeley, Jean Arthur in *Easy Living*. Men all over the place: sipping champagne, seducing women; half a dozen tongues, and she can speak them all.

On the steps she admires the doorman's livery, those ever-so-tight tights. In the foyer, she hands her fur to a maid, asks for a light, and immediately a Spanish grandee appears. In a drawing room she has a brief tête-à-tête with a French diplomat from whom she declines another glass. In the library she rebuffs the overture of a Czech businessman. In the grande salle, and sipping another champagne, she tells the Argentine beef billionaire that she is on the side of the children, and if she were Eva Peron, why she'd knock his block off! He exeunts ever so politely, all the while complimenting her ankles, while whispering to an aide to "shoot that woman!" The aide approaches her and offers to shoot his boss in exchange for – . In the dining room, a woman holding in one hand a long mother-of-pearl cigarette holder, and in the other yet another glass of champagne, and a fox slung over her right shoulder, unsuccessfully attempts to seduce her with the promise of "explosive passions" which comes out as a spluttering burst of sibilants and plosives. She merely replies that the local fireworks are probably more exciting. Seated at dinner, the gentleman next to her, a Malay refugee millionaire, shows her his "ring," and confides in her that should she join him the ring will reveal to her the "unutterable secrets of love." She says she'll "consider it." In the smoking room, a retired Japanese general lights her cigar. He says nothing to her. Could this be her man? But what of the Malay millionaire? On the verandah, an overly smart girl of twelve tells her she knows who she is looking for. "I doubt it." In the garden, she overhears two exquisitely dressed lesbians cooing. Back in the foyer, the Japanese general and the Malay millionaire are wondering who is to escort the "ever so charming" young lady home, when suddenly she sees a car driving off, and glimpses, in the window – her Man!

She bids them all a heartfelt goodnight, quickly slips the liveried doorman her address, and has her car "follow that man!"

***

Tokyo tires me out; can't figure out why people think it's so thrilling, Kaoru typically complains.

Chapter 6

HARAJUKU–YOYOGI

It wasn't easy but eventually Roberta had to ask Lang to leave and he was glad to, glad to get out, glad to get away from her for a while at least, at least to clear the air; so he found himself a place in Kichijoji, which he didn't like either, all those foreigners, the discomfort of the easy living of it all, he thought (at first), at first he thought he'd be west of everything she or at least her Tokyo represented, but eventually, soon enough really, he came to like it, came to praise the place's "charms" as he said – god he can be so condescending! – he came to see something of what all she'd been telling him: ha!, Lang came to like Tokyo – Tokyo was alright.

* * *

doo lang
doo lang
doo lang

* * *

Loves the city, does he? And they all call him insane for it? Perhaps. But look at me. My love has always only been modest and from a distance. I'm sure I've only survived the way I have because I've never allowed myself to become absorbed in and by the big bertha, the great mother, the enormous uterus we call Tokyo. No, I've worked rather relaxed, I've gotten out and come back. Time and again. Shall we call that love? Perhaps. A certain fidelity. But again, to be distinguished from he and his claims. But we are kin in our ways. There was a time I was close to what he feels; but I didn't allow myself to go that far. I figured that if it is a true love then we must mutually get to know and respect one another's habits and rhythms and thus maintain a love to last – as it has, these decades already. Yes, he and I are kin; along with a few others whom I have known, lesser men and women and greater too whom the city has, well, not destroyed, we should not say they were destroyed so much as … well, they were forever transformed in ways that they had not only not anticipated, but in ways they had never wished for, never imagined the possibility of. Now there's another story to be written: the wasted in love, the failures. Who are these people for whom love – is, does such different things? The ones who just did not have enough, once having declared their love, to respond to and to match their partner's own responding love. Cafferty wishes Lang well.

* * *

When I was young I *could* feel the earth revolve under my feet the sky above, center of all what beauty and why should no one believe me? I stride forward amongst the unbelievers.

* * *

Ah, this city, Hiroko thinks for a moment, how to get from home to Roppongi, much less Shibuya, and worse, Van Zandt's Shimokitaza-wa? Shit! (oops!), but it *is* hard to get around. Well, maybe I'm complaining. The trains are alright. They just don't run long enough, you can't always afford a taxi, they aren't what you'd call cheap, and only an idiot would walk all the way home. And if I don't find a nice guy – oh, where was that hotel, it wasn't that far? But I really do thank van Zandt for what he calls his "contributions" – anyway, why couldn't the trains run all night like I've heard they do in Paris?

* * *

Faye's idea of a "Post-Whip."

* * *

- Gorgeous!
- Wonderful!
- Marvelous!

- Smashing! – Would Audrey say that?
- Don't you mean Arlene?
- No, Audrey. I watch the classics, you know.
- Oh. Yes, yes, I think she would.
- 45?
- No.
- Sadistic?
- Guess again.
- Pimpness?
- Oh, you're too smart! Smashing!
- That'd be a nice name for a line.
- "Smashing." Ooohh, it would. I wonder if we can copyright it.
- We'd better act fast. The walls have ears, you know.
- Don't they?
- Don't you love Van Zandt's ears?
- God, they're so small and squiggly. My tongue ...
- Oh, I know, and one hand ... and the other ...
- Oh god. I can see him now. And those rough hands.
- Terrible on my nylons. But then he always buys me extras.
- Yes, he is a considerate boy.
- Man. Don't forget, those westerners like those adult names.
- Right. Man this and woman that. Why can't they settle down?
- Or why can't we grow up? Oh, what a laugh!
- So, how's Arlene?
- Oh, you know, she really is so square.
- Oh, comeon! She may be, but isn't that her charm point? I happen to think that she's also a sensitive and intelligent woman. Whether or not she wants to go out and have fun with us.
- Well, you can have her. Actually, I don't think she likes me.
- Well, you are rather pushy, Mona.
- Yes, but it's always served me well, so far.
- Perhaps, but she is a westerner, after all.
- Yes, but I've done alright with VZ.
- But that's not saying much. And besides, he hardly talks, not the way Arlene does.
- But I don't want to talk with VZ.
- I do. I like a little conversation. Have you ever talked with Roberta?
- Talked with Roberta? You mean the Holy Nun of Mount Yanaka?
- Mona!
- Well, she's hardly ever said a word to me. And besides, do you know that there is a Salon de Mona in Yanaka? So who needs nuns in my

pleasuring district?

- I don't – .But, in fact, she's hardly said a word to me either. But that's not what I'm saying. She does speak; the trouble is, when she does, no one listens.
- Oh? And what does she say?
- Oh, she speaks about many things. About her neighborhood mostly. She even told me how she and Lang first met. And she cooks! She makes a better *hiyayakko* than you or I.
- That's not really an accomplishment, Maxine.
- That's not the point. She's told me a lot about herself and Lang; and why she likes Tokyo so much, especially *shitamachi* – I can say she's even given me some appreciation of the place I come from.
- But not, pray, the place you want to end in.
- I really don't know, Hiromi – uhn, sorry, Mona.
- Has she told you about the big crisis with Lang? How he came and couldn't stand her and dumped her?
- Really, Mona! I wouldn't put it so harshly. And yes, she did tell me. I can't understand why.
- Maybe she just needed to speak, and thought I wouldn't listen. Which I did. How did she put it? Oh yes, she said that he didn't like her friends and after a while he moved out. But there was more to it than that. She said, that *it wasn't easy but eventually she had to ask Lang to leave and that he was glad to go, glad to get out, and to get away from her – for a while at least to clear the air. And then he found a place for himself in Kichijoji, which he didn't like either – all those foreigners, and the discomfort of the easy living of it all, you know – or so he thought at first – thought he'd be west of everything, even of her, or at least the Tokyo she represented, but eventually, soon enough really, he came to like it, he even came to praise what he called Joji's "charms" – god he can be so condescending! – and in the end, he came to see something of all that she'd been telling him. Yes, she said that in the end, now, that is, Lang came to like Tokyo – it was cool being here.*
- Roberta told you all that?
- More or less, yes.
- Gee, so now he's in Kichijoji.
- Yes.
- Can you imagine anyone *not* liking Joji?
- Not really. Or, maybe only Lang.
- Should we visit him?
- I don't really think so.
- Why not?

- Really, Mona. You can't have every man you want.
- Oh, I don't "want" Lang. I'd just like to "have" him.
- Well, tell yourself "no" this time, ok?
- Must I?
- Yes, "Dear."
- Stop it.
- You!
- You!
- No, you.
- But, I didn't say anything.
- Oh yes you did. Really, you're not in a movie, you know.
- Yes, I am. VZ says I am.
- Well, that's VZ. And you are Mona. Maybe she's the one in the movie.
- Right. Thank you. So, what should Mona do?
- Do? Why, do nothing.
- Nothing?
- Can't you see? It's like a comedy in its own way.
- I suppose.
- And the "nothing" we do is our "everything."
- Huhn?
- I mean, we just talk and walk like normal people.
- Really, Maxine!
- Oh, really, you!
- No, really – you!
- You!
- Us. Yes, let's walk, and talk, as you say. Saunter. Practice the finer arts – after all, we are artistes, are we not?
- Talkers –
- – and walkers.
- To the Max –
- -ine!
- My arm –
- My Dear.

* * *

All degraded and shameful practices collect and flourish in the capitol.

– Tacitus

* * *

- Take that long walk down – short by anyone else's standards.
- A few streets more and my history gets lost and confused here.
- Bamboo kids, new-human kids, remember, Marianne.
- They came in from the country for a few hours on the street, to dance and laugh, the chance to get some cheap geegaw that'd wow 'em back home –
- And it would, I've been to Gumma –
- They came to see – some boy, some girl, a style they didn't have in the rice towns; they came to be seen: and seduced, or at least a quick kiss, a feel, enough to keep country conversations going for a week or more.
- Nothing's changed; Japan's always been like that; read the classics; country bumpkin wowed by the big city; the provincial bringing back the latest styles only to discover they're long gone.
- To-ki-yo!
- But that was then and it was never me. Yoyogi-Harajuku. What did I want from it, what did it give me? Cambodian food, architecture books. No, maybe the warrens and alleys; the concrete kids' playground –
- Concrete kids?
- – the retro postwar apartment building, dirty stucco. You know, on the Champs Elysses.
- No one would think of going near it in the 80s, but now it's all boutiques. Oh, that memory of a sort of *shitamachi* here in what was making itself out to be the fashion capitol of the world.
- That's that Tokyo contradiction.
- There was a style, you could see it, sure, but behind it lay centuries of peasant indigo. What's a Tokyoite? A rice farmer. Pigeon-toed, feet clumping as they walk, sloppy at table, sloppy in bed. "Tokyo style" – those kids are just magazine articles. Concrete kids, pulp kids. Give me something severe.
- So, Shibuya doesn't live up to its name?
- Would that it would.
- Severe.
- Astringent Valley.
- A highwayman's name, wasn't it?
- Or, there's an assortment of derivations. But that sounds about right, what with all the would-be pimps trying to pick girls up – pucker up – all over the place.

–   Yes, there's more history here than one would think, ancient names, Shoto Tea, but no, not the elegance of *shibui*, something more out of town.

* * *

Why!? Ya' fuck 'em 'cos they're there, man.

* * *

Rich and strange, Hiro in a rare contemplative moment says to himself, an address book filled with bars and girls, and here I am spending the night alone. She had to cancel, alright a legitimate excuse, and she did say she wants to meet again soon. Half accepted. And then Kaoru-san had an important meeting, so I had to stay late in the office. Could've gone alone to a bar, but that would make it three nights in a row taking a taxi home. A night alone. That is definitely not rich, but it is certainly strange. Better be careful to not let it happen again.

* * *

Spent an hour choosing paperclips. Tokyu Hands, a sort of bliss.

* * *

Arlene's going dancing! Someday. Or, actually, she is dancing, with herself, for herself, perhaps even to herself. Remember that scene in *The More the Merrier* when Jean Arthur puts on a rumba record and dances to it alone there in her room, and Joel McCrea's in the hallway and he hears it, and he starts to dance himself to it, and then later they're at the nightclub, and Charles Coburn's arranged it so that they can flirt together – and all those girls ("eight to every fella!") flirting with McCrea – and that short chorus line, that first blonde girl with that wonderful smile, and the woman drummer in the background, all those extras, all that flirting ... and Arlene thinks now of Roberta's party, how after the fight about the music – what was it they wanted, Jazz or Country? Who wanted which? Never can figure out their taste, their secret codes. Maybe that's what love is. But I thought the Wiener was into American music, and Roberta strictly modern; she was listening to Berg and Webern for ages, I recall. – Lang had to up the ante, had to!, damn him, and that only made Roberta even more angry, disappointed; jeez, it was her party for him and VZ and he *so* ungracious; and how he started flirting with everyone, even poor Kazuko – Kazuo was so good, so clear and steady, Kazuko's little samurai ready to strike at the precise moment, and none sooner – the two girls went along with it, they hadn't a clue, though Hiroko stood a bit off, Hiromi all too ready to dance with Lang in a tatami corner, stumbling – he even made a pass at me, but I set VZ after him. Let them both know their place – it was enough with all those Japanese guys ogling me. Enough to watch out for Roberta. He walked all over her; hope she got hers back. If not that night, later sure enough.

* * *

Reject the art world the fashion world the music world the novel world the so-called thought and beauty worlds, whoring worlds all. You must reject them all – and still live the city.

* * *

The Loves and Death of Ōsugi Sakae

The encyclopaedia tells us in reference to the end of his notorious four-way love affair, that one woman stabbed him, another divorced him, and a third married him.

Ōsugi Sakae (1885-1923) was a lover; a dandy (indeed, his prison nickname was "ohai," derived from "haikara" (("high collar"))); perhaps a masochist (he was fascinated by the idea of crucifixion; prophesied not inaccurately the manner of his death; as a child he enjoyed being punished by his mother); and was in other ways a sadist (or if that term is too strong, let us just say that he tended to either hurt or dominate others ((he was always ready for a good fight; spat in his teachers' faces, tortured cats; and then simply look at the way he tried to handle the affair with the women: they would abide by his rules of freedom))). He seems to have had little gift for friendship; he opened Japan's first Esperanto school (1906); was involved in nine different magazines; and like his father, he stuttered. His biographer tells us, "A more willful, independent, unpredictable, intriguing – in short, charismatic – Japanese is hard to imagine. One is either attracted or repelled by him, but never left indifferent."

Contradiction and the lust for freedom define him. It is a shame that the Surrealists were unaware of his existence for they would surely have embraced him as one of their own, not only for his outrageousness and spontaneity, but especially for his defense of a love as free and mad as possible. In a lovely phrase, he wrote that the end of capitalism would release the "high scent of love." "Hands off love!," indeed.

And too there are the spiritual and artistic sides of the man (if we can separate them from the amatory). His flirtation with Christianity. His rebuke once to someone: "Historical materialism?," he retorted, "Don't talk rot. This is a spiritual matter." His remark that "Freedom and creativity are not outside of us nor in the future. They are within us now." His sketches – especially that lovely self-portrait, some calligraphy, and the "Red Skull" – certainly reveal an imaginative hand.

Ōsugi was not born in Tokyo, but in then Kagawa prefecture in 1885. He came to live in Tokyo in 1902 after having been successfully expelled from Cadet School for fighting (and receiving his first stab wound), and for homosexual behavior. (A contradiction: his father was an army officer, and Ōsugi apparently wanted to follow in his footsteps – this from a man who obviously was unable to brook any authority throughout his life. ((There is a famous story – one that reveals more certainly about the Emperor than anything else – that one day the father fell into the castle moat and emerged all muddy, making the Emperor giggle with delight, "Monkey! Monkey!"))) Ōsugi's first arrest occurred – in true and proud Tokyo fashion; would that others might follow his example today! – when he joined in protests against a rise in trolley fares. (The author recalls that in the 1970s Italians rioted over an increase in cinema prices.)

When not borrowing money, his main source of income came from translating (for example, the work of the French entomologist Jean Henri Fabre), or writing articles. What writer would not be proud to have this said about himself: "His writing is usually simple and plain, true and coherent, open and aboveboard. Then again, sometimes he writes unexpected rubbish." He also had the good sense to say that the intelligentsia had been co-opted by the ruling class, and if they really were intelligent they would play a receptive part in any workers'-instigated revolution. More interesting, and more in the spirit of this book, he has this to teach us: "Listening silently to a person's long speech is only to be swept up in a marching song: it is what is done vis-à-vis upper-class people. Among people of the same class, long speeches will disappear and short dialogues will succeed. From long monologues to short dialogues: this is the evolution of conversation. This is the evolution of humanity."

Of course, the greatest contradiction of the man with his theory of the ever-expanding and creative and willful ego was how to reconcile it with the will and desires of others. But perhaps, in a world where conflict is all, the question must necessarily remain unresolved.

While married to Hori Yasuko, he began his affair with Kamichika Ichiko when he appeared one day at her doorstep saying, "I've lost my shadow today. It's alright if I stop in." While he was most probably referring to his police "tail," it is nonetheless a wonderful line for a seducer. Kamichika was called "the first adulteress." Itō Noe, the third woman, was dubbed "the southern beauty." When the affair exploded with Kamichika's stabbing of Ōsugi, so notorious had he become an advocate of free love that he was even blamed for other person's affairs, including that of Countess Yoshikawa with – so unimaginatively – her chauffeur.

The end is sudden and well-known. On September 16, 1923, in the wake of the fears aroused by the Great Kanto Earthquake of September 1, and while people were mercilessly killing Koreans whom they accused of looting, Ōsugi Sakae, "the foremost anarchist of the Taisho period," along with Itō Noe and his six-year old nephew Munekazu, were arrested by the military police, beaten and strangled; their bodies were then wrapped in *tatami* coverings and dumped into an abandoned well. It has never been established from how high up came the order to have Ōsugi killed.

* * *

They have debased that supremely mad metaphysical color, pink. But you, Arlene, have not forgotten. I know, because I can see it in your eyes, and yes, I can see it in your lips.

* * *

-   What if I go north – disappear? Would you come after me?
-   Yes, but not to Gumma Prefecture.
-   Say: Kiss me.
-   Kiss me.
-   Say: I want you.
-   I want you.
-   Say ...
-   No. Put your arms around me.
-   There's only two of us now.
-   Then we're stupid and we'll die.
-   We die then in Tokyo, stupidly or otherwise.
-   I have seen the Tannhauser Gate, the Shores of Aldeberan, and the fires of Orc, Roberta – and still you refuse to speak to me.

That particular sort of scruffiness that accompanies that particular sort of neatness and epitomizes the Japanese landscape, be it urban or rural.

– Paul Waley

* * *

- God what a long, long walk.
- What film is Kazue in? *La Jetée* or the Wenders thing on Ozu? You know, where she's mixing her famous Margarita.
- That she learned from her teacher in Ginza?, that bar behind the primary school behind the Imperial Hotel?
- Right, that one.
- Which one? There's a million bars in Ginza.
- The one we're talking about, the one we know.
- Ok, ok.
- The city is a park writ large, a home writ large, Golden Gai writ large. A bar for every activity – one for journalists, one for communists, one for filmmakers, one for – whomever.
- A bar for you and I, Roberta, a bar that's ours. Three *tatami*, five guests.
- That's what the foreigners love, exotic Tokyo, in the middle of the highrises and electronic gizmos, these six-*tatami* wooden bars in a three-block area and it takes you twenty minutes to refind the place you got drunk in last month.
- But that's as it should be.
- And as it should not: Golden Gai will go, the skyscraper kids will wrap it up like dog shit on the street and deposit it on Dream Island.
- Right, and there'll be a little ersatz shrine dedicated to dedicated drinkers.
- One for my you-know-who – or is it whom? – and one for the road, then.
- Really, what a walk to Roberta's nine *tatami*!, a whole world.
- Is Shinjuku a desirable address?
- For who? I'd feel in the middle of – what's the difference between a hurricane and a tornado? Which one has an eye? Which an asshole?
- People get it wrong; there is no Shinjuku, unless you count it a city unto itself. It so folds in and back upon itself that it fades away. Borderless, decentered – Piss Alley doesn't up one's image – you're

lost and found here.

- Desirable then if that's what you need today. And today, I do not.
- What would Roberta say, what do you think, eh? A few months here, and then the move to *shitamachi*, that was wise, what she needed, she's not a Shinjuku woman.
- Is there such a song?
- One for the road, and that mellowed walk now across Shinjuku –
- From neon to dark to neon again –
- Sex shows to ice cream parlors to mediocre sushi –
- A group of drunk salarymen to kids on a spree. "Oh, I love scrapes!"
- To girls with permanent fits of the giggles –
- Hey, there goes Araki into Dug!
- A faux Mexican restaurant with the most glamorous toilet in the city, all silver and mirrors and hot-house flowers, and terrible food, Arturo's mother generously gave it a C-.
- Here we go then, around a corner, past the love hotels, the acupuncturist's office, the Vietnamese restaurant –
- The Thai whores –
- The Russian whores, another corner, the condom vending machine, and –

* * *

Roberta's round midnight. Paper lantern, late Debussy, and her copying Kenko. What taste: she sees no conflict between Lady Murasaki and Sei Shonagon.

* * *

rivers and hills
slopes, canals
Cupid and Psyche
in conversation

* * *

Driving in from Narita yesterday, Kaoru remembers, I got stuck in one of the older sections of the city, and I saw one of those trucks that clean out the toilets of houses without flushing. The men wore spotless uniforms. Where do they haul it all? To Tokyo's own garbage dump,

"Dream Island." Wasn't there a movie about it a few years back? Does it all just stay garbage? Do they transform it into something? Something useful? Is it used for landfill? Is it sifted through? Or is it just piled higher and higher? Was it a Sci-Fi movie? In a thousand years explorers from the Planet Zonar come to the thousand-story high Dream Island, Tokyo's twenty-fourth ward, and there they read the history of the city, what we ate, who we made love to, the crimes we committed, the money we wasted, the junk we consumed and shat. The city we destroyed by ignoring. What is to become of us? Will we challenge Fuji with our trash? Hmm, my cigarette ash sometimes a miniature Fuji. I'll have to give this more thought.

* * *

R'n'L!!!!!!

Good old Langenscheidt. No, I don't mean the dictionaries. I mean the yellow crocodile balloon in my *genkan*, the house guardian. Marianne left it to me the last time she was over.

Gotta get some decent espadrilles. The cheap ones wear out so fast. Maybe this summer I can find some in Europe.

Things Fall Apart Dept. In one week I had the Panasonic man over to clean my fax machine … then the Yamaha guy came over to fix two of the stereo components … then somebody had to come over to fix the hot water button. High-tech life, my ass.

The mind roils (what a great word) in Tokyo. Everything happening at once – as we know it all does anyway – but here we're assured of it, we experience it. You do understand me, don't you? (God, what if you don't?!)

Made a mean pesto. Better come over and get some.

What's your favorite Elvis picture? Mine – well, one of 'em, one of many, of course – is that great photo of him and some girl kissing, their tongues stuck out, just touching. I wish I had gotten the poster of that when it was used as an ad for something a couple of years back. Was it a JR ad for the train system? Or was it for a magazine? Also wish I'd picked up that book – German, I think – of just photos of Him kissing a billion different women.

I missed that great typhoon in 1993 – when the trains had to stop and even the subways were flooded; I remember driving up to Hakushu with Akashi-san from Daitocho, and his potter friend, he of the beautiful wife ("beppin" – there's even a magazine named after her), and hearing about it on the radio; even hearing of Nakano-Shimbashi being flooded and thinking, christ, that's where Kazue lives, and she's in Hakushu probably unaware that she's seen the last of her apartment – and then wondering if she'd care. Anyway, all of which is to say that I sure hope I am not out of town when the big earthquake hits. No, I don't mean it morbidly or anything like that, just that, well, forgive me for getting sentimental, it's just that me and the city mean so much to each other, how could we be apart on such an occasion?

The day my script went "into development" and was never seen again.

I think I want to collect fans. I know some people collect *saké* cups or ukiyo-e or photographs or whatever, but I now have five fans and I think that I want more. But cool ones, not that sentimental, kitschy sumi-e stuff. I'd also like to get a few dolls; maybe just an Emperor and Empress set. Old, of course. And I'd love to have a Bunraku head. And one good tansu. That'd be enough.

Oh, I lost a pen today. That nice matte black, heavy Ohto pen. Only a thousand yen, but I liked it. But I still have another 'cos I'd ordered two just in case (ah, prophetic me!). Better hightail it to Ad Hoc or Maruzen and order a slew of 'em. Not to be confused with a brace or a gaggle. But possibly a giggle.

What did Bakin say when he was travelling? (No, it's not a riddle.) Nagoyans "follow Osaka in custom and costume, Kyoto in stinginess, and Edo in literary taste. The women are pretty, but thick-waisted. There is not a single slender woman. I wonder if it's the climate?" Looks like we got off best.

Bought a penlight today. "Lost a pen, but gained a light." You tell me what it means.

* * *

It's gotten to the point now where when I go into a shoe store before even asking where the large sizes are I first ask if they honestly think they might have anything that would interest me.

* * *

In the basement there is a train set. A boy of about six years old is playing with it with his friend. The boy wears braces on his weak legs. The friend is Hiro. Occasionally, the boy's mother comes down and gives the boys sweets and riceballs. And as this is a Saturday, they leave the basement – Hiro holding his friend's hand as he struggles up the steps – and the three of them drive to Machida in Southern Tokyo to buy extra train parts. Hiro is in the back seat and as he feels the breeze across his face, he looks at his friend's face and sees that the boy seems to be feeling nothing, his face is a blank. All the while, the mother is talking about nothing and the radio is playing "Walking Blues," by Son House, "I Shall Not be Moved," by Charley Patton, and other Blues. When they arrive, there is a tremendously long overpass they must cross in order to reach the department store. Hiro holds on to his friend's hand, but the walk is so very long, the friend so slow and heavy, he fears what might happen should he let go. Hiro wakes in a sweat. Vaguely he remembers his friend from so long ago; he does not know what ever became of him. "Poor kid, we were friends. Maybe I was his only friend. Me and his train set. Can't remember his Mother ever saying much. And that music, what was it? Something from very far away. Don't ever want to hear a voice like that again." Hiro doesn't know what to do with his emotion, his very real fear. He feels restless all that day and all of the following day.

Kazuko dreams that her father is reading a letter and frowning slightly. Then he calls her downstairs. This makes her feel very heavy, in a way she can not define, heavy, but not unhappy. A Blues is playing; she likes it somehow, though she's not even sure she's ever heard a Blues, the deep stuff. They are in Machida. The letter is in *katakana*, all borrowed western words. She thinks it's French, her father German. The more they transcribe it into the alphabet the less it looks like either. Her father had thought it had to do with her studies, a note from one of her professors remarking on a certain recent distraction in her he'd noticed. This was around the time she'd met Kazuo. It was true, she'd been slightly distracted, but never at the expense of her studies, her filial duties, "Oh, no, Father, never!", she wants to scream but the music's power takes over and she and her Father all their attention wrapped in it holding hands now the way they did when she was a child and together they look out the windows of the station coffee shop and Machida has vanished, all those shops, schools, the station itself, there is only the Musashi Plain now, Father and Daughter, and a Blues.

* * *

He needed to speak with her; grabbed her hair and pulled her head back. – "Listen, man."

* * *

The costs of confusion notwithstanding, Kazuko ponders, this is Japan, and Edo presents no challenge. I know by now the train and subway systems – why aren't they joined on maps?, after all they are all of a piece. But they are all either priced so high, or one line is in conflict with another. Why can't they all be harmonious, provide the same comfort? Just be a normal city, like any other.

* * *

– What's a what?
– What's an anus but a sun spelt backwards? To walk into the sun, a view of Fuji. You and I reamed by light. The mellowest hours. Gotta remember to sort of stick near the Ome Kaido, veer right or the other way, but stick close. At least there's a bar every thirty minutes or so, "always happy to serve a Western lady." You could count down the stations, Nakano, Koenji, but what for?
– What for what?
– What's a station spelt backwards? A long walk. But a good one. No Fuji, but the immediate prospect: the wood fence with torn posters for local politicians; the weeds or should I say the bits of pavement interrupting the growth of vegetation; the dirty stucco, white or pink or turquoise for a season; the opaque windows with their silhouettes of Minnie Mouse or Marilyn Monroe in 'em, or a poster of an "idol," totally untalented but an idol nonetheless, cock sucked for three months and then a has-been, a wash-out, a distant memory without prospect, or a warrior-robot-weapon, a boy's idea of cuddliness when Mama's tits aren't around, though they usually are. The prospect, immediate: my own visible breath, my feet preceding me, time, all of it in an instant – the prospect of myself, the

Marianne I become in Tokyo.
- What?
- What's Tokyo spelt backwards?
- Wait, you can't *spell kanji*. The same thing. East Capitol, Capitol East. Not very glamorous.
- Ah, but that's why we love ya', Tokyo, we know who you really are. And you us. Ok, ok, veer, but stick close.

* * *

The money never mattered. All I wanted was you. Now I walk the streets of strange cities thinking about you.
      – Burt Lancaster, *The Killers* (Robert Siodmak, 1946)

* * *

The ordinary saint. The wife of the recluse. His small hands; eloquent, really.

* * *

The Cranes of Tokio

Lithe, they stand on one tall, thin leg; in groups, singly, underground, above the city, in the sky itself they stand. (I see one now from my window-screen.) All peace, they stare ahead unmoving, their heads swaying in gorgeous arcs (arc after arc ... ((themselves not arcs but all angles like girls on the verge of womanhood, on the verge of becoming arcs))), they begin to describe an arc and then of a sudden swing round and stop again to stare, stare at something or someone that intrigues their gaze for a moment. All gaze. But in their care for us they turn again. White markings, red flashes of light in the evening, and fiery orange bodies, they are in their own way emblems of a sexual paradise (and so many other paradises that we work on together). Androgynes, they reserve a small space for the little-egg-men that would pretend to direct them, but they, we know, are mere adjuncts that would readily could easily scatter like crows with the slightest gesture of a lover's hand. These cranes are not symbols of longevity, but of a single time, the present, which is to say the future, which is to embrace the past.

(Some years ago an American friend living in Gunma prefecture visited me in Tokyo. As we emerged from Shibuya station I remarked that we were still yet within the station, that the moon the sky the stars were simulations, that yes, thirty-story buildings were contained within the station. "And those cranes?," she asked. "Building the station ever higher, the city ever wider," I replied. "In fact, they're connected to even larger cranes outside this false canopy; those cranes – which we can't ever see – are less angular, and make very delicate arcs that join the whole city – as far as it extends so far, that is. I'm surprised you haven't heard of them out there on the skirts of the Kanto Plain. After all, Gunma is just the next suburb that'll be incorporated into the city." "Uhn, noo, no I hadn't heard anything at all," she embarrassedly admitted.)

In ponds and pools and stunted lakes, also called construction sites, their legs stand firmly in the ground – how deep, we do not know. (For that matter, has anyone ever seen them arrive? Just as one day we notice a new building on a previously barren plot, so one morning we notice the cranes in their familiar stance, working, gazing, in the thick of things. ((Nor for that matter, has anyone ever seen them leave.))) And their heads – joint, gaze, beak, desire – are in the skies.

The Skies of Tokio

(Why did they stop building the new City Hall? God, how we loved it as the buildings were a-building, growing ever higher, strange towers topped with swaying cranes, red lights flashing, regal cranes all presence making a claim on the future that entails the past as sure as anyone's grasp, cranes to rival any city or future. And then the towers were finished. Visit them now at night, a Spielbergian light show and no more – hope, desire, imagination: abandoned for a spotlight.)

A male sky over a female city. (Yes, yes they change sexes on occasion, as they choose, but largely remain thus. ((And, as this text is restricted to the skies, so the sexual discussion must be set aside for now.))) A gray sky with the occasional white or black rubbings, chalk. A dark gray sky or a light gray sky, with scoops of foam, seed, cream. A black sky – black on black, matte. A steel blue sky with shafts of white. Yesterday, a dark blue sky with flames of orange outlined in gold, and a blood red moon going down. For one week, a brilliant blue sky one wanted to soar into, a death-bliss sky with clouds one felt one could grasp, lift oneself onto, and find angels there to converse with, the two or three wings we desire (the angel's, the lover's, the poet's). Black and white skies, mournful Araki skies. Minimal skies; skies of a severe desire, an austere need (Baudelairian Dandy skies). Skies brooding on evil, Melmothian skies, wandering sorrowful skies. And skies all passionate joy. Skies all excess. Unrivalled skies that no other city possesses imagination enough to love. (Not to make other cities uptight, but just to state a truth. ((And we are, after all, only speaking of love – for the city, for its skies, for its cranes.)))

The Skies and Cranes of Tokio

Marina Vlady glances East and West; she sees me, smiles. Columbo walks up to me, shakes my hand: "compañero." They too are cranes of a sort (and so too poor Marion): eyes fixed firmly in the present, which is to say the future and to incorporate the past, the changing (changeless) city, and so the changing man the changing woman. Deep deep in the earth (concrete, pool, construction site, as you like), high high in the heavens, we build ourselves one another, man and woman, sky and city, we become cranes, firmly joined, canopy to mattress, lover to lover, we gaze, sway, shudder, and move on, recreating ourselves lovers cities.

* * *

Nadar from his balloon sites Tokyo.

* * *

Lang says it used to be a canal city. You can see the signs everywhere in the traditional parts of the city. Even Jimbocho, Ginza. But what does that mean? What is a "traditional part" of the city? One that is up to date and without a hint of its past. That's the only possible answer. So what do we mean? The old part? No, all parts being equal. The low city? Presumably. But did their old houses match ours? Were they anything like ours in scale and beauty? No, completely different histories, cultures. Low city opposed to a soaring city. Amsterdam has its canals. And yet, why did they remain in contact only with us for two hundred years? What attracted them to this species of foreigner? Even still. Isabel toiling on that dictionary. A German guy applied for a job with Amro and was sure he'd get it, had some Dutch, figuring he'd pick it up fast enough – and then they had to turn him down because three Japanese applied and they all spoke Dutch! Why did they? Who but the Dutch should ever speak it? Ever be able to? Eight consonants in a row. Curious history between us. "Dutch learning." And what's caught on? No two nations more unlike. Perhaps an unspoken longing between we two cities. Something hidden, unable to be articulated. A need to be spoken, a desire to be acknowledged. Two tongues to be desired. Ah, give me the sound of bicycles and everyone of all sizes and ages and sexes, all out at night, a white beer, a red beer, a blue beer. Young girls, cozy, and never lose sight of the edge. Amsterdam, home.

* * *

"Timeless. Temporary. Tokyo."

– Kazuo

* * *

SCENE SIX: A TEMPLE

The Woman awakes, after a heavy night of furious and fantastic masturbating, and staggers on to the bus to Jindaiji, the city's second oldest temple, located, yes, near Kichijoji – the Western Kichijoji, that is. The heavy incense emanating from the old temple adds to her sedation. The many souvenir shops only annoy her; though she does make her annual purchase of a demon-dispelling votive charm. She barely notices the row of monks in procession (though normally, her sexual fantasies run along acolyte lines), the small garden, an especially enormous tree, and the *susuki* leaves, final remnants that once lavished the Kanto Plain, playground for the Shogun's horses. Nor, of course, does she notice the man enjoying his cold *jindaiji soba* at the table next to her.

* * *

MIROKU

Don't worry, Baby,
Everything's gonna turn out alright.

– Brian Wilson-Silva

PART TWO

TOZAI! TOZAI!

- That's the shout, "Eastwest! Eastwest!" Everyone included. Good for any performance – going out at night, getting up in the morning.
- And Northsouth!, Northsouth!? Shouldn't that be included? After all –
- You're right, of course. And it is there, only more implicit. We go around the city, we go across, we wander all over – but one somehow doesn't feel that other pull. Just think of the Ginza line: the fun north end of it, and the dull commercial south. So, we'll follow the traditions in this respect, and keep that direction subtle. And, by the way, it should be "Southnorth!, Southnorth!" – *Namboku! Namboku!* I used to be able to get to *shitamachi* on the Namboku Line, get off at Todaimae Station. There's a decent wine shop near where you emerge with foreign wines, including one of the few places I could get prosecco.
- But if it's all underground, then it's all subtle.
- Not necessarily. We know all about the underground cities of the train stations, those elaborate malls and hotels, porn shops and tea shops. But they exist too in the subways, though perhaps not as elaborate, a salaryman or a girl can still get him or herself fitted for an evening. Yes, the sun exists underground too – as many names and myths, tragedies and romances – after all, the city's underground – just look at a map, think of the Yamanote as a circle, and the subway lines bursting out all around and within it – what do you see?
- Uhm, ok a circle, squiggles, a rainbow of colors, the Tozai blue, the Ginza orange. What am I supposed to see?
- A sun! And, considering that we're considering the underground – it's an anus. And after all, what is an anus but a sun spelt backwards?
- A what sun?
- Spelt backwards, an anus.
- Uh … ok.
- Comeon, let's walk.
- What, along the Sobu, east, and then down the river, along the bridges, sort of southnorth?
- You wanted every direction, sure, why not, a proper mix. After all, neglect the bridges and the subways, you do not do the city justice.

- But we won't be taking a subway.
- Oh we will – and we have quite a few choices: the Tozai, the Ginza, the Asakusa, the Hibiya, the Shinjuku lines, they all traverse *shitamachi*. And whether we do or not, the subway, as I've said, is implicit.
- So, Tozai! Tozai!
- Yes, appropriately. You know, the farther East we go, I see the West. It is implicit, always. The yellow Sobu grinds its way east. Here, Shōhei Bridge – these wonderful stone lamps, the thin river below – seen from the train it's exhilarating, and at ground level too. You know, you leave Kanda, no not the bookshops, but the students mixed with the salarymen, and suddenly these stone markers – you're not only entering Akihabara, you're approaching the River, the Sumida, not the Kanda. Walk through Akihabara, ignore the noise and toys, the Liebeskind lamp warehouse – or is it Eisenmann? – the River is beckoning. It's a hard walk, grimey, there are as many bill collectors as there are computer outlets, but the River is just a bit beyond, and that's where your focus should be. Yes, we can do this eastwest and southnorth, it makes no difference, this is the Center.
- You think so?
- I have to. If the River goes – and it is – then Tokio goes, no more.
- No more Tokyo?
- No. No more. All the conversations of all the people who lived here and loved here and especially the people who never gave it a good goddamn, and the few who did, who bothered to remember a name or some women who burned or drowned, or children who made it and moved out, or the few rebels, even the foreigners who wrote so much bullshit but nonetheless had a glimpse of willow – oh well.
- Oh well!?
- Well, the city endures.
- But you just said – ?
- Did I? Maybe I'm wrong on all counts. Oh, it'll endure – in its fashion. In memory. No, come back here in twenty years –
- Only twenty?
- You want thirty?, I'll give you thirty – but little more. No, I suppose I suffer the same Kafu-Seidensticker nostalgia. It's going – gone! How often can you write about "the stones underneath this shitheap of concrete underneath the next layer of dust under the following bag of bones" – what fire was it now?, what disaster? – well, anyway, under it all, they say, a certain legend is said to have

occurred, though it cannot be verified because all municipal and poetic records were destroyed the last time a building to last for exactly three years was built on the spot, and on and on? That can not go on. Tokio does not want a memory – we know that. But by now it is so far gone that the memory itself has forgotten its job, forgotten to remember. What's that illness dealing with accelerated growth, quickening senility. It repeats itself all over the city. Something new, virginal is built or born, grows fast, and within a couple of decades all memory of its origins is lost. It happens all over the place, is happening in so many millions of versions. And no records are being kept. All those memories lost –

- "Like tears in rain."
- Yes.
- All gone?
- All. Gone. But that's ok, as it should be.
- No!
- Yes.
- But a new Tokyo – the spirit?
- Ha! The "Spirit!" No, that's precisely the problem. The Spirit dies too. Yes, Tokio may be found West, as I've been saying. But it keeps going West, and, ok, might redefine itself, but in the process comes so far from the first, that, well, it's nothing like what it was. After all thirty million people – what balance can be found there? We've passed the Millennium, the subways are expanding –
- Anus takes over the sun, and can't be said to shine?
- Ha, yes! So, it all gets out of hand. When Roberta and I lived here, those many years, wonderful years, I was overjoyed by the idea of twenty-five millions, of all the human parts of the great machine that had found the proper balance of chaos and order, what a maze! So much fun to be a hamster – though I'd also almost intuitively, I suppose, favored the chaotic – that is how it is you know, living here, at first you see only the chaos, then begin to perceive the order, then to feel the balance, and then, finally, you see that chaos is the real order of things, but by then you have become so accustomed to Tokio, you far more easily accept the chaos, the miscellania, all that that does not seem to pertain to any certain order – you welcome it, revel in it. You are a Tokioite. But the last time we were here for a visit, it suddenly seemed to me that I'd never seen so many people, where were they all coming from, how was one to make any sense of this place? Or maybe I'm just getting older. Would I feel that way had we never left? Probably not;

I'd have grown with the place, never noticed the greater numbers. But it's not my job anymore to help maintain the continuity and change – it's yours.

– So, was there ever something you can call a "Tokyo spirit"? Surely, there must have been. That's what you've always been talking about, you and many others. Tokyo's ways are not Japan's, Tokyo's special character …

– Good question. Open question. "Was Tokio ever the Tokyo we imagine it to have been?" And when been? That's the problem with we nostalgiasts. What Tokio are we speaking of? The night Kafu met so-and-so in Ogikubo? The morning of an execution along the river? That perfect day when the cherry blossoms …? The aborted coup? The lonely afternoon when the arrow sang? The 1927 opening of the subway? (The tickets were in four languages, by the way.) The fire – which fire? – the air-raids? The day Zonar opened? The day he arrived – and was as immediately swept away on the road to Gunma Prefecture only seeing the skyscrapers of Shinjuku, not even able to visit his grave in Zoshigaya, wondering when he would ever see the city he'd given so much thought to? The day she got the broke-heart letter? The day he finally lost his virginity?

– Hold on.

– No. I can't. Do these make a Tokio? That's what I have to wonder.

– Well, do they?

– I'm not sure. Maybe this is it. You lose your virginity, you die in a fire, you hear an arrow zing by, whatever … what makes it Tokio? What is a Tokio-specific experience? Not so much that you happened to be here, but – what?

– That you associate the experience with the time, with the place?

– No. That's not it. But it's close.

– ??

– Maybe … that you associate, but you also realize – realize deeply – that while it may have occurred in almost any other place, there was also something eerie, uncanny, in that it could only have occurred here. Some special knowledge and association. I'm sure lots of people have lost their – what is it, "cherries"? – and I'm glad for 'em – well, when you've lost it here, you know there's a difference, there's a memory that includes Tokio.

– That's it?

– Isn't that enough?

– Uhm …

– No, you're right. Maybe it isn't enough. But you get the idea – ?

- Yeah ...
- Ok, good, Then it's enough for now. That'll give you something to go on.
- ??
- But you have to go with it.
- But where's that leave the future of Tokyo that you were speaking of?
- Was I? Oh, well, I'll be gone before that occurs. I have no doubt that the city will survive in one form or another; I wonder if I will like the changes, but I hope to be able to appreciate them. As for the rest, the real future, that's up to you. Try to maintain a bit of the old and the new Tokios. Try to remember a few of the stories and legends. And add more! I'll be leaving – with my Tokio – you're staying, make your own.

And so they talked, and so they walked, easwest, southnorth, the bridges and stations. He took his notes, brief, barely articulate, but he was grateful for the names and memories. He might look them up in a spare moment, but was only too aware that they were not *his* Tokyo – he kept to the conventional spelling – and while he was new at it – even his "cherry" intact (he liked that, that his cherry might blossom here) – he knew too that this Lang that he was speaking with, this foreigner who seemed now such an old-hand, had occasionally referred to a man named Cafferty, who Lang admitted that he had had briefly to rely on in the forms of some brief conversations (though it seems they were never really very close), a walk or two, and a small sheaf of notes:

"Dear Lang:
I'm too old and too used to my paths to help you now. I hear from Roberta that you've taken an interest in my beloved city, this old Tokyo I can barely discern now. Good for you. She further reassures me that your interest is serious.
I trust her.
I liked you from the first time we met – liked you, I should admit, from a distance. But, I have to admit, that I found you then too excitable. What was it? Why? That you seemed to need to intimidate her at the same time that you humbled yourself to her? Frankly – I'll keep this short – that put me off from you. It was only her reassurances to me that, well, you were confused about being here, that lead me to let up on my

earlier judgment of you. In time, of course, I saw you shake that silver mane of yours, and snap yourself out of it, saw the side of you that she treasures, the whole man, or almost all.

And then we met casually a few more times.

You are fine. (I've suffered the same way that I saw that you did.) I only wish the best for you and my own beloved Roberta, who will linger in my mind for a very long time – as long as I am given. She has told me that you have come to have a great passion for the city; not an ordinary passion, that is, as so many who come here experience and tarry, and then let go of. I suspect that you have also seen what it has come to mean to her – I mean the city, of course, but especially her few blocks of it. I trust now that you have come to respect that, those. She sees the whole city in those few familiar blocks– and you see yourself in, well, more. Both views are valid.

I will trust you, Lang. Perhaps years ago – many years – we might have become good friends and done a bit of "pavement botanizing" together. But no more, not now. I am leaving, slowly. I reduce my apartments year by year till they reach the contentment of that small pine box. No desire to speak – what could I say?, who would listen? – oh, I know you of all might, but to what purpose? – and besides, sight leaves too. (This might be my last typed letter!) But seriously: Pride, dignity, respect: what matter?

I lived in Tokyo.
Lang, surely, isn't that enough?

Therefore: I am enclosing a few notes – garnered from this and that, from a time I thought I could write – but then you read Hölderlin or Rilke, and realize the responsibilities of poetry, and it's better to simply walk away and not embarrass yourself. When you go deeper, however, you'll notice the small references. A little something to get you going – this city, unfortunately – perhaps – leads you straight into poetry; or so I have found. Maybe that is why I chose finally only to follow the city, and leave its poetry to others better than I. Can you do it? I wonder. Defeated by poetry, and won by the city, can not, certainly, be the worst of fates. I am sorry I have no more to give you – like so many lives in this city, mine too went up in flames. Long ago.

FLAMES

Of passion, certainly;

Flames too of accident.
Eastwest!

All the best,
Cafferty

The young man then looked through the envelope of notes that Lang – this new acquaintance – had handed over to him. After a short while, he was able to figure out their order, but not their poetry. He decided, finally, to leave them stand.

A.

SENJUOHASHI
"Senju Big Bridge"
"When we disembarked at Senju, my heart grew heavy at the thought of the thousands of miles that lay ahead, and tears welled from my eyes on leaving my friends in this world of illusion."
– Basho

The Great Thousand-armed bridge was the first across the Sumida, 1594, very north, and near an old Edo execution ground. (For serious crimes, the authorities really did parade the criminals through the city, as in Mizoguchi's, *Chikamatsu Monogatari*.) Now this is interesting: the temple, the Kozukappara Ekō'in, that the criminals were then buried in, was affiliated with the Ekō'in, which is the one that honors those who died in the Fire of the Long Sleeves. Not bad company for arsonists, robbers and murderers. Another: that Hiraga Gennai is also honored – if that's the appropriate word – here; after all, he was a murderer.

NB: How it all comes together along the river and the bridges and subways. The bridge in fact later became known as the Kozukappara Bridge, a bit more colorful than Great Bridge, perhaps, but the color seems a morbid hue.

(Anyway, the Bridge was washed away and doesn't exist anymore.)

B.

SHIRAHIGEHASHI
"White Whiskers Bridge"

I.

AKIHABARA

The kiosks are all different and none have Snickers, there is a "milk bar" in the station, an incongruous Akihabara supermarket and department store, but it is the warrens spelling our future that the place is known for. I prefer the small stalls in and around the station: thousands of cables, or clips, or doo-dads that only specialists understand, and the true Tokyo types selling them. They are of course dwarfed by the big stores, screens, and constant shouting (by those other "true" Tokyo types).

The Occupation, once again, did not know what it was creating when it moved a bunch of open-air shops from Kanda to Akihabara. Now it's all here, the nerd-geniuses.

C.

Sakurabashi

1987

"Cherry Blossom Bridge" – yes, the blossoms here are lovely, but couldn't they have come up with a better name? No, probably not.

D.

Kototoibashi

"Asking-for-Word Bridge"

The poet Narihara sent a Miyako-dori – a seagull – asking for word of – appropriately – the capitol (but the other one).

Green, poetic (tragic?)

Mukojima, Basho's hut, Tamanoi renamed Pigeon Street, and Kafu's great story, *east* of the river. (Where was Fuji Ice, his favorite café?)

New Year's crafts fair, a walk along the river, happier days for us all.

(All that nostalgia for the Yoshiwara too – 18 Great Connoisseurs! – astringent indeed when you think of the women behind cages, all ready for fine "conversation." Query: why did footbinding never find a taste here?)

2.

Asakusabashi-eki

At the foot the Stationary Museum, where one knight fells another with his lance, Castell. Here too two realms are united: love and writing: the Belle Grande Hotel and a Kokuyo billboard. Sorobans and felt-tips battle forever against the calculator and computer. (A flying skull?)

E.

Azumabashi

"Bridge of My Wife"

"Alas, my wife!" – a self-sacrificing deity.

1774, later 1887, steel girders.

The view of the bridges from here glitters like some pink and green lace, lingerie.

It is best viewed from a middle distance, looking east one sees the land higher than is the bridge.

F.

KOMAGATABASHI

"Colt-Shaped Hall" (or "Cuckoos over Komagata")

Pretty, elegant.

3.

RYUGOKU

An art space seems to be here – what the hell does that term mean, anyway – what is an "art space" – presumably a space allocated for art. But why separate? That's not the spirit of things! And "installations" – what are they? I come into a gallery and stay there a while – am I not installed, have I not installed myself? Does some sort of permanence or prestige have to emerge? Do I not already possess it myself?

Anyway, the big draw of course is that the sumo tournaments are held here – the blood rushing to the face, the scent of the beasts' hair rising into the stadium.

I saw the Hara Setsuko photo show here. In an art space. It was installed.

Off there to the right, looking west, by the post office, Yanagibashi, that's where the boats emerged, sailing up the river. The soldiers too.

G.

UMAYABASHI

"Bridge of the Stables"

Site of the Shogun's stables.

Yellow, galloping.

H.

KURAMAEBASHI

"In Front of the Storehouses Bridge"

In front of the storehouses, ho-hum.

4.
KINSHICHO
Wasn't there a decent Mexican restaurant there once? Was this supposed to offer an alternative to Shinjuku? What kind? Shinjuku, where the best shit was available, and I mean it literally. Now Kinshicho is all cleaned up.

(Extra: And Shinjuku was once called the "anus" of Tokyo, with people lined around the corners waiting to pick up some shit. For their small farms or gardens. Too, who was it told me years ago he – yes, I recall who, but had better leave him nameless here in case these notes come into the wrong hands – had come to understand that curious desire some people have for sex involving, well, the materials of the toilet? Said he'd been in Golden Gai, at Gold Dust, Y—'s place till she moved to Ginza – and had gone to the toilet, having forgotten that she had gone before him. Well, it seems he opened the door – no one ever bothering to lock it, the bar being so small one always noticed when someone had gone – so had he in fact forgotten? – and there she was, asquat, round, white, beautiful butt fully exposed, a few longer pubic hairs on view too – it probably was a compelling sight; and she had obviously just shat, the scent filling the tiny cubicle. The combination – the woman, her flesh, the scent – lead him to understand how that desire might occur, he said, assuring me that no, he did not have the peculiar taste for it himself. Too, it – Shinjuku still – retains its Piss Alley. What was the old black marketeers slogan – a sign at the east exit: "Let light spread forth from Shinjuku." – Anal light.)

I.
RYUGOKUBASHI
"Bridge of Two Provinces"
First to be built south of Senju, after the Ohashi; built after the Fire of the Long Sleeves; here fireworks; 1693. Joining now the sides of the river, all contained.

J.
SHIN'OBASHI
"New Great Bridge", 1912; then tragic: 1923.

5.
KAMEIDO
When the Sunday painters are in Meiji Jingu, I am admiring the

wisterias here.

Though the plum has gone, it remains in the spirit of the great scholar-poet Michizane.

This is where Osugi Sakae was put to death. No more plums indeed.

K.
KIYOSUBASHI
Named after two districts to either side, Kiyosumi east, and Nakasu west.

L.
SUMIDAGAWA'OHASHI
"Big Sumida River Bridge"
For traffic; the River deserves a far better tribute.

6.
HIRAI
Like Osaki, an in-between place.

M.
EITAIBASHI
"Bridge of Eternal Ages"
Romantic. "Crossed the bridge itself the day sky at night. Lit blue."
Now the oldest. 699, then again 1808, 1925; single span.
Like a folding fan, or interlaced fingers.
Very romantic: Nihonbashi (the last shogun wrote the characters for the bridge), Kayabacho, Monzennakacho.

N.
TSUKADA'OHASHI
Here I crossed the great river for the first time; the sun was glistening on my lover's neck, thin arms, shining on my first, late, feeble steps. And on the other side was transformation, washed by river light, the lover's light – we dove dreaming and came up for air. All bridges light.
1964

O.
KACHIDOKIBASHI
"Shout of Triumph Bridge"
(Victory over Russia, 1905)
1940, double drawbridge.

7.
Shin-Koiwa

&

8.
Koiwa

Just the other side of the Arakawa – just awful. The future of a faceless Tokyo.

What kind of shape do these notes form? Can something be made of them – something written, that is? Explore the names more? Get more history and anecdote? Study bridges? Or – ?

But I've sailed under, walked across, and behind me the setting Sun.

THE YAMANOTE

Chapter 7

SHINJUKU–SHIN-OKUBO

So there was Lang in Kichijoji, and enjoying it; it wasn't Roberta's Tokyo and so it felt like a kind of truce; she had no interest in the west, and so Lang could feel like a pioneer, he'd made his discovery – and then she made her move – it wasn't against him so much as it was for herself, she'd found a place she could finally call "home" – she moved to the low city, you know, the old city – nothing could have surprised Lang more, but Roberta was happy really, happy, she loved her new/old Tokyo – Roberta'd made her last move.

* * *

cheeks blown out
thought frustrated
hair swept back
a woman in black
the next day's train

* * *

Night, love and wine to all extremes persuade;
Night shameless, wine and love are fearless made.

– Ovid

* * *

THE HAPPY ISLES OF VAN ZANDT

"The hibiscus will flower, the coral will grow, but man will die."

Big picture of Gretchen crying out. Then wild cry across the chaotic landscapes. Ranges of mountains split open to the left; behind them boiling waves.

"Art consists in eliminating. But in the cinema it would be more correct to talk of 'masking' ... the cameraman ought to create shadow too. That's much more important than creating light!"

He wrote to his mother: "I wish I were at home. But I am never 'at home' anywhere – I feel this more and more the older I get – not in any country nor in any house nor with anybody."

He sold the business and bought a magnificent estate – it was a miniature paradise.

> The garden gate, inside.
> The night storm rages. Pouring
> rain. And trees bent low. But silent,
> the gate. A bell above it, silent. A few
> seconds. But! Now the tongue of the bell
> moves. Once. Then goes silent again, quite
> silent. But then: at the porter's window. The light
> shining out.
> – Mayer

He would spend hours gazing out to sea at a sailing boat that went back and forth there every day. One morning he got to know the fisherman it belonged to, and astonished us by asking if he could go out with him. He often did so after that, and the fisherman told my parents that their son was a born sailor!

[WH speaks of] ... headlights gliding over rain-wet asphalt in the dark city, of rough seas, a dazzling sunrise, almost imperceptible gestures, facial expressions so eloquent that they reveal the soul within.

[In *Der Januskopf* – subtitled, *On the Borders of Reality*:] The idea of the statue begins to haunt the doctor, who sees it as a symbol of the duality of human nature. He offers it as a present to the girl he is court-ing, Jane Lanyon, who refuses with horror.

"Jaorana oe Murnau tane ..."

"... endless discussion over every effect of lighting. [He listened to us and said:] 'All the things you're doing now with artificial sets I shall do one day in a natural one.' We laughed then, but when we saw his masterpiece ..."

Wilhelm was not captivated by the pretty ones; he was attracted rather by those who were sensitive or a bit odd, especially if they were witty too.

"... a sad place steeped in alcohol and jazz ... where the white man has transmitted to the beautiful, careless, childlike inhabitants his own civilization, including the Bible, brandy, syphilis, leprosy, and cheap cot-ton goods."

All the splendor had become a wilderness. My brother decided to transform it into a paradise.

"The whole world had finally become a wheel, and the sky galloped backwards around them like a fiery top ... Life can be so beautiful when one is in love and riding on the merry-go-round!"

[He shows us] an apotheosis of the flesh: the feats and canoe races are only pretexts for showing those godlike young bodies. He was intoxi-cated by them, just as [the camera] becomes intoxicated with light ... A sail unfurls like a sheet of shining silk, and suddenly the dark bodies of natives are seen among the rigging like ripe clusters on a grape-vine. Long, narrow canoes flash like fish through the transparent waters. ... In our appreciation of this complex entity we almost overlook the details, we almost forget – how could it be otherwise? – the love story.

The marble mask of the dead mother, where we see the white face of the drowning woman drifting on the gray waves of the lake.

FW in a letter: "Soon, when we have crossed the Equator, [the Southern Cross] will shine down on our books and dreams, for it is towards our books and dreams that we are voyaging."

The Happy Isles of Van Zanten, a novel by the Dutch author Laurids Bruun. (And *The Excursion to Tilsit*, by Hermann Sudermann.)

"The hibiscus will flower, the coral will grow, but man will die."

* * *

Last night I saw the lights of the city, Kazuo contemplates. The city ablaze like some huge, tremendous toy, a Disneyland of its own. And it was a sign of hope and desire. The flashing cranes all over the city, the great neon signs of Shibuya and Shinjuku and Yurakucho; the low city and the dim lights of houses; the huge apartment blocks of the high city. All like a gigantic Yoshiwara, a nightless city, a gift.

* * *

REPORT (SEIZURE); STATE OF LANGUAGE, CITY
– Fiction a Verb Necessarily
"Comeon, I want to show you my favorite public telephone."

* * *

- I fall to pieces when I talk to myself.
- So many do.
- So, is it a phenomenon to be remarked upon?
- Look, a Vietnamese restaurant next to the Colombian prostitutes who are next to an acupuncture clinic.
- And the crazy lady feeding the temple cats, don't forget her.
- All things pass, but not my way. Neither here nor there, a manly woman nor a womanly man. Who will come to me, say the word? Jeez, I'm beginning to sound like Marianne.
- Maybe the people talking to themselves are really a secret band of actors reciting scripted pieces and no one knows, no one has ever known that they are listening in on these scripts, or in fact are ignoring or walking away from wonderful little plays, monologues, soliloquies.
- But when someone does hover in to listen, it's the actor who sneers back and drifts away.
- Gee, actors who insist on being totally anonymous, or ignored, or thought half-nuts.
- Do they go home and become "normal"? Take off their crazy-person

costume, and get on the phone? Do they wear masks?
- Or – do they play their role their whole lives?
- And are we the only ones who know all this? And now that we know, what happens? And why am I half-whispering this to myself?
- Should we introduce ourselves to the cat lady? Could she be the Shakespeare of our times?
- And if people have been talking to themselves for centuries, as I assume they have, then is there some sort of secret guild, with oaths and secret signs and all? If I speak a little louder so that passersby stare at me, do I get invited to join? Am I breaking the rules by reciting my own text? Should I be speaking Japanese? If I'm not supposed to say my own words, how do I get my text? Or is it texts? Do you get a new one every day, or every week, or what? And how do you get them? Are they passed stealthily on the train? Left in a portfolio on a seat? Faxed?
- Or – oh no – maybe you only get one for your whole life. Like a mantra, I suppose –
- One text, one monologue. But a really, really long one.

* * *

Her eyes all glittering and me all embarrassed in black – and she so gaily dressed. She shook my hand goodnight and asked if my hands were always cold. "No." "Good," she told me, "it's not good for hands to always be cold," she said as if she were implying "come around sometime when your hands are warm." This from a woman who knew nothing of me (except for the book I had with me), standing there, already half turned away, and saying this simple truth. (And I never met her again.) I wonder if Roberta and Lang know the pain these recollections bring.

* * *

- Yes, but –
- But no, Hiroko; you see, don't you?
- No, but should it matter, after all …
- Well, we do live in two different worlds. What's that song? I'll take the high road, and you'll take …"
- Yes, but is the one all so bad? You seem to have turned your back to half the world without looking forward. You're only standing still, while I think I'm at least moving. You live and work now in Aoyama – Arlene's "Blue Hills" – and you seem to think that's all there is.

I'm next door in Shibuya – well, at least I spend most of my time there – but I look at it and sometimes I feel "Is this all there is?" I don't think so.

– "I don't think so." Is that all there is?

– No, but, and I know I'm not sure, but I do know there must be more. I guess. And anyway, what's so wrong about it? The low road does have its charm points. Maybe it's not so glamorous, but –

– Name one.

– Me!

– Yes …

– Myself!

– True …

– And I!

– Very charming. But look, Hiroko, if it's so charming, why do you seem to always want to leave? Are you and Hiromi still looking for an apartment in Shibuya?

– Yes, but we haven't found one yet. She's pretty persistent, stays over at friends' places a lot, but I usually manage to go home no matter how late we stay out at night.

– Not sleeping around?

– Oh, that was my earlier youth. And besides, I am fond of my mother's breakfast.

– No tea and toast for you, eh?

– Rice and fish and *miso* soup!

– You're a strange one, you know.

– No, I don't, and I don't think so. Deep down – if I may say so – I think I'm a regular girl –

– *Miso* soup …

– No, that's not at all what I mean. I'm as confused as anyone, sure, but I accept that. I have a few dreams; I don't know now how to make them real. I've made a few bad moves, but nothing catastrophic. But too, I get inklings now and then, and –

– "Inklings"?

– Well, you know, occasional flashes of … of how I might proceed. Or, of how I might better develop myself, find out what I really want to do. Ok, so I'm not exactly clear about my future, but I do think I have a good one.

– You sound pretty sure of yourself, hopeful, confident.

– Well, yes, shouldn't one?

– Of course.

– Yes, I suppose I do feel confident, or at least not wrong about myself. If only I don't fuck up.

- Have you?
- Tell me about it! But I think, I hope, those days are over.
- And Hiromi?
- Well, she may not be the best example, but she has been a good friend.
- No, I mean, does she fuck up?
- Oh, comeon …
- Ok, back to you.
- What was I saying? Oh yes, I think I'm finally making some good moves, looking forward.
- And not standing still?
- Not standing still. I'm sorry, I didn't mean to criticize you; it's just that it seems to me that you could do so much more, want so much more.
- What could I want?
- Is that it? To be in an ad company, writing copy, drinking with clients, sleeping around?
- Hiroko, there simply isn't much more in this state of affairs.
- No, there has to be. What about home, love, travel, learning something about other people?
- Nice, if it comes, but highly unlikely. I have no complaints. I like my job alright, my clients like me. I have some free time. I have some girlfriends, and I like to drink.
- And love?
- Oh comeon! I'll have a family, alright?
- And love them?
- Now really!
- Alright. … Well, as I was saying, yes, I would like to be with a man I can really love, have a family with. But he has to … you know, not stand still, know that we can change, move together, make things, make moves that most people don't even ever consider.
- You sound serious.
- Of course I'm serious. It just has to be possible. I know most people don't even consider it a possibility, but I think you can have a home and a "happy" – a happy life.
- You also sound simplistic.
- Yes, maybe. But I don't think I'm completely innocent. I have my inklings, and there's nothing simple about them at all. A couple, a family – doesn't that mean … uhm, something … moving?
- I suppose so. I don't know.

- I mean, look at Lang and Roberta.
- Hardly an example, Hiroko.
- ?
- Just look at them. He's over in Kichijoji, and she's in Yanaka. Is that what you call a happy couple?
- Well, they're not there because they don't love each other.
- Oh? They're there because they do? Because they're together?
- Yes! Am I the only one who thinks they are together, sort of.
- Perhaps you are.
- They've made their choices. *There's Lang in Kichijoji, and enjoying it; it may not be Roberta's Tokyo, and maybe it's a kind of truce. You know, she has no interest in the west, and so maybe it makes Lang feel like a sort of pioneer, like he's made his own discovery of Tokyo.*
- And that sounds like a good couple to you?
- Well, yes. Yes, I admit it looks bad. They're on opposite sides of the world – or at least you might think so. But it's one world, isn't it? She's happy, he's happy, they're both in Tokyo. She has her quiet life, and he has his excitement. Don't the two have to meet in the middle?
- Shibuya?
- That's no middle!
- Where then?
- In their hearts.
- Hiroko!
- Uhm, I mean, they will meet, together. I don't mean a compromise, really, a sharing, a compromise. Isn't that what all couples have to do?
- I suppose so.
- No, really. Sometimes being apart is the best way of staying together.
- Too abstract-weird for me. But could you stand it?
- What?
- Living apart from your husband?
- No, I'd hate it. The thing is, they've been together for a long time, and then she moves here, and then he comes after her, and then he finds out he also likes Tokyo.
- And then he lives apart from her.
- But at least they're both here!
- In a manner of speaking. They're here, but not together. So much for his "rescue mission." Jeez, one minute he's a pioneer – can't figure that one out – and the next he's a rescue artist.
- It wasn't a rescue mission! At least I don't think it was. And as for

pioneer, well, you know, the west isn't the area most westerners think of as traditional Tokyo. But maybe it was that he felt he could discover something new there, see the old in that new or however the jumble goes.

– Well, he never really wanted to come here. Didn't he think he'd just sweep her off her feet – ah ha!, now he's a swashbuckler – and take her back to, where?, Vienna?, Amsterdam?

– Vienna, I think. The important thing is that he did come here, for her sake. I think she liked that.

– Didn't think he was intruding?

– Maybe. But she also had to appreciate it. And then he began to see a Tokyo …

– A Tokyo that was not hers.

– He began to see a Tokyo that wasn't hers – meanwhile she has her own – and someday they will meet and see that their two Tokyos are a single city.

– Dream on, Little Wing.

– ?

– Hiroko, *shitamachi's* out. Get it? Roberta'll go to her public baths, buy *miso* from the local *miso* lady, slurp her noodles, do her work, whatever it is, and write perfect *kanji*, and in no time go so native that Lang won't recognize her.

– You really are more pessimistic than I thought.

– As you like. I just don't see them getting back together again, ever.

– Well, I do. You can't just take your "high road" without looking back at your "low road." And anyone on the low road will naturally wonder what lies up. I believe they'll appreciate the best of both worlds. And so should we all, dammit!

– Alright already.

– Don't you see? Roberta *made her move. It was never against Lang so much as it was for herself, she'd found a place she could finally call "home" – she moved to the low city, the old city, you know.*

– Yes …

– *And nothing could have surprised Lang more. Isn't that the beauty of it?*

– Uhm?

– The surprise! That she'd made her own move!

– Yes, but ….

– But no. She could show him a place or a sort of place that she could call home, for herself, but never against him.

– And Lang, in love with the west?

- Oh sure he's macho enough to oppose her, but he's also curious enough to want to know what it is that attracts her to that part of the city that he wasn't initially attracted to. He loves her too much, wants to know what she likes.
- Macho?
- Oh, he feels he has to know what she knows, and now she has something he doesn't. It's all natural enough. But it's also love, whether he'd acknowledge it or not. It is love – one wants to share, one's joys.
- I suppose.
- Of course, silly. And of course, *Roberta was happy really, happy* – not that she's the type to say so, but we could all see it, *she loved her new-old Tokio*, had settled in, she did it all so smoothly – oh I just wish I could act with such grace, such lithe …!
- And you call me silly?
- But she *was happy, really happy, is happy, so happy really* and you have no right to say otherwise.
- I said nothing.
- No, you needn't. Ah, what a skeptic. So sad, really sad. Really.
- Leave me out of your little dancing circle.
- Gladly – really. But anyway, the point, and the point for Lang is that *Roberta'd made her last move*. She wasn't going to move again. Oh, was he surprised! I mean, he is a man who has something to say about everything and here he was in a neighborhood *saké* shop all smoke and plaster peeling since the early 60s, and he had nothing to say, couldn't say anything, nothing! An unnatural Lang. And what a relief, I might add. She was unbridgeable, she –
- I think it's unbudgeable,.
- Not unbridgeable?
- In other circumstances, perhaps.
- Such as?
- Your big river flooded over.
- Oh. Anyway, she was …?
- Unbudgeable.
- Yes, unbudgeable. But she wasn't resisting him or anything like that. She'd just … settled. Soft, firm, her own.
- And he had to face it.
- Right, he wasn't just about to, unbudge her; he had to face that.
- ?
- But she was unbridgeable too. He couldn't get across to her.
- So why didn't he leave?
- No! Don't you still not get it? If he left it'd mean either that he

didn't care or he was so egocentric as to think that she'd follow. But he did – and does! – care, and so stayed; and his ego knew that she wouldn't follow, she was going to remain.

–   Lang injured, awaiting her to relent.
–   No! Don't you still not get it? Perhaps he's injured in a normal sort of way, but his is a healing wound – now wait, bear with me – healing because he does have his Tokyo, his west to complement her east – and they shall meet! Get it, stupid?
–   In a vague sort of way, maybe.
–   So now he will begin to feel the enthusiasm for the city that she has, she'll feel his, he'll feel hers –
–   And they'll feel each other – in a manner of speaking.
–   You do get it!
–   Sort of. But I don't buy it. Aren't they two different Tokyos they're feeling, after all? What's to say that they shall "meet" as you put it? Why can't it really mean that they'll only split further apart? Like you and I. He going his way, she going hers. Never to meet, forever separate. I don't mean to sound pessimistic –
–   I know, it's nature, not you.
–   It's not. I just don't see why they have to get together again.
–   Love, idiot! Ever heard of it, Hi – ?
–   Vaguely. I don't put much into it.
–   So I've heard.
–   But – can't …?
–   No.
–   But –
–   No.

* * *

The boy looks in, around and under phonebooths and vending machines – tobacco, softdrinks, condoms – and finds still-good telephone cards – his favorite a Ferrari – occasional coins, and once, ¥10,000, which, surprisingly, he saved.

* * *

Languishing. Tea and melons, and some Kurosawa battlesite. Daitocho. Now that was a place where I thought I wanted to be and once I got there felt my visit shouldn't be too overextended. But I'd promised our friends to look after the garden in my own inept manner and so was duty-bound to stay. Nothing died. Roberta and I needed the break. "Gotta rethink things through," we said. Or being kicked out of the house by any other name. The house, the old farmhouse, sounds like the castle in Italy Roberta stayed in. Those huge beams. Years younger perhaps, but no less not citified. But I do like a toilet that flushes. A kitchen with a proper stove and where you don't have to examine each chopstick for insect signs. A view all around you and soon enough you really do forget inside and out. A bamboo grove, and the raccoons roaming freely, stealing the cats' dinner. Never did spear one; never did scare 'em either. But the seclusion, no conversation in a rice-growing village. No video shops or Parco Book Centers. But why three hair-dressers? Akashi-san came by once a week to bring me over for a hot meal, and to show me his camera collection. Nice family. Homegrown vegetables. And his bonsai! – hundreds. A bicycle ride to look at the sea; and why all those Brazilians, and why them jumping into that cold wild ocean? A ride to the "mall" for some noodles and water. Crushed ice with syrup, love that stuff in the summer. And a hell of a summer it was, too.

* * *

R'n'L!!!!!!!

Yes, yes, a way to connect it all. Glenn, Aretha, Fritz, Buster, *Weird Tales* and the Continental Op, all of 'em, and all of us. We're on our way, kids!

Ya' know how most decent thinking people in the world want to have a home in town and another in the country? Well, I jes wanna have one on the west side of Tokyo and one on the east. Is that too much to ask? ("No, No, We like the idea, kid, We like it.")

They may've stopped making them years ago, but I still dream of laser disc shops. (I mean of course ...)

So, whadda'ya think? Are there porno films of Clarke and Carole getting it on? They must be available! Look into it, eh? I'll pay top yen.

I gotta get a copy of that book, *The Face of Buster Keaton*. What does our man Cavell say about it? – the face, I mean, not the book.

Do you know that story about Tallulah (sp?) Bankhead and Hitch when they were filming *Lifeboat*? How she'd show up on the set without any underwear, and there it was for all to see as she climbed up into the lifeboat set each day, and one day the technicians "complained" to Mr. Hitchcock, and he said something like, "So whom shall I speak with, the Costume or the Make-up Department?"

Did Warhol ever do more Elvis's than that stuff from *Flaming Star*? Was that the only one? And if so, why so? And did he ever do a Cary or a Carole? And if not, why not, dammit?

Remember Susanne, the German actress from Hamburg who was at the castle? A beautiful woman (what *did* go on in her head?), red hair (real), beautiful face (that sharp nose, the smooth, angley cheeks), a face that you could imagine in some pre-Renaissance painting, half-androgynous (which already says much); something heroic, spiritual. To draw upon a cliché, a perfect face for a Joan of Arc. But oh so much more! (The irony in the eyes, something knowing, critical, but saying nothing of what she saw. Apparently she did some Zen, too. She was a koan herself – a koan whose answer apparently I will not know the answer to in this lifetime.) At least she knew I liked her.

Also gotta find that o.p. issue of *du* on Glenn that Fritz mentioned.

No, no, I don't want to get into a "whatever happened to" mode, but, what did ever happen to the lead singer of the Shangri-Las? Did she become a porno star or a big executive or something?

I always remember – or, actually, I don't remember, I only recall that line from Wilde from the first edition of his letters on the inside covers, something about, "my handwriting once so Greek and gracious," or to that effect ... anyway, I mention it because I know how my own handwriting and letter-writing style has changed so over the years; a great part came first from reading Byron's letters, and then writing LC, and all that freedom I found, a "sweet new style to accommodate chaos" indeed, to mix it all up, me and Tokyo. As for the handwriting, I do think there's been a natural "progression" (whether, yes, people can read it or not), and maybe a lesson from calligraphy, and in the end, excuse me, as Blake says, "it is spiritually discerned." You think I'm kidding?

Did Frank O'Hara ever write anything about Cary or Carole? And yes, once again, if not, why not, dammit!?

* * *

Rich, strange, she wonders. Rich. The cornucopia. Strange. Not like others. My childhood. Kazuko-chan. Ah, at least I see Kyoto twice a year. In its own way, I can say Tokyo too is rich and strange. But does it therefore make me so? No, it enhances my experience, certainly, and I am sure, I am enhanced in some ... in some strange and rich ways, by the capitol. And perhaps, in whatever small way, I can enhance its own rich and strange ways.

* * *

- To walk across the city, you go around it.
- To walk around the city, you go into it.
- To walk into the city, you go across it.
- You can almost hear your thoughts in these caverns. Or, if you close your eyes, get still, and listen real hard – no, it drives you mad, like some multi-multi-tracked soundtrack of banks, hotels, bureaucrats all spewing ... syllables.
- The great roar that drowns out the art of speaking to oneself. Shinjuku is a sort of perverted yin-yang sign, with one half all life and the other anti-life.
- But we're on the way to the sun.
- A black hole here, stillness, a silent roar, high-rises that feel like their first floors are way below groundlevel, and their top floors only reach streetlevel.
- Metropolis, latest version, the underground city.
- The burying ground, killing floor, east meets west here at a standstill, crossroads.
- Imagine one of those cartoons where Martians have landed, postapocalypse earth, and they find the skyscrapers of Shinjuku. How will they judge us? Not as creatures who had perfected the soliloquy.
- Alphaville.
- Arufamura.
- A whistling wind –
- Dead branches flying past –
- A newspaper –
- A skull –

- A tear.
- I can hear my mother's voice, calling. Saying nothing.
- Moan you moaners, mumble you mumblers.
- Bundle up, gotta keep ourselves busy, keep these lips moving.

* * *

7. The MIDDLE SECTION of the film takes place at a sidewalk café in Shinjuku – rear projection, obviously – where we see our Woman sitting with a glass of mineral water, the portfolio on the table. She is clearly very nervous, keeps putting her fingers near her mouth, or running a palm on a knee, but she does not allow herself to indulge these tics, never bites the nail, never scratches the knee.

After a short while, in the distance we see Roberta and Marianne walking together, talking.

- And then it came, I came, just flowing, wave after wave. Funny what these funny Japanese vegetables can do.
- Oh, Marianne, you are a creative one! But I like a more direct contact – if necessary – if not, then the tumble. I also like to eat my vegetables.
- Who says I didn't?
- Of course.
- They're multi-purpose – like Godzilla.
- ?
- Don't you know, the Godzilla dildo, those scales running down his back.
- You're joking?
- No. There's Ultra-Man, too. Those silver arms, you know.
- And –?
- Of course, Ultra-Kid, for strolling, complete with remote.
- It's truly wonderful in a way. Oh, and I'll bet the girls, you know, Hi-
- Hiromiko?
- Yes, and I'll bet they each have Doraemon dildos. That cute pug nose, plug it right in and squeal.

[They both laugh, continue to walk, and then:]

- But don't you think life in the city is in a way masturbatory? You know, we run in circles, all our own, ever trying to increase the excitement and yet whenever a peak is reached we may be satisfied but oh how we want to speak with someone, share the joy, the dirty secrets, the humor of it all – you know what I mean – but just as immediately we're back on the Tokyo treadmill again, the excitement rises but the peak we're really after never seems to materialize – oh these mini-peaks are alright, sure, but are they enough?, enough to sustain one? – I see you and think of the mill, the conservatory, the relentless nights, even the great successes, but –

- Vegetables?
- Not exactly – but we need to connect with something outside ourselves, outside the narcissism of this city, connect with each other, yes, we are successful there – but connect too with something more, something –
- Roberta.
- Something, oh – "like approaching the divine" – that's how I felt once after Lang and I made love – and not just once. I know you know what I mean.
- Yes.
- Do I make sense?
- To me, certainly. This last bit, yes; but I don't know about the masturbatory Tokyo thesis. Oh, look who's here!

-
- They sit down with the Woman.

-
- So, whadda'ya' think? Does this burg jerk your head and arm right off?
- Uuh–?
- Roberta's got this idea that the city's one huge dildo in which we're all masturbatorially walking around in circles and quietly coming but failing to commune with God –
- Marianne!
- Oh, what's this? [She lifts the portfolio.]
- "My Dildo" – this week. It's certainly got me going round circles in this, what was it, "burg"? Someone left it on a train seat, and I've been looking for him ever since, trying to return it.
- Uh-huh?
- Really.
- "Someday he'll come along, the man I love, and he'll be thick and long …"
- Now, Marianne, cool your lusts. It's true. I've only seen the man from the back, and he –

–   – was all in black. So what else is new – in this burg?

[Now we see Hiroko and Hiromi approach, also in conversation.]

–   Swinging?
–   La, la-la, la-la.
–   I thought that was something our parents did – or at least their friends.
–   There are other ways "to swing," my lovely.
–   Well, you can swing a leash – but this city's no place for dogs.
–   Yes, it's a cat city. "My Pussy," like the bar. But no, not a leash – or sort of.
–   "The hills are alive …" From the rafters.
–   You –?
–   Yes, "swinging in the …"
–   All, all knotted and bundled like a package from Kyukyodo?
–   Like twelve layers of incense. My pussy, indeed.
–   Well, uhm … uhm …
–   Oh my ankles are still a bit sore, and around my arms. I mean, after all, you are suspended. But you know what I discovered, the body takes care of these things for you, it, what's the word?, it compensates. Take a little pain, get a little pleasure. Your juices flow. Liquid incense. I can't wait to see the photos.
–   The photos! Hiromi!
–   Well, I'm not going to do it everyday, and I would like to have some proof, something for my scrapbook. And yes, you'll see them.
–   Something tells me it wasn't just the two of you.
–   Oh no, there was a whole crew. Someone for the knots, someone to test the ceiling, make-up and creams. And he wanted me in a kimono – actually we did it twice because the second time he wanted me in another kimono, something more for Spring.
–   Winter and Spring bondage sets?
–   Something like that. Actually, it's sweet when you think of it.
–   Oh, I couldn't agree more!
–   Well it is. You'll see.
–   Perhaps. But you, you …
–   Yes, I know. I have to try everything once. And sometimes often! Christ on the cross. Christ in kimono. Is there a difference, really?
–   You didn't!?
–   No, but I thought of it. Anyway, I like our incense better. And we've got thousands of gods! Can you imagine, three gods in one? Isn't

there some movie about a woman ...? Oh, forget it. But you know, my Christianity is purely decorative.

- A way to get boys.
- Or men.
- And the difference is ...?
- Oh, ask me some other time. Look!

[They too sit with the other three women. Marianne begins.]

- Hiroko, Hiromi. Hi. Sit down, we were just talking about sex.
- Oh. We were talking about Jesus Christ.

[Roberta and Marianne stare speechless at one another. Then Hiromi.]

- His *Passion*, I think it's called.
- Ah, yes. Anyway, take a look at these photos.

[Hiroko takes the portfolio, and studies the photographs closely, seriously.]

- They're like a dream, some strange story where you know everything's connected but you can't figure out how, and you feel your very life depends on it.
- Straight out of the textbook. Ok, yes, but don't you notice anything else about them?
- Let me see. Yes, they're only buildings, only exteriors, and there are no people. But they were all taken in Tokyo, and –
- – right –
- There are no places without people in Tokyo.
- None.
- None.
- None.
- Can't think of one.
- So how did he take them? Or she.
- That's what we can't figure out. That, and how they're connected.
- Well anyway, seeing as you can't figure that out, what were you saying about sex?
- Oh, yes, Hiromi, of course, sorry to distract you. Well, Roberta here thinks that our lives here are spent in some sort of gigantic masturbatory ritual in which we only ever fondle ourselves and never

connect with anyone else really, the city doesn't allow for any sort of outward, other amative gesture.
- Ohh, that's sweet. Gee, Roberta.
- It was just an idea I tossed out – speculation, conversation.
- But if everyone's doing it, what sex does that make the city? Is Tokyo bi?

[As the five women begin to discuss the question, we cut to Arlene and Kazuko, walking, talking.]

- Which means the French, the Chinese, and the Turks make the best lovers? Not in my short experience.
- No, let's look at it in reverse. No food culture, no erotic culture.
- The English!
- Everyone's first choice.
- Go on, please.
- Well, the Austrians are all front, all frills. Sweet cakes and wine half water, frills and lingerie. Mere teases, and the main courses mere meat and potatoes. They only thrive thanks to overlayerings of other cultures.
- This is good. And the Americans?
- They can't decide what an authentic American cuisine is, and likewise, they're wholly confused about sex. Sandwiches.
- I always think weak coffee.
- Who do you like?
- The Dutch are curious. So many shapes to the people, pointy noses on the roundest heads, peasant faces on their royalty. Hearty meals, simple meals, tough –
- – but cozy.
- But cozy. And I like them. But this is silly, really.
- Well, of course it is! Now then, you Japanese.
- I was afraid of this. Well, if you can afford it, you can have the most exquisite meal.
- Perfectly trained chefs, perfectly trained women.
- Yes, we have done our studies. But we have our simple meals too, noodles, green tea over rice, miso soup and tofu.
- "Wham bam."
- Uhm, yes.
- The men don't match the meals.
- No. But we women do, I think.
- Too late to change either?

- Ohh ... oh, look!

[Naturally, they join the others.]

- But what were you saying about Jesus?
- Oh, something about seeing him in a kimono or something.
- Weird. But, tell me, Kazuko, does being wrapped up in one of those things give you an erotic charge, or do they turn you into something even more demure?
- Oh, Marianne, you're embarrassing her.
- Oops.
- But it is a real question. And so is ...
- The underwear question? Uhm, not so real.
- Ok, ok. Yes and no.
- ??
- Or no and yes.
- Ok, so much for Jesus and kimonos. Where were we?
- Sex, photographs, an empty city.
- Ok, one at a time.
- Or maybe not. Look at it this way. We've nearly agreed the city is or can be masturbatory – or orgiastic. It's the collection of villages and the anonymous in a crowd of twelve million. One or all. Little deaths, little Buddhas.
- Ohh, those red shawls.
- Bibs, meals never taken, love never experienced.
- And couplings, you know, Roberta, like "normal" sex?
- It's not a normal city. But they occur, yes. You just have to decide which sex you are, Arlene, and which you want the city to be.
- ?
- It's you, it's your lover, the lover you want, the lover you want to be, the lover you've lost, the lover or lovers that you will meet –
- In a gesture, a word, a turn around a corner.
- In a photograph.
- Of a building.
- In an empty city.
- You're making me wet, girls.
- Hiromi, control yourself, this once, ok?
- Ok. This once. So, who's the lover? Who's missing?
- Take a look at these. Arlene, Kazuko, you too.

[The portfolio passes hands, the pages turned, the photos seen from various angles. We hear indistinct comments, what might also be the sounds of a woman masturbating, or a couple of any sex making love, or more than a small group – or the relentless round of the Yamanote line.]

At the end of this sequence, our six women having left, the Woman seems to see a figure – her Man? – pass the corner of a building and she rushes up from her seat after him. But [zoom in] she has forgotten the portfolio on the table! Time passes, it sits there, until a waiter comes, picks it up, looks through for a name or an address, but finding none, props it up on a nearby window sill. Time passes, night comes, the café closes, the portfolio remains on the sill. Time passes, the last stragglers head for Shinjuku Station, a light breeze passes over the volume. Time passes, stillness (or as much as there can be in Shunjuku), and we hear footsteps. It is the Woman; she finds the portfolio, picks it up, and smiles to herself, her confidence assured that lost objects in Tokyo are rarely stolen, but far more often than not their owners find their way back to them.

SCENE SEVEN: FASHION STORE

The labyrinth is multiple. Parcos 1, 2, and 3, separate buildings; and between them siblings, or offshoots, wayward paths, dislocations and distractions, which, once inside, one can sometimes regain one's focus and actually find a way into a Parco; and within these – both the neighboring shops and the Parcos – the very small shops like homes in *shitamachi*, bars in Golden Gai – or equally enormous competitors, Tokyu this, Tokyu that, or from on top of the hill of Koen-dori you can look down onto a Marui (oh yes, there are others), the zigzag pattern of the visible escalator, hive; all those windows and yet all those racks of clothes, racks of shoppers – a variety of boutiques, some repeated or af-filiated, some permanent or temporary; restaurants and art galleries; the usual array of stairways and elevators and escalators, some stopping only at certain floors; the basement levels invariably given over to the least likely to succeed and yet these become the most popular, the Yamanote version of Ameyokocho's food casbah. And the labyrinth of money. And the labyrinth of fashion itself: mix and match or miscarry; this week's in and last's out and next's to be – and as soon vanished.

And so, trembling, she enters, on the scent of her vanishing case. The BGM – from Bob Marley to Strauss to Roy Orbison without a blink – is not noticed by her. Could he be buying himself a white shirt, or some lingerie for a lover? Perhaps the latest photography books, or some jewelry for a lover? Maybe he is ordering new bookshelves, or buying a favorite wine for a lover. A sweater for the approaching Fall, one for himself and one for a lover. Lingering over some magazines, and ordering flowers to be sent to a lover. New stereo equipment, and a CD for a lover. Eating sushi, before he meets his lover.

Perhaps the BGM itself – from "Sukiyaki" to Haydn to Buddy Holly without missing a beat – conceals a code that predetermines all his and her movements – how else to justify this maddening order? Is it earthquake-sensitive? Can it predict the winds? Where a man goes, what shirt he chooses, whom he falls in love with? Who is responsible for selecting the music and its order? Will I find happiness?

* * *

A complete blank. The moon-face of Hiroko – "I can feel it. Something special is about to happen!" – Yakushimaru, star of *Satmomi Hakkenden*, stares at me meaningfully from a poster as I cross the road.

* * *

Osen and Sōkichi

We turn to fiction for the truth of events – events which more truly lie in the scarlet of a crêpe undergarment, a sudden rainstorm, a style of hair-do, some stolen rice crackers. They also lie in the associative techniques of fiction: how a vision of a prostitute's white face will suddenly coincide with the moon, and that – the ever-sliding signifier – with the Buddha, and then as suddenly the memory of one's mother's breasts. Feelings, visions, memories, names – strung together they form a rosary whose beads we tell in honor of the love suicides of Myōjin Hill.

Tokyoites live bifurcated in time and space. We live here in the immediate present – and in the previous decade. We live here in the great city, this secret capitol of the world, and in the city or town from whence we first came.

How many tens of thousands of today's successful businessmen, doctors, entertainers, and other professionals had not too long ago arrived in Ueno or Tokyo stations, their long journeys from Sendai, Akita, Fukuoka and smaller cities over, their heads aswirl at the immensity and jumble of the city where they, only seventeen or eighteen years old, are to begin in two week's time their university studies, and yet for an instant they are babes again ready to rush back to Mama's loving arms – and yet within six months they adopt the city as their own, call themselves Tokyoites, and visit Mother but once or twice a year?

As for the double time we live, it seems that we all succumb to a certain nostalgia for something we never knew, we feel as if we have missed out on or been deprived of some essential experience, one without which we can never call ourselves whole – for we have all arrived too late. It is a sort of secular original sin. I arrived in the Eighties, and have a great regret at not having been here in the Seventies. I am also intensely envious of those of my friends who were here not only in the Seventies, but also the Sixties and even the Fifties. I feel I will never truly know Tokyo as a result of not having been here then. (Or I will only know a half-Tokyo, that of the immediate present and prospect.) Oh, I know I can turn to films and prints and photographs, and yes, they may give off certain airs, but they jealously maintain the secrets of their time. Fiction is another matter: nostalgia burns brightest there (and much of the prose is at boiling point). The Master of course is Nagai Kafu, whose works are filled with regret over a passing Tokyo, and especially for an Edo *he* never knew. This *decade before* nostalgia can also be seen as a complex temporal-urban variation of the *furusato* (hometown, invariably rural) nostalgia that the Japanese like to indulge themselves in. The latter is easily satisfied: twice a year you take a train to your family's ancestral home (and where no doubt you are officially registered; the state makes it hard for one to become an official Tokyoite), visit your parents, relatives, old schoolmates, as well as the actual ancestors, in the local cemetery; and three days later you rush back to your *home* in Setagaya or Suginami or Nakano Ward. But the true Tokyoite's longings can never be satisfied: having renounced former cities to wholly embrace Tokyo, he can never go home again, never resurrect time.

The story is a simple one and can be found in volume 20 of the *Kyōka zenshū* (that is, *The Collected Works of the Great Izumi Kyōka*), Tokyo, Iwanami Shoten, 1973–76, under the title *Baishoku kamonan-ban*, one of those Japanese titles whose erotic pungency fades somewhat when literally translated: *The Prostitute and the Bowl of Noodles Topped with Duck Meat and Scallions*. Around the turn of the century, seventeen year old Sōkichi Hata arrived in Tokyo from Kanazawa, ready to enter medical school. A few youthful missteps – his first drunk, some missed classes, an expensive coat – and he was on the street, expelled. He fell in with the wrong sort – "shabby politicians, businessmen of the lowest order, charlatans, and a few who were working toward their goal of becoming policemen someday" – finally becoming a day laborer and acting as a sort of houseboy for the pimp Kumazawa and his mistress Osen. Penniless, helpless, ashamed, he was humiliated one day by Osen's hairdresser who attempted to shave his eyebrows – the young woman came to his rescue – and then found out by Kumazawa and his thugs for having stolen some rice crackers. He decided to do himself in by taking the hairdresser's razor and slitting his throat at nearby Kanda Myōjin Temple. Osen sensed what was afoot, and again saved the boy. Together they fled the house on Myōjin Hill and hid out in Okachimachi, where Osen continued to ply her trade in order to keep Sōkichi in school. Then one day, having just serviced a customer, she is arrested. While being lead away she folds a paper crane, kisses it ("the marks of her lips showing faintly red against the crane's bluish-white body"), and hands it to Sōkichi telling him it contains her spirit. Unbeknownst to him, it truly does possess her spirit, for shortly thereafter she goes mad. Jump ahead to 1920. After having taken a five year sabbatical to further studies at Leipzig University, Sōkichi Hata, M.D., has returned to Tokyo to assume the position of head of internal medicine at Tokyo University Hospital in Ochanomizu. He boards a train, gets off at Ochanomizu Station when suddenly a furious spring rain-shower commences. He goes to a compartment to wait it out. Inside, "the first thing that caught his eye was the scarlet of her crepe undergarment, bright as flame and dappled with cinnabar." It is of course Osen. Two women are taking her from the brothel where she has served these two decades to a home for the clinically insane. She does not recognize Sōkichi. He introduces himself to the women, takes Osen to his office nearby – and there he draws a razor.

That's all, an all too common and trite story. (And one that was adapted by Mizoguchi, another *feminist* author – in the Japanese sense, that is, of making them his primary subject – and who we are never sure whether or not he truly likes and respects women.) But its significance lies naturally in the details, details too that make it a decidedly Tokyo story. These concern, as the reader has surely guessed, time, place, and those "superficial matters that compel us most," the things of everyday life that contain the eternal truths. In the story, also known as *Osen and Sōkichi*, we are given two different times: circa 1900 and 1920, two decades to play with. They are contrasted by the shady Myōjin district of the earlier period and university area of the later; by the bright cheer of the young Osen and her later madness; by the despair of young Sōkichi and the successful man of the world of late Meiji. The dilemma of the Tokyoite split by space is "negatively dramatized" by there being *no men-*

tion whatsoever of Sōkichi's life in Kanazawa, or Osen's in wherever she came from. (And *that* is quite another story, again all too familiar: the young girl who comes to the city filled with hope, works a week as a waitress, or even a DJ (see the Kuwabara pre-war photo), and is systematically, almost formulaically crushed by the city into prostitution. But even more than this is the generous sprinkling of details that evoke a specific time and Tokyo (and only Tokyo: my point is that no story of Osaka or Kobe would be written like this, no such loving attention paid to these kinds of details): the crimson crepe, a sash, the classic Shimada hairstyle, the seven sen for a bag of ricecrackers ("Sōma crackers that were made and sold in an alley in Miyamoto-cho, just at the bottom of the steep flight of steps running down Myōjin Hill ... salted and crisp, flecked with soy sauce, and marked with horse-bit patterns"), the brazier on the station platform (and the waiting booth), the red cap of the station master, the tissue thin paper that fans the coals in a brazier, the various blossoms of the various months and seasons, the far off views then available (Shinagawa, Kuramae, Asakusa). It is all a Tokyo that you and I shall never know, Reader, but one whose truths continue in their many ways in our own stories, our own fictions.

* * *

Ah, this city!, Cafferty peruses, the best years, each year, and they proceed. How many more, Lords? Constant delight, continuous surprise. Or is that the reverse? better look them up once again; ditto principle and principal, and throw in capital and capitol – which one is Tokyo? The city a spelling lesson.

* * *

Kazuko is spending her first year at university, sharing an apartment with three roommates in Tama New Town. She is extremely depressed. (Tama is a "new town" on an old river. Actually, it was once called ((it still is)) "new town," but it is better to consider it just another part of the westward move of Tokyo.) The willows of the Ginza came here. It was supposed to be one of those models for a comfortable life in the sprawling metropolis. But it has been absorbed by something greater than itself – the spirit of the city, so that by now, apart from a bit more greenery than usual, and some apartment blocks that look just a bit the other side of the ordinary, it looks like "any neighborhood, Tokyo" – and is the happier for being so.) The three other girls, having successfully entered their particular school and thus graduation guaranteed, are now only interested in partying. Besides, this is their first time in Tokyo. The opportunities are endless. Kazuko wants to be easygoing and friendly, and so occasionally she wastes a Saturday with her roommates. On this particular occasion, she is in an apartment in Tama where one of the girl's boyfriend lives. Whiskey seems to be the order of the day. Already Kazuko has drunk too much. Two boys are fighting in one corner, play wrestling, but it will conclude with a serious accident. The apartment gets bigger as the dream goes on. In another corner are Lang and Roberta and Van Zandt (whom Kazuko did not know at this time of her life, of course), eating sandwiches. Now her roommates are berating her, needling her for being so studious, threatening to frame her for cheating (which she has not done, of course), threatening even to have her raped by three of the boys at the party. Kazuko is totally helpless, on the verge of tears, she is too drunk to see or think straight and to get out; she can not call across to her foreign friends. The only soothing thing happening – the last thing she remembers before passing out (and hence to enter a dream within a dream) – is hearing Coleman Hakwins' "Body and Soul."

Marianne is at a party playing her alto sax. She is wearing a very short black skirt and a pink t-shirt. Her body is glistening with sweat. She is very thin and her hair is all curls. One moment she is the center of attention; another she is in a corner, mellow. She is only playing tonight, and refusing to speak Japanese. She is in what her friends call her "Polish mood."

* * *

It was Roberta's worst night in the six months she'd been in Japan. It began with the disaster of van Zandt's film in Yanaka – or at least the disaster she created. The plan, following the successful premier, was for everyone to head back to Roberta's small apartment in Yoyogi, and then continue the evening with a party celebrating not only van Zandt, but her finding a new place in *shitamachi* – she was to move the following day – and to equally honor Lang, who'd decided to stay a while longer, and had recently found his own apartment in Kichijoji (and thus too becoming less of a burden on his estranged wife). Following the disastrous film showing, however, Lang and van Zandt decided they would *walk* to Yoyogi. By the time they arrived at Roberta's, some three hours later, they'd consumed a good deal of beer and *saké* from vending machines, and had shared many confidences concerning the woman who had once been van Zandt's best friend, and Lang's loving wife. For some, the temperature rose considerably when the pair entered; even the two electric fans were useless.

What's more, everything about Roberta's party plans had gone wrong. (This the Roberta who only a few years earlier had gone through her delightful "party phase" – parties to which all were required to dress in red (and VZ came in white), or bejeweled, or as their literary hero. She was *the* expert hostess. "Anyone who can afford the booze can give a party, but it doesn't guarantee fun.") The Japanese she invited – the vegetable man and his wife, the old woman on the first floor, some young people she'd met in the neighborhood – were overly dressed and polite, and obviously unable to eat the cold cuts she offered them. And her overly casual western friends too were not keen on *natto* and the various country pickles they were offered. On the other hand, the Japanese guests freely offered the whisky they had brought, while the westerners happily shared their *saké*. The alcohol level was rapidly rising while the level of mutual incomprehension remained at an absolute zero. The girls too were at an impasse: Should they translate? Should they eat some *natto* as well as prosciutto? What should they drink – some Japanese wine (and thus possibly make everyone ill)? And what about van Zandt and Lang – whenever would they show up?

And when at last they did – to continue from the paragraph before last – freely drinking whatever was near to hand, swallowing makeshift combinations of *sembei* and camembert, swearing in half a dozen languages, including Japanese – all hell broke loose. But not before the three men from the corner sushi place knocked and entered bearing three large round lacquer plates of sushi, courtesy of Lang. They – no one more working-class – were his new buddies – and he who could often be the most elitist of individuals. They were very polite, while also becoming rapidly drunk. Almost no one could understand a word they said, whatever was this sushi chef code anyway? Meanwhile, Lang and van Zandt condescended to all the others – no prejudices here – or almost all, van Zandt came on too roughly to Hiromi, while Lang scorned one of Roberta's student friends by insulting his knowledge of *kanji*, while also refusing to admit that he, Lang, was wholly incompetent in the language. "You don't need a goddam school to learn a language. You need the streets, you need lovers, you need to get drunk, man, drunk on the word! You need to fuck the language, that's right, fuck Japanese, then you'll understand what it's capable of!" Roberta was horrified and ashamed, and only too happy that her Japanese guests had no idea whatsoever what this madman was saying – or almost none, for Lang's gestures were fairly clear to all.

"Stop it, Lang," she tried to say calmly. And he, just as calmly, ceased to talk, rose, walked to her small stereo, said, "Ok, if you like," and he stopped the *gidayu* recording (Roberta so hoped to come to appreciate this art too), and replaced it with some Thelonius Monk. "Now there's a man who would understand me," he proclaimed.

Roberta shouted. She'd had enough, and was near tears of rage and shame. She grabbed Lang's arm; he shoved her back and she fell on to the floor, hurting her wrist, spilling some food and drink on a couple of guests, and only becoming more embarrassed and ashamed. The Japanese all together rose and left quietly but not too politely. The girls were too aghast to giggle. The other guests tried to leave – "No, stick around!," Lang exclaimed as he poured them more to drink. Half-drunk already, and half-afraid to disagree with him, they too soon became wholly drunk, or ill, or argumentative. The next day there was a story of one of the couples getting into a fight on the street. Van Zandt began to go home, but stumbled down the stairs and fell asleep in the small *genkan*. Lang – made of stronger stuff – Monk's man, recall – managed to get away, never revealing to anyone how the rest of that night proceeded for him – or even what little he remembered.

As for Roberta, she was haunted, in close-up, by that awful night, that awful party (and awful film too, she would forever insist), and for weeks thereafter would cry herself to sleep, saying over and over again, "I only wanted to do good. I only wanted to do good."

* * *

He greeted her in the Dutch manner, three kisses. What a wonderful custom!, she thought. Why stop at the sober and merely friendly two, add this small excess, this promise of three meaning four and four ... the night.

* * *

It's a terrific city Tokyo, but tormented -- and tormenting. But terrific, Hiro reels.

* * *

The whole damn thing? Nah, can't see it. Where are those quotes from Bernhard that Lang gave me? Oh yeah, here. "VZ: Catch the spirit! See you on the pavement, Lang." Let's see ...

"I hate nature, because it is killing me. ... In fact I love everything except nature, which I find sinister ... I fear it and avoid it whenever I can. The truth is that I am a city dweller who can at best tolerate nature."

Ah, now that's the Lang I know! Probably can recognize two types of trees – bamboo and willow – and three at most flowers. Tulip, Iris, Rose. Girls names too. (Is Tulip a girl's name? In some country, sure. Are bamboo and willow?)

"For in the country the mind is drained just as fast as it is recharged [in the city] – faster, in fact, since the country always treats the mind more cruelly than the city ever can. The country robs a thinking person of everything and gives him virtually nothing, whereas the city is perpetually giving. One has simply to see this, and of course feel it, but very few either see it or feel it, with the result that most people are sentimentally drawn to the country, where in no time they are inevitably sucked dry, deflated, and destroyed. The mind cannot develop in the country; it can develop only in the city."

That's our Lang! Now there's no arguing with that, surely? Didn't Lang tell me once that he isn't a native of Vienna – and that I should never let anyone know? That he spent his first few years in the countryside? Only he'd be embarrassed about something like that.

* * *

– Two questions. One, Thai food tomorrow night in Shinjuku?
– Yes, of course, but why not the new place in Jimbocho?
– Two, will you love me tomorrow?
– Yes, of course; but why not the new place in Jimbocho?
– That's all I wanted to know.
– We're agreed then – the new place in Jimbocho?
– One more. What new place in Jimbocho?
– Will *you* love me tomorrow?
– ...
– Depends on the new place in Jimbocho?
– Forget Shinjuku.

* * *

Keep my lips moving, for what? For whom? For no one. I wander, wander who? Oku-Tama, sounds like someone from a cowboy movie. And why not, the city's wild west. Oh, who did write the book of love? Did I miss some chapters? Can it be rewritten? Is there a sequel? Can the crazy cat lady help me? Something brief. Just so. An encounter. "An encounter in sensible shoes." Now that sounds dowdy. I am witty, I am not unattractive. I only lack nerve. Gentleness. "Nous ne pouvons vivre ..." Or some rough stuff? Could I really? Oh, I suppose. But gentleness. I want a man. No. I want a woman. I want a voice of my own. What would the Cat Lady say? What would Zonar? They'd understand. Who writes the script? This is silly. Ok, in Japan I can walk around and talk to myself. Or can I? But back in the Midwest? No way, Sister. A lover. No circle, no giggling girls. No lesbian club, no bar. Like Japanese kids on a date reading separate comic books, we'd lie in bed back to back, talking to ourselves. Occasionally listening in. We'd go for hikes, she goes this way, I go that. We'd send each other postcards about our adventures, "Dearest Arlene." We'd write kanji on the back of each other's hands. And we'd walk hand in hand – in the Midwest, and in Tokyo. The rest of the world would come to understand.

But for now, I must keep walking, perhaps head back to the city, keep talking. To myself.

* * *

Yoshiko is in love with her music teacher. They visit the "B Flat" love hotel, a pink synthesizer in each room, "wrinkle chapeau" condoms too, with a cute Godzilla saying "I love you"" on each wrapper.

* * *

Van Zandt thinks of Hiroko's eyes, pools perhaps but no space for sinking, all the more reason he thinks to forget about Arlene as he thinks of Arlene, her lips, her voice as he forgets about Hiroko whose eyes. ... And he recalls what he said to her that day of the frank talk: "Geez, Arlene, you've come only once and that with a woman. Fine, why would you want to forget that memory, what are you scared of?" And she had no response, other than to add that now she would be content the rest of her life just designing paper clips, or better, post-its, all those pastels, helping people retain their memories.

* * *

"The California River is at its widest one mile, at its narrowest, a stream through which young lovers regularly wade in a few tense moments of hand-holding that has determined a great number of families. It is located high in the hills of Nagano Prefecture in the center of Japan."

All I want to talk about is you – or is you not – the whole he and shebang of it all plain as the setting sun – what does Carole say – "Whenever there's a chance to take the spotlight away from me ... if I start to tell a story, you finish it. If I go on a diet, you lose the weight. If I have a cold, you cough. And if we should ever have a baby, I'm not so sure I'd be the mother!" – ah, two butterflies in the window, a double halo – like that walk of his describing greater circumferences – perhaps he will encompass us in time – he's performed other miracles I certainly never expected – I want to talk – I have an address, an ID, fingerprinted – and where do you lay your silvery head tonight? – one of us must go – isn't that a song? – no, neither of us need go – stay if you like but for chrissake, for our sake, yours – my circumference here – I need only a few steps in all directions – oh, you try not to listen but I know you're there – to talk about you – and here I am still wet with you – whole bereft happy and ... what's the word – the turtles were screwing under the rosemary plant – you haven't changed much in how many years has it been now we've had more or less together – "I can change, I swear" and other crap – no you see you just don't see, don't swear, show, put out, prove it as some singer says – but do I expect any change – maybe I did at one time but you know me – I'm a fast learner – should I care – about you changing I mean – well I do and I don't mostly – but there's oh so much more that you'll see in time I hope – not lose like Lisa in *Letter* – a moment ago you were here and now you're gone so what else is new – ah, this is: the address is mine and you're jealous of a city I have made my own and you're only now beginning to realize – you've never been so slow before – jealous that the love you proclaim for the place is not being reciprocated – well, what did you expect, is it a true full love or the half-measure – your style of love is not the city's – and though yes you feel a great deal for the scene – feel really far more than almost anyone who says they love the place – still it's not enough because we both see through you – see you have to change your style of loving and that means oh so many changes – and now only now are you beginning to wonder about mine – now when I am so obviously at home here – now when love presents me no problem you see the love I have always offered you – this totally committed thing isn't so scary after all, in fact its very comfortable exciting even – never seen me so content before have you – and neither of us even really chose the place – it was a place to go an available opportunity to arrive – and see now the changes that are being wrought – O damn you – yes perhaps sometimes you've seen who I am – but this time the love the city is mine first and you do not know what to do with it – I'm not flaunting, just stating the fact, ok, with pride – but do nothing with it other than accept it see it for what it is and work with it not against – I brought my love here – and that did not include you – you see we each can have our exclusionary policies our extraterritorialities if that's the word – oh yes you're welcome – but on my terms this time – I have my long-term visa and you can only renew yours a short number of times before its not even back to go but you're off the board completely – we'll deal with that if it comes to it – all my love that does not include you – but so much does too – remember those early years – me in your Europe – you in my America – we seemed to contain a future and now all present and alone sir – it's not even a question of … no matter no matter now – there is so much now that I no longer have to deal with – god how I loved you tried to make you see that love – but enough – I have come to love the city that I chanced upon – the city of chance – la bella fortuna – and I will stay and you might leave – never wanted to be here and now that you can go you – which can't you bear to leave, the city or me? – which? could it possibly be both? – no, you needn't choose, we'll see – yes because I love this tortured and tender city sometimes it seems even more than I love you – she reciprocates after all, she talks to me she walks alongside me in her own curious step but never missing a beat – I love the prospects that are no prospects the city that is not one but all these villages and this one is my own I love my vegetable seller my fish monger and my rice lady who laughs at the thought of me eating brown rice the sushi shop around the corner where I stop once a week on the way home from work and a few restaurants in town to meet Arlene Kazuko and I love the dry cleaner and the tailor of whom I make extraordinary demands but to him I am just a crazy woman foreigner and he accepts me and when the earthquake strikes I know his family will take me in if need be … I love my moldy walls my *tatami* that need to be replaced the one and a half *sakés* a night I love the noisy kid next door but not so much his long suffering mother because she's made a cult of it and those friends who are beat and broken and need a new visa and god knows if I am breaking the law in giving them a place to stay – and I certainly must love the dirty cat who comes begging every morning after all I've given him your name – and no I can't say that I love them but let's say I am enchanted by the advertising and the TV and radio stations but this is silly this list who cares what I love – oh jeez but I love everything I do, everything, no matter what it is no matter how trivial I give it all I've got and I love it – so who cares what but the lover responsible for it all – walking alongside, that curious step of hers – we talk well together on our walks – yoo-hoo are you listening! – the kids just got up and it feels like rain – and your love – could you ever love – oh sure I know Arlene is in love with me but she'll get over it these infatuations – I know I do that you love me really love me – you have you do – sometimes – but will you ever be able to love me really the way I need – but that is you and this is me and I no longer want or expect change much less try to bring it about – if it wasn't meant to be – definitely rain refreshing – oh I tried – you know that much – the early years – we sound like a record collection – for serious collectors only – Europe California – a citystate – for serious lovers only – my big bed and breasts that summer ... yes some talk remains fine – or me going down on you for an hour or more and then you came and I giggled – my parents who couldn't stand the thought of you – the very – and we walked all those cities all night talking – and all our friends and all the parties we gave each other – in the cities and in their countries – all those homes we were together in – and then the first in a series of splits, divisions, you from me me from you – I gave myself a few months on you here ... and I lingered and you couldn't take that this time I wasn't coming back – finally for once it was you who didn't like the tone and turn of things – now you who'd always denied tones to anything weren't keen on the tone of my letters especially as their frequency decreased – ok so you had to come and retrieve, rescue, claim me, whatever offensive term like one of those guys who gets kids out of cults as if I were being held hostage against my will you thinking I'd made some sort of mistake been fooled by some Japanese she can't surely be happy there you were going to play the hero but you couldn't even see then that you had nothing to do with me but your own insecurity don't you get it yet you were threatened by ... by what? by Tokyo by me liking it by me feeling comfortable here by the very thought of me not needing to be with you I couldn't be happy here on my own and without you and with a group of friends I was lucky to make on my own and whom typically you claim for yours that's ok friends are ... no you couldn't be happy with the thought ... oh damn you! – and then here you were here check in and get out with her quick mission and now look at you (look at us!) so much longer later.

I've stayed all this while and you've managed to maintain two homes though the time spent in Europe has decreased noticeably as of late and ... it's written all over your face you can't quit the place it's not me you can't quit you're free to stay or go I can take it can't you still not see that I've been able to for quite awhile now even before I came here – but you didn't see that then never did its ok stay or go just make up your own mind – but as I said only a few hours ago this really is the last time together or not however it's to be it will really be irrevocable our permanency will no longer be a matter of when you or I decide to stay or when to wander it is time for me to stay in one place and to choose how many pillows are to be on my bed no more design changes thank you – I'm in Tokyo for now, where are you going to be?, that's all there is to it – the city has come between us –she walks and talks with me – perhaps he will with you – (and by the way no the sex of the city doesn't matter if it is a city it's all sexes or any as it chooses) – I have a present is what Tokyo gives me a present of myself to myself and the chance to create whatever time I want to stay or to leave as I like ... but no I don't want to talk your kind of Tokyo talk – I've done my own Tokyo research and been about the place in my fashion it just doesn't all of it interest me – and that you can't stand either – but you know I know that whatever Tokyo becomes yours mine will not mine will remain mine – oh I'm talking about me now as much as you whom I want to talk about – god I love sunsets – god – like Aunt Patsy, no softie – what would she have to say about all this – "It's the bunk" – what lead to it all – oh I think we both know – your widening circumferences increasing overlapping – the films the essays the music the shirts – and I was pulling back in content with one film every week or two a slow read old familiar clothes the repeat button leftovers – it's ok it really is nothing was not against you it was for me and I'm proud I did the right thing by me and now get some proper pride yourself – it's all ok – boy the way people fight the thought of someone wishing them well – I can't stand striped furniture, gotta get the chairs repainted soon – friends consolation – why is it friends have always been easier to communicate with than lovers – I remember the night I went out and got drunk – O was that needed – just three friends women – why do I still specify – that's when I began discovering Tokyo on my own – little by little narrowing it down – Kunitachi was nice yes and Yotsuya the house-sitting in Azabu and then a bit too far up there across the river the Edo living in "a poorer thing than the public latrines of later years" and then finally my own Yanesen – a few friends – a city of women having a good time – until that too began to get out of control – but this time I could see it coming and knew when and how to withdraw – knew Arlene had a crush on me – I know in time I can get along – what is it Zasu and Zonar, Gypsy and Jezebel – no now what is it ah yes Mona and Cheri no I mean Maxine great names actually – they're not always silly I've seen that – that always may be small but let's hope we can expand it – and so what if I shouted at VZ the man deserved it his movie simply did not move and again I say goddammit it did not move and maybe now he is – oh dammit these leftovers of your talk – hey I can even talk sense with Marianne – usually – oh but she's a delight – if she stays here long enough I think I can learn quite a lot – and even if it's all only about her that's guaranteed to be some something nonetheless – but how long can we expect her to stay – she must wander – O Marianne what ghosts what ghosts – and sweet Cafferty now there is a real education the old hand – oh but the cities we all have walked – all the women I have known and their trajectories – a catalog of cities, an atlas, we have covered continents, A Woman's Guide to the Globe ...– all those cities – why can't there just be one or two – Tokyo – Hollywood, for the first time since the ancient rule of the Amazons, a colony of economically independent women – Carole, actress, producer, businesswoman and more, "the complete filmmaker" – when it comes to engraving the saints names you and I are low on the list and these are at the top – these few, and a very few more– is this how Marianne survived too? – those who gave me a place to stay to rest my weary head – I was never but a temporary permanent guest – gone now but a home – for a girl – a girl, can you imagine me one – I was always theirs, will always be – coming and going, leaving soon enough – a faith in love, no distance to overcome – that even parents don't have – alright then – no I don't want to talk about you I want to talk about me – I like the smell of a good cigar you smoke 'em I'll smell 'em – the few who supported me without questions – said ok go, Europe, Japan, here's a place to rest to return – but I don't want to talk about leaving because the home there is gone and I can not ever go back and I need to make a new home here – we both know this world without memories is all – no not without memories but a world all leaving – oh I so want to talk about so much else and all of it entertwined – what did Arlene say – you listen you hope you listen to the crap you hope there's someone behind it you take a chance having decided that the crap is tolerable because there are so many other redeeming factors you open up you screw like gods the first night like titans the second and then the age of iron sets in the real bullshit that's been there all the time makes itself known and you finally see it there in the kisses and in the fucking and in the talk it permeates but we put the blinders on – well that's one way of looking at things – your *Gertrud* another – "I have loved," "Amor Omnia" – but not on my tombstone – though yes I have and you have not seen – baroque flowering splendiferous surrounding … suffering in the best saints senses … you think you can talk of thighs let me talk of thighs – no only two lips a word a kiss – a Lang once and perhaps no more no longer – no langueur –so be it – it's a love and a life I can live with – I am a thousand palms a blue dress blue eyes and sometimes red underwear long white legs black short hair sometimes long red eyes crazy hair wet dry a cunt moist spring fingers don't talk to me about thighs about blondes and smiles I cannot account for them myself lips all over and all over again – no, no space – you if you're willing – and if you're not – I am only beginning to imagine to talk to myself as much as I do – lips, as they say – it's in the kiss – and here the kiss is mine – mine me where you haven't come yet – me inside.

* * *

The costs of confusion notwithstanding, Hiromi carefully considers, I'll have none of it. I live here; he and he and he live there. The last trains leave then and then and then. So: no cost, no confusion. I know where I am going, and who's coming with me.

* * *

The coffee was awful. We should have gone to Doutor.
  – Cathy O'Donnell, *They Live by Night* (Nicholas Ray-Silva,
1948)

Chapter 8

TAKADANOBABA–MEJIRO

Lang came to love Kichijoji, but it was only his own, he felt only more distant from Roberta, isolated, and after all he'd come here for her for them to see how or what they were, what they were going to do and there she was an hour's train ride away and she happy rarely leaving her home her neighborhood – and so he became jealous of it all, jealous of the city for what it had done to her – had done to him.

* * *

I was born when you kissed me. I died when you left me. I lived for a few weeks while you loved me.
– Bogart, *In A Lonely Place* (Nicholas Ray, 1950)

* * *

- Went book shopping today.
- Anything good?
- Some great book covers. "Real men wear black," ya' know.
- A book?
- Should be. No, a shirt.

* * *

R'n'L!!!!!!!!

I remember knowing truffles first as chocolates before I knew them as mushrooms. But when was the last time I ate either?

The other day there were these three Indian kids on the train beating each other against the head with their shoes. All the other passengers (except me, of course) were aghast.

How can I die with my boots on when I don't have any boots?

Jee-zuz what a Tokyoite. I got three DVD players.

Saw that new Proust in Kitazawa today. Remember that great clerk they once had, Junko? She wound up working for *Eureka*. Also taking classes with Akira Kasai.

Oh yeah, but the best was that after years – hard, miserable, lonely years, my friends, years that you or anyone could or would only ever understand if you had been born in the very same circumstances as myself, only if, you had … yikes!, enough – after years of looking I finally found a copy of *Notable Names* in Dante. A great book, an encyclopaedia. Yes, at Kitazawa, and yes, at ¥25,000.

The day I broke the record.

I beat my head against the wall remembering all those years reading newspaper items about Elvis being on tour and Elvis canceling the tour and Elvis checking into a hospital for exhaustion or to lose weight or whatever and Elvis and Elvis and oh *why didn't I or any of us see* what was happening, why didn't we storm the Colonel's gate, talk with, implore the King, kidnap him if need be and snap him out of it? (And then I have to ask myself, honestly, darkly, what if we had done all that and he'd listened to us and then after a moment of silence he'd turned to us and said, "Ah 'ppreciate your concern, kids, but ya' see, I kinda like the way things are goin' right now.")

I once had a liquor store lady who was an absolute shrew; her husband was like the delivery boy, always moving crates around. She wouldn't let him near the cash register. Next place I lived in the local store was run by a family. Big macho guy; his mother who was old but happy to be working; and his big macha wife who had this long gorgeous hair. God was she sexy, like a Japanese version of a Fellini woman. Now the current place is also run by a family, same set up. Kindly old grandma. Nice husband. But I was wrong I admit now about the wife. She at first seemed to me to be resentful at being in this liquor store situation, as if she deserved greater things. Her hair done up tight, the shaded glasses. But then after a while I realized that what seemed to me to be a fake smile was in fact her real smile. And that she was always smiling, a real smile. And then the other day when it was raining and I had a paper bag of stuff, she went out of her way to unpack it for me and put it in a plastic bag. Very sweet. She's great. I love her. So: never prejudge, lest ye be so. I learned my lesson, Lordy me.

Then there's the rice lady next door. Always amused as hell that I order brown rice. I asked her the last time I was there, and she told me that all of 2 – t-w-o – people in the neighborhood eat brown rice. Amazing. She's very cute. One day in one of our wandering conversations I mentioned Araki to her, and she said she didn't like porno. Too bad, because I lust after her. Anyway, so one night I was home playing some music; about 1AM the doorbell rings. It's her! I think, "her husband's out of town, and now she's ready to surrender herself to me." No way: she asked me to turn the music down.

"Oedipus, schmoedipus, just so long as he loves his mother!"

I gotta go out and take some photos. / "We'll master the keyboard yet!"

* * *

The costs of confusion notwithstanding, Hiroko confusedly says to herself, what a phrase. Yes, it does cost a bit to get confused when I go out. I become late, my make-up isn't perfect, the lighting is always wrong. No, no withstanding about it at all. Perhaps I should study my map a bit more.

* * *

"Years, punishing years." Good years too. Let all these cities claim themselves for my birthplace! I was neither conceived nor born: I appeared one evening from out of the shadows, sexy, speaking five languages, and with all my papers intact. Like Melmoth needing to undo the bargain she tramps across Europe, from Lisbon to Berlin, from Palermo to Paris, with stops in Vienna and Nice, Copenhagen and Madrid, and all other points in between. Picking up the languages, the men and women, a great variety of eating and drinking habits. Picking up everything but herself, wandering and getting nowhere. Unable to create, unable even to destroy. What's Lang say Jimmie Stewart says, "Oh, just wandering." And look where it got him. Occasionally leaving things with my mother in the hills. Visiting her for a while, two old women speaking of the different centuries they've lived in. The occasional job or performance. Money never seeming to be a problem; can't say where I picked up that survival technique. A lucky inheritance and an apartment in Paris I still call a garage. A base, a bed, a place to lean. Is that what keeps me from complete craziness? Did my parents see the potential and put me through the fast survival program: money sense, gardening, music lessons, languages. I am more process than product. "Oh for sure," as Arlene says. How'd she do it? Never been anywhere and she's rock-solid. Could I have ever remained home? No, I was born to wander. And how did she and I come to be in Tokyo? And me with all these languages and about all of a hundred words in this one. But I don't think Tokyo quite matches up to my madness. It's mad but it's not me. And that's how it is.

* * *

- Isn't that great O-bon sequence from *Sans Soleil* taken here?
- Is it? I'm not so sure.
- Could be Anytown, Japan.
- "The beat beat beat of the *taiko* ..."
- Golden Globes.
- ??
- Don't you remember, that sumo wrestler and the busty naked woman wrestling?
- What, on TV?
- No, they were this display on top of, I don't know, maybe it was a pachinko place, and they went round and round like on a music box, but it was the roof of a building, and you could see it from the train. I don't know why they took it away.
- That's like the Statue of Liberty on top of the New York love hotel in Kichijoji; you'd actually see train passengers do a double take as they saw it all lit up as the train zoomed by.
- I don't think the Statue of liberty is at all like a sumo wrestler and a naked lady.
- I'm not so sure.
- No, Roberta, I mean in that they were both on the tops of build-

ings, they could be seen from trains, and now they're gone.
- But the Statue of Liberty isn't gone. I saw it last week.
- Did you go in?
- No.
- Alone again.
- No, you're right in that neither can be seen anymore – some new buildings in Kichijoji have gone up, so it's been obscured, you can't see the statue anymore – or from the train, at least.
- So, why'd they take away the naked lady?
- I don't know. It was more fun than, than what, pornographic, I suppose.
- Yeah, I suppose someone got uppity.
- But Takadanobaba is sort of pornographic, isn't it?
- Is it? It's a student area.
- Well, they got crazy glands.
- Yeah, but why call it pornographic? It's just a hard working class area that happens also to have a university in it.
- It's not exactly non-descript, but it's got some color.
- Right, it's where it's headed along the Yamanote where the porno begins.
- Mejiro pornographic?
- Well, let's say it skips a beat and then.
- Hmm, maybe.
- Doesn't Araki have his studio around here?
- So why do the Waseda guy students have uniforms, but the girls don't?
- Good question.
- Anybody got a good answer?
- Wait a minute, Mejiro is more nondescript than porno.
- Oh, but it also has its elegant moments.
- Isn't that where you saw Dominique Sanda?
- You saw Sanda? You never told me.
- You're right, where was it, Chinzanso?
- That's not really Mejiro.
- Well, I thought it was.
- You saw Sanda? What was she doing?
- Posing. Being beautiful.
- Nothing pornographic about the place, then.
- Not in your mind, perhaps.

* * *

Tortured, twisting Tokio, Kazuko ponders, we pray for you – but at what shrine?

* * *

At about eight that evening, work finished for the day, Kaoru joined a small group of coworkers for a typical evening out. That is to say, drink, eat, drink, talk, drink. The first place they went to was the nearby hostess bar his company frequently used to entertain clients. There they snacked on dried fish, nuts, and rice crackers, while drinking a few very expensive beers, as well as some Suntory whisky. (Kaoru had only had imported whisky once in his life, and it did not suit him. Too good, he thought.) While putting in a comment now and then to the conversation – the current job, the clients they had to deal with – he was more interested in observing the hostesses as they seemed to take shifts in their movement from table to table. His group was turn and turn about visited by an obvious novice to the game. Slender, perhaps eighteen or nineteen, she had already learned how to make light talk, light cigarettes, keep the men drinking – thus increasing the tab – and meanwhile pouring her own tea, disguised as whisky. Too thin for Kaoru, he politely but indifferently kept her busy hands at bay. It was the foreign woman who kept his attention. But she was in demand from the five or six tables of businessmen, and so she had little chance to converse with Kaoru and his friends. Her short skirt, low décolletage over what looked like large breasts, set his imagination afire. During the seven or eight times she sat next to or near him he was able to learn that she was studying anthropology at Tokyo University, and planning to study the folklore of Akita prefecture. While he could have maintained a conversation with her in English, she insisted on speaking Japanese with him, even tracing various *kanji* on his palm from time to time. It was exasperating. She knew that his view of her thighs and breasts would keep him in thrall to her, while at the same time he could only gaze – and converse. A third hostess was somewhat older, perhaps in her late twenties. She was adroit at all the hostess's arts, from cigarettes and drinks again, and especially to saying nothing while seeming to say everything – the promise of a night. A night, he knew, that would come to nothing. This woman was for him the best of all; while not young, she did have the figure he craved. Too, she knew when to be quiet, or better, when only to sigh and nod assent. Compliance was what he wanted. No one who would talk back to him, no jabber. He missed his wife back in Takasaki as much as he felt indifferent toward her. And she? No, he decided, only loathing. She had his steady income, their children. Sex had never interested her – or so he had convinced himself. While not an arranged marriage, it had come to be so, merely an arrangement between them to save their families' faces. Enough of that. Kaoru however had never had the nerve to pursue his sexual inclinations. An occasional flirtation, perhaps, but nothing ever beyond that. He had always hoped that somehow the woman – any woman; this hostess here – would make the overture, invite him for a private drink … and then the night. But no one ever had. He wondered why: I'm not bad looking, I present no risks, I may not be a great conversationalist, nor love-maker, but I am, well, steady, dependable, upright. Surely those qualities are attractive to some sexy women. (Yes they were – to his wife back in Gunma Prefecture.)

After a couple of hours, one of his colleagues suggested they move on to the next place, this being a *yakitori-ya* near Shimbashi. There they could converse more freely about the things that really concerned them: baseball, the office girls, the slow service at the local post office. Besides the *yakitori*, they ate ice-cold tofu, some fried chicken, a variety of vegetables and roots and radishes, and finally green tea over rice. *Saké* was the drink of choice, with an occasional beer. A group of young people was at the next table. They too were eating and drinking the same, but they seemed so much more lively. No displays of affection, but such zest in their gestures. Kaoru's fantasy mechanism began to run at full speed. He imagined the young men – so self-confident – easily taking the girls home, and then their sexual acts. His vision – he was easily half-drunk by now – kept blurring between sights of the young women – in t-shirts and slacks, sweat-shirts or short leather jackets – as actresses in the porno movies he occasionally rented from his local shop, going home with pairs of boys, sucking their cocks submissively, happily, them spraying their sperm on the girls' hair – and the actual women in front of him, going home with only one of the boys each, making some goodnight tea, watching television or reading a comic, and then going to bed, and at most, simply masturbating or fellating him because she was having her period, or he was drunk, or simply they were both too tired to even undress.

He broke out of it. He and one co-worker who lived nearby, took a taxi in a mutual direction home, but before going there they went to one last "restaurant." This was a small *ramen* stand – a push-cart with a battery to keep the stove running, an upturned bench for customers. *Ramen* was his favorite meal. His father had subsisted on it during the post-war years, and had instilled in his son a taste for it as being a real man's meal, "you could survive on it. I did." By now the *saké* had run out, and so they were left with *shochu*, that hard wheat-based distant cousin of vodka. The conversation was minimal; there were no women present.

On his short walk home Kaoru stopped into his local video store. He rented three porno films. Though a well-known customer, he'd never had the nerve to ask about under-the-table, uncensored movies, those without the masking over the genitals. But the presence of the masking didn't really bother him, it only fired his lust more.

Home at last, he poured himself one last *Suntory*, and proceeded to watch the videos. The first featured Shiomi Mizutani, a newcomer to the scene. A horsey mouth with large lips, she was ever over eager to undress the all-too-familiar cast of men: the bodybuilder, the student-type, the dandy. But oh how she sucked cock! This was her drawing card. The (seeming) enthusiasm, the slobbering all over, the rapidity with which she could move from one to two to three without missing a beat, even the most 'hardened' costars expressed wonder at her skills. But for all her delights, she wasn't having the hoped for effect upon Kaoru tonight, and so he switched to a video with both the hugely breasted Akiko Ito and Rika Sugai. In this, they played "bat girls" to a baseball team. Swinging the bats around, gazing upon their length and breadth, one thing lead to another, and soon the girls were fucking the pitcher, catcher and an umpire. It was all too silly, but briefly, very surprisingly for this man who was not inclined to serious thinking, while pausing on the close-ups of the women's breasts, he wondered if this were indeed the source of our fascination with film. Finally, he put on the film with Masumi Tachibana, his favorite of all porno actresses. Her breasts were too perfect, perfect in shape and size, nipples the size of ten-yen coins, stretched taut tips. Her crow-black hair like a perfect helmet. A thin waist, long legs, a nectarine ass, and smallish cunt (through the filter). And her face: a long, thin smile, pert nose, and oh so Asian eyes: perfectly dumb. For Kaoru, Masumi could do anything and it was a turn-on; add being fucked and sucking cock and he was over the ass-shaped moon; it was enough to watch her bend over to grab a prick to excite him –her ass raised just so, her breasts hung within the shot so that Kaoru could see both them and her submissive cock-sucking (the man obligingly out of frame). She took her time, sucking slowly at first, then furiously, and in some strange reversal of power, commanding the man's submission.

Kaoru watched in wonderment. His whisky was forgotten. He stroked, he pulled, he tugged at his cock. He squeezed, he stretched. He wanted to moan, to cry out, but did not for fear of his neighbors. Finally, when one small drop of sperm emerged, he cursed his prick ("fishpaste!"), and knew the night was over (he might try again in the morning). He recalled the sexual pleasure he had experienced with his wife during the first few months around their marriage. It had been a real sexual joy. But now he felt nothing. Or almost: while he knew that all was not lost, that he was not wholly lonely, he also knew that he would never eat ramen with his father again, that while his colleagues were all nice guys, he missed a few people from his youth, from better, less stressful days. He felt the same loneliness that he was sure Lang felt, that Roberta possibly sometimes felt too, that certain times could never be recaptured – that first sexual attempt in his second year at University; that walk in Yoyogi-koen with his then fiancée; the birth of their daughter followed by her mother's milky breasts; the sex they enjoyed some months afterwards; their second child, again a daughter, no, he would never even have the luxury of every man's right, a son; the coldness that later set in; the job transfer to Tokyo; the occasional visits back home and the less than occasional and all too workmanlike sex they then had; the real loneliness he sensed everyday at the borders of feeling.

* * *

Worldly passions bring enlightenment,
life and death embody Nirvana.
– *Kodama Ukifune*

* * *

Marianne is wandering around Lake Shiroyama. We see the Lake, and then we see some hills variously resembling Switzerland, the Piedmont, areas in Japan. Marianne is alone, working on her Japanese verbs, occasionally humming "I Can See Everybody's Mother" to herself.

Liang did not know at all how he'd come to China all the way from the hills of Lake Shiroyama where his dream began. He is in Shanghai, where he runs into a van Zandt who is not quite the VZ he knows. He reads a billboard about "ten-thousand generations of flotsam and jetsam." He sees a black building missing a wall; and then a woman in red whom he feels should be holding a fan – "Where's her fan, dammit? What happened to her fan?," he keeps shouting to passersby. He sees another billboard, this time advertising "Headgear worn by a good for nothing young man from a wealthy family – or for a literary hack." He wonders if VZ had written it as a taunt. He runs into Roberta and has to explain to her, "I meant it literally: at the Szechuan restaurant the waitress puts her hand in to your wallet. I never meant it to hurt you, to make you jealous." Then within the dream he has another horrible dream in which he is living with van Zandt – again, the "different" VZ – and six others – bikers, Chinese bikers – a gang that includes an abacus whiz. The radio is playing a Gospel song; Liang hears Marion Williams singing. Then the radio suddenly switches to a Japanese narrator telling the story of the love between Blue Snake and White Snake. Liang thinks of Mei Lanfang, and his last thought is a desire to see Roberta.

* * *

A beautiful sentence this, from the Patsy Cline bio.: "I guess you could say he was what you'd now call a swinger." The speaker is lost, afraid, adrift, hesitant, would make a hell of an historian. But listen again: the sentence itself *swings*! It reminds me of Barbara Stanwyck.

* * *

- Awful.
- Awful man.
- Awful people.
- Awful woman.
- Good beer.
- Fair.
- Good *tsuyu*.
- Middling.
- Cute waitress.
- Awful teeth.
- Nice smile.
- But awful people, really.
- Really awful.
- Are you thinking what I'm thinking?
- The waitress?
- No, no, those people.
- "Those people" – isn't that what they usually call us?
- Perhaps, but I'm not thinking about we Japanese.
- Then of whom?
- Those – you know, those Americans.
- The ones we run into now and then?
- Yes, yes.
- Roberta and Arlene?

- No, no, Roberta and Lang.
- But Lang isn't from America.
- He's not? Oh well, what matter, same difference, all the same. Where is he from then?
- Europe. Austria. Vienna.
- Is he now?
- Oh yes, but I think they met in Amsterdam. And they've lived in America too. Perhaps that's what confused you.
- How could their having lived in America confuse me? He's a foreigner, I assumed he was from America. There's nothing confusing there.
- Nonetheless, not all foreigners come from America.
- Perhaps not; nonetheless.
- Yes, I see your point.
- Vienna, you say?
- Yes, you know, the waltz.
- Oh, I know.
- Do you? Have you been there?
- Yes, I have. Before entering my company, with a few friends.
- Is it – is it …
- Like in the movie? Then you know the Tora-san.
- That's not exactly what I was about to ask.
- Nonetheless, it is very much like.
- Lots of us Japanese go there.
- Oh yes, we're not unlike, you know. Baby-talk, finger-food, a glorious past. Wonderful people, really.
- Some might not see that in a positive light.
- Then they haven't the spirit of "gemootlick …" – or however you pronounce it.
- [Whistles a bit of a waltz.]
- But Lang, really, from Vienna? Hardly seems like it. I'd never have thought it. Doesn't seem the type, really. No, no, hard to believe. Nonetheless.
- Yes?
- Oh yes, nonetheless, an awful man.
- Yes, and Roberta.
- That must be why they are together, you know, two awfulnesses attracted to one another.
- But each awful in his or her own way.
- Oh certainly. Separate awfulnesses, united only in their being awful.
- But are they indeed united? I thought they'd split apart, or separated.

- Oh yes, clever that – united in their separateness. In their awfulness.
- But they are apart. He's living in Kichijoji, and she's at least an hour away on the Chuo line. Lives somewhere in Bunkyo-ku.
- Not another gone native? What do these people see in our culture?
- Oh she's not too far gone as far as I understand, nonetheless.
- Yes, but going. And he's in Kichijoji, you say? Can't see a Viennese liking it there.
- You've got a point. Perhaps Setagaya-ku would be more to his liking. A little more toney, that is to say.
- Yes, better housing, cleaner children, a certain elegance in the women. Less fun really is what we're talking about. A good place to grow old in. Perhaps that is why he is in Kichijoji. An awful Viennese – can you imagine it? But too, what is she doing in Bunkyo-ku?
- Oh, the atmosphere, one assumes. You know, those Americans.
- Yes, all over the place. Poking their noses, poking their elbows. I wonder who is jealous of whom.
- Japanese of Americans, of Viennese, you mean?
- Oh no, no, Lang of Roberta, or vice-versa.
- But jealous of what?
- Well, there must be something that keeps them together?
- But they're not together!
- Of course they are; this living apart is just an indirect way of expressing their longing, their bond, their inseparable union. You don't understand these foreigners the way that I do. I've been to America too, I'll have you know. I've seen the old world, and the new.
- But they live on different sides of the city!
- Of the same, single city. And besides, they are both awful people. They are a hegemony. They have the same laugh, you know.
- Really? I hadn't noticed, but now that you mention it.
- Oh yes, I've heard it often enough, really, how an Austrian can learn to cackle like an American, it's surprising really how low one can go.
- That bad, eh?
- Awful. Have you also noticed or not that they always order the same foods in restaurants? But I will say he is a bit more daring when it comes to sushi, and she genuinely does seem to like *natto*, I will give her credit there.
- Yes, yes, credit there, credit there.
- No, they are not stupid when it comes to food.
- And her Japanese is quite good.
- Oh now, how preposterous!
- No, no, I have to say, that she really can carry on a conversation, she

goes on and on from one point to another and somehow manages to maintain a thread throughout, carries you along though often you're not sure what she is getting at, and manages to tie it all up together at the end too. Snap! And it is conversation too, a real give and give.

– Give and take, she's American recall.
– Yes, but no, give and give. Oh, she speaks Japanese alright.
– A mystery. A mystery to me. Well, I am not convinced.
– I'm not trying to convince you. See for yourself. She'll be visiting my home next weekend. She takes calligraphy lessons from my mother.
– Oh, this is really going too far!
– I thought so too. But the truth is, she does have a certain feel, a genuine touch. I certainly do not.
– Nor I, I am ashamed to say. But really, she is visiting you next week?
– Well not visiting me, the lesson is with my mother. But as we are acquainted via our mutual friends, I do join them during their tea break. Seriously, you're more than welcome to come. There is also a good sushi-ya nearby, we could go there in the evening, and perhaps Roberta would join in.
– Perhaps I might. Whereabouts do you live, Hiro?
– Setagaya.
– Ahh, and with your parents? Of course, after all you are single.
– Yes, well, I'm in no hurry to leave. I fulfill my duties, and we leave each other alone.
– Living together and living alone.
– In a manner of speaking.
– Do they interfere?
– Oh, the usual.
– I envy you, I do.
– "A place to grow old in"?
– "Toney."
– Oh, come now, it's not a retirement village, after all.
– No, it's not. If I lived in Tokyo, or I should say, if I were a proper Tokyoite, I suppose I would want to live in Setagaya. It has a good balance of the old and the new.
– I haven't thought of it much, I must admit. I have no idea what sort of character it has; it is fairly large, after all.
– True.
– And some greenery. And it has the river.
– The river?
– The Tama. Is there another?

- Uh, well, some of us might think so. Yes, we'll ask Roberta, on the weekend.
- But you, Kaoru, you live in Gunma Prefecture, don't you? Whereabouts, Maebashi?
- No, a small town outside Takasaki. Been there all my life in fact. Except these past few years that the head office has wanted me here.
- And still with your parents?
- Oh no, no, they passed on some time ago, while I was in university in fact. Now there's just my sister and I. Well, I shouldn't say "just," after all, she has three children, and I have two.
- Is that a fact?
- Yes, yes, nine, ten and eleven – those are my sister's kids. Ours are three and five. Girls both. But I'm not the best of fathers, too much like my own, I suppose, rather sloppy. Not home much either.
- So much work?
- So much whiskey.
- Of course.
- But it's not so bad, really. An old high-school girlfriend owns a bar, and I sometimes stay at her place after hours.
- Oh, a bonus, Kaoru.
- Occasionally. Usually I just stay in my non-descript apartment and contemplate my normal-dreary existence.
- Well, it doesn't sound too bad, nothing out of the ordinary.
- Oh, it's bad alright. I have no illusions about that. No love lost between my wife and I. I hardly know my children. The bar owner is not so much a dear friend as ... well, let's say we admit to a desperate clinch, and then we are off on our separate ways come morning. I'm walking forward to my grave, like most of my generation, like my father's, and I daresay, like yours will do. Don't get me wrong, I do not condemn it. It isn't even worth analyzing. It is simply the way things are here. You know what I'm talking about, don't you?
- I suppose I do. Yes, yes I do.
- Shame about the girls, though. You try to keep them cheerful, all the while knowing you're lying to them, and they will find you out sooner than you think. They'll find everything out, and only pass on the same lies to their own children. And we will then indulge our own grandchildren in the same way, senile enough by then to think we can undo the lie. But again, don't misunderstand me, it is simply the way things are here.
- Do you think things are different elsewhere?
- I don't really know; I expect not; perhaps they are; but why should

- it matter to me? Other places are not Japan.
- No, no they are not. But don't you have any hobbies, something you enjoy?
- Hobbies!? You mean like reciting *Noh* ballads, or photographing the irises in Meiji Park? No, no hobbies – commuting, whiskey, the bar woman. It's a bit unfair, really.
- But you say she was an old girl-friend.
- Well, not in any happy, childish way. We just both happened to admit the convenience of our mutual recognition – you know what I mean – emotional indolence, sexual need. And we've continued to enjoy getting together now and then – but nothing more, no commitment, no ruining a perfectly good thing by getting all emotional about it.
- A perfectly good thing?
- Well, you know, you stick it in now and then, share a few laughs – that's about all the positive side of things as far as I can see. That's all you take with you. Mutual sucking and licking, mutual laughs. But cunt doesn't really taste all that good, you know, but it has to be done really, to keep things all in their proper balance. Ah, but she's a sweet woman in her own way. And you?
- Well, I suppose I have to admit that things are not really all that different for me; they may appear so on the surface, but I can see how my entire pathway was long ago laid out for me, through to the end. It's funny, it is no tunnel with light at the end, you know. Instead, it's all so clear and sunny, all the signs posted along the way, and no chance for a detour. Even if an earthquake strikes and a million people die, I will probably know what my next steps are to be. I might even be able to choose my own wife, but I'll never really know if she was in fact my own choice, if she hadn't somehow already been chosen for me unbeknownst to me. I know that at work certainly I have no choice; but it's comforting in a way.
- Yes, it is. We are like tiny chips on the great motherboard called Japan – no, better, call it Tokyo, just the great capitol, and that motherboard works – that is the great thing, the comfort. There is our pride. To be even a small part in this great …
- Yes, yes, you're right, I'm sure. Funny how others would see this all so negatively.
- Yes, after all, who complains here? Oh sure, a small minority, but we Japanese accept our lot, we don't have too bad a time of it. Time is on our side, after all. So, you say there is a good sushi-ya near your house?

- Oh yes, so, do you think you'll come on the weekend?
- Yes, it sounds fine. My own calligraphy may be rather slipshod, but I do appreciate a good hand. Your mother's a teacher?
- Oh, amateur, you know, the occasional group exhibitions, a few students.
- And all the fees working their way up to the top man, eh?
- Of course.
- Will Lang be there with Roberta? Or any of their other friends? That quiet one, what's her name, Arlene?
- Oh no, these are lessons for Roberta alone. She is serious about learning calligraphy, really, I am impressed. I doubt that her friends are. And Lang, no, he would never accompany her on such a task.
- No, I suppose not.
- Well, it might be interesting, going out to dinner with her, having a chat.
- Yes, yes, I always feel rather tongue-tied around her. I don't know what it is. It's not that she is a foreigner, oh it may have been that at first, but no longer. Maybe I just feel dull next to her.
- Dull?
- Well, like we said, our lives are already laid out for us, what could we possibly have to say new? What contribute? Whereas she seems to be making out her own life, carving a path, laying out the road herself, complete with detours, sudden turns, you know the way roads and walkways go every which way here.
- Interesting that you think this of her. But there is everything to discuss with her! What does it matter that ours are one-way streets – there is still conversation. A few words never changed one's direction, only distracted one along the way. Mutual amusement, not abusement. Yes, Hiro, talk is our only gift, when all the clinches have been forgotten, it is all we can offer. Yes, I am sure that she will be able to learn much from speaking with us. She is so enthralled with life in Japan, we certainly have much to enlighten her about. What does she know, after all, of the salary-man's point of view? Of Gunma Prefecture, of life among rice-paddies, of real Japanese women, traditional women with more than one-point-two children? Or of Setagaya-ku and its own traditions? No, she will be able to gain much from our mutual intercourse.
- I admire your confidence. But I'll have to think hard about that one, "Setagaya-ku's traditions." Maybe I'll ask my mother.
- Yes, yes, you do that. I'd like to know too, after all. It will also be good for me to see a bit more of Tokyo than Marunouchi.

- And you get along with Roberta?
- Oh, well enough. She has always been pleasant to me. I don't know why, really. I can't see myself as being at all interesting to her. Maybe because I get along with everyone, with her other friends, those girls, and maybe because I introduced her to Cafferty.
- Oh, how did that come about?
- He did some work for my company once, and one day I happened to run into him and Roberta at the same time in Ginza. They seem to like each other. Anyway, she doesn't seem to mind me.
- Do you think she's attracted? You know how foreign women are always curious about Japanese men.
- Oh no, nothing like that at all, I'm sure. I don't even think I would be interested.
- Good for you!
- Well, in any event, it should prove to be an interesting afternoon.
- Well, I'm very glad you'll be coming. I'll let her know beforehand not to plan anything else for after her lesson.
- Do you usually have dinner with her afterwards?
- Oh, no, I usually walk her to the station; once or twice we've gotten noodles together, but nothing more.
- Well then, it will be a first for the three of us.
- Hmmm.

* * *

THE NAMES OF LOVE

Who are these people for whom love?
Who these cycles of names?
Who this Roberta, this Arlene, Marianne?
Who this Lang, this van Zandt, Cafferty?
Who are these people for whom love?
Who this cycle, who these names?
Who this Hiroko, this Hiromi, Kazuko?
Who this Hiro, this Kazuo, Kaoru?

Who are these people for whom love?
Who would love?, who would love and want to love?, and who would – perhaps – love?
Who would love many and love one?, who love many, thus losing

himself?, and who would leave love to chance?

Who are these people for whom love?

Who would love and love and love?, who would insist on love?, and who would love once and – no more?

Who would play at love?, who has loved once and will only once more?, and who questions love, indeed, calls it "the big whatsit"?

Who are these people for whom love?

For whom is it a Poetics of Union?, for whom a State of Desire?, and for whom a Prospect on to the Infinite?

For whom is love the Condition of Knowledge?, for whom a Situation of Plenitude?, and for whom is it an act of Denying, of Refusal?

Who are these people for whom love?

For whom it is the Realization of both One's Self and Non-self?, for whom is it a Fall from All Future Grace?, and for whom does it form the very Responsibilities of Memory?

And for whom is love a Fateful daring of the Absolute?, for whom an Acceptance of his Mastery, and for whom, finally, is his love a Refusal of any and every Surprise?

Who are these people for whom love?

Who are these people?
For whom love?

* * *

Like some pure demon the blackest eyes reddest lips whitest skin float off the page the poster the billboard hover over and haunt me – and yet, by the mid-90s Miki Imai is wholly benign.

* * *

– Nakano already?
– Born walkers, nothing can stop us.
– So, what do we do now?
– What do you mean?
– Well, isn't it most people's impulse to walk along the Chuo line?
– You mean on the tracks? That's dangerous!
– No, but alongside, you know.

- Not my impulse.
- Why would anyone do that?
- Because if you think of going west from Nakano – well, what's the first picture that comes to mind?
- Uhm, next comes Ogikubo.
- Yes, but comes where?
- Along the way, you know that.
- No, but visually, where does it come.
- Do you mean geographically?
- No, visually.
- Topographically?
- Ok. When you imagine in your head the path from Shinjuku to Nakano –
- Is there a path? Is that what you're getting at, a path along the tracks?
- No. If you imagine the way, the two places on a picture, what kind of picture is it?
- You mean like a photograph?
- No, but, yes a printed picture.
- A map.
- Right!
- So, there's a map, Roberta, what's the big deal.
- I forget.
- I don't – it has to do with how one goes from Shinjuku to Nakano.
- Right, and all I'm saying is that most people imagine a straight line from one to the other because they have this Chuo Line map-image fixed.
- I don't.
- Me either.
- Not me, I drive, so I think of the roads.
- Not me either, I take a bus.
- I have my scooter.
- I don't think I've ever gone from one to the other – or at least walked it like we are now. I just go by whatever means are available. So what are you getting at, Roberta?
- Yeah, it sounds like you're the only one who imagines this Chuo Line straight line.
- Ok, ok, I give. It's no big deal. We'll just keep walking – away from Shinjuku –
- You can still glimpse it a bit –
- And past Nakano, Sun Palace and all, and –
- Into the sun!

- The real Sun King's palace!
- Right, well, due east at least.
- Right, due east.
- Anyone got a compass?
- Not me.
- Not me.
- How are we gonna know we're going the right way?
- Think we should try to keep it straight?
- Like – I hate to say it –
- Go ahead.
- Like along the Chuo Line?

* * *

I saw that van Zandt guy the other day in Roppongi with Hiroko and Hiromi, Hiro considers. Very late, and all three very drunk. A girl on each arm. Lucky guy. I'd certainly like to have either one of them make me happy. And I saw Arlene the other day too, in a coffee shop. She was talking with a Japanese woman. They each had a stack of books and papers with them. Were they working? Arlene. Very pretty. But too quiet for me.

* * *

Okoi

The most famous of modern geishas was destined for heartbreak; after all she was born into it: her parents had married for love!

All we know are her stage names. First there was Teru, and then Okoi, Carp, known as her biographers tell us for its "voluptuous grace." The careful reader could do no better than to view her life in light of Saikaku's *A Woman who Loved Love* and Mizoguchi's version with our beloved Kinuyo Tanaka, respecting the differences between all three of course.

We know nothing more of the parents, unfortunately, other than the fact that their livelihood (lacquer) soon came to a stop and they were forced to give up the four-year old product of their love to a 'tea' house. In turn, her foster parents too lost their small fortune and once again, now aged seven, the little girl entered another house where the foster parents became servants to an aging geisha. (In time, they would become

Okoi's servants.) The little girl's charms eventually lead to her becoming a geisha. She made her debut in 1893 at age thirteen in the Shimbashi house Omuja.

Waley tells us that "She possessed an unusually striking form of beauty: full lips, a pronounced chin, a slender nose; hers was an intelligent mature face, quite different from the other faces – childish, demure or featureless – that peer out of the photographs of the geisha of her day." We can't help but noting that things have not changed very much in the decades since Okoi's prime.

Within five years she was so well known for her many skills that her first patron, Heizo Yajima, a stock-broker, set her up in her own teahouse. Soon enough, her fame grew and the great rake and Kabuki actor Ichimura Uzaemon became infatuated with her. And she was starstruck. So too was Yajima. He was so taken by being so near the center of attention that he voluntarily acted as Okoi's go-between for her marriage to Ichimura, who, having won his prize, soon forgot her. Though she remained starstruck: she eventually spent her fortune covering the debts accrued by his profligacies. In time (Waley says two years, the Longstreets say four) a divorce was worked out. Heartbroken, Okoi had had it with men: she opened a new house and this time was hell-bent on *her own pleasures*. She was soon enough back in demand: this time by two sumo wrestlers, whose names should be recorded, Araiwa and Hitachiyama. The two behomeths dueled in their fashion, the former won, but was refused marriage. Of poor Araiwa, it has been said, "He was a simple simon of a fellow – all lard including his brains."

In 1903, our heroine was introduced to Taro Katsura, who three times would be Prime Minister of Japan. His was no temporary infatuation. He first redeemed Okoi for two thousand yen, and in 1906 married her (Waley), and she was now a respectable and settled woman. None of this will be found in the history books, of course. But still, hers was not a happy lot. In 1905, for example, the Russo-Japanese war was concluded with an unfair-to-Japan Katsura-negotiated treaty which incensed the nation. Okoi was reviled by the public as "the mistress of the betrayer of the Sun God." Katsura died in 1913, and Okoi mourned him for five years. And then her past life beckoned once again: she opened the National Bar in Ginza, and then another house in Akasaka. And then in 1934, her patron's "crooked political dealings," brought on another scandal, and again she became the victim of the mob. But, we are told, her "innate pliability ... shrugged off suicide."

In 1938 Okoi took the tonsure. For the last ten years of her life she either lived in a temple in Meguro Ward or did charitable work. For example, she traveled through China during wartime, praying for both the Chinese and Japanese victims. She also played a part in preserving what remains of the Temple of Five Hundred Arhats in Meguro. At the temple where she lived we can find a statue of the great Goddess of Mercy Kannon – it is known as the Okoi Kannon.

Perhaps there is something to contemplate here, some moral lesson to learn – something about this *karyākai*, this "flower and willow world," something perhaps especially Buddhistic and Tokyoish about the heights and depths of great passions, about the waywardness of both poverty and wealth, and that one's only refuge is renunciation. Perhaps.

* * *

She made love like he imagined a lesbian to. Clinging, sucking, wanting to get "under his skin," as Arlene had told van Zandt once in a rare drunken state. Needing so much to penetrate.

* * *

suddenly went mad
suddenly blank
suddenly – saw you

* * *

ONE THING LEADS TO ANOTHER

(To the memory of Thomas Bernhard)

Marianne is tall and thin, with full, (*artistic*) breasts, large eyes, a round face and a "young" American-sounding voice; pretty, but not beautiful, she speaks fast and is also a bit confused as to why she is in Tokyo, but *excitement* at being in Tokyo and even and perhaps especially *excitement* at being confused as to why she is in Tokyo predominates, for she is one whom *excitement* naturally *attracts*, and who reciprocally is naturally *attracted to excitement*, the costs of confusion notwithstanding, posing no barrier to the *great resonance* that resides inside her delicate breast – physically, spiritually, intellectually, indeed, even and perhaps especially emotionally – a resonance resident in that breast that is all *ex-*

citement. She is pretty – in an odd way; this is really to say that she is very attractive. After all, who is wholly or simply "pretty" or would even want to be considered so? – there after all lies dullness, resignation, death even, death of the face and of the spirit, and what deaths could possibly be worse? (For the face is the spirit's window and too the reverse, the spirit draws us *excitedly* to this face and not to that, the one leading to the other.) No, it is far better to be pretty, or handsome in the case of a man, in an odd and not a conventional way, as Marianne is, in an *opposite way*. And so too, appropriately, Marianne *walks* in an odd way: she walks *in the opposite direction*. In an odder confluence (or is it coincidence?, no, confluence is wholly appropriate), she speaks much the same way as she walks, that is to say, she *walks and talks in the opposite direction, excitedly*. She speaks against the grain as she strides forth boldly, assuredly, enthusiastically, *excitedly*, when suddenly she comes to a stop, appears momentarily confused, but the costs notwithstanding, she is *excited*, struggles to drag her way forward again, until, suddenly, *excitedly*, she again breaks into her confidence-filled and forthright stride until, again, she half stops and seems to drag herself forward – *excitedly*. It is very difficult for almost anyone – I do not include myself here – to walk with Marianne, but it can be exciting – and here I most emphatically include myself. As one converses while walking with Marianne both participants' words seem to go in and out of a perfectly melodious synchrony and a cacophony, the one leading to the other. However, the important point here is that the "misunderstandings" that arise are not half as exhilarating, and not a tenth, not even one percent as *exciting* as the poetry that results, for it is a poetry that results, an *exciting and essential poetry* that results when one walks and talks with Marianne. But who will or ever could know this about her unless I say it here and now? There is much more, pages, volumes more that I could say about Marianne were I so inclined at the moment, and I am very much inclined, that is freely admitted, but were I not so preoccupied, so very much preoccupied that my pen cannot maintain enough speed to keep up with my thoughts so that I must write furiously and stop momentarily to arrange my thoughts, so much so that I wonder if writing what I am so *excitedly* composing *now* is not unlike my beloved Marianne's walk, my most dear Marianne's talk; were I not so preoccupied with saying even more *essential things* about this *opposite direction*, about *truths and lies*, and other no less important matters, I would say more, much more about Marianne, the most beloved Marianne of so many of my thoughts and dreams, real dreams of for me a very real Marianne. But that will have to wait for the moment, that will have to be momentarily halted, postponed, put "on the back burner" as they say, and perhaps someday when I have or am given more leisure, though I have serious doubts of that day ever occurring in a life that is filled with preoccupations of such a pressing and demanding nature to say what is *essential*, then I will say all the more that I want to say about my dear and beloved Marianne. For example, I will write how she, even she, the very guardian of our dreams, Marianne, the bearer of that most mysterious, magnetic, exhilarating name, is not even sure – what an enormity! – not even she its bearer is sure how to properly spell it, there being so many variations. Marianne; Mary Anne; Marie-Anne; Mary-anne; Mary Ann, and so on and so forth. I could also talk about her voice, her letters to me and the photographs of her that I possess. But all of that will have to wait – for, whether they be truths (in Marianne's case) or lies (in all but a few other person's cases), one thing always and naturally leads to another. If I were to describe my "real-life" (village Switzerland, outside the book) friend Marianne, and the description (sex, voice, dress, breasts, walk, talk, gestures, that whole lyrical angularity of the woman; recurring phrases, reading and listening habits; passions spiritual and erotic, joys and sorrows; artistic and intellectual tastes; and more, not forgetting that splendid, ringing *laugh* that would raise the saints from their meditations, or that *stare* that overtakes her at moments as she looks into your soul), and if this description corresponded exactly with my "character-in-a-book" friend Marianne (the capitols of Europe, inside the book), if I were to undertake such a description in that thoroughly fanciful moment of leisure that will probably never occur in a life obsessed with saying what is *essential and true* and naming all the hundreds and thousands and millions of lies that I have listened to and endured to the point where my actual physical constitution is at stake for the sake of holding on to a very few but wholly indispensable truths, truths without which I cannot live, truths upon which this very fragile constitution depends (and, it goes without saying, truths upon which the constitution of this description depends), if, as I say, I could and were to undertake this description of my (outside) friend Marianne, and what I said corresponded note for note and word for word with my (inside) Marianne (or however it is you spell her name), if I were free (!) to describe the one, the real, outside, village Swiss Marianne, who also, by the way, is not sure how to spell her name, this most gentle and *artistic* and pained of all life's creatures, and this description corresponded to that of my (inside) Marianne, this equally artistic and least consciously literary Marianne – though Marianne has read a great deal, is in fact a better-read person than even myself, and has written some few, not many but a very few, extremely valuable pages that she has allowed me to see and some to even copy and that are far worthier than these I am writing now – this Marianne whose breast – heart, soul, sensibility – seeks as it also expresses something higher than the literature of the marketplace where the ridiculous novel-whores – not to mention the art and film whores and dance and music whores – no, this Marianne, my Marianne, whose artistic sensibility came about as a result of years on the gallery circuit and even more years on the treadmill of the conservatory, followed by many more years, punishing years, years demanding to the highest *artistic* and human degrees possible, years spent in the cabarets and worse places, worse even than the worst imaginable song-and-dance dives of her native state, and all of these years spent in pursuit of the *most essential artistic truths, truths that could only be pursued and found by choosing to go in the opposite direction– and to go until she finally succeeded*; if, as I say, the description of my equally gentle and pained, well-read and artistic village Swiss friend Marianne (outside) and my (metropolitan, remember) Marianne (inside) fit one to one, exactly and without the slightest degree of slippage, though I could forever (as most readers would no doubt prefer) claim the former a fact, the village Swiss (outside) Marianne a fact and the latter a fiction, the cosmopolitan (inside) Marianne a fiction; or better, if pushed to it, I could proclaim them both fictions – or both facts! – simply because Marianne (country or city, outside or inside) by the nature of her being, of her embodying truth, is not and never could be a lie, can only and ever be *essentially true*. But, as our good, dear and departed friend T. has written, "it is not possible to communicate and hence to demonstrate the truth," and, as he has also said, "to write about a period of one's life, no matter how remote or how recent, no matter how long or how short, means accumulating hundreds and thousands and millions of falsehoods and falsifications, all of which are familiar to the writer describing the period as truths and nothing but truths." I see her (and Lang, and Roberta) *here* (in the 'mentis acie'); I hear them *now* (mental ear), talking as palpably as I am walking with them, now, here, at this very moment and place as I write in this state of complete and entire *excitement* and lucidity. And as T. has also said, all attempts at saying the truth become simply lies to anyone who reads them, because after all, when one realizes that to try to write and to tell the truth that one will never succeed, that the truth will always be taken as a tissue of lies, that "the description makes something clear which accords with the describer's *aspiration* for truth but not with the truth itself," then fatefully and *excitedly* one goes in the *opposite direction*, in that direction where one thing leads to another. Come now, you ask me, you certainly do not believe in these characters of yours, in this preposterous idea of a city (these "styles of walking and styles of talking") you are proposing? But isn't that it? It is, it must be preposterous to maintain any parcel, or segment of truth, of something *essential* and *essentially true*. To acknowledge the impossibility of communicating any truth just as one ridiculously, absurdly, flies against all the facts in attempting it. (And perhaps too to be smashed down and crushed like a gnat in the attempt – yes, one also accepts – indeed, even welcomes – that very distinct possibility.) To talk and to walk with "facts" and "fictions" (the one leading to the other) hand in hand all the while going in the essentially true and opposite direction: to be with Marianne (Swiss, outside) and with Marianne (European, inside), fiction or most decidedly otherwise; to talk with Lang and with Lang; to walk with both Robertas. But few will ever understand this, could ever be expected to comprehend this, this which is *most essentially and excitingly true*. A phrase, a woman, a word, *one leading to the other*, and suddenly one is caught, wrapped up, enthralled, and *excited, one thing leading to another*, and one is forever off in that *opposite direction*. Lord, how when one was younger one was content simply – joyously perhaps but not *excitedly* – to talk and walk with one's friends. But now they are gone – into their *excitements*, their fictions, their *essential truths*, and one must make do alone, in memory, a phone call, an occasional letter, a more rare visit. I speak of my Marianne of the artistic breasts, speak of the *essential excitement* I found once in just being in her presence, her truth, her conversation, her *essential* and unending *excitement* without cease, *one excitement leading to another*; found once in a conversation at midnight in a bar in Tokyo with Lang, a conversation punctuated mostly by our deepening silences, silences deepening as an awareness of what we were saying to one another grew upon us, an awareness of how *exciting and of how essential* the truths we were expressing were (there were many other such conversations, all ended now); found once too when silently walking across the city with Roberta (and never revealing to her the great love I bear her); and having been within that real knowledge, real truth, within those most *exciting and essential* truths each leading to another – having gone, that is, in the *opposite direction* and seen how one thing most assuredly leads to another when one is in the midst of such exciting and essential truths as these my friends, I am free to write and speak now as I please, and to reject and condemn forever whatever lies, falsehoods and accusations the rest of the world may try and defile me with, even if their source may be you, Reader, no matter how dear you may be or might become to me, because after all – I know whom I am addressing in this two-way street where one thing leads to another.

* * *

On March 30, 1989, while riding the Ginza line to work, he saw the ad for "Lang's Whiskey," and, while not a whiskey drinker himself, resolved, out of pure auspiciousness, to not only get a copy of the ad – advertising so saturated his city – but also a bottle of this his whiskey, have it available for friends.

* * *

–   I've been saved by this neighborhood. "Woman saved by neighborhood!" Really, who needs the rest of the city?, needs the High City, the Yamanote? Who needs it? Ok, ok, maybe some people do – "Man Saved by High City" – but for now I can relax, wend my leisurely way – still can't figure out the way around the Jōmyō-in – is that it? – the way the road curves and then you're – where? – that's the point, isn't it? – a right way to live – history is made in the daytime too – just by walking along the wandering paths – let the history writers try to catch up with us – but they can't – they live outside of time – to them it's a thing – a timeline and all that – here it's just the living, the doing of it – it's own reward – no wonder the people are always so amused every time some foreigner or historian or whatever kind of academic comes up to them, asking some question about this or that – how many generations has your family made these paper balloons? – please tell us again the distinction between western and Japanese ice cream – would you mind being in a picture with me, please? – what, again, is Japanese swimming? – really, they are never exasperated – are they just amused at the human inability to get things? – or the weirder human desire to – to what? – well, not to know things, but to know things in these ways – and at the expense of knowing them by doing them – but again, they never get angry – would I? – yes, at this point – maybe not later, if I live here a few years – ah, the ice-cream place! – "Woman saved by Japanese ice cream!"
–   So, Roberta, what is Japanese swimming?

* * *

Ah, this city, van Zandt quickly reflects on a morning after, a walk through Sendagaya, run into Maria, we go to a bar, meet Stefan there, in comes Johnnie, jokes, obscenities – jeez, he knows the best dirty jokes!, some girls at the next table, flirt, a couple of name cards. Come home. Messages from Sabrina, Inez (who so rarely calls). Not a bad day.

* * *

Three Encounters.

1. I was approaching the station, eager to get on the train and to continue trying to read one of Calvino's early Palomar stories in the original. Two young men and a woman – art-school types – came up to me and asked if they could take a picture of me standing in front of a poster for a pop star's concert, the pop star silly, dressed in pink as a working woman in front of a refrigerator. I oblige. I give them my address, and they promise to send me a copy. (They never do; not intentionally, they're just broke I suppose.) As they're leaving, I ask them why they wanted the photo, or rather me, in it. One of the young men quickly responds, "because you're cool."

2. I was on the train standing in front of a small group of boys, about ten years old. I am silently reading my Pushkin, occasionally glancing round the page at the boy's playing their silly games (or gazing anxiously into some distance, anxious about – what was it?, I wonder now). Most of the boys by now have gotten off the train. At one of my side glances, one of them grabs my attention with a smile that in a decade's time will stop women a bit too often, and I hope not cruelly. Silently, speaking with eyes and gestures, he gains my agreement to engage him in a fierce struggle of scissors-paper-stone. He does not smile; he is intrigued by this curious foreign man who somehow represents mysteries he feels he'd like a short glimpse into. We face off; two out of three. I trounce the kid. He snaps his fingers in mock-disappointment, reaches into his pocket, takes out a five-yen coin, hands it to me, and he gets off the train. He smiles at me from the platform and I return to my Russian.

3. I was going up what seemed to be an endless number of stairs and stairways in a station I had come to for the first time. Damn, I remember thinking to myself – it was during those first years here – not only am I climbing all these steps, I'll probably take the wrong exit, too, and then have to backtrack half a kilometer or more. Three-quarters of the way up a final flight of what look like hopeful stairs, I passed a group of three boys in school uniforms and those heavy leather book bags on their backs playing scissors-paper-stone. As one wins he gains a

stair; as one loses he steps down. It occurred to me that this could go on eternally, and I imagined the boys, their mother's bringing them their meals, fellow schoolmates helping them with their studies (their diplomas delivered by motorbike messenger), phones and faxes set up on the stairs (they are portable, able to go up and down the stairs as the game proceeds – a shower and toilet too) so that the boys – men now – can work and support the families they have propagated (in the discretely placed beds, also portable) ... until finally, decades hence a small temple has already been installed anticipating the day when the three boys will become saints and worshipped as examples of friendship and stick-to-itiveness. I remember that I laughed to myself at the silliness of the fantasy I'd just fashioned and had just emerged from the station – aha!, it was the right exit. – and I heard a great triumphant shout, and a second later, an equally great moan. Had a soul been released? But it had been no fantasy: I really had been present at the birth of a myth: one boy had been liberated, up another rung closer to the light of day, while another had been sent hurtling so much deeper below. I make a mental note to come back to this station in a couple of days.

I think of these encounters now, think that I participated that small much in the real, the natural, the deep life of the city – but that in all three instances – being cool, winning five yen, seeing the birth of a myth – I had only a functional part. It was not me, it was not my life that was involved here, I instigated nothing: any other foreigner would have been just as cool; the kid would have a good laugh at dinner when he told his parents and then forgot me; the boys on the stairs took no notice of me, the myth was only seen by me, it will live its life without me. I was not, in short, a part of the city. I would that the city would love me back, and yet. These thoughts leave me bereft. (And in that do I become a part of the city? Is my bereftness that of a man or a boy? Am I that much more a part of the city in being ignored by it – and is this in fact an acceptance of some special sort?)

* * *

On his deathbed, near Uguisudani, the poet Masaoka Shiki wrote of the things he most wished to see: "moving pictures; bicycle races and stunts; lions and ostriches in the zoo; ... automatic telephones and red letter boxes; a beer hall; women fencers; and Western-style theatre. But I haven't time to list them all."

* * *

SCENE EIGHT: MUSEUM

It's an opening at the Hara Museum. Japanese Art Deco, former residence of an Imperial relation. The art crowd, the diplomatic
crowd, the fashion crowd, the hangers on crowd. A small crowd of
people interested in art; a smaller crowd of artists. A small building
with twists and turns, a spiral staircase that leads two ways, either a
white-tiled, scallop-curved room, or the roof (one imagines as a helicopter pad, or a place for assignations: "Don't fret, no one's going
to suspect we're up here, they came to be seen, not to see, to glide
across carpets, not to walk on gravel.") Two gardens. A café, a gift
shop. Lots of people, lots of talk – no one looks another in the eye;
instead, the eyes look in two different directions at once, one to make
sure someone is looking at you, the other to see who has just entered
and with whom you can engage in more small-talk; or is it the same
at any opening? Probably so, so let's leave that at that. The only place
to be sure of meeting someone at the Hara – or this or that museum
or gallery or reception or cocktail (in one's "smoking" – even Gardel
sings of it) – is the staircase.

   And there she stands her ground. She can't miss him now, no
sir, no way. She hears snippets of conversation. "Teaches at Musabi, but
it's all crafts, you know." "His wife is the real force." "*Japan Times*? You've
got to be kidding!" "Elemental, my dear, elemental, never seen anything
so profound. So like our own artists – who did it first, you know" "He
does stuff for boardrooms, eh?" "Well, she's kept up with her art magazines." "Pretentious shit." "Scribbles with a ballpoint, eh? And they call
that art?" "My six-year old does similar stuff." "She dresses weirder than
her art." "Korean, is he?" "Site specific? So, where's the site? Oh, here!
Ha, ha!"

   She can't stand it any longer. She thinks the art is good. Well, some
of it. She wants to go back to the white room. Yes! That's where he'd be.

   She enters. She is alone. No, she senses his presence. He is so silent,
and she respects this silence. She cannot turn to look at him. It is something about the room, the white tiles, but warm in some soothing sort of
way. He opens the door – and leaves.

   But the white holds her back. White on white – she's changed costume for tonight, is herself a combination, white suit, white-on-white

blouse – it holds her still. White, whiteness. The light to fit all. His steps, the closing door, such stillness.

She walks to the roof in order to recover, to feel the cooling air. She re-enters the room. Now it is all dark, except for some flickering lights lining the wall. They are LEDs, numbers flashing continually, an installation by Tatsuo Miyajima. There is something eternal about it, high-tech and Zen, this garden of darkness and lights. And again she senses his presence, but is too transfixed by this odd, unexpected peace, this garden, to approach him. He exits.

She does not regret it, being so close, as she is so still now. But oh so close! And so unable to speak. ("Mister, is this your portfolio? I was on the train when …") What is it that stops her, is it the room, the curve, the white?

She breaks free and rushes to the roof, sees the taxi speed away, off into the maze of streets, the city and its mysteries, lights flashing on and off, a mystery of signs saying nothing forever. Garden city.

In the cab, he wonders momentarily about his portfolio, if it will ever turn up. He shrugs the thought away, recalls the attractive woman who had entered the room, but admits that he left suddenly as a courtesy. It is not a room to be shared.

* * *

Then one night in a beer hall hallucination – a beautiful painter in the background – Cafferty sees Roberta and Lang, van Zandt and Arlene, Hiromi and the boy, and all the others together again after two or three decades, the dead the abandoned spurned lost, failed … loves, brought again together for a moment – loves, once, lost.

* * *

Strange and rich, a phrase Hiromi stumbles upon. That's the way to go. Well, I have rich parents, and they're sure strange. I hope my clothes are. And I think my taste in Pop music is the taste of the nation's. I could learn a little more about shoes, though. I'd better talk to Hiroko about this.

* * *

Yes, of course I can understand him, I'm capable too, as Roberta knows all too well and ill, of such tremendous passions, overwhelming obsessions – Ophuls, Sternberg. By all means the city. To think I once wanted to leave – but then. My early, whining period. To get drunk, to love madly, to take that chance (at "a mistake as long as eternity") – otherwise what?, dying and never knowing. But this question, this matter of loving the whole city the way he does, the kit and kaboodle as Cafferty might say in a lighthearted moment: ah, this is a different matter, more in kind certainly than in degree. Let me see: yes, I love the city. No, I do not love all of it. I do not know all of it, and I doubt that anyone ever could –without becoming an utter boor that is. No, I do not want to leave the city, but not because I love it so much as I find a certain freedom here; call that a love. Perhaps. But it's like a cat, the city that is. It does not require your love; you give it yours and it can just as soon walk away. Is she, to give the city a sex for the moment, is she a great mistress, a great courtesan? Ready to spurn, to crush the lover underfoot, after having reduced his dignity and wallet dry. Whatever Lola wants, indeed. Perhaps that might be the metaphor and the narrative he really should be writing. But would he then play Sternberg or Jannings to Tokyo's Lola? (Or Tokyo as Lulu?) Probably both. But to go back: yes, I can say that I "love" the city in a manner of speaking, but I will not allow myself to be ruled by it. And as much as I admire, am attracted to, desire to know ever more intimately the city, I can still all the meanwhile stand back, see it for what it is not – see, for example the drastic perhaps irremediable shape it is in – and see it for what it pretends to be, see the false lover behind the true (And thus see myself? Getting close here, Lang.), and be prepared to renounce it should that time and event ever become necessary, which I pray will not occur because, well – I love the city too much. Perhaps he is on to something – perhaps not.

Chapter 9

IKEBUKURO–OTSUKA

Roberta's Tokyo – they'd meet once or twice a week, she chose the places, a classical café in Nakano, tempura at the Hilltop Hotel – you know, the writer's hotel – they carefully avoided the west and ... and eventually they extended their borders, began to explore Nishi-Ogikubo, Kokubunji, Kunitachi – and he began to explore the city more, both directions, came to be intrigued as she'd known he would and hoped he would, the Lang she knew, the Lang she suspected – Lang, liking almost all of Tokyo, hers his.

* * *

BOYS IN PINK HOUSES

A lingerie shop named Revenger
A mansion named Gloria
A studio named La Quan

* * *

My horrid ability to imagine the worst. Woke up this morning from a dream in which I discovered – I couldn't even be there with them! – that Lang and Roberta had died. Van Zandt had left me a note, and all he said was, "cut yourself out of it, man, cut yourself out as soon as you can!" And Arlene had left without a trace.

* * *

R'n'L!!!!!!!!

I remember reading that Kyoto was never officially undeclared the capitol once Tokyo was so declared. Meaning that the country has two capitols. I thought it was in Waley, but my third reading of the book proves me wrong. (Now I am convinced that books are haunted and can read their reader's minds. I mean, I was *sure* that info was in Waley. Now I suspect that the reading ghosts or whatever they are read my thoughts and decided to play a trick on me. Or maybe we are each born with book hobgoblins. They aren't peculiar to each single book, but to each reader ((or lover, or film-maker or whatever)). I mean this has happened before – and I don't think it's a matter of a now-failing once-perfect memory. You know that book *Isles of Gold*? I was convinced – no, I *am* convinced – that I read in it the location of Hiraga Gennai's grave. Now: pfft!, can't find it. ((You don't know where his grave is, do you? Or was it the museum I was looking for?)))

Where was it, in Tsukadajima?, that those three children just re-fused to be photographed, but kept teasing us to try? Finally got 'em though, and a good one. I even went back a week later to give 'em a copy, but couldn't find them anywhere.

I remember always being aware of *Bringing Up Baby*, but I can't re-ally remember when exactly I turned on to Cary Grant – saw the whole truth and shebang and accepted him as my personal savior (as should we all, and then, in Jackie deShannon's phrase, "the world will be a better place / for you ((bop bop)), and me ((bop bop)) / you just wait ((bop bop)), and seeee").

The day I lost it completely!

Speaking of the 80s, I'll never forget all that late-night TV porno, the pantie diaries, the girls on their knees eating bananas. And besides the porn, remember the laughing prankster Jesus? Christ, can there have ever been a better decade in TV?

I remember getting drunk last night, but not the first time I ever got drunk. One should, I think. But I do remember my first drink. Which I can't tell you about. (Actually, now that I think of it, that was my second drink; the first I just remembered.)

I remember my first sight of Tokyo all too well, because we passed right on through it and boy was I ever disappointed. Can't quite remember the exact date of my first day here though, but it must've been about May 1980. Jeez, that's great, Spring, a new decade. Sweet.

My bed was always falling apart and I had to fix it every other morning, and one day I told Kathryn about it and we found out we were sleeping in the same bed – so to speak.

There's all that talk about Elvis's heroes being Dean Martin and Perry Como and the like, right? So what? They were every young pop singer's at the time. But don't also forget that Elvis said he wished he had a voice like Clyde's. Now dig *that*, my friends.

And I remember – oh, yes I do – Lang saying how anxious he was to get out of Tokyo. And then how anxious he was to get back.

I remember always thinking what a great memory I have, and then SJ proving me so mortally wrong.

Anyway, don't forget to put a little love in your heart. (Always did like Jackie de Shannon – gotta make "When You Walk in the Room" my ringtone.)

* * *

And they call me mad? A-ha! I like this now. Of course, he only wants to out-do me here. Show me your love. Heard that line often enough. Said it too. And had the love shown. Bodies, loves, tears, slop. Tra la la, the city goes tra la la and tumbles out of my arms. Tra la la I stumble to my bed and bid ye all ... Morpheus rises, and pins me against the walls of memory and dream; we embrace, fuck our ... fuck our what? ... and from our copulations the daughter-son called Tokyo is born. Is that what he wants to hear? Is that the love he professes? He may understand the city street-level, and even the vast underbelly; but what does he know of a city's dreams? Copulate and dream, hallucinate the city; see it for the hallucination that it is – not just the ghosts of history, not just the drunken roiling crowds, not even just the erotics of everyday life – but be hallucinated in turn by the city. The monk in Ginza with his begging bowl and hat that covers his eyes; the parking lot attendants at Seed; the college girl getting seven hundred yen an hour waiting tables at Cozy

Corner: could he come up with them? And their dreams of life and the city? Or could they hallucinate him? Would they want to? But they in their own way also join Morpheus and together copulate with the city they give birth to. He has much work to do. Tra la la, Marianne.

* * *

Kazuo is blessed, a challenging job, international clients, good friends, and Kazuko. Once a week he joins his coworkers for a post-work drink, followed by dinner, and then on occasion an extra drink or two, The girls in the office – to whom he is invariably polite – could envy him, could desire him, but his own grace precludes those possibilities and only renders them the more selfless. His male and female colleagues like to work with him as he pushes them further without anyone getting hurt. They trust him. And his superiors keep their eyes on him, grooming him along for a future executive position.

Surely, there must be something wrong.

This week's office party is not unlike any other. The round of beers, the variety of foods, the good cheer and jokes, the flirtations, the bosses leaving early (though not before leaving a good sum towards the bill) so that the younger workers can relax. At a neighboring table, one of the girls notices some former university classmates, and invites them over. Among them are a recently arrived foreign couple. They are young and fresh; they've come to Japan for two years to teach English and pay back their student loans. Their Japanese is awful and so everyone has a good laugh. The man is interested in high-tech gadgets, and has heard a lot about Japanese TV comedy shows; his wife finds bonsai fascinating, and also wants to take flower arranging lessons. She has bonsai at home, in fact is a member of an international bonsai society. No, they don't know much about Japanese advertising, though there certainly seems to be a lot of it, the man remarks, "I mean, we've been bombarded with it since the minute we got off the plane. You hear messages from loudspeakers on the streets, all the neon everywhere, the ads on the trains, gee, it's just really everywhere, and a lot of it in the four different writing systems. But the beer commercials seem very good." With that another round is ordered. Kazuo takes it upon himself to offer a few remarks about the Japanese approach to advertising, and also manages to introduce his own firm's work, the client-company relationship, the top-level art directors, the independents and mavericks. The couple is surprised to learn that one can find advertising industry magazines on the racks in bookstores, and copywriters and art directors, pop stars in their own right, appearing on TV talk shows. Talk turns naturally to pop culture. The couple is also amazed – "weirded out," as they put it – at all the cuteness they see around them. Kazuo is unable to offer any sort of explanation. A couple of the office assistants try – to no avail. This frustration results finally in an order of *saké*, and more foods, and naturally, a discussion of Japanese food. Both of the Americans like it – or much of it. "Boy, one of those sushis was so tough I must've chewed it thirty or forty times, and I still couldn't swallow it easily. Finally, I just had to wash it down with a good slug of beer." This amuses the Japanese, and Kazuo remarks that there is no special method, no one can soften up some of those "sushis," and that the thing to do is chew it only a couple of times and then – yes, wash it down with a – "slug?," a good swallow – of beer. "Well, I'll be!" exclaims the man, a remark which no one of the Japanese seems to understand, but to which they nod agreeably. Some *eda-mame* are ordered and this the couple likes very much, their hands going back and forth repeatedly popping the soy beans into their eager mouths, a couple of the girls hiding their giggles. The woman then remarks – flatteringly, it must be admitted – at how good all of the people at the table speak English. This everyone quickly denies. One of the women asks if it shouldn't be "well" – and the Americans exchange puzzled looks, without answering. Kazuo replies that their English may be just passable, and that he and his colleagues have no illusions about their lack of facility in the language. (Though in this regard *he* is being overly modest.) He adds though that his company sponsors English lessons for all of his colleagues, an offer that most of them take advantage of. Reciprocally, he wonders if the couple plan to take Japanese lessons. The woman answers that before leaving home they took a three-month crash course, but now that they're here, it's like they're back in class, day one. But they'll give it a good try. And then she orders a little more *saké*, and more of "these here green beans."

More and more good cheer.
Surely something is not right.

But there isn't.

And Kazuo sleeps well that night.

* * *

You've been tried and thrown over, Tokyo, but I won't be, Hiromi defies.

* * *

No, not for the first time in the two or three weeks since he's returned from those four months in Middle Europe, does van Zandt pick up a paper to discover five stories on his small, generally unheard of hometown. In the six years she has lived in Tokyo, Roberta has come across seven such items concerning her equally small town in Northern California, the last being the September before last, this being Halloween midnight, she sees no end in sight.

* * *

– No, no, I'm sure it's here somewhere.
– I think they tore it down.
– No, they wouldn't have.
– But we don't seem to be getting anywhere near it.
– Well, was it by Ikebukuro or by Otsuka station?
– Or in between?
– Uhm …
– Oh, Kaoru!
– Maybe it's just between his ears!
– A point of light, eh?
– And you say you saw it once from the train and thought you could see all of Tokyo in it?
– Definitely between his ears.
– What kind of light? A point? There must be a million points of light around here. It's certainly as bright as Ginza or Shinjuku.
– Or Shibuya.
– Right, how do you expect us to find one single light?
– Well, I suppose we have to let it catch us off guard.
– Oh, so we're not really looking for it –
– It's looking for us?
– This was after a little boozing, was it?
– No, no – it's got to be here somewhere. How could I make up anything like this?
– That's a point.
– I remember a nice bar here. I looked into a glass and thought I could see the next five years – and I did: lost my girl, lost my job,

had to move back to the country and start all over again.

- Are you sure you want to find this point of light, Kaoru?
- Hey, I've been to the same bar!
- Must've drunk out of the same glass.
- Yeah, let's go look for a glass of whisky.
- Hold on just a bit more, guys.
- Ah, we're getting closer to the porno theaters. You can see a lot there, a special perspective.
- Front row, and you can see the world.
- Is the Seibu here still the world's biggest department store?
- Why?
- Just wondering.
- No, I think the Sogo in Yokohama is now.
- Well, I suppose it doesn't matter.
- Why would it?

And they continue in the long curve from station to station. Kaoru was drunk that night, but he wasn't in Ikebukuro, and he did see the light.

- Now can we get a drink, Kaoru?
- Yeah, how 'bout it? There are lots of places in Otsuka.
- Yes, but you have to be careful, there are lots of gangsters around here.
- And not only Chinese.
- Look at that old lady with all the cats.
- Say, here's where that great acupuncturist has his office.
- He's Banana Yoshimoto's acupuncturist, you know.
- Really?
- Yes, Maria's too.
- They say he really is a miracle worker.
- Well, I'm in the mood for only one miracle right now.
- Strange area out here.
- Reminds me of Ueno – you know, lots of people in from the country for the first time, sort of shabby, but in a rough, pleasant way.
- Peasant way.
- Rowdy.
- Yeah – it can be fun.
- It can be rough, too.

* * *

"Rich and strange," it occurs to Hiroko, I'm certainly not rich and I don't think I'm so strange, like van Zandt says. I'm just a downtown girl trying to get uptown. Is that so strange? I don't think so. And I'd like to be rich. Now that's not strange. But all those rich stars on TV are all a bit strange. Hmm.

* * *

DEATH LETTER BLUES

Got a death letter for ya', baby,
gonna mail it C.O.D.;
a death letter with your name, baby,
for that time you fucked with me.

* * *

We watched her – and we watched each other watching her.
– *Anatahan*, (Josef von Sternberg, 1957)

* * *

BAKIN AND THE *EIGHT DOGS*

How even to begin to describe *The Biographies of Eight Dogs (Nanso Satomi Hakkenden)*? And yet, except for a few pages, it remains untranslated into English. Here is a lovely paragraph.

"Shino had gone to bed, but could not sleep in his impatience for the dawn. His head was filled with thoughts about the future. He realized that he was alone, that there was no one to stop him from leaving, but he could not help feeling unhappy that he was now to go far from the graves of his parents and the place where he was born. Hamaji, who regretted his departure no less than he, slipped out of bed and, taking care lest her parents now snoring in the back room should waken, those parents toward whom she felt a resentment she could not voice, she soundlessly stepped over the threshold of the barrier of her maiden reserve, which had hitherto kept her from going to Shino. Her knees trembled, and she could scarcely walk. How dreary, sad, bitter, and hateful the inconstant world now seemed."

The fall of a great house – the Ambersons comes first to mind, among other examples – is often more compelling a story than the rise, or fall, of any individual. The house's restoration offers no less a satisfaction.

In 15th century Japan, besieged and near defeat, the general Satomi Yoshizane shouts out that he will give his daughter Fusehime to anyone who can bring him the head of his adversary. It is done: by his watch-dog, Yatsufusa! Fusehime herself keeps her father's promise, and the new couple go away to live in a cave. A year later, Fusehime is accidentally shot by an arrow meant for her canine husband, and in her death throes a white vapor emerges from the wound and envelopes the rosary she wears around her neck. "Eight beads rise into the sky, each marked with the Chinese character for one of the Confucian virtues. The eight beads are subsequently found in the hands of the newly born sons of eight men whose surnames begin with the word *inu*, Dog. The eight heroes meet and separate many times, but finally they assemble and by their efforts restore the Satomi family to its former glory." (Keene)

His biographer says that Bakin "interpreted an age to itself," with the *Eight Dogs* being called "the grand culmination of Tokugawa culture." Zolbrod goes on to say: "His life exemplified a social trend that led to the Meiji Restoration and the modernization of Japan. The same forces that drove Bakin to wander as a masterless samurai, struggle as a popular author, and attempt to "restore" his family caused many samurai to shift their loyalty from their overlords to the forces working for the overthrow of the Tokugawa government."

The "hermit of Edo" was born into a samurai family in 1767. As a young boy he waited on his lord's idiot grandson. When his father was slandered by a fellow retainer, the family stipend was reduced by half. The lifelong themes came into being. As they are for this author too: as separation was the theme of his life; so (re)union would be the theme of his art. In Bakin's case this especially meant restoration of the family (even his name means "restore"). The father died when Bakin was eight. At the age of thirteen, he left his service and became a *ronin*. Eventually, restless, resentful, he renounced his samurai status and began years of relentless wandering, working here and there as a comedian, a calligrapher, a fortune teller, until he became seriously ill and was nursed by his self-sacrificing elder brother. In 1785 his mother died; the next year, a brother. In 1798, his beloved elder brother. Bakin was all remorse, regretting the unfilial years.

He began to write. Apprenticed himself to Kyōden; lived with the bookseller Tsutaya. Published chapbooks, averaging ten a year. From about 1796, he supported himself by selling *geta* and teaching calligraphy, until around 1806 when he could support himself and his family solely on his writing – the first person in Japan to do so, with the possible exception of Rokitsu in Osaka.

In 1793 he married the uneducated, insulting, hysterical and chronically ill widow Aida O'Hyaku, of whom he would eventually write that the best years they had together were these when they lived in separate houses. In 1798 Sōhaku was born, the son upon whom Bakin placed all his hopes for the restoration of the family name.

His writing grew ever more popular. And thus the great conflict of his life came into being. A samurai at heart, he wrote popular fiction that expressed samurai ideals; this he hoped would give him the wherewithal by which to regain his family's samurai status and so be able to abandon this lowest class of writing; but as the decades went by, and his fame and skill increased, the prospect of restoration receded ever further.

The work was historical, and drew upon every form of Japanese fiction, poetry and drama, as well as Chinese popular fiction. It was plainly didactic, the large themes being the reunion and restoration of a family, filial piety, courage and sacrifice. It was also prodigious: thirty novels in ten years; the 181-chapter *Eight Dogs* taking twenty-eight years to write, the longest novel in China or Japan and possibly the longest ever, anywhere. Scores of essays, poetry collections, literary criticism (*Edo Authors*, a history in which he becomes the culminating point of Tokugawa period fiction), comic poetry, plays, miscellania. His work "included material about shrines and temples, foreign songs, famous courtesans, authors such as Hachimonjiya, Jishō, Ejima Kiseki, Chikamatsu, and Ihara Saikaku, place names, interpretation of dreams, the Archetypal Hero who as an infant is abandoned to the sea, poetry on rain, Japanese gods, semi-legendary heroes, the history of Iidamachi, the Kantō dialect, children's stories like *The Monkey and the Crab*, *Peach Boy*, and *The Tongue-cut Sparrow*, holiday observances, animals, plants, genealogies, astrology, travel, love-suicide, and Chinese poetry and fiction." (Zolbrod) The comparison between Proust and Lady Murasaki is often and tiresomely made. That between Bakin and – who? – yes: Balzac, rarely so, but the fit is obvious.

He lived in an age of repression, when each and every act "had to be thought through ten times" for fear of arrest (look at Utamaro's fate). He was ever fearful of giving the government displeasure. An 1806 portrait shows him tall and thin and sitting in an urn; the legend says, "Within an urn the universe." Conservative, traditionalist, short-tempered, he preferred to be alone. In 1816 he attended his last public gathering for twenty years, and withdrew from "the floating world." Cantankerous and even cruel, he criticized all his colleagues. His few "friends" he rarely met; fortunately for him – and for them too, perhaps – they lived far away and so could only correspond. He was mistrustful, careful, distant. For all the enthusiasm and affection in his fiction, there seems to have been a near-total failure of all personal relationships. He wrote this horrible sentence: "It is a pleasure to be without friends." He seems never to have known "the pleasure of any love affair." The son in whom he placed all his hopes died young; unfortunately he appears to have lacked any imagination; Zolbrod calls him a "self-pitying parasite." Only in very late old age did Bakin express any affection: for his daughter-in-law O'Michi who was his amanuensis during his last decade of blindness.

In 1836, twelve years before his death, under the pretext of celebrating his seventieth birthday, he held a "writers and artists party" for more than seven-hundred prominent guests. The actual purpose was to raise funds so as to purchase a samurai patent for his grandson, thus finally restoring the Takizawa line to its former status. In this Bakin succeeded.

* * *

In her dream, Roberta is in Meiji-no-mori National Park in Western Tokyo, and where she mistakenly expects to find the tomb of Hirohito, the Showa Emperor. (Later, upon waking, she will wonder whatever drove her to go there.) Instead, she comes to a staircase made of white opaque glass. On either side are doors of the same material. Behind them she hears voices and can just make out the faces of a few relatives – an aunt, an uncle, a couple of cousins she liked – and the few friends of her childhood. They are all either speaking Japanese or their voices are the various instruments of the various versions of John Coltrane's "My Favorite Things." Despite her inability to go forward and see her family and friends, Roberta is content – content to be once again so near to these few loved ones, to her adopted language, and to a piece of music that she discovered when she was twelve.

Curiously, at the same time that Roberta is having her musical dream, Cafferty has a dream in which he thinks to himself, "I should have been an accordion player." In his dream too, of course, we hear 'Trane.

* * *

City beating in your heart –

forcing the blood to flow
your hand to compose
your mind to revolt –

forcing you to kiss me.

* * *

–   Whew, this city never stops, does it?
–   Are we still inside the city proper?
–   Whatever could you mean by that?
–   You know, inside the twenty-three wards? Is Ogikubo part of one of the twenty-three wards?
–   I really don't know, sorry.
–   I really don't care. What is this talk of "the city proper"? What's a "proper" city?
–   I only meant classical Tokyo.
–   What's "classical" Tokyo then?
–   The traditional twenty-three wards. Isn't it?
–   There is nothing traditional about them. They've changed boundaries, they've changed names, and they've changed number too. I think there used to be sixteen, and at one time as many as forty or so. Maybe.
–   Maybe?
–   The point is that they have not always been twenty-three.
–   Have they ever been forty-seven, that would seem to be more Japanese.
–   I don't think so. Another point is that they can change again.
–   Change to forty-seven?
–   If necessary.
–   That's a lot of wards.

- But why are there twenty-three? That's not much of a Japanese number.
- Well, it's almost half of forty-seven.
- ???
- I don't know why there are twenty-three, there just are – for now.
- So, what about Ogikubo? Is it part of one of the twenty-three wards?
- No, I think it's part of one of the cities.
- Part of one of the cities! It's part of Tokyo.
- Yeah.
- Right.
- But Tokyo is made up of twenty cities, or around twenty. I think.
- Wait a minute, you're saying Tokyo has twenty-three wards – for the moment, though the number can change – and that it has another twenty or so cities – even though it itself is a city? That doesn't make sense.
- Well, Tokyo isn't a city!
- What?
- It sure feels like a whole country sometimes!
- Technically speaking, Tokyo is not a city.
- Oh, yes, not a proper city.
- What's a proper city?
- What's an improper one? Take me there.
- But it's always called a city.
- It's not a member of the United Nations.
- Does it have its own army?
- It's certainly got its own economy!
- Ok. The city of Tokyo has wards and cities but neither technically nor properly is it a city.
- It's also got islands.
- Does it have mountain ranges too? I'd love to go hunting and hiking in Tokyo.
- Uhm, yes, it does have mountains.
- It what?
- Yes, it does. Tokyo's big.
- No one's denying that. We all know it's big – just look around you – and after all, we have come this far, and we know, or I think we still know, that we're still inside it – and as big as it may be, there have to be limits, and I'm not so sure, that by my definition of a proper city, it should include islands and mountains.
- But it does, it really does.
- You're insane. What kind of a place is Tokyo anyway, by your

standards?
- Well, I'd call it a city.
- But you just said that properly and technically –
- I know, I know, but you said that it's a city that contains cities, and that doesn't sound quite right to me.
- I know, but the fact is –
- More like the fantasy is.
- But what about Ogikubo?
- What about it? Is it a city too that contains cities? Will I turn out to be a city – not technically or properly speaking of course, I beg your pardon – that contains cities?
- No, all I wanted to say was to get back to the original question: is Ogikubo part of one of the twenty-three wards?
- Well, no one here knows for sure, not anymore.
- So, let's go into that bar and ask –
- And linger over the question.
- Good idea, Kaoru

* * *

Monday. It was the evening before the Emperor's 60th anniversary, it was the same street I'd dreamed of – a gray sky like a monk's robe, a suggestion that it had recently rained, the few pink leaves of the cherry blossoms scattered here and there – so all this wet pink and gray all like a tinted photograph – and it was my street, the street leading to my home!

* * *

Notwithstanding?, but shouldn't the costs be a delight? Why negativize, Cafferty, as usual, connects. I delight in not knowing where I am going – apart from those promised appointments, about which I am exact and punctual. To discover the city, to make it my own ... what does Henry James say? Oh, I'd forever rather be lost in Tokyo than found in any other city.

* * *

- You slippery fish, I know you, van Zandt, I know you through and through, like I know ... like I know .. uhm, whaddo I know? .. like I know my mother's backside – uhn, no, that's not what I meant –
- Your mother's backside!?

- Wait a minute. Like I know, my mother, my backside.
- Your backside!?
- Frontside, too, ha! But no, like I know … the way home from the station in the snow when I'm crawling dead drunk like I will be tonight if I can't catch my last train. How d'ya' like that?
- You're comparing me to a zigzag in the snow?
- Not very complimentary, I'll grant you. Let's see, no, I know you like I know all 47 ronin. No, too complimentary.
- Ouch. But do you really know them all?
- Oh yes, they were my heroes when I was a kid. But no matter. I know you like I know my bankbook. No, I don't, my wife knows that, I certainly don't. I know you then like I know … oh damn, you're a foreigner, what is there to know? No, don't take that in the wrong way, please. It's just that we Japanese tend to see you all alike.
- Oh, I know that alright. Thanks very much. And so do we foreigners tend to see you all alike as well. How's that?
- Undeserved! But you are a foreigner, and a rather different one, I'll grant you that. Hell, van Zandt, maybe I don't know you at all.
- And I'll grant you that.
- But I don't even know your first name.
- Van will do.
- … an ancient race …
- Do you know him?
- Who? You? I just said I don't.
- Not what I meant. But skip it.
- Hop, jump. Two more beers?
- By all means.
- I take it you're not American?
- No, Dutch.
- We have long relations with your people.
- Yeah, yeah, but you do not have such a long one with me.
- True. So, do you think you know me?
- Can't say that I do.
- Then we're off to a good start.
- Start? I thought we were finishing. I do have a last train, you know.
- I know alright, just as I know that it's not for a few hours yet – and quite a few more drinks I hope.
- That's the spirit. Waitress! Two more, please.
- Anyway, Kaoru, as I was saying, or trying to say, we've met a few times now, here and there, and I am glad we happened to run into each other tonight, and have a chance to talk alone. We've met at

a few gatherings of mutual friends, not really met or talked together, so I was just happy that we could get together casually and by
chance this way. Get to know each other a bit more, you know.
Those other times we've never really talked, you've kept rather to
yourself, and if we are going to keep being in the same room to-
gether now and then, I thought it might be a good idea if we got to
know each other a bit better. You know, instead of, as – what's the
phrase? – nodding acquaintances.
-    Is that a Japanese phrase? It ought to be.
-    I'm not sure, my Japanese isn't that good.
-    I know that.
-    But good enough to know who my superiors are.
-    Then it must be very good.
-    Not really. Set phrases.
-    Like many foreigners.
-    Now don't start generalizing again. I'm certainly not about you.
-    No?
-    No. I have no idea who the hell you are, but as I say, we do keep
     running into one another, and so maybe I ought to have a better
     idea of you.
-    Yes, have a better idea of me alright. Instead of a bad idea, is that
     what you have?
-    No, I mean that I have no idea, good or bad. All I know is that
     you're a salary-man, and that you lived in Gunma until you had to
     come here. And that we have a couple of mutual friends.
-    Oh yes.
-    Yes, and they are good friends of mine. Lang and Roberta, Hiroko
     and Hiromi, your friend Hiro. How do you know him?
-    Hiro? Oh, he's a nice kid. Lives with his parents in Setagaya-ku.
     Works for a PR company. His company did something for my
     company once. That's how we met. When the work was finished
     there was a party at the Imperial Hotel. Hiroko and Hiromi were
     there, working, you know, like waitresses, pouring drinks, lighting
     cigarettes, that kind of thing. Afterwards, we all went out together,
     seems he knew them outside of their work. We kept in touch, Hiro
     and I. Some time later he invited me to a party and the girls were
     there, and so were your foreign friends.
-    My friends who happen to be foreigners.
-    Whatever. One thing lead to another, and now occasionally I am
     invited to parties where all these people are. It is an interesting
     experience.

- What is? The parties?
- No, being among this group of foreigners whom I do not really know. They're always talking.
- Well, that's what people do at parties.
- Yes, yes, of course. But they are always talking so well. The foreigners talk about their life in Japan, and the girls respond in their silly way that is not always so silly, they seem genuinely interested in the foreigners, and they all talk together, if you know what I mean.
- Uhm, I think I do. But is that all so strange?
- Strange? Perhaps not, just not part of my experience, you see.
- Not really. I don't know you, after all. I don't know your experience.
- Well, there has been very little with foreigners, until now, and I have to confess, I do not always know what to say.
- Such as?
- I am used to making what you call small talk. These people want to make what you might call big talk. I cannot do that with a foreigner. I always think he or she wants something more from me than I can offer.
- Kaoru, we too are experts at small talk. Big talk is just talk, like you and me now, making conversation, talking about whatever interests us. No big deal.
- But sometimes it seems to me that you, they, want to know secrets, how we feel.
- What's wrong with that if it's sincere? It's just a way of getting to know a person, getting closer.
- That's what I mean. Why would anyone want that?
- To know another person.
- Again, why would anyone want that?
- You're married, right?
- Yes.
- Then presumably you know your wife.
- More or less, sufficiently. What's your point?
- You know her feelings.
- What does that have to do with anything?
- You do, don't you? Or don't you?
- She is my wife, we have a family, I have a job and responsibility. We respond to one another, our feelings are not a part of it.
- Then are you saying that you do not know her?
- No, of course I know her.
- Does she know your feelings?
- What feelings?

- Look, I do not want to sound too much like an American, but don't you think that a husband and a wife have to share certain feelings together?
- You mean our intimate relations?
- No, or not necessarily. But to understand one another day by day, the things you do –
- What I do is my feelings. What she does is hers.
- I see.
- Do you?
- Not exactly, but that's good.
- Good that you do not see?
- Good that I can see somewhat.
- Maybe. I don't understand.
- I maybe don't either. But that's ok. So, Hiro introduced you to the bunch, eh?
- You mean Lang and the others?
- Yes.
- Yes, he did.
- And what do you think of us all?
- Oh, like I said, you're a curious group. That Roberta's ok, she speaks Japanese alright too, I have to admit. But that husband of hers, that Lang. Let me ask you – are they really husband and wife?
- Well, yes and no. You see, they once were, really were. That was in Europe, some time in America too. Then she got it into her head to come to Japan. He never really wanted to, come here, that is. So they took a break, their marriage took a break. But then it lasted too long. He always thought she'd come for a few months, have her "Japan experience," and be back in his arms again. But she liked it more than ever, and he couldn't handle that. Thought he'd have to come here and get her back, back to Europe, that is. Or at least I think back to Europe. He'd had a passing interest in Japan, everyone does – no offense here – but he could only imagine a full life in Europe, and with her, as wayward as he may have been in the past – I think that's over now – and so, anyway, he came here some months back thinking to retrieve her. Trouble is, she held out, and he had to make his way here, hold on till she saw the light, and was ready to leave. So he lingered and in time, he got to like the place too. In his own way, of course.
- Yes, I've heard parts of this story here and there. But how do you fit in?
- Me? Oh, Roberta and I have been great friends from long before she

married Lang. I was able to get here on a grant, I had an idea for a film. Well, to make a long story short, she helped me out when I first arrived, then I got to work, liked the place well enough to extend my grant, and really work on a very serious film. I got to the point where I thought it was pretty well finished and decided to show it at Image Forum one night. Well, to make a short story even shorter, Roberta hated it and said so. And that was that.

– What do you mean?

– Uhm, well, just that Roberta and I have not really been the best of friends ever since.

– All because of a movie?

– Because of my movie. My movie about my Japan.

– But you're still friends or not?

– We speak to one another. Can we change the subject?

– And Roberta and Lang?

– Well, she was living in Yoyogi at first, that's where she was when Lang first arrived, and then she moved to *shitamachi*, and did not want to live with him. It wasn't so much a rejection of Lang as simply a move for herself.

– I cannot understand this at all, but please continue.

– So he found a place for himself in Kichijoji.

– They were on opposite sides of the city.

– Yes, where the famous twain never meet.

– They never met?

– Oh no, they met. They proffered compromises to one another. *They'd meet once or twice a week, she chose the places, a classical café in Nakano, tempura at the Hilltop Hotel – you know, the writer's hotel – another restaurant in Nakano-Shimbashi, the Vietnamese restaurant in Okubo – they carefully avoided the West and ... and eventually they extended their borders, began to explore Nishi-Ogikubo, Hakusan, Kunitachi, the Pond, that street where the calligraphy shop is – and eventually he began to explore the city more, came to be intrigued as she'd known he would and hoped he would, the Lang she knew, the Lang she suspected – Lang, liking Tokyo! – all of it, or almost all, hers was becoming his, theirs.*

– I cannot understand at all, but please continue.

– So this is where they are at now. From east and west they met in the middle, then they extended their borders. Lang is quickly becoming an expert on the low city, and Roberta is slowly taking a liking to points west. In a word, Kaoru, as I see it, the couple uncoupled is becoming one, a union of all points, center and circumference, or

better, no points but where you are and that is everywhere and that is Tokyo, man and woman, the two and the one, the many and the single.
- Single?
- Singly.
- Divorce?
- Union.
- Separated?
- Let no man declare asunder.
- Then they are together again?
- Not quite.
- Why not?
- They are a difficult couple. Quite separate.
- But not separated.
- Geographically, yes. Marriageably, I hope not.
- But?
- But yes. But no.
- What will happen?
- Happen with what?
- To them!
- Them, who?
- Roberta and Lang!
- Oh, them! Oh yes, what was I saying?
- Van Zandt! You were saying that they might or might not get together again!
- Was I? Oh yes, yes, they might or might not, as you say.
- No, as you said. What will happen?
- I have no idea. What do you think?
- Me? I have no idea. How could I?
- Well, I haven't either. Maybe it's up to you.
- Up to me?
- Sure, why not?
- I hardly know them!
- Precisely, all the better.
- What?! But what can I do?
- Drink up, Kaoru.
- I don't want to drink – I want to know what will happen to your friends.
- My friends and I will be alright. You're a friend, aren't you? You'll be alright, won't you?
- I don't know. I mean, I hope you and I are friends. I think I'm al-

right. Are you alright?
- I believe so.
- Then we're alright.
- Yes, you and I are.
- But Roberta and Lang?
- Well, we're friends, aren't we?
- Yes.
- Then we are alright – and they are alright.
- Are they?
- Why shouldn't they be? Do you know something I don't?
- No, van Zandt, of course not.
- Then we either know everything or nothing. Either way, we're alright.
- And does that mean that Roberta and Lang are alright too?
- How should I know? Don't you know?
- No, I don't.
- Then how are you going to find out? What are you going to do about it? It'd be a shame if they were not together all because of a good friend such as yourself.
- But I hardly know them, what can I do about it?
- Be a good friend.
- But that won't bring them together again.
- Who says it won't?
- Van Zandt, you are drunk.
- Kaoru, you are drunk.
- Yes, but you're not being a good friend now.
- You're right. Waitress!
- Ok, van Zandt, what can we do about Roberta and Lang?
- Oh, that depends.
- Depends on what?
- On them. After all, it's up to them, what do we have to do with it all?
- But you just said –
- Yes I did, Kaoru, and I meant it, but there are limits, you know.
- Limits? Limits to what? To friendship? No, I won't accept that.
- Then what will you accept?
- That we must do something about the situation.
- What can we do?
- I don't know. I don't know at all. It's all rather confusing to me. But we must be able to do something.
- True. Or maybe not. Where are they at, after all? Galivanting about

the city and meeting nowhere. Where are we? Started out in Marun-ouchi, then to Akasaka, now in Kyobashi. (I had my first beer here. My first in Japan, that is.) We wheel about the city, going in circles, one city all cities. No, that's not true, one Tokyo, one Roberta and Lang. Maybe that's it.

– What's what – what "it"?

– Well, they've started their mating dance, don't you see? Wheeling about the city. Like some esoteric Buddhism.

– I'm sorry, but once again, I do not see at all.

– Ok, I mean that we wheel about, we go round and round, well, not exactly, not even round and round, but zigzag and round and twist and shout and turn about and … no, not meet at any center, too many of them, but, well …

– Well?

– Well, they've got a map, I'm sure they can make sense of it all, whatever sense is available, make their own map – that's maybe it. You see, don't you, like I described, they came together – when he arrived, say, he had nowhere to go, but to stay at her place for the first couple of weeks, and then it was clear she wanted to be alone and so he had to find his own place, and he did out west, and slowly they began to come together again by meeting in what they thought were neutral locations, anywhere in between the end-points, and then from that seeming center they branched out till they got to the point where they were in one another's original territories, she sharing *shitamachi* with him, he showing her the splendors and miseries of the high city of the new west. So that's where they are now, but they have to go even further yet. They've only begun to encompass the city. They really ought to take a vacation far west, and one to the tropics too. That's Tokyo too, don't you know. You see what I'm driving at?

– Uhm, not exactly.

– It's simple, really! They use Tokyo, they see it and explore it as a way to get together again! As a way of finding out who each other really is. Old Lang, new Lang, east Roberta, west Roberta, high Lang, low Roberta and vice-versa. Center and circumference, everything exploded, everything coupled. Union, Kaoru, union!

– Union.

– Now you've said it, old friend.

– New friend.

– Now you've said it.

– Have I?

- Certainly.
- I have?
- We both have.
- Ok.
- Ok? Ok yes, or ok maybe?
- Ok, ok.
- Ok double – you have said it.
- I guess.
- So.

* * *

Ah, this city, Lang writes in a private notebook, got to you in time, Man! Just when you needed me and me you, eh? So be it. We wrestle, make love, conquer one another, and transcend, transcend, as Patti says, lots of work to do together yet, lanes and lines to discover, exploration, meditation (sounds like Van) – and then we become one!

* * *

The earth reels. Tokyo suffers. Too sudden a change in the weather, and people lose the ability to converse, they stumble to work, shift subjects in mid-sentence, and become generally unfriendly. It is not a pretty sight to see, and children should not be exposed to this uncanny phenomenon. Science has no explanation, nor psychology. Come to Tokyo only if you are fully prepared to discover this within yourself, this known only to Tokyoites.

* * *

- Last time I ate sushi in Tsukiji at 5AM was in my university days. But then I could take it, staying up all night, drinking with my pals, but now I feel it all day. Don't even seem to recover till late afternoon, and then for only a few hours till I start again. I also knew the way home. Don't even know where I am right now, what's around the corner. What do they say, a glass of alcohol takes an hour to get out of your system? At that rate I won't sober up for a year and a half. If I stop drinking entirely right now. That doesn't even rate an if. What about tobacco? Do the lungs clear up at a similar sort of rate? If I have cancer now, will my lungs clear up by the time I die of it?

–   So why stop, Kaoru, if you're having fun?

* * *

–   So now do you understand?
–   All too well.
–   Well said.
–   As well.

* * *

I have watched
the city from a distance at night
and wondered why I wrote no poem.
Come! yes,
the city is ablaze for you
and you stand and look at it.

– William Carlos Williams

Compare:

Chiamavi il cielo e intorno vi si gira,
Mostrandovi le sue belleze eterne,
E l'occhio vostro pur a terra mira.

– *Purgatorio* XIV, 148-150

* * *

SCENE NINE: OFFICE

It was a strange building in Shimbashi that revealed to her that Japanese architecture, or rather, the city of Tokyo itself taken as a single piece of architecture, is all parts of an enormous jigsaw puzzle (one of those that want to get into the record books) that have scattered all over the place (for whatever reason, earthquake, a child suddenly rushing in, the scurrying of the players to prevent a drink from falling on the already assembled parts) all over the place. Many still remain on the table, but quite a few thousand are under the table or the piano, on chair seats or stuck between the cushion and the backrest, against the walls or on the lower bookshelves, one or two inside a pant's cuff, even one is later discovered in the hostess's hair. It will be a full three weeks before all the pieces are finally found. Or almost all, a few simply disappear: one is found three days later in a nearby gutter; another winds up behind a neighbor's fishtank; and a third in a child's toybox.

The specific difficulty with this particular puzzle is that once it is about half assembled, it suddenly becomes apparent to the players (for that in the end is what they are) that it seems to be a trompe l'oeil picture, and not at all the flat representation of a helicopter shot over Shinjuku that was depicted on the box. Instead, it seems to be an interior, it looks like an office – when viewed from a particular angle. When viewed from another however, it is also an interior, but this time a home. From yet another, the interior is an office building lobby, and this is the most difficult perspective from which to assemble the puzzle as it is the most boringly minimalist (to adapt the art term to what is essentially and usually one of those dead blank spots of architecture the world over); and finally, from a fourth point of view, the interior is a floor of a department store, women's clothing.

The woman enters the office that perfectly matches the one in the puzzle. Rows of desks, papers piled high. More noise it seems than is on the street: conversations, some loud, some whispered; electronics; a radio coming from one corner; little laughter; the constant pouring of tea and lips smacking (management only); the steady clack clack clack of outdated but still useful office machinery; paper being shuffled, torn, dropped, rumpled. One man is shining his shoes; two women are distributing tea; three men are at a table in a reception nook discussing something important; lots of cigarette smoke; a few partitions, but nothing to separate personnel by degree of authority, experience or salary. The only sign of such is that at the head of every two facing rows of desks is one set at the perpendicular. Bad travel posters are on one wall; lots of calendars, one or two from last year still (purely oversight, not for the pictures certainly); there is one rack of current magazines and newspapers; a very long set of shelves overflowing with professional journals; another shelf of documents, records. For all the seeming basic order – rows of desks in a neat arrangement – the woman still has to wend her way about: this person to avoid, that pile of old papers not to knock over, this flower pot not to bump into, and those computers on the floor (to be thrown out). She surveys the scene, takes a deep breath, and begins to walk, to inspect every face in the place; she begins at the left side of the room (the east side of the city), and goes on her way, up one aisle and down the next, determined to inspect every face, but how can she be sure that by the end of her route she will have seen every man's face in the office as there is so much movement taking place? She is well aware of her predicament – but can't just shout out, "Will everyone just stop!" In fact, she suddenly wonders to herself, isn't it uncanny how she seems to have gone unnoticed? Wouldn't she have expected to be greeted by someone and asked her business here? But no, nothing of the sort has occurred. But she is too busy to figure this out right now. As she has no one's attention it will be that much easier for her to accomplish her task here. She has determined that if she walks the room two-and-one-half times, then the probability is that she will have encountered every face in the office.

She begins her careful, methodical walk.

She finishes, and alas, has not met her man.

She leaves, somewhat frustrated, but determined. Surely he can't be purposely avoiding me, she wonders to herself. He has no idea of my existence. I'm only trying to help. And surely he does want his photos back. I wonder what they mean exactly to him. He can't have any idea that all I want to do is return his portfolio to him.

Don't I?

*　*　*

Marianne's eyes were like JK's, deeply set, the irises small and intense, the lids heavily and darkly made up, and in any variety of colors the effect was always the same; depth was also added to by the long thin bangs that seemed almost to sink into the sockets, that the wind waved this way and that never allowing one a clear whole view into her deeps and adding that much more to the changing, changeless mystery that was the ever changing Marianne.

*　*　*

You take a poor mid-western girl and put her in Tokyo and whadda'ya get? A poor mid-western girl in Tokyo. No big bones about it. Everyone says I'm so well-grounded, rooted. To what? Tokyo? Tokyo's no vacation, and it sure ain't no home. While I am here, I am here to ... well, do all that stuff a body'd do in any city where you have to make a living. Couldn't I just not make a living for once in my life? Nothing exotic, just something interesting for a change? All I know of Europe is from what I've seen in the movies, the television ads, high-school history lessons. Let's see, the Treaty of Westphalia, the Battle of Limoges – no, not Limoges, that's a perfume I think, the Battle of Utrecht or Breda, no, that's the surrender that came at the end of the Battle of whatever that kept the Turks out of Europe thanks to Velázquez. Kant was the city's timekeeper. Pascal is a woman's name, a film by Rossellini, who married Ingrid Bergman – is that circumferential? Was it a mole or a horse that drove Nietzche over the edge? The bakers of Vienna saved Paris and that's where we get croissants from. Coffeehouses, little girls, and the assault on language: Kakania. Crêpes Suzettes were a burning failure that pleased the king's niece. And polaroids were invented because Land's niece asked him why it took so long to develop a picture. No, that's an American story. Rembrandt's wife was named Saskia which I hope I will be named in another lifetime. The stirrup. Amounts of rainfall. Vlad the Impaler. California grapes in France. Dreyfus. Blériot. People used to really riot at premieres. Hugo. Was it red caps they waved? A history of caps, or hats as history – as good as rainfall. Why not shoes (Dante's sandals)?, or shirts? Or fans; Byron's letters. Three poets dead of Roman fever. Well, more or less Rome. Italians no longer eat, or drink soup, and Italian men are the only ones who think they are sexy in a suit and no socks. "Thanks, Mama, for the one hundred lire, I'm on my way to America." The Romans shaved, the barbarians did not. The Italians eat horsemeat, but we cowgirls don't eat our best friends. The guy who loved Laura invented tourism. The Goths, great names, Visigoths, can't remember the others. The Hun. "The Boshe are no man's fools." Foreigners working in Japan are the equivalent of the Greek slaves in Rome.

* * *

I have heard the cicadas in Meiji Jingu, Kazuko ruminates. And I have seen the irises in Kameido, and wisteria and plum and cherry blossoms. But why would the morning glory be the city flower? Why not the iris or the wisteria? Oh, maybe it's the name: sunrise! And the remaining marshes and reeds of the Musashi Plain. I have also seen the hundreds and thousands of small gardens or plants in windows and verandas. Yes, I have seen this green Tokyo.

Chapter 10

SUGAMO–KOMAGOME

Lang was changing, it was clear to us all, and Roberta liked it, liked this Lang, a Lang she'd always suspected; and Lang liked her: she was an unsuspected Roberta, a neglected Roberta, and a Roberta she too acknowledged she had neglected ... a Lang and a Roberta they both needed to know, to acknowledge, and more – a Roberta he'd long refused to see and one he now had no choice but for now they stay united on separate sides of the city – they have no choice but.

* * *

Oh, baby, don't you want to go? California, and our sweet home, Shi-

-nagawa
-mbashi
-mokitazawa
-nsen

* * *

I can see myself in six months, Hiromi projects. And I have an idea of what I'll be wearing. But who will I be with? And I can see myself in ten years. A mansion in Setagaya perhaps. And I want to have two vacations a year. Oh, nothing excessive, but I have certain needs. One in the summer to a beach, Okinawa, Hawaii, wherever, but a nice, cool beach. And in the Spring or Fall to Europe to buy clothes. And one of them I will take alone, or with Hiroko, but definitely with my husband.

Children? Well, I guess I'll have to do my duty.

* * *

THE FLOWERS OF EDO

All this love this city all surprise and each of us a village a poster (a face, a machine and a landscape and a face reprised) concentric rings blazing together into a love mad drunk pronouncing the word as we wander the city – the very moment! – a boy and a girl their mouths from which fires pass through one another linger and again pass into you as you through me – you! – this inferno-city ablaze street-level.

* * *

HIRAGA GENNAI AND "DUTCH LEARNING"

What do we not owe to the Dutch? Friendship, the air of freedom, the fullness of the flesh, the openness of the mind, the expansiveness of the spirit – what it is to be human demonstrated everyday at what seems, from the perspective of our depravity and poverty, a more than human level.

And what does Japan not owe to the Dutch?

Knowledge – moral or intellectual, botanic or cartographic – sometimes seems like a fit, St. Vitus, a stepping forwards and back in starts and stutters, a pulling oneself together and continuing on or giving up and embracing the ghost. Sometimes it seems that people – (almost) all people – prefer to remain stupid. Something compels them to put on their blinders and walk backwards. A classic case is the one that begins, "Whatever happened to China?" (referring to its developing science suddenly stopped in its tracks). Another – the will to ignorance personified – is Japan during its two and a half centuries' period of isolation.

But some small spark of the will to knowledge lingered, and its center was the tiny island of Deshima in Nagasaki Harbor. Here began that peculiarly Japanese romance and flirtation with the "Southern barbarian," and that ensured that Japan was not wholly unprepared when the Black Ships of Commodore Perry – representing in time the entire compass of barbarians – came knock-knock-knocking in 1853.

It was called "rangaku" – or Dutch Learning (the "ran" coming from the middle syllable of the corrupted "Holland" – "horanda"), The 16th century had seen an influx of Portuguese and Spanish visitors to Japan. The Shogunate did not take a liking to them, however, what with their proselytizing and *that message* brought in by the Jesuits and so antithetical to the homegrown pantheon. Persecutions soon followed, and then complete isolation. Almost – Deshima, where a few Dutch were allowed to trade, and to talk (and to walk – biannual visits to Edo). The Japanese appreciated the Dutch for their lack of missionary zeal.

Trade had brought in clocks and firearms, eyeglasses and tobacco, but soon enough interest grew in Dutch – Western, really – learning in every field: chemistry, botany, mathematics, astronomy (a revised calendar) and geography (maps, atlases and gazetteers of the world), medicine (the first human dissection), and in the arts, the study of perspective, and oil painting. The Meiji Revolution was being well-prepared for.

It can be a fascinating story. The Japanese were so careful – paranoid in today's parlance – that they had one of their own interpreters executed for suspicion of telling the Dutch too much (but what could he have told them?). The Japanese were of course fascinated by the foreigners. One poet wrote

Dutch letters
Running sideways
Like a row of wild geese
Flying in the sky.

The hosts at one time even came to believe that Dutch was a universal language! (The Dutch themselves once thought their's was the first, the original language.)

On the Dutch side, the "Japon" – the kimono, or its lighter version the yukata – became a craze among *gentlemen* of means. Invitations were written with instructions to appear "in Japan," or out. One historian writes of Dutch burghers being amused (or is it offended?) by this "foppishness and dandyish pansy frippery" (what a phrase!). (One might also reflect here on the history of the word, "Japan." Here it is a noun for a dressing gown; elsewhere in Europe it was an adjective – "Japanned" – for something that has been lacquered; or as a verb, "to Japan something.)

There are many heroes in this story – Will Adams, Engelbert Kaempfer, Philipp Franz von Siebold on the Dutch side; Sugita Genpaku, Nishikawa Joken, Miura Baien, and many others on the Japanese. But foremost among them all is surely the man whom one encyclopaedist calls "one of the greatest figures of his time," and a historian calls him nothing less than the "extraordinary man who seemed to embody the entirety of Edo culture."

Hiraga Gennai (1728-1779) began life as head of a samurai household, renounced that role for that of *ronin* (masterless samurai), and ended it in prison. He began his professional life as a botanist – and throughout remained devoted to the art of classifying, with all of its imaginative possibilities. He also "experimented in making asbestos cloth, thermometers, and Dutch-style pottery, in addition to conducting surveys for ore deposits. He also tried his hand at wool manufacturing." But even these do not begin to encompass the great polymath's scope. He was also a philologist and compiler of dictionaries; he wrote on subjects as diverse as music, law and the martial sciences. He was the first in Japan to make asbestos and an electrical generator, and the first to paint in oils. He wrote satires and *joruri* (plays for the puppet drama). Pen names included "Dove Valley", "Wind Rider," and "Wanderer from Abroad" – all of which hint melancholically at his longing for something outside of the confines of his island home. Hiraga seems to have been drunk on knowledge – and to hate any restrictions put upon its pursuit. The works for which he is best known are biting, vicious satires with names the likes of "A Treatise on Farting" and "The Tale of a Limp Prick." His masterpiece, *Fūryū Shidōken Den* (The Dashing Life of Shidōken – the "story" concerns one Fukai Shidōken, who learns to fly and thus visits all of the known world, and many parts unknown, including, of course, Holland, and a visit to the legendary Island of Women) seems a combination *Gulliver's Travels*, *Utopia*, *Impressions of Africa*, a dash of *Finnegans Wake*. Along the way, he upsets every possible notion of truth, lies, fiction – language – the very bases of society, then and now. (In an earlier work, he writes of "the Buddha's fraudulence, Lao-tze's and Chuang-tze's balderdash, and Lady Murasaki's zillion lies.")

It is said that frustration in various mining projects due to a rank-conscious society lead to mad fits of rage and despair. One such lead him to *kill one of his students* – for which he was imprisoned.

* * *

- This area must've suffered during the war.
- Why do you say that?
- Well, for one, you don't see much of anything very old, only a cou-

ple of temples; and then look at the buildings you do see, built overnight, cheap materials, no character, no plan.

- Sounds like a lot of Tokyo.
- True enough.
- So, one area was saved by a few lucky winds – just beyond, Nezu and around there – and others, like here, were wiped out.
- That's about it.
- And these buildings get built because no one expects them to last anyway?
- I suppose.
- What do they expect, another war?
- No, not that, but earthquakes, and, you know, natural disasters.
- And manmade.
- Definitely manmade – just look around you.
- Oh, that's a nice attitude. Romantic, sick.
- That's the trouble, it is romantic, all that sentimental gush over fires and earthquakes.
- Couldn't it just be a sort of compensation to ward off the real depth of sorrow?
- Now, that's romantic!
- Which means then that the whole city is in a state of mass delusion.
- Sounds possible.
- Probable.
- Like a Fifties horror movie.
- More and more probable.
- And what's also manmade is to blame it on nature.
- You mean we can prevent earthquakes?
- No, but we can deal with them a lot better than we do.
- Isn't that what Shinto priests are for?
- Hardly, I'm afraid they more often call up the earthquake gods than quiet them.
- Kazuo, do you really believe –
- No, silly.
- Nice name, Sugamo.
- An artist's name.
- A sumo wrestler's.
- Komagome.
- Sounds like a ketchup.
- One of Godzilla's kids.
- Magomeko.
- But it's not all so dull.

- No, not at all – no place in Tokyo is.
- After all, Rikugien is here.
- I know a good tempura restaurant nearby, eel.
- And one of the Kichijojis is here too.
- Some hilly paths.
- Nao, wood front and pure fiber within: a great *washi* shop. And, all these blue-and-white buildings and suddenly one a fiery red sun – a red hat shop.
- My grandfather loved Rikugien, used to come here on holidays; he knew all the Chinese literary references, which flowers would blossom when.
- Was he a Sunday painter? A calendar photographer?
- No, not at all. Just a salaryman who loved this park.
- Sounds like a nice guy.
- No, not at all. I think he cheated on my grandmother, probably should have been put on trial after the war, was a lousy investor and lost the family fortune … and worse –
- What?
- Yes?
- He had a romantic notion that Tokyo would rise again like the phoenix!

* * *

A tree-lined street and cinema.
Ginza, spring, twilight.
The quiet rhythmic world.
Business and pleasure.
A blue-gray shirt, a gray-blue sky.

* * *

Rich and strange, Cafferty muses, a resplendent richness matched by sensuous strangeness that I have made my own. In an appropriate manner and measure. The city I found myself in and in which, in whom, I continue to discover and create myself. What measure of happiness. But apart from a few select passages, have I ever really been able to communicate it to another? A boy briefly, a woman once. Ahh.

* * *

The bees got in from somewhere and then knocked themselves silly and then dead banging against the window. Then the ants came in from somewhere and ate the bees. "I'm spending a month in a castle in Northern Italy." I couldn't believe it either. Roberta, you lucky woman. And then I tried to draw the castle, an outline, to orient myself, all those staircases going this way and that, and I just had to get a penlight to find my way back to my apartment at night. That night we came home from dinner at Maddalena's – and that funny story about her son-in-law who thought he was going to lord it over all and now he's bussing tables – and that night coming home and crossing the courtyard and the leaves on that tree I swear were white. And then everything became green. Driving around Costigliole d'Asti and to Torino all those greens, that deep dark violet with even a hint of a red but it was all a green, and a gray green and a golden and a yellowy and a silvery green and everything was one shade or another of it, green. God it was ... Marianne was right, it is part ruin, part très moderne, post-mod before the term, oh this section from that century and this tower from such a period (the six-cornered tower, bricks and granite). Getting lost, discovering the white room, the wine cellars so cold in mid-August, the big round room in the basement, ought to be a cabaret. The cobwebs. I swear it was haunted that one day the bathroom door opened as I approached and then slammed after me. Andrea suspended his big TV from the ceiling in an hour and watched all of half. The green room with the neon beam. The pink stairwell with some of the older decorations. Quiet, water-drinking Ernst, until he makes a quick remark, and then the sharp, short laugh, self-amused and self-aware. A cat named Telemaco. The view, just hills and houses and vineyards, and I thought the castle was kind of smallish and then driving back from town there it was, looming. And the peace. (And in the town meeting Rita, pretty, forensics, inviting me to an autopsy. Must do it someday.) The peace. Solitude. The Day of Creation. Didn't read a newspaper for two weeks or listen to a piece of music – finally put on some Glenn, Bach and Schoenberg. The mind so solid, deep like the high ceilings, all that space it could wander in and always return focussed, solid. Hours and hours alone in Irene's apartment, free to read and write, you could go a day or more without seeing anyone. One day three people are staying and another twenty – handsome, happy and hardworking Giovanni; Christine of the ripe flaxen hair and perfect smile; redhaired Susanne, the actress teaching philosophy. Intensity, calm. To work – a perfect environment. And all left in peace and all there to work, to repair a roof or an apartment or prepare a performance for Hamburg or Sardinia; but then we would meet, friendly, kind, and usually but not necessarily everyone assembled at dinnertime and those wonderful dinners – increased my working recipe book a hundred percent – and the wine and talking late, or not. And then the kids returned from summer camp, Zora and Ivan, and Wladimiro joked "la vita tranquilita è finita," and it was not. Couldn't be. Peace – Burio.

* * *

Hmm, I don't think so. And besides, I wouldn't want so enormous a love. You put in your time, you do what you can, you move on. Like any place, there are some things you like, some you don't. The good outweighs the bad, and so you can live with it. Oh, a few extremes here and there perhaps, but there's nothing particularly special about Tokyo. No romance. When it's time to go, you'll see old Arlene on that "big silver bird."

* * *

And the city, walked through for so long, began to walk through him as he had covered it. There will be that hour outside all perceptible time when just as in a photograph album, the city's infinite deck of cards will go on opening up in the hands of the person who had known them one by one, drawing them out of the pack and separating them and putting them in order, and which now will give by themselves, from themselves, Shinobazu Pond while he's walking down Shibuya's Spanish Steps, a doorway in Higashi-Ginza ("kobikicho" – for Kabuki and other pleasures to be had there), when he's talking with friends in a Gotanda dive, the city leaping at the eyes like one cat at another, the falsely immobile city spreading herself out toward him, invading him in the middle of a thought or a shower, accepting him as her own with a brilliant flash of Nezu warrens and paths, the song of a *chindoya* band opening up a new *pachinko* parlor, or the smell of *ramen* on a late-night *ramen* cart near the station, climbing up into his memory and leaving in the same moment like a person who barely looks at one photo before moving on to another. And that's how it is, but in other ways, because the player and the cards are no longer two different things, what comes up in the hands of the involuntary memory is born of a long-fought conciliation, now the city knows that she can give herself to the traveler, her former crouching rancorous passivity becomes an unexpected visit, a sign of freedom for someone who also sought it freely; a double acceptance and a single pact, joining freedom to freedom, the only true love. And, therefore, the same as with passion or friendship, hands will loosen, contacts will become simpler. Now, day by day, we will be the city that is us day by day, beautifully, we will recognize her in every new piece of knowledge and she, who knows us now, will, in turn, recognize us in every new direction we take. But just as with love or friendship, and above all with poetry, which amounts to the same thing, the unknown will still be there.

– Julio Cortázar-Silva

* * *

– Well, if that isn't it, then what was?
– Was what?
– What you wanted to say?
– I forget now. You know, I had a dream the other day that all the capsules in capsule hotels were really flying vehicles, the hotels were like mini-airports, and that there was enough space in the sky that no one ever got hit. The sky was filled with these needles going all about. And then I thought better if the people inside could eventually discard the capsule coverings and become like Blakean angels, you know, long and thin and ethereal. And it was all localized, I mean they weren't intercontinental people-jets, just within the vicinity.
– So people could get from, say, one station to another. These capsule-people eliminated the train system?
– Yeah, doesn't it sound great?
– No, it sounds dreadful. It's just cars in space instead of on the road. Why anyone would want to eliminate our public transportation system is beyond me. Oh, I'm sure your dream is non-polluting, but I sure don't want to see a bunch of sewing needles criss-crossing the sky, Blakean or otherwise.
– Well, like I say, it was only a dream.
– You know what dreams of flying mean, don't you?
– No, what.
– I don't know, something I suppose, maybe nothing.
– Do dreams of levitating qualify as flying dreams?
– I'm not sure. That depends on what dreams of flying mean. Why?
– I also have recurring dreams of levitating. I can will myself up and move from place to place – oh, tree to tree, room to room, nothing like China to Yokohama –
– Like your needle-angels –
– Right, this is just very local. Anyway, I recently had this dream

where I told everyone that I had this recurring dream, and there was a girl there who admitted that she had the same kind of dream, and we both levitated together. The thing is that it was like a dream within a dream and so I was all the more convinced that it was real, reality.

- You dreamed about flying away together with a girl?
- Yeah.
- Let me assure you, V-Zed, it was a dream, and it is not like reality at all, it is like Hollywood. I think you'd better find out what flying dreams and levitating dreams mean – and then find out how to stop having them. How's your film going, by the way?
- Real good.
- Tell me more.
- Well, it's an over-haul of the earlier version, the same but different, you know.
- No, I don't, I don't even understand that sort of language, don't even want to.
- Ok. If you saw the two –
- You've saved the earlier one, the one Roberta so hated?
- Yes, despite all I said, at the time I wasn't about to just get rid of all that work, flawed or otherwise.
- I'm glad to hear it. A sort of "V-Zed Hero."
- Whatever. Anyway, this one might remind you of the earlier one, but it is its own piece. It's still about architecture, women and photography. Remember I told you about crossing the street one day and crossing the other way was a woman who looked like an East-West cross between Dominique Sanda and, uhm, what's the name of that actress who played in *Kamata Koshin Kokyu*?
- Uhh, I know who you mean, I can't recall now … Korean.
- …
- Keiko Matsuzaka!
- Yes, of course. Beautiful woman. Anyway, I ran across her again – the woman crossing the street. She's beautiful, and she's playing the lead, the woman in the film.
- The one who goes wandering across the city with the portfolio of photographs?
- Yes, she's a natural, seems just to float across the screen. And I have her dressed so severely.
- Still black and white? The film I mean.
- Almost always.
- Ah, Spielberg.

- Cafferty! Give me some credit. Think silent film.
- Ok, ok, just teasing.
- I hope so. Anyway, she's a wonder to look at. I've added some close-ups of her looking at the photos, holding them up against the sky, against the buildings they depict, holding them against her chest – no, her white blouse, and no, she won't let me touch her, to anticipate your next question – and you see her questioning and her understanding in those depthless round eyes of hers.
- Round?
- Nearly, she actually is Eurasian. So she holds the photos of the buildings, and she seems to stop time, holds the city still.
- You really are excited.
- I tell you, Cafferty, it was an awful thing Roberta did – and it was a brave and good one. I only regret that she'll probably never know it.
- Oh, V-Zed, it's still that way, is it?
- 'Fraid so. Why should it change? What do apologies amount to? The damage is done, it is not undone by a few words.
- No, but … Or, yes it is, of course it can be. Otherwise, what do you want? Roberta to cut out her tongue and deliver it to you as a sign of her sincerity? Abase herself to your great artistichood?
- No, of course not. It's just that I don't know how the damage can be undone. You can't return to where you were before. And so I make a new film – same but different, and not giving a damn about her opinion.
- Well, of course not, but you shouldn't have in the first instance either. You shouldn't care much for your own opinion either, I'd daresay.
- What does that mean?
- Oh, it's just the way I've always interpreted that phrase no one likes to hear but keeps secreted away nonetheless, art for art's sake. You see, it's not for your own sake or much less society's that you make art, that's assuming there is a you for it to be made, and farther yet a society that might appreciate it. No, you make it for the art itself, and in that making and in that made thing you discover that much more about who you are, who you were, and who you might be, all assumptions cast aside. That's the theory, at least. And if it doesn't reveal anything – hell, it might even be better art. But my point too is that your film probably taught Roberta more about her own limitations than it ever did about yours. And listen to you now, talking about the new film, you're obviously exceeding yourself, going deeper so as to go farther out. Capsule Boy.

- Directed by Capsule Boy! Starring Capsule Girl! Curious speech, Cafferty.
- Just give it a thought later, alright?
- Sure. Maybe you have something there. But nonetheless, I really don't know what to do about Roberta.
- Do? What's to do about her? Do something about yourself.
- Shoot.
- No, you aim – at yourself.
- I too often have. Do you think that first version was too self-indulgent?
- Very. I'll go one further, it was self-destructive. Whatever were you trying to get at? Cheap-jack editing, bad pun super-impositions, an oh so sincere acting style, and knowing film referential winks for all the cinephiles out there. You were imploding when you thought you were illuminating. An explosion inside a cave, no one ever notices. Capsule Boy was sinking hard that night.
- Hmm. Why didn't you tell me this then?
- You wouldn't have listened. And besides, Roberta did. And you didn't listen.
- Self-indulgence as self-destruction, eh?
- Something like that, something equivalent.
- Well, I'll grant you the self-indulgence – but I thought I was being more than merely clever, I really thought the material was good.
- Oh it was, good and sometimes very good – but it was dishonest – it was pointing a finger at itself while also pointing one at you, when it should have been pointing past you, beyond itself.
- Why is that dishonest?
- I do not mean that you were not being honest with yourself, no, you're a good artist, but that you were being dishonest with your art. You don't make art to show us how wonderfully clever you are – little boys do that with their mothers, who are there to indulge them – you make it to show how full of wonder art itself can be. And if it is, if it succeeds, then your reflection will be there too for those who bother to notice. No, if you want to show off your cleverness, your great wit and learning, well, you sit down and talk with your friends. I might add, that I suppose that too was a part of Roberta's protest: you were being dishonest with her. That film was the stuff of your conversations, it was a draft, a taking-off point, Capsule Boy, but not a finished flight by any means.
- And now?
- And now what?

- What am I to do about Roberta?
- That I cannot answer. I am sure you both hurt, but there's a mountain of pride between the two of you preventing either from making the first humbling step.
- You're getting moralistic, Cafferty.
- Behind every aesthete – who more than Oscar?
- Did he humble himself? Did Bosie?
- Oh, Bosie never, he simply never had enough imagination to do such a thing. But Wilde? Yes, probably, in his own self-flattering way. But he was already a broken man, remember – and on top of that, or to top that, he had to take an already crumbled edifice and bring it down further yet. Shame followed by humility, and yet a breath of air, please, and so the self-posturing to the end. What a man! So complex, self-knowing. And so it is no wonder that we get the Oscar-Christ of *De Profundis*. Such overcoming and yet maintaining is rare. I couldn't do it – could you?
- What do you mean you couldn't do it? Have you ever had to?
- V-Zed, how long have you been here, two years, two and a half? And I – decades. What do you know of me? You look at what seems to you a mellowed man. Do you think I was born this way? How long, for that matter, have Lang and Roberta been together, more or less, together, that is? Nine, twelve years? Don't you think they have had some overcoming to do, just as I? I've spoken with Lang – the pride he's still swallowing to remain with that remarkable woman.
- Yes, but what about you?
- Oh, short stories, long stories. I opened myself up to Japan, let her come flooding in to the point where I'd completely forgotten myself. Oh not in any Zen sort of way, I just did not care who I was anymore. But what I was not doing was caring about whom I was becoming, much less whom I might be. I, as your generation says, went with the flow. A Bosie of my own sort. And then came the reckoning. I had not recognized that my feelings were being used – in this I also let my friends down when I did not listen to them, to their warnings – I just thought we could float along so effortlessly forever, the cash was flowing, the vital juices, and slowly but equally effortlessly I was being worn away, physically, emotionally, all of it. I'm sorry I can't tell you details now, and it sounds so melodramatic – and it is – just let me say that it took quite some time for me to recover and to learn. You see, in my own perverse way, I had enjoyed it, I had to recognize, enjoyed watching myself self-destruct, enjoyed that openness to everything that had begun it all. No, I did

not enjoy the pain. But I did learn a lot about myself, my tolerance, my being able to set my self aside for the sake of another. My what, then?, porousness, this talent for absorbing almost any experience, letting it sweep into me and then drain away. I've accumulated quite a lot in my time, I tell you. But you see too, it is not the stuff that records are made of. If I were to write a diary, say every night before going to bed I write down the day's experiences, in the morning my memory of those events would be forgotten – and the pages blank. That's why you and your friends consider me a dilettante – but in fact I do not pretend to be anything at all. You want volumes, memoirs, collections, snapshots. I want to remember, but cannot. I'm a layer of shadows, V-Zed, transparencies. Embrace me three times and three times you will wrap your arms around yourself. Oh, I could tell you stories, tell you about the past, my past – but I wouldn't even know if they were true. Are they really my memories, something I've read, made up, dreamt, like your dream of dreaming levitating with the Sanda look-alike, dreamed so deeply that you thought it real? No, my stories are like Blake's dying songs, "not my own, not my own." But what could you possibly want to know? My sex life in Japan in the 60s? My wanderings about the country? Remarkable meetings? What the country was "really like" back then? My sins, lovers, heartbreak? Lovers have walked across the city just to make love to me in the morning. There were some months of bliss with a young couple. I saw a man knife another straight in the face, and then the two embraced like long lost brothers. Or a child running through the streets, his temple pierced and the blood arcing in the air. The bodies of a couple smashed on the pavement – their parents had forbidden their marriage. There are so many stories, happy stories, sad stories, my own heart bleeding of heartbreak or joy – I actually cried when I first saw Kyoto – but I am like those tears in rain, washed away, and that is best.

– [clears throat]

– But not washed up! Not washed up. I didn't mean to get carried away there, V-Zed, but I just want you to know that your woes with Roberta and with yourself are not any different from, well, mine or hers and Lang's either, I suppose. Speaking of whom, how are they doing? Will they get together again? Will he leave? Is he finally enjoying Tokyo? Is he still so filled with resentment? You know, I like him, I like him very much – there's a man walking with a great load of secrets. How well do you know him?

– As much as he allows.

- Just as I thought. No wonder he can't let Roberta go. And so, how are they?
- Hard to say. Maybe there has been a thaw recently. You know they're living on opposite sides of the city.
- Yes.
- Well, after some tentative steps, forays into the areas in between, they began to explore one another's turf bit by bit. Seems Lang has begun to appreciate the old city, and Roberta is no more so dismissive about developments west.
- The old criss-cross then? The exchange. The one for the other.
- Yes.
- Well, I am very glad to hear it. Lang too making a move. Remarkable man, still able to overcome and make the required changes in himself. This is what we've been talking about all this while V-Zed.
- What you think I can't do myself.
- Oh no, I never said or implied that. Quite the contrary, I do believe you can, you obviously have the imagination for it, just look at what you're doing in your film. No, no, I apologize if I gave you the wrong impression. All I am saying is that it has had to be pointed out to you, you've been so focussed elsewhere, so dedicated to the film in fact, that you have only neglected your own good health. Physical too from what I hear of your carousing. But now that it is pointed out to you, or signaled clearly, and not in Roberta's rather abrupt manner, I believe you can only proceed in the way indicated.
- Yes, Master.
- Sorry, I really should have phrased that differently. Let's just say, I trust you'll do the … do what you have to. Is that more Hawksian for you? Are you good enough, V-Zed?
- That's more like it, Cafferty. Yes, a world where Hitchcock and Hawks, Murnau and Lang, Roberta and Lang, myself and Roberta, Bresson and Ophüls, you and your past, myself and my future, can reconcile and live together.
- Green tea and coffee, brown rice and burgers, *tatami* and chandeliers!
- And again, Roberta and Lang.
- Yes. Above all and by all means.
- *Yes, you know, it's clear to us all now that Lang is changing –*
- As I ever suspected he could.
- *And Roberta is so pleased*, you know. He's like a *new, hidden Lang, one she'd always suspected.*
- Oh, I'm sure she is pleased. As too I am sure this is not the first time he has had to change and prove to her his mettle. I do wonder what

has gone on before between them, in America, in Europe, when they first got together, if they've split apart before. And what she has gone through on her own here, these many months.

- *And he seems equally happy. She is like an unsuspected Roberta, a Roberta he'd neglected.*
- Good for him. To discover the lover anew! To keep being able to surprise one another – and one's self.
- That does seem to be the case here, she's like *a Roberta she has acknowledged she has neglected.*
- I can see that. You know in all this talk of overcoming, we too have been negligent. After all, the center here is Roberta. She's the one who struck out for Japan on her own. We too often look on it as an act of bold creativity, and yet, perhaps it was something completely negative.
- But –
- No, no, hear me out. From what I understand of their last year or so together before she left, she was in an awful way; and yes, he may have, probably did neglect her, but she allowed him so much advantage, and you and I know that he is one who will take it when proffered. Sounds to me like she'd completely lost touch with herself, with whatever it is that had kept her strong and kept her and Lang together. I'm not surprised at all that she left – and came here of all places. It was a last chance, last ditch move. Yes, alright, positive in a life-saving way. But look at what she has done here. She eliminated all trace of the earlier vibrant Roberta, reduced everything, and has slowly built herself up again from scratch. Think of the risks she's taken – among them the risk of losing such a friend as you – look at how she's chosen to live: the modest apartment, the everyday routines, and especially the elimination of the habits of a lifetime: the films she loved going to so many times a week, the time spent with friends – what did you tell me once?, that she sees her friends only one afternoon a week now. These are not the actions of someone in search of a Zen way, but in some ways the wise sacrifices of a person who knew she was near her end, and had to save herself. But think of the faith too that she must possess: she left Lang, planned this course of life, knew Lang had almost no interest in Japan but was never wholly sure that he would in time come here to get her back – she took that risk, said nothing to him, no, "Look, Lang, I'll be in Japan, if you want me, come get me." No, all she said was, "I'm going to Japan, Lang, goodbye." She never asked him to come for her, never challenged him. She knew that this time she had to act

on faith alone – and take the great risk that he might not come. You just have to admire a person like that.

- Yes, and now it is as if *they have almost rediscovered a mutual Lang and Roberta that they need now to know again, to acknowledge, to recognize.*
- Yes, but rediscover and recognize anew, like new. The Roberta she has been digging out of herself during her time here might never have been discovered but that would not have made her any the less Roberta. We have infinite depths, you see, V-Zed, infinite depths, this is what I was saying to you earlier.
- Yes, it's curious, Lang seems to be in love not only with his old Roberta, but this new one, or rather, *a Roberta he'd long refused to see and now has no choice but.*
- And a Roberta she'd long refused to see and now has no choice but. And what will their next move be? Move in together again? No, too soon, she still has some way to go. I am sure they are too smart to make that move until the time is right, no matter what they will have to pay for separate apartment fees. Have you ever wondered how many couples that hate each other stay together simply because of the money they can save? Anyway, Lang too has some way to go yet. After all, he is on his own Tokyo journey now, and has to remain open to the changes that will have on him; but neither has to worry about that as any kind of threat. While the city has broken many a couple apart, it has also brought many together; the more wonderful is when it brings them back together.
- I suspect that for now *they will stay united on separate sides of the city – after all, they have no choice but.*
- Yes, I suppose you're right. They can continue the criss-cross, the exchange. They'll cover a lot of territory that way, and stay out of one another's lairs when they need. Lang must walk down the mountain and bring roses to the Low City. Roberta will ease her monkish ways and once in a while enjoy the high life. I assume Lang already knows the better restaurants out in his area. I assume he already knows the better ones in Roberta's area as well. Ah, but all this high city low city talk, I've never felt comfortable with it. I know the reasons why we use the terms, but why do they remain? The city is simply a curve, a side of a bowl, a swing. You know the phrase "*bura-bura*"?
- As in "*Gin-bura*," wandering about Ginza?
- Yes, well, it literally denotes a swinging motion; and from that it has its sexual connotation. This is more appropriate for Tokyo than this high-low division. I want to see people fucking more, not compet-

ing for position. This is the real Tokyo spirit.

— How can I help?

— I'm sure you're making your own spirited contribution, V-Zed. So,let me see if I understand you correctly. You say that *Lang is changing, it is clear to you all, and Roberta likes it, likes this new hidden Lang, a Lang she'd always suspected; and that Lang likes her: she is an unsuspected Roberta, a neglected Roberta, and a Roberta she too acknowledges she had neglected … a Lang and a Roberta they both need to know, to acknowledge, and more – a Roberta he'd long refused to see and one he now has no choice but, and for now they stay united on separate sides of the city – they have no choice but.*

— That seems to be the case, yes.

— Well, it's a nice case, a rare one certainly. Could you see it as a movie?

— You mean an old one, has it been done? By who – Bresson?

— Ophüls? No, it would have to be a combination of the two. By you?

— By me? Hmm. Lots of talk, I'm not sure I'd like that.

— Oh, but it'd be one-sided.

— Lang. But how to show all that Roberta has gone through? It's all in her head, isn't it?

— Yes, but you'd simply show her life in the city. The reality of the streets, the simplicity of her apartment, the repetition of her actions. And then you'd have Lang's discovery of the city. The city would be their emotions.

— Hmm … No, not my style, a story, all show. That's not a Tokyo story to me.

— Oh?

— Lots of talk – regardless of what I just said, this is a different sort of dialog – lots of pictures, but they don't necessarily go together; the viewer makes the connections, fills in the gaps, puts the "story" together.

— By the way, you don't mention Roberta being in the new film. She'd be marvelous, you know. That voice, the talk.

— Don't think I don't know it. You'd be marvelous in it too – that voice, the talk.

— Sorry, you've already said it's a girls only production.

— A voiceover?

— No, no, this is one movie I only want to admire.

— I hope you will.

— But really, what about her in it?

— How? What can I do, say?

- You go up to her and say, "Roberta, would you like to be in my film? I would like you to be, and would appreciate your saying you would." Or is that too long?
- Sure, Cafferty, I just go and ask her to be in the film.
- Yes, you do.
- Maybe, I do.
- You know what it would mean?
- For the film?
- For everything.
- For me?
- For all of us.
- Yes, I know.
- For you?
- For you. For me too, yes.
- I don't know, Cafferty.
- Yes you do, V-Zed, you do know.
- That voice.
- That Roberta.
- My film ...
- Your friendship ...
- Just ask her, eh?
- Just pop the question.

* * *

She had spoken away her lipstick and now was a bit drunk, her boyfriend moreso. Was it just because she was from the Midwest that she really didn't know what to do, how to kiss him? With all attention on each fumbling footstep, she would reach beyond his friendly goodnight and aim at the mouth and hope its message went not unminded; but his intentions – at least this night – were honorable (as they used to say), and so her aim was slightly off and she somehow slobbered half on his lips half on his cheek, but semi-drunkenness excused all, but too yes the message was well received as subsequent events proved.

* * *

Ah, you city, so you're it, eh? Where I make some decisions? Why are you punishing me like this, making me so extravagant? Am I some plaything of yours? How did you choose me? Were the Ms next in line? Oh, Tokyo, if you're up there – what'd that guy say – if you're up there, wiggle your ears!

* * *

-     – I see you everywhere ...?
-     – But ... uhn, but fail to ...
-     – find you!
-     – Good. I see you everywhere, but fail to find you ...
-     – hmm ... find ...
-     – find you ...
-     – No. Fail to find you ... find, ... but fail to see!
-     – It's a good one. I see you everywhere, but fail to find you.
-     – Find, but fail to see. Yes, very good.

* * *

A TOUR OF THE MARIANNAS

Mary Anne:

Within you and around you, cities hovering above, in our single heart beating in a triple city. Shake your hand; I'll lend you a shirt – an indefinite loan.

> her imprint fades
> the scent of it
> sheets of it

- Ohh, it's so cold, cold here.
- No, no, Mary Anne – there is no more emotional place.
- No more emotional man?
- No more.
- And this woman?
- A conversation – cold emotion.

She pulls my face towards her on her haunches.

Twenty years ago gangly and nervous with our own natures and now look at them slipping into one another this long sliding thing our nature.

slipstream
streetcar:
there you are!

Your Memphian feet in Chinese slippers;
Memphian thighs in black Chinese slacks
Your Memphian breasts in a red Chinese blouse
Memphian skull – speaking those Memphian words – in a Chinese hat.
Your Memphian cunt in this Chinese face.

–   I don't know what I'm doing.
–   You have a choice?
–   I don't know what I'm doing.
–   You're supposed to know? to do?
–   I don't know what I'm doing.
–   Don't. Don't know.

Your heart in my hand, no, on my palm – firm, standing, beating and all the best adjectives.
She strides standing naked, high breasts – standing still, naked, striding, unconversant.
The night awakened by the voice, the cry, "try me."

And I will love you till I know it's wrong.

– VZ

* * *

–   Ever westward!
–   Onward!

- Eastward!
- Upward!

- Isn't there supposed to be a ghost somewhere around here?
- Ghosts are all over the country.
- No, but, oh where was it?, oh yes, in Inokashira Park.
- No, those are college kids running around naked at night.
- Lots of sex taking place there.
- Which means lots of voyeurs.
- But wait, yes, I know the story.
- About voyeurs? What's to know?
- No, about the ghost.
- See.
- She's the ghost of a woman who was spurned by her lover, and now she lives in the pond, and she splits apart any lovers that go for a stroll there.
- Really?
- Well, yes – if you want to believe it.
- Lots of people do.
- Really?
- Yes, really; in fact lots of girls do not want to go for walks in the Park with their boyfriends.
- Oh, so it's just the people who come here for sex, is that it? They're under no illusions, and figure there's no love involved, just a good time.
- Could be.
- Still, you do see lots of couples in the park. Families even.
- Yes, but are they together? Will they stay together?
- Maybe someone ought to do a survey.
- Alright, enough already. We could get stuck on legends and stories every few blocks and never get to where we're going.

- Ever westward!
- Onward!
- Eastward!
- Upward!

- Kichijoji's the best.
- Well, Lang's certainly gotten to like it.
- But it is!
- Why?

- Because it combines east and west, old city, new city. The scale is perfect. And historically, it embodies the history and direction of the city.
- Huh?
- Well, look, for one example, the original Kichijoji temple was located way over in *shitamachi* somewhere; then the fires, this is in the Edo period, caused it to be moved west – there's one in Sugamo – and finally here. Money-wise, too. This is where people used to have their second homes – or, one of the places, Shibuya's another – and now its keeps a bit of its gentrified side – just look at the big houses behind the main streets – and all the greenery, too – and you'll see what I mean.
- Yeah, and you get young and old too. The old families, and all the kids from the nearby universities.
- "Joji," as they call it.
- Right, and lots of 'em prefer it to Shibuya.
- Well, you have the train connection. But a lot of 'em do stop here.
- Well, a lot of 'em also come from rather far out, too. They have to stop somewhere.
- The point is that they are happy to stop here.
- I certainly am.
- And you have a lot of foreigners – or Japanese with foreign experience – and so you get the three or four supermarkets with foreign foods available.
- Gee, you guys are really making a case.
- And isn't it a writer's place?
- Right, again the universities, and so there are a lot of academics.
- No, I mean real writers.
- Yes.
- Didn't Dazai do himself in around here?
- Yes, that's right. Was it in Inokashira Park? Or the river?
- Lots of good food here –
- And record shops –
- And clothes –
- Parco –
- Clubs –
- Lots of stuff –
- Something for everyone –
- Ok, ok, we're not writing an ad for the place –
- Right, we're beginning to sound like copywriters –
- But we are –

- No, we're not, not now anyway.
- We're walkers –

- Ever westward!
- Onward!
- Eastward!
- Upward!

* * *

Hiromi (or was it Hiroko?) hadn't seen van Zandt in a week. She'd tried to leave him messages, but he'd not left on his answering machine. And then, he wasn't the type to return calls anyway. And, he'd told her to never visit him unannounced. She'd walked – in that deceptive light skip of hers that made everyone think her unaffected by events – to his two or three hang-outs in Asakusa, and again he hadn't showed. Was he on a binge?, with another girl?, ditching her? Hiroko (or was it Hiromi?) did not know what to do. Call Roberta?

* * *

There were three couples fucking. A gay couple visiting. VZ and a woman I wanted. Someone else whom I can't recollect. And I lived there. Sure, I was happy for them, the more fucking the better. A bit noisy, with those thin walls in such a small house. And I was only too mindful that the sex that was not mine – I remember her skin, her smile, the eyes never modest in that demure Japanese way, but exultant. So I felt like a guest in my own home. Was this fair? Or maybe there is a truth here that I failed to recognize. Tokyo is my home, and I am its guest. More and more sex then, for the city.

* * *

This waitress is too old for Hiro, that one too young, this one too skinny, and that one too fat. This beer is too cold, and that one not cold enough. This fish overcooked, and that one under. This colleague too silly, and that one overly serious. This office lady too demure, and that one too brash (that loud laugh). This manager too ostentatious, that one too faux modest. This *saké* too sweet, and that one too dry. This morning too cold, this evening too warm. This restaurant too loud, the one before too quiet. It is the third of the evening, an *akachochin*, its outdoor paper red lantern a bit battered. It is a dive, the type of place Hiro used to take a certain delight in. But tonight he is all unvoiced complaints. Why won't his boss – the ostentatious fellow with the green bow tie with polka-dots – trust him with a decent expense account? Does he think he'll waste it, not use it properly and on the proper clients? All he wants is a break, just one decent chance to prove himself capable – and on and on so he begins to sound like a parody of some American melodrama. Damn!, he's burned himself holding a match too long while he was lost in this reverie. Now everyone's laughing at him. Ok, force a smile, Hiro, show them that you aren't over serious about yourself. No one bothers to help him. Why not? Not even that nice new office girl, the one who dropped out of Waseda. What did she say she studied? French literature? American? Why not Japanese? Doesn't she have any patriotic feelings? Is she ashamed of our literature, our hard-working writers? But when he thinks about it a few seconds more, he remembers that he hasn't read a Japanese book in quite a long while. In fact he can't even say he's read a real book in quite a long while. Comic books, weekly magazines – that's his fare. Why did he sit so near the boss, anyway? This means that he can't make much conversation of his own, has to pay attention to what the boss says, and pour the man one drink after another. Shouldn't the new girl be doing that?

Two dives later, finds Hiro in a bar that looks like a concrete garage with a few stools and formica tables strewn about. He doesn't care that the sleeve of his suit is lying in spilled *saké*, that there are whisky stains on his tie, and that at the previous bar the new girl had clearly rejected his advances – but then he can't even remember what he said to her; he only has a vague idea that while he tried not to be rude he did want to make his message clear, apparently the wrong strategy – but then what would he have done if she had consented to come home with him – pass out in her lap? No, he'll have to make up for this lapse some time. But then, he asks himself, what's been eating him so recently? Why all this anger and resentment? It can't just be on account of an expense account?

A half-hour later, having walked in the door and telling himself that this kind of nightlife has to stop, and just as his head is about to hit the pillow, Hiro's breath stops as he foresees a life like this, an eternity of boredom and resentment, of pettiness, and unfulfilled desire. "Fuck it" (or it's Japanese equivalent), he mumbles to himself as the lights go out.

* * *

Shores of Aldeberan, Clouds of Magellan.

Boiling blood, the great god descends. Post-murder, he falls back on to the red satin sheets, yellow-eyed. Once omniscient, sputtering now how he no longer knows. What kind of god is it who can "no longer know"? Spitting blood – "Keats' black mouth blood" – the American, orphaned, strides the streets and elevators of his adopted city.

He walks alongside you, Arlene, blood-caked, Memphian, blonde. Roiling.

* * *

The costs of confusion notwithstanding, Van Zandt. I'll figure it out. Haven't I already? I mean, I got my canals – is that what he calls 'em? – corridors, whatever, I know how to get from here to there – and to get laid – isn't that enough? What cost? What confusion? Dammit, Lang, stop upsetting me with your shit.

* * *

Cafferty is back at his old job in New York. The fashion magazine of which he has recently been promoted to assistant editor will hit the stands in seventy-two hours. Suddenly he realizes that not only has an important advertiser been indirectly insulted in a humorous piece that Cafferty oversaw, an equally important credit has been left out, and there is a perhaps too explicit homosexual reference in another piece. He tries various ways to halt distribution, to explain the situation to his boss, to save his skin. He calls a friend, the "friend" has no sympathy. Another suggests a double martini. A third talks on and on about the possibilities of new careers, how to get out of the jam, how to place the blame on someone else. Cafferty is in a great panic. And what happened to the office muzak? Why is it playing that Negro religious music? (It is the mighty Ira Tucker and the Dixie Hummingbirds having their church – "In the Morning" – that our man is unaware of.) Cafferty goes to his window to further think through his situation – and he looks on the mountains and hills and rivers and valleys of the Okutama and Chichibu regions of Tokyo.

Upon waking – all asweat, shaking – Cafferty will shower and wonder why this dream recurs every six months or so. He'll also recall the various events that lead to the actual circumstances of the dream, the circumstances under which he did leave the magazine, of how it all lead eventually to his arrival in Tokyo, and the friend who betrayed him. He will curse for a moment, and then he will thank what he can only call Fortune.

Kaoru is reporting for work at the mountain resort hotel. Suddenly there is an earthquake. The hotel manager rushes out to calm the nerves of his guests and employees. Frustrated, he shouts, "This is my house and you will behave as I tell you to!" Kaoru goes to the locker room to put on his uniform. Naked men. Gospel music in the background? Why not. Then to the cafeteria to have lunch. The line moves slowly. All the food is Japanese Western: strawberry and cream sandwiches, puddings, waffles, weak and overly sweet coffee. There are large pitchers of water on all of the tables, at none of which does Kaoru sit because he is new on the job and shy about introducing himself. He puts his tray away, and reports for work, but he opens the wrong door and comes out onto the stage of the ballroom where a banquet is being held. Then the hotel changes to a mountain spa where Kaoru recently stayed on a work holiday with fellow office employees. Now he is a guest, getting drunk. The hostesses are old, dressed in yukata, their gold teeth flashing, and telling obscene jokes. He grabs one by the ass, and unlike the actual occasion, this one lets his hands go farther.

* * *

PURGATORIO MONOGATARI

Cimabue's out
the Gion Bell

A boy
thrown from a boat

A nun
– Fortune's wheel –
sword at throat

* * *

Down down the round we go. Let's say it is an erotic universe, or better, city, as Araki and I would have it: then what of that waste, all that life, lost for the city? Yes, I am lost for the city, like Patti sings, "Oh God, I fell for you." A little bit of life destroyed in just a word from a friend.

Arguments among us soon come to resemble a state of drunkenness. You can't resist the impulse for just one more remark, drive it to an excess, and wake up the next morning feeling lousy and aware of the time you've wasted. Arguing in Tokyo: two steps back. Life fails, falls friendship.

The memories the city is constantly evoking, not just the name of a bridge or a slope – that's a history I want to live with – I mean the name of a magazine or a stationery company or some random sight: these remind me of him, her, you, me. The whole place can be a city of pain for me some days, and yet I must live with that pain, and trust that the cure *is* in the poison, trust the city to sustain me. Sublunary: that's the word usually applied. Sublunary in mid-August when all my sins pore from me. The Sublunary City of the Sun. The sun goes down, the moon comes up; the moon goes down, the sun comes up. Memories die – where do they go?

"Why be bored, who scared you?," as Iggy says. The City of the Moon and the City of the Sun: they shall be One. Or we perish, outside of time, day or night. For example, my conflicts of walking – in my case wandering the city, usually in search of a book, a record or a shirt. Is it a waste of time?, an avoidance of responsibility? Or a delirium?, a plunge into the plenitude of the written/walked city? "Oh, it'll only take a short time," I always tell myself, and it winds up devouring my day, as some small sight, more often commonplace than not – a skirt, some silly young couple, an ad – leads me forward. And me wondering who has co-opted who – the city or me? But the answer is already there: my time has been taken, all spirit exhausted (exalted?), and my flesh swept into a vacuum: and no time to write it. The cafés are not attractive and hardly conducive to writing (or reading for that matter); I write very little each day, a fact that gnaws at my conscience; my social life – women, friends – demands that I be away from home at least four nights a week. And when I am home, what? There is the mail to read and respond to; the day's notes to look over and organize (for what?); another drink or two (or too often more); and then finally into bed, exhausted. Where I find myself unable to fall asleep. The mind is free to roam in its own mode of walking over the day's events, the people, the women, the places. More notes need now to be taken; phrases reworked. I get up from bed half a dozen times – paper, water, find that article. Friends who know I am rarely home before midnight begin to call. No matter the physical or mental conditions, going to bed never relaxes me – even alone, it excites me. I never fall asleep from physical exhaustion, horizontality has nothing to do with it. Rather, body and soul mutually work themselves through until they are satisfied that the day's work is accomplished, and the night's can begin. And then I wonder: have I walked it as I have talked it? And I wonder: will I – in dreams?

Faces. Words. Lies. Invariably. They will bring you down. You have devoted yourself to them, and yet, your friends will bring you down: will encourage your every weakness, encourage you to encourage theirs. "Multi-cultural" Tokyo, and suddenly the Brits are proud and complaining about the French who are proud and pissed at the Greeks who are superior in every way to the … and everybody has something awful to say about the Japanese. There is a bad joke waiting here somewhere – and you will laugh with them (you might even make up the joke). Down. All sinking. Reclaimed land and what we hoped were our reclaimed lives, all come here to drown. The city is a cruel Master/Mistress (What *is* the sex of this city? Why can I not determine it?) – a great Seducer, Corrupter. The city will bring you down. We come here having experienced all corruption, viewing all the possibilities of pleasure and innocence regained within it all … only to discover we have been had, the City has deceived us, and one day we look into our souls and see there all corruption, like a Dorian Gray portrait multiplied beyond even Wilde's vision of corruption; Oscar again teaches us to look and look again until a new angle is revealed and all the world is undone. Malebolge.

Look at Lang, if ever there was a wasted soul. And he says he knows what he's doing. Not the Poe Man of the Crowd he pretends to be, but to be pitied. And Roberta buoyed by our false faith that she does know. And perhaps she does – if she's smart enough and lets go of us. Or "Van Zandt and the Abuse of Women." The man is just unconscious and unconscionable, and will never become aware of himself. The New Man is the Old Man. Arlene – yes, let's go through the list then – Arlene, all complacency. She *must* make her move, but expects it to come to her. Will she ever see? Kaoru: a pure contempt for life and even a man I detest. But pure in something at least. Intolerable his intolerance. Kazuo: a graced man perhaps and without a worry – and *that* should worry us. And his girlfriend, well, Kyotoites do tend to live in a cloud. Hiromi is just another all-too-common loss, not even counting as a casualty. Her pal Hiroko, so much potential – the city is sure to devour her; she'll wake up someday next to her salaryman and kids and three-generation mortgage never knowing what hit her. She'll have the occasional dying memory of better times and write it all off as a dream. And Hiro. Guiding the nation forward falling. Cafferty. a "stringer," a cowardly streak, wary that his greatness here might have been a mediocrity there. And Marianne. Mad, surely, but not mad enough to be the saint she fools herself into thinking she is or might be, I'd hate to have her dreams. That leaves the author. "They shall bring you down"? No, I shall take them all down with me. The Sleep of Reason. I shall be some Goyesque imp forever shitting on the pile of my characters' corpses.

I no longer know, and so I walk the city, howling silently, and have made that walking enough for me, a way to avoid myself and all of my responsibilities, half a man inside, walking and talking to myself. Malebolge.

* * *

R'n'L!!!!!!!!!!

Would you buy a samurai helmet or a sword hilt? How do you choose good calligraphy? I saw some Beardsley's for sale recently.

Just Asking, or Ignorant Medicine Dept. Can you get a headache from the arms of your glasses? You know, as the metallic covering rots away. Can it affect the brain?

Did you ever notice how much Wladi reads labels of whatever's in front of him?

Remember JG saying to Chris when CT said a novel should be encyclopedic, "so why don't you write an encyclopaedia?" Need I comment?

Maybe I'll die of passive smoking; what a death rattle that'll be.

Speaking of which, I wonder who buys the good cigars at my local tobacco shop? I've n-e-v-e-r seen anyone smoking cigars around here. And I've only seen two pipe smokers in all these years, and no one who rolls their own – and yet all that stuff is available, and apparently someone is buying it.

The little black cat lost one if its eyes (is that a blues?). Susi picked it up – the cat, I mean – and plucked out a thorn, looked for the eye – and it was gone! Just all this flesh, no lens. Yuck. The cat was ok, though; a little wobbly as it ran to its food.

I think that Hagiwara line applies to almost any situation. Eg, Wladi has been talking for the last twenty minutes about his dog and after a while one feels his poetry getting crazier as his intoxication rises.

But wait, the beautiful Agnese approaches. I am unable to write in her presence.

As per yer inquiry, yes, *Elvis and Gladys* is a good read.

Remember Miss Imbrie in *The Philadelphia Story?* "I can't afford to hate anybody. I'm only a photographer."

You know that Chinese restaurant in Ikebukuro? They get their tofu flown in from Shanghai every day. Try it, you'll feel the difference.

* * *

- Doesn't Hiroko take tours of Tokyo, too?
- How should I know, Kazuo? Who's Hiroko?
- She does, yes, but not the same kind I do. Where she takes random busses on her own, my company has the strange policy of entertaining out-of-town-or-country clients with rides on commercial bus tours of Tokyo, complete with tour guide girls in cute hat and white gloves keeping up an endless patter about Tokyo sites, history, legends, songs, which they warble so nauseatingly on.
- Sounds –
- No, it doesn't. Any kind of bus tour in Japan is a distinctly Japanese experience which the Japanese or foreign visitor should try his or her damndest to avoid. I, however, can not. For some reason known only to my boss, this has become my special assignment. Oh I put up with it.
- Maybe it's just your good-nature.
- Man, I've seen Tokyo by Night, Tokyo by Day, Tokyo through History, Tokyo by Waterway, the Shogun's Tokyo, the Emperor's Tokyo, Movie Tokyo, Architectural Tokyo, Legendary Tokyo, Archaeological Tokyo, Future Tokyo, Kid's Tokyo, Eco Tokyo, Student Tokyo, Woman's Tokyo, Computer Tokyo, Commuter Tokyo, Museum Tokyo, High-tech Tokyo, Crafts Tokyo, Garbage Tokyo, Paper Tokyo, Government Tokyo, TV Tokyo, Shinto Tokyo, Buddhist Tokyo, Foreigner's Tokyo, Food Tokyo, Pensioner's Tokyo, and so on and nauseatingly on.
- Sounds –
- Yeah, I suppose. It's not always so bad.

* * *

SCENE TEN: MARUZEN

Having had an expert adjustment made to her favorite Waterman fountain pen, and picked up a new Pilot double-lock pencil – the forerunner and far superior version of what is unthinkingly referred to today as the mechanical pencil – she commences her investigation, in this the tenth photo-site. But first a quick coffee. She then passes the bespoke shirt department, declines to be fitted for a new blouse, glances at the traditional Japanese crafts, wants so to look at the display of maps but duty first, sweeps by the pottery sale, and finally the area devoted to various sorts of British sportsperson's outfits and accessories and essentials. Where is she? This being Tokyo, why she is in a bookstore, of course. "Gee," she wonders to herself, "did Soseki buy books here? And Tanizaki? Must've, they lived nearby, didn't they?" But now the store is filled with salary-men and office ladies from the Marunouchi, Kyobashi, and Nihonbashi (finance, trade, steel) areas; clerks from Takashimaya department store, assistants from the many fine restaurants – this being after all, one of the more traditional areas of Tokyo, the very spot from which all roads lead away ("You are leaving the Capital" ((This the most decisive moment of all – and all it receives is this ordinary phrase? No danger sign, encouragement to reconsider. Is this all there is?))). Like the many people lingering at the magazine racks and bookshelves, she too will take her time here. If her man is half the one she thinks he is, he is an avid but careful reader, and will also be found to be lingering.

The bookstore is arranged not unlike the city. And so she wanders among the shelves and sections.

Politics (clean and dirty), economics (secrets to success!), serious literature (Dostoevski and Mishima), non-serious literature (Mishima), children's literature (from Grimm to Atomu), theater (Shakespeare, the Chikamatsu of the West), history (the Decline of the West), Japanese history (What Nanking? What Korea?), philosophy (every latest trend!), technology (train lore, the wheel in Japan), women's studies (what non-Japanese women want), art (pastels, pastels, pastels; Japan's influence on van Gogh, hence, Japan, source of modern art), Nihonjinron (the theory of being Japanese: different brains and hence a different language known only to those with this sort of brain; a special stomach enzyme that weakens the system against alcohol), foreign languages (learn at your own risk!), reference books (train timetables of Meiji 18), religion (Christ died in Akita), crafts (Japan: at one with Nature), architecture (the Japanese house: source of the modern), film (Have you seen Ozu?), test preparation manuals (Warning: four hours sleep pass, five hours fail!), crime (the fish knife in contemporary murder), etiquette (must-reading for the modern female!), and so on and on.

Curious, she wonders, we're the most literate country in the world, but does the world have any idea of what we actually read? If literacy were gauged by quality as well, where would we be on the list? But then she notices – or does not notice but rather becomes aware, for after all how can one notice what is not there? – that there is no section of what the country most enjoys reading: Maruzen is devoid of *manga*. Uncanny, how can it survive? After all, Kinokuniya bookstore devotes an entire floor to the stuff.

Finally, she purchases a volume on architecture and photography, figuring she ought to know more about the double subject. Resignedly, she admits that once again she has missed her man.

* * *

I am in thralldom, in throes, Tokyo – are you?, Hiroko wonders.

* * *

–   I came in here for a drink, and –
   – ... and found a memory. What else are we here for – but to remember?
                                        – *Ruthless* (Edgar G. Ulmer, 1948)

* * *

That great exchange of telegrams – that mutual utter incomprehension! – remember? The former mayor Goto Shimpei, now in charge of reconstructing the city after the earthquake, fires one off to his friend, the city planner Charles Beard, "Earthquake fire destroyed greater part of Tokyo. Thoroughgoing reconstruction needed. Please come immediately, even for a short stay." And Beard responds: "Lay out new streets, forbid building without street lines unify railway stations." "Lay out streets"! "Even for a short time"! What tenderness!

Chapter 11

NISHI-NIPPORI–NIPPORI

And then Lang had to return to Vienna for a few months, there was no choice, an unfinished job, a previous commitment, I forget what but there was no choice– we all felt sorry about it, not knowing what would develop – Roberta seemed to take it alright, and I emphasize the "seem"– apparently they wrote and spoke regularly … but she was never sure if he'd return– and then she surprised us all, she visited him, they got away and were together – wherever they were.

* * *

He described to me his reunion with Tokio. Like a cat who's come back from vacation and as soon as he's back immediately starts to inspect familiar places. He ran off to see if everything was as it should be – the Ginza owl, the red "Tokyo" neon sign in "Asian lettering" just up the street from Ark Hills, the Shimbashi locomotive, the English books section of Maruzen bookstore, the Temple of the Fox at the top of Mitsukoshi department store, which he found invaded by little girls and Rock singers. He was told that it was now little girls who made and unmade stars, that producers shuddered before them. He was told that a disfigured woman took off her mask in front of passersby and scratched them if they did not find her beautiful. Everything interested him. He who didn't give a damn if the Dodgers won the pennant or about the results of the Daily Double, asked feverishly how Chiyonofuji had done in the last sumo tournament. He asked for news of the Imperial family, of the Crown Prince, of the oldest mobster in Tokyo who appears regularly on television to teach goodness to children. These simple joys he had never felt – of returning to a country, a house, a family – but twelve million anonymous inhabitants could supply him with them.

– Chris Marker-Silva, Sans Soleil (1982)

* * *

I remember seeing my parents making love, Hiroko recalls. That's when we lived farther out, all in that cramped room. My father on top and then my mother, and she just sounding so delirious and happy and he so happy in making her happy. And I just watched. I couldn't really see much, they were under the covers. I was happy to watch; I didn't want to say anything, I was just happy to see them happy, my parents. And they still seem happy. I saw myself make love once. In a hotel. I guess I seemed happy to myself too.

* * *

Kaoru has a day off. He wears only his underwear. He is sitting on the floor at the table, with a large can of beer. The floor is covered with newspapers, weekly magazines, and comicbooks. His wife has gone shopping with the kids. This Sunday he is too tired to accompany them. "I'll see the kids next Sunday," he says without either contempt or apology. After another, smaller beer, he is bored enough to go for a walk. He walks down the five flights of stairs to the street. He sees the Christian neighbor who takes her wheelchair-bound husband to church everyday, their two boys following. He sees the young girl with large breasts talking with two boys on motorbikes, and wonders when she'll turn eighteen so he can see her in a porno video. He sees a couple of American soldiers from the nearby Yokota airbase. They are laughing, and he is sure the joke is on him. He silently curses them. A couple of Americans in the local liquor shop are singing a Country song that he vaguely recognizes. He thinks America must be a wonderful place if it can produce such music. He sees other families, apparently happy. Finally, he runs into his own family, and before they can say anything, he suggests they go out for spaghetti and ice cream tonight. He is in America, on a bus. An American acquaintance – some guy who works in the International Section – is a few seats before him. The bus stops. There's a bar. The American gets into a fight. The American is now black, he's fighting with a white guy. A knife, a death. Kaoru is in the car with the white guy whom he hardly knows but who seems to know Kaoru well. There's an exchange of knives. Kaoru is in a car in America with a knife in his hand, the murder weapon, wondering how he got here. He awakes in a sweat, his wife stirs for a moment. He goes to look after his children, sweeps the dream away, walks back to bed.

Hiroko is wandering around Yokota airbase in North-Northwest Tokyo. And then it becomes her old home in *shitamachi*. Her grandmother is adjusting the picture on the television. Her younger brother is reading a comic-book. Her mother is holding back tears. Her father is in the shop on the first floor. And Hiroko is supposed to be finishing her homework, but in fact she is daydreaming about a boy in her class and wondering how she can get out of the house tonight to see him at the school playground. Then, she has just said goodnight to him; she is restless. It is almost midnight. She runs to the station and gets the last train to Tokyo station. She walks to Hibiya, and wanders into the Imperial Hotel. She is fifteen years old, but she is a thinking woman. A businessman offers her a drink. She accepts. He invites her to his room. She refuses, but she does accept an invitation for a walk in Hibiya Park. There she allows him to fondle her, she gives him her panties. She accepts ten thousand yen for the twenty minutes. She returns to the hotel, and stays in the coffeeshop and lobby, reading Kafka, an author she's chosen just because she liked the name, "kafuka." In the lobby, Hank Williams's "Lonesome Highway" is playing, again and again.
Hiroko, awakes in a panting sweat, remembering the night.

* * *

She sits dripping over his face, his eyes strain to still the image.

* * *

Van Zandt, that coincidental man went walking. One step after another, steady, certain in their grip of the ground below, but uncertain of their destination. At the train station he saw a young, rice-skinned woman in red and black on the platform opposite, and thought. A few hours later in another of the hearts of the city – it doesn't matter which – he saw her again shopping for a pencil. He was shopping for some paper. That evening in another – what we have called here – the "hearts" of the city, yes, he saw her again, alone, drinking, and he thought. One woman, three hearts; three hearts; one city.
One man, one van Zandt.

* * *

- Not quite your kind of area, Hiro?
- What, why do you say that?
- Well, I can't really picture you spending too much time appreciating the finer delights of the older city.
- Oh no?
- Not really.
- When was the last time you got stuck – I mean, you were here?
- When we went to that all-tofu restaurant.
- Oh yes, that was two or three years ago.
- Excuse me, but I don't think that was quite the last time, Hiro.
- Shh!
- Oh, comeon, no need to keep it a secret.
- Oh, alright.
- What?
- What?
- Well, what's the main thing you notice when you're on the Yamanote Line and it swings past these stations, Nishi-Nippori and Nippori?
- Uhm, the signs?
- The ravishing beauty of the view!
- That one can see Mt. Tsukuba from here without interference!
- The clean air!
- The silence!
- The luxurious housing!
- All the greenery!
- The cables and poles have all gone underground!
- The happy faces!
- Relaxed!
- Loving!
- Everyone speaking English!
- Or French!
- Or any language, as well as Japanese!
- Ok, ok, comeon, seriously.
- Ok, ok, the same thing you notice from anywhere along the Yamanote Line.
- The filth!
- The garbage!
- The human degradation!
- The meanness and sullenness of the people!
- Their evil insularity!

- The concrete and steel!
- Alright, alright, seriously now.
- Ok, what?
- ???
- The love hotels.
- That's it?
- Well, there are a lot in this particular area, don't you think? Between Ikebukuro and Ueno, all the spillover.
- Mmm, I'm not so sure.
- But other in-between areas have lots of love hotels.
- Maybe they're just bigger here. Taller buildings, you know.
- Maybe.
- So, Hiro, what you're saying is that this entire area – which does have personality, and a lot of important history too – of all of it, all it makes you think of is its love hotels?
- Well, uhm, yes, or all I'm saying is that that's what you notice from the train.
- Not me.
- ?
- ?
- ?
- I notice the light, endless. Look!

* * *

My cunt lies to the east, rises for you, easterly. Talk to me, cunt of mine, I want to be the little man walking inside you as you walk – easterly.

* * *

The costs of confusion notwithstanding, no place else I'd rather be, give me an address, make me a map on a scrap of paper, I'll find you, discern the system, read the signs, *chome*, *machi*, whatever, gizmo shop, soba shop, no confusion, no cost, Columbus-Lang discovers the city the way he unravels a memory or dream!

* * *

Baudelaire on the splendors and miseries of living outside the loop: "The complex elements which go to make up the painful and glorious decor of civilization."

* * *

Stop, enough! One bead of cum; licked away, the rest for breakfast.

* * *

1657: The Fire of the Long Sleeves

"In every look that comes my way, every woman says: within my sleeves the whorl of pain."

Tokyoites are not blessed with that capacity for memory that Kyotoites possess. In the ancient capitol, for example, if someone mentions "the war,"' you will not be certain if your interlocutor is referring to the Second World War or to one that occurred in the nineteenth century, or even the sixteenth or twelfth! As for Tokyo, if one speaks of a fire, well, that would probably refer to one that occurred just last week. But if one were to speak of a "great fire," then most people might immediately think of either the air-raids of 1945, or the earthquake of 1923. But if one were to press the point, then memory – or deep reading in history – might bring to mind the Yoshiwara fire of 1911, or the Kanda fire of 1881 (Kanda was actually said the be the "best place for fires" ((in what respect, having them or viewing them?))), or the Ginza fire of 1872, or the fires of 1834 or 1829. Going even further back, one might recall the fire of 1682 that destroyed a great part of the city. (And it too is a story for which we must make space in this book, for it involves love.) But for the true Edophile, the greatest of all fires occurred in 1657: The Fire of the Long Sleeves.

"The Flowers of Edo" they're called. Could any other city create such a *festive* name for those disasters that have so often – "no fewer than ninety-seven major conflagrations between 1603 and 1868" – brought devastation to the city? The author knows something of the spirit. In Spring 1994 a fire destroyed a home just two houses away from my own. While people were concerned and somewhat afraid, there was too a definite ebullience in the air: the whole neighborhood out in its pajamas, people scurrying here and about for a better view, the excitement at watching those quintessential Tokyo heroes, the firemen, at work.

Edo was barely half a century old when it occurred; indeed, one might say that 1657 marked the city's second birth so great were the changes the fire brought about. A site that had been constructed as a military fortification suddenly had to face the fact that it was indeed a city of people: over-crowded Edo had to be expanded; firebreaks and fire-brigades created; whole areas had to be rethought, rearranged, removed. It was a moral lesson too: out were the flamboyant mansions done in the Momoyama style; in was a greater austerity. In fact, large parts of the present-day city only came into existence because of the fire. What is now the great fish market of Tsukiji had never before existed. Tsukiji was founded on reclaimed land as a result of the pressing need to expand the city. Scores of shrines and temples were moved out to areas such as Asakusa, Yushima, Yotsuya and Azabu. And besides the new firebreaks, most importantly, the first bridge across the Sumida was built, Ohashi (the "Great Bridge"). (Simply read Waley: like a running theme in his book we keep coming upon phrases on the order of "this came about in the wake of the fire of 1657.")

And why "long-sleeves"? The reader might know that kimonos with long sleeves are worn by unmarried women. The legend is this: A certain kimono was worn by three separate young women all of whom lived in the area of Honmyōji in Hongō. The first woman died lovelorn; the other two both died after having just worn the same kimono. Before any more unfortunate deaths might occur, the priests of the temple decided to get rid of the kimono by burning it. While attempting to do so, however, a strong wind caught the flaming garment and whirled it here and there, to this roof and that as if it were the embodiment of the haunted, unsatisfied souls of those three young women.

The kimono no doubt was finally devoured by flames – and so too was the city. Three-quarters of Edo were razed; more than 100,000 inhabitants died – one-quarter of the population. And a fifth of that number were to be found piled so high in the Kanda River that sight of the river itself disappeared. Even the gold in the castle keep melted.

A more prosaic account of the fire would speak of eighty days without rain; tremendous winds sprinkling layers of sand and dust over thousands of already highly flammable thatch-roofed houses. And then the flames began. Three days of raging fires that only ended when finally it snowed.

The dead were honored in a new temple, Eko'in, which also suffered its own horrors: it burnt down in 1916, and again in this century's other two great disasters. But somehow it not only absorbed all this suffering, it dedicated itself further and drew into its embrace the memories of those who suffered in further disasters (more fires and earthquakes), the aborted, babies who died in childbirth, those who died in prison, even animals.

We could go on, but enough horror. The only romance about it all lies in its name and the legend of its origin. Perhaps someday the "long sleeves" will be forgotten and the great disaster that recreated the city will only be recalled by its alternate, or "official" name, "Meireki no Taika," the Great Meireki Fire ("Meireki" referring to the name of the period in which it occurred). Perhaps, but that is unlikely, this being Tokyo.

ɢɢ ɢɢ ɢɢ

Fires have no narratives – or none known to this author. Let us indulge ourselves though and simply create the space here and now for that other fire mentioned earlier. It is a short, sad tale and again concerns the flames of unfulfilled passion.

In 1682 a fire broke out, again destroying much of Edo (including Bashō's hut). The house of a grocer in Komagome was among those destroyed. He and his family took refuge in a nearby temple. There his daughter, soon to turn fifteen, the young and lovely Oshichi, fell in love with one of the temple's acolytes. But within a few days, the house was rebuilt and the grocer's family returned home. Oshichi was desperate. So much so that she dared – so as to see the young man once more – she dared by her own hand to burn down her own family's new home – and she was caught.

The law was clear: Arsonists under age fourteen were banished to live on a distant island. "But when fifteen years of age and over: Burning at the Stake." Oshichi was lead to the stake along with five other arsonists. As the wagon in which she stood drew past the crowd, all could see that the fair young girl was unrepentantly noble, self-assured and unafraid for she had done all for love. (One thinks of Anne Wiazemski in Bresson's *Joan of Arc*.) And the city's heart went out to her. She was memorialized at Enjōji, where, it was thought, the Bodhisattva Jizō elected to take on the burden of her sufferings. And even today people pray at her grave, laying flowers and other offerings. Before they play her role, Kabuki actors come, too. (Just as they also pray at the grave of Oiwa of *The Ghost Story of Yotsuya*, jilted and slain, forever haunting the man, her face horribly disfigured.) In his *Five Women Who Loved Love*, Saikaku too wrote of Oshichi.

ɢɢ ɢɢ ɢɢ

But of fire and its horrible effects we have spoken enough.

* * *

Why this sudden spiritual crisis? Why does the young woman suddenly hear the names Kukai, Dōgen and others? Why this dream of the sacred giant dragonfly under her pillow?, the dream of the fat woman who saved her from embarrassment (and saved the insect from the viper who lay under the absent lover's pillow)?, the dream of the religious leader's convention where they all entered with their heads completely covered, swathed in endless cloths, covering their own never-cut hair, even their eyes covered, a bit of gauze to see through, these signs of the ego's denial, why, the woman wonders, at this time above all, why this burst of spirit?

* * *

Our bodies sets of lips, chests, drifting, imploding into one another, all tongue and penetration, a single blood-stream, cum-stream.

* * *

– Here you are.
– *Mugi-cha*! Makes the summer almost bearable. Shame they don't export it.
– I knew a pregnant woman who spent her summer in department stores for the air-conditioning.
– She didn't shop too, did she?
– Oh no, just kept cool. How do you manage?
– I was born cool, Cafferty, haven't you noticed?
– Inside-out.
– Well, that's what people think, so why disillusion them? That is true of you too, isn't it?
– I would like to think so, but alas.
– Alas what?
– Alas, I am of your party.
– I knew we had something similar.
– Probably more than you suspect.
– Oh, I hope not.
– Whatever for? What could you mean?
– Oh, Cafferty, you would not like to be like me. Trust me.

- Well, I certainly do trust you. And I like you – how you carry yourself, your conversation, your –
- My conversation? My weird talk, you mean.
- Call it what you like, it is fascinating.
- Incomprehensible. Hell, I even confuse myself much of the time.
- You're not after lucidity, are you?
- In my own weird way. It would not be unwelcome, believe me.
- But you are lucid, Marianne – in a weird sort of way.
- Thanks, I think.
- No, I mean it.
- I think of lucidity as being in some way reasonable, communicative.
- Not me, I think of it as illuminating. A flash of light, a beam thrown on something that had hitherto been opaque.
- Oh, come on now.
- No, I'm serious. That other kind of lucidity is just rational talk that makes the days go by, makes us ignore the slings and arrows. It's convenient.
- Cafferty, I do not pretend to poetry. And if you call my talk poetic, I'll deny it – poetic only in the worst sense. A car crash in a movie that takes place on a beach.
- Have I seen that movie?
- No, I just made it up. And believe me, it's a bad movie.
- But there's a lot of poetry in the movies.
- And a lot of bad dialogue that some people believe is poetry.
- True. But do you really confuse yourself so?
- Oh, I don't know if that's the right word, really. I certainly surprise myself. I often say to myself, "Did I just say that?" Confusion, surprise – I provide my own amusement.
- And ourselves with wonder.
- Well, it's a wonderful world.
- You do think so, don't you?
- Of course. You don't?
- Let me respond later. Back to you.
- What's on your mind?
- Wonder.
- Ok, I will.
- No, I mean your sense of it.
- Oh, yes. The branches of a tree. How they hold up. How do we? All the punishment, outrageous fortune. A child on his bicycle. How his father teaches him. Bread rising in an oven. A woman at a window. What does she gaze on? Is she turning away from something?

Waiting for the bread to finish, expecting some word? The telegram that releases her? That will doom her?
- Are these movie references?
- Oh a couple, I suppose. Does it matter?
- No, I was just wondering.
- Watermelon. Do you remember that scene in *Late Chrysanthemums*, the actor and the maid who is the only person who tells him the truth, that he stinks on stage?
- Vaguely, yes. Why?
- I don't know, it just occurred to me. I love that scene. Maybe because it's summer.
- You'll stay in town?
- Haven't decided yet. Maybe I'll go on an inspection tour.
- Of your islands?
- Yes, I haven't seen them in a couple of years.
- But you'll still be in the city, you know?
- Of course, I couldn't bear to leave, you see.
- Nor I. I used to go away every summer, unbearable.
- Did you see the fireflies?
- Oh yes. You still can, in pockets here and there, you have to know where though.
- And I assume you do?
- I'm not keeping it a secret. Why don't we go sometime?
- Oh, Cafferty, I'd love to. What an honor, thank you. The fireflies of summer. Dragonflies. What are bluebells, by the way, insects or flowers?
- Does it matter? They sound like both, don't they?
- Do they sound deadly, poisonous?
- Blue, bell. No, not at all.
- We should make them the official Tokyo flower-insect.
- I think we just have. But let's not tell anyone just yet.
- Ok. But are there any in Tokyo?
- Does that matter? There are now.
- Yes, yes, there are.
- What else is there in Tokyo that only you and I know about?
- People like you and I, Marianne.
- Ha ha. True. But I hardly know you.
- Better than you think, I'm sure.
- I'm not so –
- Try me.
- Love life.

- I've had one. Or two or three.
- Or four or five?
- Or six or more.
- But you're not telling.
- Oh, I don't mind telling you. But it would be nothing new to you, I'm afraid.
- Really?
- I'm sure. I think that I love like you – full-speed ahead, and then things get sloppy.
- Slip on your tongue and all that.
- The whole rigmarole.
- Work life.
- Various. Editing, PR, office work of many kinds, private secretary. Nothing special but it enabled me to drift through and pay the bills along the way. Not at all like your experience, I'm sure.
- Not unlike if you count waitressing, hostessing here, some office work there, barely paid the bills, though.
- No, not unlike, I suppose.
- Friend life.
- Blessed.
- Very like. Benevolent bluebells.
- Hummingbirds.
- Irises.
- Cafferty, you're a dear.
- Marianne, you're a charm.
- Merely?
- In the other sense.
- Do I have antlers?
- In the other spelling.
- I accept.
- Japan life.
- Where's that?
- Here.
- Where here? I see no Japan here.
- What –
- Improve the question.
- Tokyo life.
- There you go.
- Tokyo life.
- A charm – in both senses. No, I'm positive I would not be anything like me had I not come here.

- Then I'm not wrong.
- About what? Me?
- No, the city. The city and I. It does that to one, doesn't it?
- If what I'm thinking is what you're thinking, then yes, yes it does do that to one, doesn't it?
- I think you're thinking what I'm thinking. And yes it is, it is doing it to me, isn't it?
- Seems to be so, yes.
- Again. Tokyo life.
- Personality, anonymity.
- Oh, I love that answer. More.
- As they say, skinship.
- That too. More.
- To be anyone you want. To finally have a chance to create that.
- Like paper that dissolves in water, or those kids' bathtub toys that flower in water.
- Both, yes.
- Another.
- Mugi-cha.
- Oh, that's not specifically Tokyo.
- Sure it is, if we say it is.
- Ok, I do.
- I do too.
- Does that mean we're married? I've always wanted to be married. No, I don't mean that, not that way – but married to you sounds like fun.
- Well, it wasn't in the past.
- But I thought – ?
- None of your guesses are wrong.
- How do you do, Mrs. Cafferty?
- Believe me, you'd be the only one now. You've the imagination for marriage.
- Is that what it takes? I've always thought so. But most of the world seems to think it's bicycle lessons, and baking homemade bread.
- Well, for most of the world it is. And that's why most marriages are so decidedly dull.
- Dull, dull, dull.
- Dull, duller, dullest.
- Betrothal, death throttle.
- Speaking of marriage –
- Oh, let's leave them for later. This is too much fun for Mrs. Cafferty.

- Ok, ok.
- Marriage life.
- My past?
- No, my future.
- Uhm, alright, let me see. *Mugi-cha* in the summer certainly.
- You sweet man.
- I get up early, so you can count on a good breakfast.
- Can you get muesli in Tokyo?
- I have my sources.
- Oh I'm sure.
- Well, that means two breakfasts.
- I'm sorry.
- No, no, I'm pleased. Maybe we'll meet in the middle in time.
- I hope so, I'd like to meet your middle.
- Uh-hum. Now then, as you know, I know every variety of restaurant, tempura, soba, sushi …
- Is this going to be an eating marriage?
- Wait, wait, I'm just getting started. Lots of movies, of course.
- You bet.
- The best friends.
- Spread our love, the light, the bluebells.
- Tokyo at night.
- Tokyo in the morning?
- Dawn.
- Will you give me the wintry sky, that blue, that clarity?
- I've just signed it away to you. You're clarity itself, Marianne.
- You're the only one who thinks so.
- Why would I any longer need the wintry sky when I would have you? – my bluebell.
- Cafferty, I'm devoted.
- Marianne, I'm … I'm enthralled.
- So marriage can work, can't it?
- Oh, if people can talk, walk. It only takes imagination.
- Only, yes. I'll bet I can out-walk you.
- Bet's on.
- Shall we?
- How? Walk and talk? Walk in silence? Or linger a bit more here, talking?
- Here, it's far too hot outside.
- …
- I used to live by a rose-garden. I used to live by a tofu-seller. I used

to live by a yard filled with kids' bicycles. I used to live by a street where the traffic noise never stopped.
- I used to not live in Tokyo.
- Horrors!
- I could never leave. That would be my doom. I used to live in the countryside.
- Oh, you poor man, you.
- By rice-paddies. Never been so depressed. Women permanently bent at ninety degree angles. Men with leathery faces. Cheap *saké* their only relief. Bicycles.
- We're in the big city now, Dear, we'll make our way.
- That sounds like the kind of copy I used to write.
- Is that what you do?
- On occasion. It more than pays the bills. Allows me a bit of travel, some indulgences. How about you?
- Like I said, bouts of hostessing, save the cash, lay low for a while, then back to the willow world.
- And – ?
- Oh, it's alright, really. A woman needs to know how to handle it, that's all. I don't agree with all the criticism of it, it's taught me a lot of how things work here.
- I'll bet it has.
- Art life.
- What? Oh, yes. Uhm, movies mostly, trying to read Chinese classical poetry, I was here during the heyday of *Mono-ha*, what tremendous art, what a breath of fresh air, Lee, Suga, Sekine. Those artists should be better known.
- Actually, I meant your own art.
- What art?
- I thought you ... that you wrote or ...
- Or painted or composed? Oh no, never even tried. Well, I may have tried in a certain manner, but no.
- But all this talk of the imagination, of conversation like sparkling movie dialogue?
- Marianne, that's for living. No, no, I'm no artist. Sparkling movie dialogue? Well, I've dubbed a few movies, but nothing you or I would want to see more than once. No, I recognized quite early on that I did not have that in me.
- Why?
- Well, the dedication, the ambition, maybe even the ruthlessness. No, I wanted to enjoy life. Cultivate friendships. Converse, congress.

- I'm surprised, I really am. Now I'm maybe even more enthralled by my new husband. Really?
- Really, Dear.
- And all this talk about imagination?
- That's not the sole property of artists. I'd go even further – it's our nature.
- !
- But you're an artist, aren't you?
- I hope you're enthralled now. No, I'm not, not really. I've posed, I've been in a few movies because I walk well I'm told, strike a certain presence, seem "mysterious," but no, I'm no artist, no actress.
- But I thought you – ?
- No, Dear. A lot of people think so. But that's just their projections, their wishes. I wouldn't presume.
- Presume what, to be an artist?
- Well, yes.
- No presumption involved. They're just doing what we are all capable of, given the chance.
- Given the society?
- I'm not sure, really. I suppose so, but I wouldn't care to get into a debate about it.
- What-you-do life.
- As I said – talk, walk. Love, occasionally.
- Me?
- Forever and always.
- That's a country song.
- Is it? I had no idea. Can't say I like the stuff.
- Our first argument.
- Forgive me. I'm old enough to learn new tricks.
- I don't insist. "Hear the lonesome whippoorwill." Lonely bluebell. Music life.
- Classical. And Duke Ellington.
- Well, I'm young enough to learn new licks. Ouch. Life life.
- As you see me. As I am.
- As we will be?
- As we will.
- Oh, Cafferty, why didn't I –
- Let me finish: why didn't I meet you decades ago?
- So, why?
- Well, you weren't even born, Dear, not even –
- Let me finish: imagined. But you are an artist –

- Well, it depends on how you define the term.
- By your standards.
- Then perhaps I am, but I wouldn't apply the epithet myself.
- Epithet, is that all?
- Why want more?
- You're too modest.
- No, too sure of myself.
- Are you?
- By now, yes.
- Will I ever be sure?
- I think you already are. That's what makes you so special, Marianne.
- But next to you –
- If only ... decades, you know.
- The brush of a wing, sound of a bell, firefly. Dodecahedron plus.
- But you are sure, I can sense you are.
- Can you? That makes me happy. I don't know. I sometimes wish I could change, but then I always wonder, change into what? When I think of the possibilities, there's no one, no way I'd like to be but the one the way I am now.
- The one way.
- Well, mine. For now, I suppose.
- So there might be change?
- There always is, I suppose, but I force nothing. For all the weirdness I'm thought to be, I am not discontent to be myself.
- Nor should you be, you're radiant, really you are. You have no idea of your wonder, qualities.
- Confusion.
- Is that bad?
- Well, it can get in the way in a job interview.
- I imagine. But you manage.
- I do, yes, I suppose.
- But are you genuinely confused? After all, you do manage.
- Oh, confused only in that others think me strange and I only wish people could understand the curious things that I say. But that's just truly the way I have to articulate what I see.
- Well, we're having no problem. And obviously, you have strong friendships, and people like Lang and Roberta and the others seem to understand you, seem not to be confused by whatever you may say.
- I suppose you're right, yes. See, I don't really think of myself as confused; nor do I think of them as confused. Just that –

- That it doesn't measure up to the world's rational definitions of human discourse.
- Well, that may be one way of looking at it, not exactly the terms I would use.
- And, don't forget – we are talking, now, and haven't missed a beat.
- No, we're each other's rhythm section alright.
- Marianne and the Bluebells. But are they insects, or flowers?
- I really don't know, Marianne, and I hope I never find out. I only want them to be what you want them to be.
- Well, maybe in the summer they'll be insects, and I'll keep them in little bamboo cages. And the rest of the time they'll be flowers.
- Perennials.
- Oh yes, like the way you and I must talk, perennially.
- I'll do my best.
- Oh, I know you will, you do.
- I haven't always.
- I can't believe it, my love.
- Sad but true. Maybe I've always only ever spoken too clearly. Maybe I should take lessons from you.
- Oh no, you wouldn't want that. Don't you see? We compliment each other. And besides, your clarity is a form of imagination too. It's your term.
- Perhaps you're right.
- Oh I'm sure I am! So tell me more about "sad but true."
- Well, by your terms, maybe my partners couldn't see the imagination behind my clarity, and only saw it as a certain dullness.
- Then they were the dull ones.
- In a way, I have to admit that they were.
- Left you?
- Yes, and that's what I can't understand. Not that they left me, but that all my friends always thought that I had undermined the relationship. I never left anyone, always wanted to stay. They left me. I was not the problem. They were their own problems. Probably still are, with whatever exciting dullards they've wound up.
- You're not in touch with them still?
- No, I've never had that gift. Goodbye has always meant goodbye to me. Besides, they'd written me off.
- Poor souls.
- Perhaps. Perhaps they're actually better off now.
- Their loss.
- Who's to say?

- I am. My gain.
- Marianne, you flatter me.
- You flatter me.
- Is that an order?
- No! Yes, ok, yes it is.
- You're a sweetie. You're my clarity.
- And you're a bluebell.
- See what I mean?
- Clearly.
- Blearingly.
- Endearingly.
- Ikkyu. Sesshu.
- Is the museum still open? Should we go?
- See the Sesshu? It's incredible, isn't it?
- Ikkyu's face.
- How he must have talked!
- And walked. How many sandals?
- How many brushes? Do you think he turned some of those sandals into brushes when none were available?
- And where did the ink come from when that ran out?
- The blood of bluebells, of course. How else could he have written such poetry?
- And the winter poems?
- Poets can draw blood from flowers too, you know.
- Mizoguchi kept a portable toilet on his sets.
- Lang had thermoses of soup on his.
- Ozu kept records of the bottles of whiskey drunk as he worked on his scripts with Yoda.
- Joan Fontaine was born in Tokyo.
- Cary Grant's last film took place here.
- Ophuls admitted his Yoshiwara was his worst film.
- Still, it has its moments.
- Buster Keaton rigged a portable toilet to surprise unwanted users; the walls would flap down and embarrass them.
- Buster Keaton went to China. Proved every child's dream.
- Oh god, Cafferty, you're talking my talk!
- Should we go to China?
- Whatever for? We have Tokyo.
- We'll always have Tokyo.
- Will we always have had Tokyo?
- You mean like Rick and Elsa?

- I mean like Rick and Elsa.
- You don't plan to leave, do you?
- Whatever for? Clarity? I have you.
- Then no, we'll never leave. Whatever for? I have no plan to leave, do you?
- Whatever for? It's home. I am possible here, understood.
- And I can invite confusion finally.
- Better to be confused …
- Better to be clear …
- Than clear or confused …
- In any other city.

[Much later]

- But weren't we supposed to talk about something else today?
- What matter? No, oh yes, you're right. Roberta and Lang. Haven't you heard?
- No, what?
- *Lang had to return to Vienna for a few months, there was no choice, an unfinished job or other, a previous commitment, I forget what but there was no choice– we all felt sorry about it, not knowing what would de-velop– Roberta "seemed" to take it alright – apparently they wrote and spoke regularly … but she was never sure if he'd return – and then she surprised us all, she visited him, they got away and were together, were happy being together – wherever they were.*
- No!? Really?!
- Yes!
- Are they're both back here, now?
- I'm not sure. I hope so. Or at least I hope they're together wherever they may be. But together. Tokyo or no.
- But they'll always have Tokyo.
- Yes, yes they will. Like you and I, Cafferty. We have our bluebells, they have theirs, bluebells or whatever else they choose.
- This is great news. Roberta and Lang, together again.
- That's also a Country song.
- I'm beginning to like it already.
- Roberta and Lang. I can hardly believe it.
- Cafferty and Marianne, imagined at last, I can –
- – believe it.

* * *

Rich and strange, Van Zandt thinks to himself, for all my wanderings, even in my own room, or my neighborhood, hell, the whole city, nothing changes – what's the rest of the line? – wandered Paris, wandered Amsterdam, now I am wandering Tokyo, wandering girls. Changes, changes.

* * *

The sea we turn into salt-seed moon-rise.

* * *

It cannot be comprehended, seen whole as one. As I walk in one direction across the city, someone else moves in the opposing direction, burying my tracks. This guy will do the same again tomorrow. That woman will be sleeping with another man. That shop will become a park (yes, we can reverse history). The only way to comprehend it all, to perceive the whole city entire, to fully express my boundless love is total acceptance of that shop, woman, man, and so see ourselves completely one multiple heart, an onmi-directional love. And so we survive, perceive, whorls within.

* * *

R'n'L!!!!!!!!!!!

I wish I could do hand-shadows.

During my first few months in Tokyo I was taken for a Jew, an Arab, a a Greek, a Sicilian, but never for what I am.

There is so much *shit* in the air. You must swear to me that when I am on my deathbed (assuming I will have one) that some Wolf or Hawk or Debussy will be playing. I could not abide going across the river, as Stonewall put it, and having some pop crap as the last thing on earth I hear. The thought horrifies me.

I remember when I first met Elfi, I asked her if her name was the German form of Elvis.

The annual survey. If you had a magazine, what kind would it be? If you had a publishing house, what would you call it? (Me: Eight Dogs Press, even though I hate dogs.) And a record label? And a restaurant? And, of course, a band?

Ways I might die. Well, the first, obviously, is being hit by a car here (they can't walk, can't drive). The other day a woman was making a left turn and looking right; almost hit me. She blithely drove on, smiling at me. The second is from a knife wound – I'm always dropping them. I'm cutting vegetables, drop the weapon, it goes through my foot and into the floor. Bravely, I lift the whole, call the hospital, but too late, gangrene sets in, the foot is amputated, then the rest, part by part. Most probably though I'll fall down a flight of stairs in some station because I can't keep my eyes off some looker.

How do they get the cranes up there, on top of buildings when they're building them? Do they first build a ground floor or a roof and assemble a crane at the same time, or somehow drive one up there and then continue building, 'cos otherwise they gotta have an even taller crane to lift another one up there, right? Or am I wrong? Do you know, or is it one of the mysteries?

So, do you guys think life is disappointing? I mean, I know it's a wreck sometimes, but after all, we got you and I – or is it me? – nah, it ain't a disappointment ... yeah, maybe it is. I don't know – and anyway *Tokyo Story* happens in Kamakura.

"I opened my eyes to the whole universe and I saw it was loving." What a pretty line. Here's another: "I could be in love with almost anyone. I think that people are the greatest fun." Ah, the California sun!

The waiter had a shirt just like the one Carrie brought me from Hong Kong.

Pascal was right you know – about leaving home. (I also like what his father told his daughter, Blaise's sister that is, when she remarked that she preferred poetry to geometry: "To be human, one must be both delicate and exact.")

I was just glancing around my room and realized that I have five images of James Joyce on display: the *L'Arc* cover, the Svevo book, a copy of a Freund portrait, the JJ playing cards, and the picture Marianne took of me at the grave. And the King?

One of the regrets of my youth: I never saw Chiyonofuji – did you? Oops, gotta go, there's a Velázquez in town.

* * *

Our bodies the name of god, every letter, syllable, character signed in the world in our arms.

* * *

IN THE CITY

There are women, she knows, there's a friend.
There were men, she knew, is there a man?
There are lies, she knows, there'd been a truth.
There is the loneliness sometimes, but it passes.
There were children, she recalls (and one was lost).
There's a mother, she calls every other weekend, there was a father.
There was love, she thinks, there is him.
There were dreams, she dreams, and now there's this *situation*.
There were words, she says to herself, two or three remain in her bones.
There was Lang, Roberta remembers, now there is me.

* * *

–   But it doesn't stop here, you know.
–   There's a Marui in Koganei, yes, but that's not the end of it, not at all. If we keep walking west. We've still to come to Kokubunji, Tachikawa, and more yet.
–   So, where's it stop?
–   What's the next prefecture?
–   Does that matter?
–   Sure, doesn't it?
–   Why? It's just an extension of Tokyo.
–   So, where's it stop, the border of the Kanto Plain?
–   Why should that stop the city?

- Kobe then, where it drops off into the water?
- No, they'll build a bridge.
- Well, it's gotta stop somewhere! Shanghai sure ain't no part of Tokyo!
- Who says it isn't?
- A billion Chinese, for one, I'm sure.
- Ok, ok, let's say it does stop somewhere.
- Yes, that'd be nice.
- But why should it stop?
- Oh comeon, you mean that Tokyo should just keep expanding until it just swallows up everything?
- Would that be so bad?
- Well, I believe a few or more people would feel some discomfort.
- I feel some right now, just thinking about it.
- But there have to be boundaries to the city.
- Oh, alright, I suppose, but in Tokyo's case, I think they're harder to define.
- No, you get mapmakers and other people and you draw lines. Here's Tokyo, there's outside of Tokyo.
- But don't those people perhaps feel like Tokyoites?
- See, hard to define.
- So, do you think there are a bunch of Shanghai-ites who feel like Tokyoites?
- Could be.
- Oh, comeon!
- Ok, ok, maybe not, but we have to be open to the possibility.
- Ah ha! – now that's a different story.
- No, it's not.
- Why not?
- Everything's still fluid, open – like a good story.
- Well, I, for one, have no idea what you guys are talking about.
- I don't either.
- Well, the subject's open, we can go back to it another time.
- Or not.
- Well then, someone will – of that I am sure.
- Well, I for one am sure that right now, or real soon, we're going to be seeing the sun. That's all I need to know.

* * *

The breathing ear listening to the petals come to rest.

* * *

Ah, this city, Arlene feels, you exasperate me, excite me, frustrate me, delight me, talk to me, fuck me, cry to me (isn't that a song? – did VZ play it once?), oh, you make me want to stay and leave. Oh, To-ki-yo: you make me want to learn again how to make love.

* * *

Roberta hadn't wanted to go shopping, especially in the second biggest department store in the world. But she needed new clothes. That was a fact. New clothes certainly never made her feel particularly better – as they obviously did Lang and Arlene. Roberta was one of those light, arbitrary shoppers, and a lucky one at that. She figured January would be a good time to shop: The bonus season, Christmas and New Year's over; money, energy spent. She had not counted on, was wholly unaware of, the sales. Nonetheless, she was a lucky shopper.

* * *

Straddled thighs, bursts of lust – two cunts, four breasts, eight limbs – the infinite kiss.

* * *

Kazuko is blessed, a challenging job, international clients, good friends, and Kazuo. It's a sayonara party for a friend who is temporarily leaving the company cooperative to study abroad. While there are only women present, it's always been understood that women with serious male attachments can invite their partners. Kazuko mentioned it to Kazuo last week, but forgot to do so again. Oh well, he's probably forgotten. Maybe there will be a message on her phone machine when she returns home.

- We all envy your going to Paris, Shoko, and we'll really miss you a lot. Please write us when you can, ok?
- Can I write to you in French?
- Not if you want us to understand your letters!
- But what if I forget how to write Japanese?
- Oh, that can never happen!
- Oh, don't worry, I'll write – and often.

- We know.
- But you just have to make sure?
- I suppose.
- But don't let the company fall apart without me, hear?
- Oh, we won't let that happen. Now we'll have to work even extra hard without you. Right, girls? Everybody for extra overtime?
- (Universal groans.)
- I'm just sorry I didn't pull my own weight.
- What weight? You're going to look marvelous in those great French clothes.
- Oh yes!
- And live in a rue in an arrondissement.
- Oh, it's just a street and a ward.
- But they're in French!
- But without tatami!
- Oh, what a sacrifice!
- I'll bet the French have lovely stationery.
- But so does Japan.
- Too cute. Shoko, will you send me some French stationery?
- Yes, of course, Yoko.
- And you'll wear French lingerie.
- Shall I send you some of that, Miho?
- Would you?
- Uhm, I think you'd better visit me, and pick out your own, ok?
- I'll be there!
- And who are you going to wear it for, Miho?
- Now now, Miki, Miho will get her man yet, you'll see.
- Well, sooner or later.
- Let's order some cakes, shall we?
- (Universal agreement.)
- And French shoes!
- Red leather!
- Yellow!
- Blue!
- I hardly think I'll have enough money to be buying either French shoes or lingerie.
- Oh but your beau will.
- Oh, now I have a beau, is that it?
- Yes, and he'll set you up in a big lovely apartment where you'll give the most glamorous parties, and you'll be the envy of all the guests. The French women will study your Japanese grace, and the men will

all be enthralled with your Japanese mystery, and –
- Yuriko, I think you've seen too many French movies.
- Oh no, one can't see too many French movies!
- Ok then, she hasn't seen enough Japanese movies.
- Well, none of us have.
- And I think this "beau" you're speaking of is better called by another name.
- Oops, sorry. Well, you know what I mean.
- Uhm, sort of. But remember, I'm going there to study. So that I can come back and re-join the company, and make us even stronger.
- To make us strong, you mean.
- Stronger.
- Good for you.
- Do they really call the worst seats in a theater the Heavens?
- I really don't know, but if they're the cheapest, then I'm sure you'll find me in Heaven.
- The Opera!
- The Louvre!
- The Louvre doesn't have seats, silly.
- So? It is the Louvre, and she can see the Naked Maja, without her French lingerie.
- I think that's a Spanish painting, and it's not in Paris.
- Well, you know, that famous one, of some naked lady.
- Yes, but I think she's dressed – in a dress – and she's smiling. Or naked ... Oh, but there are so many women in Paris either naked or dressed!
- Oh.
- But you will go to the theater and the museums and tell us all about them, won't you, Shoko?
- Yes, when I have the time – and the money.
- ...
- "Boulangerie!"
- "Patisserie!"
- Hey, they rhyme with "lingerie"!
- But they make you fatter, so they don't rhyme – not if you want to look good!
- (Universal laughter.)
- Ah, Gerard Philippe!
- Jeanne Moreau!
- Brigitte Bardot!
- Ugh.

- ?
- Who's she?
- Before your time, Miho.
- Oh.
- Girls, I'll write you everything … promise.
- Will you? Will you?
- (Universal smiles.)

And so the party goes on.

But Kazuko doesn't envy Shoko. She likes it here; she has come to like Tokyo very much – with a few complaints, but only a few and those mostly minor. Of course, she'd prefer to be home in Kyoto, but there is the company, her friends and colleagues, Roberta and the others. And Kazuo, who really can't leave Tokyo. And then the door opens and she sees him. So do the girls, and they look back at Kazuko and a few of them forget Paris for a moment and envy her.

* * *

No, perhaps it was really just in the nature and not necessarily the materials of the work, I convolutedly decided to myself: the city, my way of loving – I had tried to look *with* not *at* the lover – the language I have been fumbling with so as to speak with – well …

Lang had suddenly found himself in this cruel city – that is, it can sometimes appear to be cruel to one who is not prepared to see it on its own terms, terms that can also be very playful when not sticking to a schedule – so here he was, estranged more or less from Roberta and tossed between two or three choices that he wasn't really wholly aware of, and suddenly a man of few words, and most of those the same, repeated, unlike the even more self-convoluting VZ, or the delirious Marianne, or the more athletic dash dash dash of Roberta, or the ever-sober Arlene, or the careful, insightful Cafferty, and so he was, in a word, at a loss for them, but not yet happily so. He, I, could not yet feel as light as we felt bereft. So for that time then it was enough – enough! it was overwhelmingly consoling – to have these friends with and around us. But Kazuko, Hiroko and Kazuo, even Hiromi, Hiro and Kaoru, and their styles of talking? I wanted to consider them friends too, they were Tokyoites, after all, more or less, as were the others, or were becoming so, certainly … But could I ever become more than the material of the thing, more than the one who simply wrote the city?

*   *   *

His bulb in my mouth, my petals in his.

*   *   *

URBI ET ORBI

Amsterdam, a song
Brussels, a bar
Cahors, some photographs
Dublin, a bar
Easter Island, an ad
Frankfurt, a newspaper
Ghent, Lang's shirt
Hollywood, a hair salon
Istanbul, a menu
Jena, a bookstore
Kamakura, Ozu's train
Lima, DR's home
Mariannas, her islands
Napoli, an ice cream
Oberlin, a school
Paris, a boutique
Quebec, a sculptress
Shanghai, a visit
Ùstica, the sun-god
Vienna, a woman
Warsaw, a record shop
Xian, a source
Yorkshire, a friend
Zürich, Marianne's photo of me at Joyce's grave

*   *   *

–   And so what's new?
–   We haven't spoken in so very long.
–   Only so many?
–   Ah, your Italian accent!
–   On whose account?

- Who's counting, indeed?
- Indeed, Lang?
- Inaction, indeed.

* * *

Buddha's balls, Buddha's cunt.

* * *

- How long do you think it would take us to walk all the way there from here, Otemachi to Shibuya?
- Why would you even want to? That's what the subways are for, and the busses, and taxis.
- I know, I know, let Lang walk all over the place if he likes. But how long would it take, do you think? Let's say I aim for Ginza first, twenty-five minutes at most; then Kasumigaseki, twenty; then Roppongi, maybe forty, that's an hour and twenty-five minutes; then Shibuya, forty, that makes two hours and fifteen minutes. Could that be right? I'd have thought about three hours. Hey!, we missed my station. Oh well, we may as well walk to the next, eh?

And he does, and does, and does; on to the next, and to the next, and to the next. Hiro's instincts were right, and a surprise to us all – and then he tried it again, Aoyama to Shinjuku; and yet again, Shinjuko to Ikebukuro. He began to discover another Tokyo, and reported it all back to us. Some months later he started a club of "Tokyo Walkers" – he may even have met a girl.

* * *

As reading becomes writing. Some years ago reading heavily in a subject and projecting a two or three years' reading schedule ahead. A curious allusion lead him on to what he thought would be a short detour and while on that track he was lead further again astray on one more digression of reading (to which of course his whole interest was given) which, it goes without saying, lead him ... and lead ... and ... Needless to say, that initial reading is years behind him now; as much perhaps as he has tried to keep the whole and origin in mind, and even managed on occasion short trips back to various crossroads, which naturally entailed their own new detours until these many directions swept him into the whirlwind of an unimagined reading where all these echoes (with their own multi-directioned ways) of books read, unread, to-be-read – the whole a part the parts a whole: all of the innumerable books, the read and the unread now bound in him as he walks the library of Tokyo.

* * *

Her small breasts surmounted by nerve ends – meridians of the compass rose – his hand under her blouse, the moon silvered under the stars.

* * *

Tragic, trivial Tokio, Cafferty says.

* * *

–   Where is it, Kaoru?
–   Takasaki? It's in Gumma, one of the prefectures bordering Tokyo. Perhaps we are becoming a suburb, but we have our own culture, our history, our uniqueness. I know Lang and Van Zandt say they hated the place, but they only spent one weekend there, how could they appreciate Takasaki?
–   What did they say?, they said it was either an overgrown village with a department store or a stunted city that was pockmarked with rice paddies. VZ said there was no talking to be had with farmers' daughters whose teeth were either gold, missing or black, not blackened. And as for the men, well, the leisure suit has a permanent home in Takasaki. Lang said that the only local traditions were to be found inside a whisky bottle in an ersatz 1946 Ginza nightclub, or siting on mildewy tatami so as to give the all-weather insects easier access to one's already weak blood. And that the children had all just emerged from the forest, their parents not having had the wisdom and compassion to strangle them at birth. And that as for –
–   Enough. They cannot appreciate Takasaki. They are so, so wrong.
–   Really, Kaoru?

* * *

Coming up for air, wiping the hair from her tongue.

* * *

SCENE ELEVEN: SOBU LINE

The train is a piece of mobile architecture, yellow, cutting east-west across the city – whoosh! under the bridge at Ochanomizu – they say there is an Aleph there – and as it moves east to west she walks backwards in time; she walks through the train to the end; when it reverses directions, she does likewise. But within each train car she needs to inspect every face of every passenger, and so accordingly as she walks one way in reverse to the train's direction, she also describes a squiggle as she weaves in and out of the standing passengers. And of course, these various motions and directions and feints as the train lurches or comes to a halt or as passengers jostle against one another and against her, are all again repeated when the train itself reverses direction on its way, well, no, not "home" – what is a train's home but the track?, or the "yard," cold, dark, and anonymous (see *Human Desire* for this). But then too it is a part of a train's function to allow ingress and egress at each stop along the way (she *would* have gotten a local!), and thus we find her also moving in a direction perpendicular to her movement in time (double: the train and she on it moving forward, she walking towards the past, ground already covered), perpendicular too to the circles and weaves she describes, like a bloated crucifix – or in fact, like a … well, a train track, ties and all.

But with all this movement, starting and stopping, getting on and getting off, transferring, jostling of bodies, overhead announcements, television screens in the trains – with all of this, is it any surprise that she does not, once again, find her man, and instead only comes home late, exhausted, grimy, ready for a whisky, a foot soak, a turn with O-Dildo-san, and a sleep on the tatami with the gray buzz of the television providing the background soundtrack to her dream … of a train ride.

* * *

I won't insult him by taking him seriously – unless this declaration of his great love for the city is to be read as a suicide note – he's had crazier notions – to connect the world is one – no, no, to think through the consequences of his actions has never been one of his stronger suits – just look at his finances – to take on the whole you must be grounded first – any adventurer knows the value and necessity of a, oh, what's it called?, I hate being stumped for a word – of a, well, "safe-house" for the moment – "safety net"?, no, that's not quite it, either – but, no, he just lurches forward – and where will we discover the body? Not that I can claim to be so sensible – the wrecks of my youth are there for all to see – but I do have a few survival techniques up my panties – and much else too, another survival tool – but in a city this size and this wonderfully superficial, and … well, not so much confusing as excessively hectic, why would anyone ever want to go after the whole thing?, why this need for comprehensiveness?, these encyclopedic novels? – No no, not me, thanks, gimme the short stuff – I likes my neighborhood and I stays in it. The city, all of it, can come here if it wants, if not, fine, I'll never know what I missed, and so not miss it, what I'll have had will be all that I had, and so that too must qualify as its own totality. The whole city then in a few blocks. The whole thing? – well, I wish him well – as I know too well, the great loves *are mad*.

* * *

There are ten billboards, three posters. The first is a close-up of a face, smiling, bored, all joy, contemplative, it doesn't matter the look or to whom it belongs; it is a close-up of a male face (and it is momentarily difficult to determine just what product is being advertised); it is repeated three times; the second is a medium shot of a thing, a machine, an instrument, electronic, certainly, gleaming, open, offering the open viewer all the world; it is repeated three times; the third is a very wide view of a landscape, and again, whether desert, tundra, forest, mountain range, or even a great city, it does not matter which; it is a landscape, and it too is repeated three times. All of it then thus: face, face, face, machine, machine, machine, landscape, landscape, landscape. And then again, in a perfectly elegant and unexpectedly emotional reprise, capping this lovely sequence, the end of the sentence of the poem, and all of it viewed within a matter of seconds between Sendagaya and Shinanomachi stations – her face.

Chapter 12

UENO–AKIHABARA

Roberta returned to Tokyo; Lang finished his work – there it is – here they are!

* * *

Tokyo Nous Appartient

          – Jacques Rivette-Silva

* * *

–   Marriage then.
–   À la mode?
–   No – in a manner of speaking.
–   What's Ophuls say, most married couples come to hate each other after just a few years together, but most of them don't come to realize it.
–   Max on the mark once more. Max and Garbo, what that might have been!
–   Are they extending one of the subway lines, by the way?
–   I don't know. I hope so. As far as Akita, down to my islands.
–   Right, live in Kyushu somewhere and commute to Tokyo.
–   Why not? I'm sure they'd make the trains comfortable, and fast.
–   Super-bullets?
–   With bed capsules.
–   And bars.
–   Karaoke.

- Soap cars!
- Tunnels of love. Looking at it like this, it sounds a definite possibility.
- I give 'em twenty years at the outside.
- The millennial mobile. No, that's too short a time. How about the centenary of Taisho?
- The mad king, "democracy."
- How about more monorails?
- Like *Metropolis*, yes.
- I say bring back the pneu, you know, those tubes that wind around inside buildings so that you can send messages through.
- My old library had that kind of system.
- Do you think Paris actually had one, I mean, going all over the city? That was how they delivered their mail, wasn't it? Or at least that's the impression I get from their books.
- But what would this do in Tokyo? I like my mail at the door in the morning; I can't imagine all those magazines zooming through little underground tubes; and what if a rat got caught inside? He zooms through, gets pissed off, you reach in for your mail, and there go two or three fingers!
- No no, I agree with you. I was thinking more of a larger, thicker pneu in which people could zoom through.
- Oh, so now you reach for your mail and some guy who's just been ignitioned from across the Tama river only twenty seconds ago, now it's his turn to take a chunk out of you because he's stir crazy?
- I guess you're right, but maybe there is something there. Or maybe not. Maybe we'd just better stick to our dear train and subway system as it is. Anyway, I do think they're adding on to it, and it can only get better. That's one thing the city has not screwed up.
- Help me, Jaysus!
- But if only they didn't stop the trains running so early. Or at least had a late night system, you know, trains every half-hour or so.
- Sure, but then all those capsule hotels and bars and all night cafés would go out of business, you'd have less vomit on the platforms, the air would not be so redolent of eau de puke.
- Oh comeon, you know what I mean.
- I was kidding, of course. But the office workers have to get home and a good night's sleep so they can be back at their desks in the morning.
- Do you think that's it?
- And get those teenagers off the streets and in the love hotels where they belong! Of course that's it. Social control – you've heard of it

haven't you? They're masters here. They've created a society of sleep-walkers. History really is a nightmare they're desperately trying not to awaken from.
– Do you really think that?
– Oh in my off days, yes. In my better moments, I believe in Our Lady of Lunacy. And high-school baseball.
– And girls in sailor uniforms?
– With the roundest eyes! But no, you know how I feel about being here.
– Yes, but that's different from how you feel about here. But I think I know how you feel. Much the same as I.
– Do you think? Can you imagine?
– No, perhaps I spoke too soon. I always seem to speak with the random search button on, I have a sort of jog and shuttle verbal apparatus.
– Oh, comeon, you're not that bad.
– Oh but you know that I have been known to cause a few "Did-she-just-say-what-I-think-she-said?" looks.
– True, but …
– I know, cute mistakes, all the more endearing. Anyway, I won't let me off the hook, so you needn't either. But, how do you feel about here?
– Where here?
– Japan, of course.
– But I'm not in Japan!
– Well, you're not on the Moon either.
– No, all I mean is that I'm in Tokyo, and there's a great difference.
– Do you really think that too?
– Simple: people outside of Tokyo follow everything that goes on here, right? Fashion, speech, trends, manias, whatever. All the social changes originate here, all the dirty politics, all the international stuff. Do you know many Tokyoites wanting to put on *mompe* and sit on the verandahs sighing all day long about the weather and eating *sembei*?
– A bit simplistic to me.
– I suppose.
– And anyway, the dirty politics begins in the countryside hometowns – where was Tanaka during all those shadow shogun years, or all those other guys, where do they come from? And fashion and ma-nias, do they really amount to much? The fashion system is tied to something larger and of which Tokyo is only one sub-center.

- Great! Tokyo the city of sub-centers itself a sub-center!
- Hmm, that's not bad, is it? But then it's only the fashion world. And the trends by definition are not lasting. I mean, a summer's desire for a gilled lizard doesn't really make much of a cultural mark on a country? Speech, well sure, but you get that all over the world, don't you? The Midwestern model in the States – you don't hear too many Southerners on CNN – and Standard Brit on the BBC, and whatever they call it in Paris or Madrid or wherever.
- Do you think Parisians wax melancholic for the pneu?
- Oh, I' m sure, but don't change the subject.
- So what are you getting at – that Tokyoites really do want to take themselves back to the country, and nibble on *sembei*?
- Well, they do wax sentimental for the country home, you've seen the O-bon dancing. Those city girls and boys have practiced their steps quite well. They do have that country feel. Look at the way they exult – it's not just the rhythm of the drums doing that to their bones.
- Then it's not a sexual throb?
- Of course it is that too – but not the sex of the city. And a country music analogy is not too far off. What's *enka* after all but their form of it?
- Arlene, you're on a roll – and no feet in orifices either.
- You're one to speak! We ought to have a talk show – the incomprehensibles. Ha, we could set back English education here by decades.
- What a great idea. We really might be a hit, and besides, English education here is such a shambles anyway, that probably no one would notice the subversion. We'd probably be an improvement on things.
- We could have a chain of schools.
- Sleep with the cuter staff too. Boys for me, girls for you. No jealousy.
- Marianne! I'm afraid I'd be more the den mother type.
- Lion's den. Lionness's.
- No, a simple Arlene den.
- Simple?! But tell me more about your countrified Tokyo.
- Well, I'm just talking off the top of my head here –
- From where else would you?
- Oh, somewhere else is possible too, I'm sure, but not now. All I mean is that I haven't …
- I understand the phrase. Go on, please.
- Ok, anyway … O-bon, yes, I mean, that dancing is something in their bones, it's deep, they dance so well because they feel the country so. It's almost primeval. A hankering.

–   Is this going to get anthropological? Psychological? You aren't going to start talking wombs and mothers and that sort of stuff on me in a minute, are you? 'Cos if you are, bye-bye for me in a split second.
–   Don't worry. At least I think not. Ok, maybe primeval is a bit too too. But you know what I mean.
–   Let's say sort of. So are you saying the great capitol is a deception, that we're awash in a sea of hicks?
–   Not quite, but close. I mean, you know what happens when you go to any store here, how the clerks kowtow, grovel in that slimy way. Is it in *Chikamatsu Monogatari* where you have that clerk always groveling, on his knees whenever someone buys something, and that shrill *Arigato-gozaimasu! Arigato-gozaimasu!* – what is that but the deference of the country bumpkin to big city money?
–   I thought it was a class thing.
–   Oh that too, probably. But the behavior is straight out of Tokugawa country.
–   Is that a branch of music, too?
–   Probably. And what about all these drunk salary-men? Oh, they have to act the sophisticate in business – especially when dealing with foreigners – but wherever do they acquire any sophistication? – you know about those "how to" guides, how to order wine, how to dress properly, how to drop the right names – anyway, at heart, that is, when in their cups, all they really do is hanker for the simpler life of the country. The sophisticate has to prove his rustic side.
–   It's true; I've often wondered about that in the bars.
–   And the girls, the women. The bow-legs, the awful dirndl-like dresses, the country damsel demeanor, my god, and then when they become mothers; comeon, Arlene, you've been outside the city often enough to see country women dressed in layers of quilts, feet wrapped in I don't know what kind of tortuous material, those full fresh country cheeks. Same here.
–   True.
–   And then their fate as mothers and wives. Where is the citified woman there, tell me?
–   No, no, I don't disagree, Arlene.
–   No wonder they go home to the country when they give birth. No, the countryside dominates and determines not so much where the city is going, but what is allowed according to the most ancient traditions. Buruma's book sort of makes the same point too, I suppose, though he doesn't spell it out like I just have.
–   Have you written any of this down?

- What for?
- It's just –
- I know, off the top of my head.
- Well, maybe we can make it one of the topics of our talk show.
- Ok.
- Let's see, "You can take the city out of the country, but you can't take the country out of the city."
- "Super-models in *mompei*."
- "Primitive Modern."
- "Tokyo, the ancient capitol."
- "Arigato-gozaimasu! Arigato-gozaimasu!"
- So, ok, I'm half-convinced, where do we take it from here?
- Where? Nowhere. I mean, we gotta live here. I don't mean to burst any bubbles, yours or mine.
- Seen Roberta lately? What goes on with her, her and Lang?
- Haven't you heard? She's back. *Roberta returned to Tokyo; Lang finished his work – here they are!*
- What do you mean here they are?
- They're here, both of them, back in Tokyo.
- Back in this country backwater, both of them?
- Yes, together again.
- No, I hadn't heard a thing, I only got back a few days ago, you know.
- Well, yes. Remember, Lang had to go back to Vienna some months back, right?
- Yes, sure I remember, who could forget the peaceful but nervous sayonara party, the waiting for all hell to break loose and it not?
- Oh don't be so –
- So what?
- So I don't know, but don't.
- I wasn't, I was just kidding.
- Ok, ok. So, he had to go back, had a previous commitment that he had to fulfill, and that apparently he wanted to. It gave him a break from here, to clear his head about here, about Roberta. Apparently too it gave him quite a bit of money.
- Really, what was it? He has so many fingers in so many pies.
- I'm not sure, it may have been two jobs in one, something about script doctoring, and helping someone with an architecture book. Something like that, in that direction. But it paid well, and will allow him some leeway here.
- Good, super.

- So, Roberta seemed alright with his going, remember? I mean she seemed to maintain, but who could tell? After all that time, from when she first came here, neither of them knowing what was up, what would happen, other than that it seemed most likely that they were finished, what with Lang completely out of touch for such a long time, and Roberta just lingering, so slow then, remember?
- S-l-o-w is hardly the word for it. *Nosferatu.*
- And neither of us able to do a thing for the poor woman. And then the break with van Zandt. Doom city, Robie. Oops, I forgot, we can't call her that anymore, can we?
- Where did that ever come from, anyway?
- Her Cary Grant phase, she wanted to be a cat burglar.
- ?
- Don't let it bother you. Back to –
- Doom city.
- And then he was here. Remember when Lang arrived; there's a letter one day, and him on the doorstep the next?
- "Hello stranger, how long has it been?"
- And then the party, and then him moving out, Kichijoji, and then him gradually beginning to actually like being here, and their going back and forth –
- Back and forthing.
- To and froing.
- Hither and thithering.
- Hither and yoning.
- East and westing.
- High and lowing.
- Yamanate-o-ing.
- Ok, ok. So, it seemed they were doing well, and then he had to leave. But she seemed ok. In the air perhaps, but different from when she knew absolutely nothing about where she or she and he were at or what would become of them.
- Cut already!
- Stop?
- No, to the chase!
- Oh. Sure. So, while he was gone, it seems they spoke a lot, he called her, regularly. He even had flowers delivered to her on her birthday – from Europe! Or at least the order was placed in Europe. And then, of all things, she visited him, in Vienna.
- Like Joan in *Letter*, "revisiting the scenes of our youth."
- Yes, exactly! But he didn't go away saying he'd be back in two weeks,

and she pregnant. By the way – just give me this little digression – have you read that take on Max, in, where's it from? Oh, I can't remember. But it's about the "Collected Letters from an Unknown Woman." I'll dig it out for you later. Anyway, where was I? Oh yes, so there they are in Vienna. She even went hiking with him. And of course lots of movies. She never minded that, of course, But she can also live with just two or three a month. If I were such a film freak, I guess that's what I'd call love: Lang coming to Tokyo and going without. Ah, what a sacrifice! What a man!

- Are you serious?
- No, silly. Well, maybe a little. I mean he has given it up you know, has had to, given Tokyo's lack of any real film culture. Anyway, apparently, this time round, Roberta liked Vienna, reconciled herself with their past there. Obviously, she doesn't ever want to live there again, but she has made peace with the place. I wonder if they're country bumpkins too.
- Yes, some of them. The rest, worse: bourgeois.
- Ok, ok. So, where was I? Yes, of course: she liked Vienna alright – and then they came back! Just a few days ago.
- And, what now?
- Well, get this; like I said, these jobs he had made him some extra money; enough to take care of his place in Kichijoji, and to help her out too. They'll maintain their separate places –
- There really is no better way to live together, you know.
- I wouldn't know.
- Arlene, do we really want to be on TV?
- I don't know. Don't you?
- Only if I can get laid.
- Marianne!
- Ok, ok. Speaking of which – any news?
- News, what kind of news?
- Oh, tinker, tailor, girls in sailor suits. The rice lady, Hiromi, Hiroko.
- Oh, that kind of news. Not really, I'm working on it. I'm thinking.
- Thinking about it is working on it? What do you do, send out thought waves? How can sitting at home thinking about the direction of your love and sex life be working on it? Do you actually send a vibe out to Hiroko and she feels the warm moist coming on, down there, and responds with a phonecall?
- Marianne!
- What?
- Well.

- Well what?
- Well, I'm not telepathic. Are you?
- Yes.
- Ok. No, that is not what happens, obviously, and yes thinking about it is doing something about it. Getting laid, as you put it, for once speaking like my countrymen, and women, may be a part of it, but so are a lot of other things. Like knowing what one wants, and accepting it, and preparing oneself.
- You're showing your midwestern roots again, Arlene.
- So?
- Ok. So, you're taking your time. Seriously, it is good, and I admire it.
- Seriously?
- Yes, yes. But Hiroko is cute ...
- I know, I know.
- And contrary to received opinion, there aren't many more like her where she comes from.
- Do you see that too?
- You mean you do too? See what?
- Oh, that for all the silliness and shrillness and the following after Hiromi all the time and all the allness of it all, all that stuff that they buy and talk about ... that behind it all, or before it all, or above it all –
- Ok, ok, steady your compass.
- Ok, well, for all of it, or despite all – the girl's got something.
- Well said. "The girl's got something." Care to be specific?
- Oh, she has potential, she has a brain and eyes that apparently she wants to learn how to use; maybe she's a late bloomer, but she seems serious about it. You know how with siblings the younger seems to follow the older around a lot, and then suddenly one day the younger just shoots up and it's like you're looking at a new person where before you'd only seen an obnoxious copycat, that's what it seems like.
- Some people call it growing up.
- Well, that's not entirely right. After all, the two of them are grown up in terms of having the minimum that this society is ever going to require of them. But I'm speaking of something more, something more than just "growing up" or even "maturing" in a mundane sense. Something more ...
- Maybe that is it: the something she has is something more.
- Maybe.

- Let's hope so. Oh, Arlene, I agree entirely. They're a curious pair. You know, my first impulse would be to split them up, tell Hiroko, "Hey, come over to our side, you've got a lot more going for you than your silly pal," but –
- But, I agree. That would be an entirely false move, wrong.
- Hiromi's her own pal, is that it?
- More or less.
- She'll grow up – and more?
- But she has. She's alright.
- Alright?
- Alright by me. Why expect so much of people? We do what we can do.
- You're not talking just about Hiromi? Are you?
- Hiromi. Just?
- Not justice, but only.
- No, no, I'm not. Leave people alone. And no, I wouldn't dare to say to, say, Hiroko, "come over to our side." That too is silly.
- Yes, I suppose you're right.
- She'll come of her own accord. If she wants to. Maybe she won't.
- Stay cute.
- And why the hell not? It gets most people through.
- But the loss!
- Loss of what?
- Loss of –
- Marianne: we're born dumb, we're born cute.
- Yes?
- Do we need to change?
- But I thought –
- Thought what? Something Lang or VZ said once? That I or Roberta may have? Those things don't matter. You know to leave well enough alone.
- Yes, yes, you're right. So what comes next?
- Comes?
- Yes, you for instance.
- Comes. I may.
- Or may not.
- Isn't it up to me?
- The coming? I hope it's with a partner.
- Me too! And it will be.
- Oh, the summerflies, the winter skies ...
- Ok, so I'm not as dynamic as you – but still you'd find no better

co-host.

- Oh, Arlene, I do love you.
- Likewise, Baby. Butterflies and all. Of course, I'm shy, and a mid-westerner. Sorry, I kinda like "American coffee," but I have come to prefer green tea.
- And girls with swimmers legs.
- Amateurs.
- Lovers. That's what the word means.
- If you like. I do.
- So, Hiromi and Hiroko forever.
- Japan.
- City and country.
- Why not.
- Alright. Bluebells.
- And you?
- Me?
- Bluebells? What's to come for you, Marianne?
- Oh, I'm doing alright. Like all of us, I tend to exaggerate.
- Do you now?
- Of course. I come – now and then. I meet a boy, a man. We play.
- Play?
- It's fair.
- For both?
- Yes, yes.
- I envy you.
- No, I envy you.
- Why?
- Insects, flowers, your style, tastes ...
- Tastes, style? Sort of maybe. Yes, I suppose. Maybe I have a kind of openness.
- It's a gift, really it is.
- I'm not always so sure, but.
- I don't have it.
- But you obviously do now. Midwest or no, look at you. School marm type comes to Japan, seeks nothing in particular, well maybe some new experience to look back on in old age, falls into a bunch of bohemian types, does not get laid but wonders what it's all about and then finds out she's –
- She's what? She's got a lack of imagination, is a bit too academic, and is not really attracted to men. What would my parents say?
- Well, what would they?

- Oh, they'd probably come around after a while, thrashing it all out on a few talk shows.
- Vive l'Amerique!
- Oh, comeon now.
- And would you appear? Could I come with you?
- Marianne, the only talk show I would be on would be ours, and it would have to originate in Japan.
- "Originate" – so you think we'd be distributed internationally?
- Yes, of course, and because I always want to be sure of our audience.
- And sure of our friends. I don't think the film crew would appreciate our being on TV.
- Not unless they were regular guests. But no, we'd better drop this idea right now.
- What idea? You don't think I really …?
- I guess not. Maybe we could make a film about ourselves as talk show hosts.
- No, maybe we can drop it altogether – I do not want to be forever hostessing.
- Hadn't thought of that. So, you think I should sort of take Hiroko under my wing, so to speak?
- Sure, why not? Give it a try. And no, it does not have to blossom into a sex thing. Not necessarily. Two wings, by the way. God, those crows can be loud here. Sure, why not? Just start being her friend, see how she responds. Take it from there. Spend time, talk. I'm sure she could teach you a thing or two too.
- I'm sure she could too. What?
- Oh, well, she is from *shitamachi*, you know. And her family sounds delightful. That sort of setting can be quite comforting – for a while.
- Oh yes, see a bit of country style living in the big capital.
- I really do not want to see you in quilts.
- Isn't quilting some sort of thing here, with the over-thirties?
- I think you're right. *Little House on the Prairie.*
- Little thatched roof on the Tokkaido.
- Is she related to the Anne of the *Green Gables*?
- I don't really know. But in Japan I suppose she is.
- Why *do* they wear those sailor uniforms?
- Or why aren't there more eye operations? I've always thought it had to do with the Meiji reforms, you know, the Germans taught them about the military, the English about schools, that stuff.
- Was it the English? Do the English wear sailor suits?
- I have no idea.

- I think those graduation dresses are cute.
- Kind of butch. But aren't they rather heavy? I can't imagine school kids wearing those everyday.
- No, I suppose not. I've got it! We switch the boys and girls uniforms!
- Cross-dressing?
- Yes! These girls can be pretty dykey when they want to, you know. God, they'd look so good, so severe. Cut the uniforms just right, really make them femmy. And the boys – all those little sailors. We get rid of the skirts, keep the tops, with adjustments …
- We get rid of the skirts. You still have them in their underwear.
- What's wrong with that? No, you're right. What kind of pants? Let's see. Why not the same as the girls, their old pants, waists hitched up high. Would that match the tops? Aren't there school uniform shops?
- I know one in Waseda.
- Maybe we can go there and try out different combinations. Get some boys and girls to help us. Then they'd really think we foreigners are nuts. Can you imagine?
- Wasn't there a film recently –
- Yes! Where all the boy parts were played by girls, and most people couldn't see the difference. Yes, it was alright.
- And the boys grow their hair longer, and the girls shorter, like in manga.
- Hiroko.
- Hiroko?
- No not our Hiroko, Hiroko Yakushimaru.
- Whatever happened to her, by the way?
- I think she got married. Maybe to some pop star, and then she sort of faded away. Like most idols. She was near the heights for a while, but just couldn't sustain it.
- So what about her?
- Did you ever see her first film? Some gangster thing, and she was in high-school. Maybe her father was a yakuza or something, but anyway, she joined in the gang, in the mayhem.
- That's another example – that yakuza series where the gang is ruled by the old *oyabun*'s wife.
- Yes, with that great actress, you know, the sister of Tora-san's sister. Anyway, the poster for the Hiroko Yakushimaru movie was of her in sailor suit, holding up a machine gun, and a trickle of blood flowing down one round baby cheek. Very sexy. I have a copy somewhere around here, I'll dig it out for you later.

- This is better than talk TV. High-school will never be the same again. And it's so appropriate too, don't you think? This country has to wake up to its sexual selves, it's been in denial for too long.
- ?
- Well, maybe not.
- Time to have fun! Puberty's sure going to be even a lot more fun.
- Puberty, fun?
- Oh yes. I had a great time.
- Mine was awful, I had no idea what was happening to me, no control.
- Yes, I've heard that can happen. It doesn't have to, though. But, we're going to redress the nation! Now what about the salary-men and office ladies?
- Ugh, what a challenge. No cross-dressing there.
- Right, let's deal with them later. I do like sushi chef's uniforms.
- Me too, they stay the same.
- I know: elevator girls.
- Yuck, those awful hats, Matsuya, Takashimaya, each department store trying to out-awful the next. The gloves, the gestures.
- I see them in lingerie.
- I'd like to, too, but ... let's see ... why uniforms at all? Why not just dress as they like, except for something that identifies their job – like a belt, or a scarf, or even a hat? But something really striking, let them maintain a shred of self-respect.
- You have a gift, Arlene.
- I may have a calling. Who's next?
- Uhm ... taxi-drivers!
- Oh, those blue suits. Doesn't that material prevent the circulation, or kill brain cells, or something?
- It must, they never know where they're going. How they qualify for their jobs, I'll never understand.
- I think it's because they keep the city clean, they've been mistakenly classified, you know, those long feather dusters they're always wiping their cars with.
- And gloves again!
- And doilies!
- That country groveling again, too.
- So what do we do with them?
- You mean after they come out of the getting-to-know-the-city class? Well, hell, again, why uniforms at all? The cab itself is uniform enough, and that little ID that's always on the dash board.

- But why uniforms at all?
- What do you mean?
- Only that maybe there is a reason for all those uniforms after all.
- Think so?
- Sure, after all, the whole country agrees on them, no one complains about it. Have you ever stepped into an elevator and seen an elevator girl complain about her uniform, her hat and gloves, her very role?
- No, but then I've never seen an elevator girl with anything that resembles a human emotion.
- But maybe that's it?
- What?
- Well, that it is just a role, and the uniform, no matter how awful, is your costume for that day's performance. Let's say you're an elevator girl for two or three years, or selling towels or doilies in Mitsukoshi, well, those two or three years are how long your show runs. You have the same costume and you say the same lines, that's a play. And you know as well as I that those same elevator girls without human emotions as you say, or those salesladies or office ladies or salarymen all have lives outside the ... well, when they come off stage.
- Hmm ... Maybe. Then my calling is all in vain?
- No, not necessarily.
- Why not?
- Well, the elevator girls and taxi-drivers and all the others are all adults. They've chosen their roles. High-schoolers have not, and they're at an age where their roles, sexual and otherwise, haven't yet jelled –
- You mean solidifed, concretized.
- Right. So, anyway, they're at an age where they're still open to, well, open to every possibility. Society demands them in uniform. We just change uniform, change the look; the kids'll take care of the rest.
- Sounds good.
- Sounds promising.
- Got a sketchbook?
- Yes.
- Boy or girl first?
- Boy-girl, girl-boy.

* * *

Oh, city, oh you – you have become home – for now – perhaps for me and Lang – could he ever accept – but in the meantime – the balance of it, one roof – ah, what you've given me – this unexpected unsuspected rediscovery – for the moment then – this city oh city you!

* * *

– And from Akihabara you get to Kanda, and from Kanda –
– Oh, from Kanda you can get to Tokyo, sure, but from anywhere you can also get to anywhere else, that's the beauty of it –
– Part of it – of the beauty.
– And that the Yamanote doesn't contain the city; it's just a convenience to stay inside or outside the loop –
– The lasso –
– The great wheel –
– Sounds like a game show –
– It is!
– After all, more of the city is outside than in.
– Ok, so what's on the other side of Ueno station?
– Asakusa, for one.
– Four or five wards.
– Two more rivers, one frontier after another.
– That's it, isn't it? Frontiers on either side –
– No, frontiers all over, what is it to walk even here in Ueno but adventure –
– The unknown!
– No man's land!
– Everyone's!
– Almost literally – Saigo as the Statue of Liberty welcoming the huddled masses.
– Pretty huddled for sure.
– Pretty unpublicized.
– Our drunk, our homeless, our own accursed.
– Driven from Ueno –
– Driven from Harajuku –
– Driven from Shinjuku –
– And back to Ueno –
– And driven again.
– Something's gotta give.
– Here.

- Here.
- Look there – do you see what I see?
- Uhm –
- Too late. Gone.
- Kazuko, are you alright? Shall we take a rest?
- No, no, I'm fine. I was just thinking about home, about Kyoto, about – no, let's keep walking.
- Sure?
- Yes.
- Straight on?
- Is that possible?
- Or shall we take a detour, see the river, reminisce?
- Which river? Reminisce about what?
- I don't know, I thought that's what rivers are for.
- Amongst other things.
- And then what, head back, back to Chuo Dori, on to Akihabara and past –
- Kanda –
- Full circle.

* * *

- If I stay?
- Go then.
- And if I go?
- I stay, regardless.
- And if I go?
- You'll return.
- And if I stay.
- I'll be here, Lang.

* * *

- Hey, doesn't anybody want to dance? Why's this party so dead? Hey, does anybody hear me?
- Hiromi, it's 3AM, comeon. Let's go home.
- So early? I wanna dance som'more.
- If we go home, I promise I'll fuck your brains out.
- You did that this afternoon.
- And this morning. I didn't hear you complaining. In fact I heard you asking for more. I also heard –

- That was then, this is now. And besides, I dance even better than I fuck.
- True.
- ?
- …
- I mean I like dancing even better than fucking.
- Oh?
- Well, proper things at their proper places.
- Proper?
- Oh, you know what I mean.
- Ok, one more, and then we go home.
- Oh, you sweetie.
- But what if I'm too tired when we get home? What if you exhaust me on the dance floor?
- Don't worry about that. Hey, where did everybody go?
- You mean working people who have to get up early in the morning?
- Ok, ok. I'm ready to go.
- But I gotta finish this last beer.
- I thought you wanted to fuck?
- I also want to finish this beer I just paid for.
- You're so mercenary.
- And cute – you told me so.
- Did I say that?
- Yes, you did. Gimme a kiss.
- Not here, not in public.
- What? You talk – you shout out loud in a disco about fucking, and then you can't even kiss me?
- They're two different things.
- Are they?
- Yes.
- Well, I suppose, but –
- But nothing. Kissing is … kissing is … it's like a sign, it's tender, it's a –
- And fucking?
- Well, fucking is something else.
- Some people call it making love.
- Yes, some people.
- And you?
- Well, it can be that. But it can also be something else.
- And with me?
- It's *something else*!

-   Uhm, thanks.
-   Don't mention it. Did everyone really go? So early? Why?
-   I told you why.
-   Oh yeah. Mmm, this is good, what's it called?
-   Brandy Alexander.
-   Like the Greek? I studied history, you know.
-   No, I don't know. Comeon, Hiromi.
-   Comeon what? Wanna kiss me?
-   I thought it wasn't proper?
-   Everything in its place and time.
-   So, can we go home?
-   Is that proper?
-   At 4AM, I think so.
-   Will you fuck me again, properly?
-   Improperly.
-   Promise?
-   Promise.
-   Ok. Remember, you promised.
-   I promised.
-   God, what a dull party.

* * *

Oh you're true, and you're duplicitous too, Tokyo. I have your number – and I have hers.

* * *

SCENE TWELVE: RESTAURANT

A restaurant in Yanaka, three storied, wood, Taisho Period – really, a monument to that era, here in *shitamachi*, what an older Tokyo resembled – *kushiage*, everything on sticks, good if a bit monotonous, not cheap. All of the private rooms are taken (a fashion magazine party; a tryst; a sealed deal). There is a "waiting room-cum-coffee/tea shop" next door. A row of tables, a thin aisle, a three-tatami kitchen, and so unlike the restaurant in its minimalist décor, quiet mood. They are a pair, big sister and little, trad girl and modern, tea and coffee with cream.

But this is her last photo, her last chance to meet her man.

But it is also too late.

In slow motion – like something out of Jean Epstein – we see the woman enter the now empty restaurant – how had she missed the departing customers? – except for an attractive woman, the shop's kindly owner – apologizing, explaining that they have closed, is something wrong?, can I help you? – and then she sees the portfolio in the Woman's arms, even seems to recognize it: "Oh, I believe this belonged to that nice gentleman who just left. Is he a friend of yours? He mentioned that someone might be coming by to pick up a package for him. Here, he left this for you." And she hands the Woman a portfolio filled with color photographs of twelve different buildings in Tokyo. "He said you would know where to find him."

END

As the credits for the film roll by, behind them we see footage of van Zandt's original film, the one that caused the rupture between he and his once closest friend Roberta.

We see the legs of the man, going up a flight of stairs. We hear a door slam. We hear a muffled argument between a man and a woman. We hear a door slam and a man's steps rushing down a staircase. We then see the Woman rushing out of an elevator on the same floor where the argument occurred. Too late.

Marui in Shibuya. We see the great escalator system, the shoppers like ants or bees bringing their food – blouses, skirts, accessories, bags – back home. She rushes in. A crowd of young shoppers. The sound of the man's rushing steps. She stops and buys an accessory – cheap, kitsch – on the first floor.

A helicopter shot of Shinjuku that circles in on the station building. We see the woman get off the Seikyo Line – why has she been north? Interior: She climbs a flight of stairs but it does not lead to any exit, rather another mall of shops and fast-food stalls; she goes down another flight, turns left, no not that way, doubles back, finds at least a place to turn her ticket in, but still no station exit. This goes on and on, the woman rushing towards what appears to be an exit but in fact is not and only leads to many more false leads, banks, copy shops, cafés, and so on. It is – Roberta was right – almost a parody of Kafka. At the end of this sequence, she half kneels in exhaustion, hiding her face in her handkerchief – as we see the man's legs pass directly in front of her.

Two cars approach as two pedestrians approach. A screech, a scream. A moment of silence, a siren.

The steps of a station. All feet rushing. No faces. The rush of feet; the Man's feet; the Woman's. Doors shut before the Woman can get in.

We see a car stop, a door opens, a hand appears, shoes are handed out, laid on the ground, feet and legs emerge and fill the red leather shoes. The car takes off. Are they the Woman's leg's? This last is repeated and varied over the remaining credits, in increasingly closer shots on the woman's feet and shoes until the colors of flesh and leather merge into a blur that resembles a photograph of … the first building.

* * *

So today they asked me what I think of his idea of loving the whole city? Do those idiots really expect me to take away from the company's and my valuable time to respond to such an absurd question? Absurd for what I should think would be obvious reasons. First, you don't love a city, you live in it and work in it. If you make enough money, you can enjoy more parts of it than I can. If you don't, well you enjoy what you can afford, a few friends, a few bars and restaurants, maybe a park if we had any. You don't even love your home, you take care of it, like your family. If not, then you're out. Second, can this even be considered a city? It is a monster, it's unnatural. It would take an unnatural love to love this thing. I can't waste my time on this, I have work to do. ("Kaoru! We need you for a minute.") If he wants to "love the whole city," let him do it without bothering me any further.

* * *

She walked pigeon-toed at an angle that put her face before her feet, as if she were forever about to stumble, as if she had learned to walk going down a flight of stairs.

And when she sat she would put the toes of her two feet together and stare at her two-tone, round-toed shoes, wondering why both those boys van Zandt and Lang wore pointy-toed shoes, "points," they called them. Points? She didn't get it.

She wondered if she would forever be doomed to walking the streets unrecognized; why did fame elude her?, where were the hordes of screaming fans outside the city's television stations that were her birthright?, why was it that she so often spent time – alone – in cafés, gazing at the passing crowd, flipping through magazines and comics and only looking at the ads and the nudes? And speaking of the crowd, what was that word van Zandt had taught her, agoraphobia?, at least it was easy to pronounce, and reminded her of one of her favorite Spielberg movies. Why, when she preferred the cheap and good coffee at Doutor, Pronto and the other chains, why did van Zandt prefer Rilke in Shimbashi or Poem in other places, for that matter why did he get his hair cut at Dante? His style of doing things was certainly not that of her usual crowd of friends. Would she ever understand him? And if she did, would that lead to fame? Would he ask her to be in one of his films? And if she did achieve fame that way, would she then have to share it? Could she?

Her eyes really did look as if they had been formed thanks to a short, quick slice of a razor; barely emergent, like some small beast's, one looked more at the slit than the feeling or intelligence behind or within or wherever it may be.

When she worried, like that guy in the Richie film, she rubbed her nose.

She was incontinent – just a small trickle – when she was sincere.

And she would squeal: at the zoo (the sight of a panda); the first tinklings of the glass chimes attached to the blue and white banners announcing an ice cream stand on the first day of the summer heat; at the sight of a handsome foreigner.

And what was it Lang had told her when she had told him that she liked hiking, day trips outside of Hachioji and around Mount Takao? What was it he said about he being a hiker too – that there was Dogen-*zaka* (cigars at Tokyu), Kudan*zaka* (North Indian food), Nogi*zaka* (a detour), and a "Rat Slope" and others with weird names, and one that reminded him of how much he loved Roberta, and all the other slopes worth hiking up – that he was an urban hiker? She just could not understand Lang like she could van Zandt, if she could go so far in saying.

* * *

R'n'L!!!!!!!!!!!

The day my first single got into the Top Ten – with a bullet! – and then the day it went platinum!

How about *dis*connecting everything, see what happens, see even if it can be done (maybe not)?

Just got a copy of *The Locket*. (Flashbacks within fl'backs w/in ...)
Wanna come over and watch it with me? ("Yes, we do ((we do (((we
do)))))," as the Shangri-las sort of said).

Ah, Tokyo my Tokyo, ten days in the country and how I'm gonna
miss 'ya. Ten days, Christ, and I've already packed clothes for twelve.
Besides probably three books too many. Hey, I figure you never know
when you're gonna be stranded – earthquake splits the world in two
leaving you hanging – or invited to a glamorous party. And then I bring
my Tokyo maps – some people set up family photos when they travel,
I lay out my Tokyo books and maps – just in case anyone asks me very
minute particulars.

Tokyo of the future? – Tokyo Baroque.

Oh so much to do, so much to read and write, and .... "I only want
to be with you," as Dusty said, and of whom Jenny gives a mean imper-
sonation, and speaking of whom I had a high-schoolish dirty dream last
night. Boy, was I surprised! (Boy, was she!!)

I still haven't fixed that door Hiromi cracked. Maybe I'm keeping
it as a reminder.

I'd love to have six months off just for rereading.

The day I escaped from you-know-where, hightailed it to Tokyo
and became a man of the crowd. I ain't never looked back, never.

So, are we connected?

Oh, hey, before I forget, we still got so much stuff to talk about: the
party for the kids; the plans for August; getting copies of those Screw-
balls, divvying up the photos, and etcetera!

Elvisly yours,

* * *

The costs of confusion notwithstanding, Marianne says to herself,
confusion indeed. Christ!, how can Lang say it is a systemless system?
Did he ever try to read a street sign – what street signs? Try to find an

address? So why else do I always have to apologize for being late? It ain't me who's confused, dammit. But costs, why no, none whatsoever.

* * *

Cafferty, his mind fast, eyes weak, knowing he has gradually been losing his sight these last few years, accepting this inevitable, had begun walking his beloved city with eyes closed (to the sun, to the moon, to the wind and rain), had finally arrived at the point where he could walk the city with eyes closed and know exactly where he was, know what building had replaced what building had replaced what ... and describe them all to you but this last (as he has never seen it), or could get in a taxi, tell the cabbie a destination, a direction, and know what street he was on, what bridge he was crossing under or over, what building stood at the corner of the light they had stopped at (and tell you what building had replaced what building had ...). Cafferty knew the city now as a lover knows the loved one's body, the he and the she of it, the continuum, the contours, crevasses, the extra flesh here (the less there), the stray wisp, the nerve gone wrong, the endless wonder.

And walk he could: straight (as the heavy wooded rulers he remembered from school), bandied (rubbery, clowns on TV), limp (Little Tramp), as a new bride (jitters), a Midwestern stroll (cornfields gently swaying), a Venetian (the rhythm of the waters), in the DeNiro manner ("Watch out, Buster!"), in the Sanda (woman in a man's suit), and more ... with a twitch, skimming the surface of the street, as a footballer, a great lady, as one who has lost everything: in a word, as a Tokyoite.

It was felt, as he always said, in the testicles.

Where had Cafferty come from? He'd once – decades ago – written about Tokyo (some few fugitive essays for airline magazines); he kept now largely to himself, occasionally seeing a few friends (though rarely mixing them); spoke little to newcomers to Tokyo: "You'll see it yourself if you stay long enough." He was said to work now and then for a large financial company, writing reports, but surely that was not enough to live on; there were rumors a-plenty: a lover (female, male?) of long ago now in Hong Kong, a stipend from an actress friend. He'd met Lang two or three times via Roberta (the last of his newcomers – she just seemed so at ease), but was in that mood when friendship, as much as it may be desired, would come no longer; he'd remarked to himself that night he and Lang were introduced, "Ah, too bad we hadn't met thirty years earlier – how we would have explored the city together!" Friendship now was an impossibility, they might form a "relationship," a correspondence filled with anecdotes and queries, but no, not what Lang needed. Cafferty knew that what he could give Lang Lang would have to find for himself on his own or within his own circle of friends; it was lonely, granted, but it was gratifying too to become a Tokyoite alone. Lang knew this too, and accepted it. After all, it was his city, too.

* * *

She was standing there behind the wall, and the wall was transparent, like water.

What was ineradicable was the knowledge of that sudden, momentary opening up of the walls surrounding him, which had then resumed their former position, swaying like curtains falling into place.

– Doderer (both quotes)

Arlene stepped into the café, sat, put down (for good) the bad translation of the novel about Vienna, and, thinking of a phrase Hiromi had once tossed aside, fixed her gaze on the wall beyond the window opposite.

It was child-shit yellow, with twigs and various "industrial materials" visible, antiquey-looking and only two decades old; cheap curtains, a piano in the kitchen, and the bedding on the verandah. Not my idea of Tokyo, but Tokyo nonetheless. (Which deserves perhaps to be a fourth recurring phrase.) And then the wall opened up, divided, and there was the street, the falling apart bookshops, the dry cleaner (run by a once-lovely fat woman with teeth all askew), the large electronics shop, the favorite bar, some few large family houses, old and solid, the women's college, and beyond that the arts university and that great sprawling park that was rained out the one time she had gone there to see the cherry blossoms. (Was she becoming sentimental in only her second year in the city?) The wall remained, front and center and on the edges no matter how far she gazed beyond it. It was thanks after all to the wall that she was able to gaze through it. But the wall came first; she had acknowledged its impenetrability the second she had fixed her gaze on it, and accordingly, it had allowed her to see all that it contained, possessed, solely as wall because she had (again) acknowledged that there was no "beyond."

"Ohh," Arlene thought in a daze, "Now I'm really on my way."

And then she saw Lang and Roberta and their break; she saw Hiromi, the once thin face now bloated with resentment; she saw the city as a simultaneous film set and the contents of a hard disk; she saw Lang alone in Europe, struggling to overcome his resentments, to come to terms with this surprise of a Roberta; she saw a lustful Roberta, and an ascetic Marianne. And then the vision ended and all she saw was the shit-yellow wall. And seeing for her really was finally believing.

What was that line van Zandt was singing these days – "You can't fool me / I can see it in your eyes."

She *would* know this city, dammit, even if it meant losing her soul – but gaining her sight! – for it.

It was in front of her eyes. Who was there to doubt it?

* * *

A woman in a window, a woman emerging from a car, a girl on a bicycle, a girl behind a boy on a bicycle, a woman bound in ropes and smiling, Cafferty recounts, Tokyo in the late 40s, Tokyo in the 50s, in the 60s, in the 70 and 80s, and Tokyo in the 90s and in the 2000s. I have seen all this. Ah, this memory of mine, shades all round. Boys in uniforms on their first drunk, and their fathers in their uniforms on one long permanent drunk. And their mothers – women in windows.

* * *

Kazuo feels that San Francisco is not too unlike his home Yokohama. The proximity of the sea .... and then he comes to a stop. Perhaps it resembles Kobe, the hills. And again he halts mid-thought. The houses, the hills, the views, the parks, the whole *urbanity* of the scene – it is unlike any place else on earth. Well, perhaps that is a bit *extreme*, but then his subject is the city in which he spent so little but so *invaluable* time. It may have its problems like any other city, but it is so *liveable*. Yes, it might be a bit small, a bit provincial, but who has ever *hated* the place? And then, this nicest of nice fellows, has so many – perhaps not *many*, but so preciously enough – *friends* there. Not like the relations he has formed in Tokyo, no, these are of a *permanent, of a deep and imaginative – of a San Franiscan* nature. He loves the bookstores; an Italian restaurant near a church he knows from a movie; a few bars; a certain waitress; some cinemas; a young girl, and two or three young women; a bakery; a basement apartment he sometimes dreams of; and so many more *emotions*.

THE WAY THEY LEFT

The way he left her, he just called, spilled the facts, said he'd never felt a thing for her, or not at least what he suspected she would have wanted him to feel for her; he was sorry if he'd led her to have any illusions but certainly she should have known, sensed something was missing – why hadn't she?; was she so swept into her own emotions that she could not feel his, or lack of them?; yes if she insisted he could give her reasons, something solid, but no he didn't really want to; what was he to say – he didn't like the way she stepped out of a car, the way she was always doing her nails, was so disappointed when she cut her hair, didn't like the pillows on her bed – what kind of talk was this anyway? – look, all those may or may not be true, they don't really matter, no of course they don't amount to anything serious, yes, there is other stuff, but again, it's just too uncomfortable to say, to lay out, no, no, you're a wonderful person in many ways, really, maybe it's just me, my peculiarities. He really was sorry, what could he say, she'd have to, he hoped, she would sooner or later understand certainly some way some how. No grief, ok?

The way she got rid of him she just waited didn't say a word to him for so long let him find out for himself let him ask the questions (and what little answers she gave him) come to his own conclusions that's what hurt him so her sheer unwillingness to talk to say a thing no conversation whatsoever when most he needed it almost refused to meet but again when they did it was a one-way conversation his monologue his pleading his making up stories trying to understand justify it all and asking her to deny or to confirm to help him and she only looking away saying nothing, acting the role she was born for some princess or raven or raven-princess. Nothing.

The cruel way he left hell abandoned her cruel they'd lived together five years had been childhood sweethearts had planned joint careers hell lives and had finally gotten married, few lives were so joined seamless few destinies so wrapped together; and then slowly the rot came in, the dissimulation, a small career change, missed appointments, and finally on an anniversary that meant so much to her during a party with most of their friends attending he makes the announcement tells her to pack and get out, offers no explanation no name of any other lover just says he's fed up with it all (what all?) and wants her out love is d-e-a-d; and so she goes, first to their bedroom – with two friends, two alone who understood, compassionated, those two alone stood by her and cursed the others for going on with the party (can you believe it?); so she grabs a few things for a quick departure (how did she stand?, walk?, not break down the body the soul entirely? from where such faith?); and as she's leaving she paid him no mind he had ceased to exist for her – and so to her friends' place for an evening only one and a new life I hear she is doing better now. From where such faith?

* * *

More than an illusion, she is an oasis:
1. Last weekend she was dressed in two shades of pink, and three of turquoise.
2. She has driven three years now and has had only one accident: she hit a parked police car!

And yet: and yet ... there is a poetry in her and hence her presence here. An almost bestial and near inarticulate blindness that sees and suffers all and yet still can laugh. She is the juncture, the split, the blindspot that sees all. Her small hands occasionally eloquent.

Hiromi: some kind of woman (some sort of love).

* * *

THE TOKYO OF FORKING PATHS

The Tokyo subway system, like the space in which its daily bustlings back and forth are described, is vast and rich in possibilities: ramifications, intersections, connecting points, one-way journeys, roundabout itineraries, parabolas, half circles, ellipses, dead ends. To examine the map of the subway system is to yield to memory, to escape to delirium; to accept utopia, fiction, fable: to visit the monuments, the abominations, the horrors of the city, one's own monuments, abominations, and horrors, without ever having to leave home.
– Juan Goytisolo-Silva

* * *

So rich and and so wonderfully strange, Lang considers, me in this city that I hadn't wanted to come to at all, had no wish nor interest in, and yet now I know I have arrived in a heaven-of-a-sort – my Tokio. And Roberta hers. Rich and strange indeed.

* * *

- Soon, the sun.
- Always, the sun.
- And night?
- The sun's sister, lover, the consolations of the moon.
- So you think it's female, too?
- No, I think it's male too.
- They're both both.
- So, they're no different from you and me?
- Well, one's hotter.
- But no more passionate!
- The passions of the sun!
- The lusts of the moon!
- The planets, spinning, desiring!
- The love that moves the sun!
- So silent, Kazuko?
- Look, the light –
- Sun over Kokubunji –
- Sun over us.
- Guide, as we walk backwards –
- Forwards –
- Sun behind –
- Forward –
- Moon for –
- Ever. Yours.
- Kazuko?
- Oh yes.

* * *

FROM LANG'S NOTES

The inapproachable heart of the city.

Every house seems to keep the concept of the city (small gardens).

Structure of the buildings depends on the plan of the garden.

Tokio and the differences of tempo.

The tower that would contain a whole city.

Silence among the towers of Shinjuku where all you see is the reflected weather.

Shinjuku, two cities: nightless (east) and silent (east).

Tokio's differing tensions: the body (stations) connections (only) to nowhere.

In making ourselves a place to live in we first spread a parasol above our heads so as to cast a shadow on the earth. (Tanizaki?)

The station – heart of the city's constant reversal (as opposed to Europe where stations are an entry to the city).

Shinohara's House in *Uehara* – the more it remains autonomous, the more it fits into its environment.

The Yamanote and the "sub-centers" (Shibuya, Shinjuku, Ikebukuro) are the delineators and distributors of the endless city.

Tokio, horizontal and without depth, a linear city, fragments of an ideal image, of the mega-60s, ideal remnants of an historic city.

Like the ritual path and place, at a festival, they delineate the growth form of the village – the procession itself expresses the community's social organization.

* * *

Hiroko is in Kabukicho, Shinjuku, which has been displaced to the UNESCO Village/Lake Tama area in Tokyo, due North. The scene is overwhelming – the neon, the hawkers and barkers, the clubs and bars and sex shops – and the people. Baby Face Leroy's "Rollin' and Tumblin'" is blaring insanely all over the city. Boldly, she walks into a bar that is frequented mostly by foreigners. She orders a Belgian white beer. Her English is fine. She is talking with a young American, and then she sees Hiromi with VZ. She continues talking with the young American. Hiroko feels great.

Roberta is back at her childhood home. She is playing some Blues on her stereo, and reading *Vogue* magazine. She gets up to sneak a drink of vermouth, which she's only recently taken a liking to. She sneaks upstairs where a cousin is staying; he sleeps naked and she wants a look. She looks through her parents' things, especially the underwear, the dildo and the douche. She shrugs it all off. Each day her breasts are getting larger, and her mind going farther and farther.

When she awakes she will remember this time of her life as just the prelude to ever more exciting years. She will go to her stereo and put on those few precious tracks of Baby Face Leroy, and play his masterpiece – one of the Songs Common to Dreams – again and again and again.

* * *

AUGUST

- Isn't it funny how –
- – time fades away?
- No, nothing fades away.
- That's funny?
- Wait – isn't it funny how some things –
- – fade away? But they exist in time, so –
- – no, wait. How some things make you think –
- – yes, and others repel thought.
- Stop.
- Ok.
- How some things make you think of other things? Isn't it funny?
- Such as?
- Well, besides our just having performed an example – and, by the way, time slips, movies have fades – now what was it I was thinking of that made me think of this, what was it that I'd never thought of, uhn, before?
- Can you repeat the sentence?
- Probably not, but why should I want to?
- Ok, so, some things make you think of other things?
- Yeah, you get me.
- So then, do some things not make you think of other things?
- Yeah, I suppose so.
- Such as?
- I don't know, I'd have to think of them first.
- But that would lead nowhere.
- By definition, I suppose. Or everywhere.
- ?
- Well, now just hear me out – some things make you think of other things, all down the line, not fade away. While some other things do not make you think of other things, they make you think of that thing you're thinking of, but as that certainly can not stand alone,

while also not making you think of other things, then those singular things must in the end make you think of all things, of everything! And all of it, I suppose, at once!

– Uhm, where do you get these ideas?

– I don't know. They just come to me. I guess I just start to think of something and that … makes me think of other things. Why? Are ideas supposed to come from somewhere?

– From things, I suppose.

– One thing leading to another. It's kind of nice when you think of it.

– Yeah?

– You know, a deep look into the eyes, a smile, a kiss, here, put your hand here, then another kiss, ya' get me? – one little thing lea-ding-to-a-no-ther …

[FADE]

* * *

HE SAID / SHE SAID

She said she loved his voice; it was deep, all of him, his passion, experience, his fears and hopes.

He said that with all the women in his life he had loved he had first fallen in love with their voices.

He said that he loved her breasts, that they excited him even more perhaps than the excitement she felt when he felt and kissed them.

She said she loved his chest; it was so smooth, the few soft hairs, the vastness of mutual sensation, the heart beating underneath, the map of kisses.

He said that she had to leave.
She said she did not.

He said he loved her walk, cool, long strides.
She said she admired his, steady, with an occasional indecisive jerk, a mis-step.

He said, between her, that he was straddling values.
She said, straddling him, that there was no between, that she had sight now of the once-distant shore.

He said that having lost so much in love that he was afraid now to love.

She said that to love was to suspend one's fear, that having lost everything, well.

He said that all he had learned he had learned from her.
She said that all she knew she had learned from a few magazines.

He said he did.
She said she did.

He said he didn't.
She said she didn't.

He said there was only one moral choice.
She said there were two, maybe three.

He said his life in this city was a constant bereavement of memory.
She said her life in this city was one of a constant renewal of the will.

He said he loved her blouse.
She said she loved his shirt.

He said that if they had met thirteen years earlier they would have destroyed one another.
She said that that they could have created one another.

He said that her blue dress deserved a poem.
She said he should get rid of his blue suit.

He said the greatest director was Mizoguchi.
She said her favorite film was *L'Atalante*.

He said he had performed a massive act of forgetting and that his earliest memories could not be reconstructed except in dreams.
She said that her earliest memory came to her in a dream about eight years ago and that it was of her birth.

He said that he wished she spoke English better.
She said that she wished that he spoke Japanese better.

He said it was all so hard and takes so long to live an honest life in a world of pain.

She said yes it is hard and yes it does take a long time but, hell, it has to be attempted, that was all.

He said he did not believe in God.
She said she believed in the gods.

He said she was his man.
She said he was her man.

He said they should have some champagne.
She said that she usually preferred *saké* but yes, champagne would be nice.

* * *

AUGUST

- Tell me again.
- What? That I love you?
- No, silly! The line from the movie.
- Which line? What movie?
- Oh, the one you were talking about the other day. What was it …? Comeon, you know. Don't you remember?
- I didn't take notes, sorry.
- Ok. But wasn't it about love?
- How should I know? Probably. Aren't most movies about love – in one form or another?
- Maybe, maybe not. Anyway, if you remember it, let me know, ok? Or write it down for me.
- Ok. If I remember it – and I have no idea what you're talking about.
- Yes you do; yes you will.
- Anyway, what's the big deal?
- Oh, nothin.' It just sort of struck me, and I wanted to remember it, you know, write it down, think about it.
- Alright, maybe you're right and it will come back to me.
- Like you came back to me?
- But I'd never been here before!
- You know what I mean.
- Ah, ok. But did I ever leave you? You left, after all.

- I didn't go anywhere. I only came to my Tokyo. You came to yours.
- Hmm, maybe I came back to myself.
- Too heavy for me right now. Let's just say you arrived.
- In time.
- In time.
- But let's get back to this leaving. I seem to recall that, regardless of whether or not you came to your Tokyo, you also left – me.
- But I had a ticket and everything, what was I to do, cancel?
- That's your excuse? Now wait a minute, you aren't going to get out of it by –
- – and it was an expensive ticket.
- And it was a one-way ticket!
- Of course it was, you yourself just the other day said you couldn't imagine leaving Tokyo for quite a while yet, and I've never heard of plane tickets that are good for five or ten or even fifteen years, have you?
- But that's not the point!
- Oh yes it is, I worked hard to pay for that ticket!
- The point is that you left me!
- I got on the plane without you – you didn't have a ticket!
- But you never told me you were leaving!
- You never asked. And anyway, you should've known.
- Then you admit that you left me?
- I admit that you stayed behind.
- You're too much.
- Ain't I though? Now, tell me again.
- But I can't remember the line from the movie.
- No silly, that you love me.

* * *

He loved her so much that he agreed to visit her for a month in the country where she'd gone to observe "the local ways." "But Tokyo's are the ways of the world," he protested to no avail, and so went down.

He endured the earth, the trees (clouds being enough for him in the city), the dearth of record stores and friends with espresso machines. The people were "close to the earth," as the phrase would have it; it made him think they suffered a permanent diarrhea. He tried to begin a conversation with a goat, which was in no mood for talking, butting him away; followed the cow in its path, looking for signs of a latent street system; he visited the local school, and felt like weary Gulliver. He played sound effects tapes to the birds, in the false hope that they might learn and sing him back the city's songs, the children's cries, the lover's shouts, the mothers' lyric conversations, the office workers' low hum, the machines' fits and starts, the traffic of it all.

He weakened. Lost weight fast. Neglected his usual fastidious habits; wore the same shirt the whole day long. (Long days indeed – in the country, he discovered, when the sun goes down the people go to bed. Did they at least dream?, he wondered.)

She in her infinite wisdom and compassion, sent him, at the end of two weeks, home for the weekend, where, as Blake remarked upon his return from Lambeth, he was "back to display my giant forms again." He arrived, read his mail – stacks of letters to answer!, books to be ordered!, invitations to turn down and others to accept!, familiar and new restaurants to visit!, and friends!, friends to speak with, see, encounter, to know.

But first, he walked; and then, he called her. How, he wondered, could he love her in two places at one time? And, what did that mean in terms of the city? She as city, but city without her? He played tapes of her he'd made in the country; the birds responded, traffic stopped. Yes, it was her voice the city and he were one. And he visited her again and he came back and then she came back.

* * *

AUGUST

Bliss
Clyde's voice
Ada & Eve Café

−   That's pretty. Who wrote it?
−   Yours truly.
−   Did you experience it, too?
−   I wrote it, didn't I? ... Actually, I'm not sure.
−   ?
−   I mean, I imagine it to be a bliss – obviously I've experienced each separately – I seem to think I've experienced them together – but I couldn't give you – or myself – the full assurance.
−   We could always go there and see if they have his CDs.
−   Nah, that'd be forcing things. Anyway, it's better this way.
−   It's very nice. Needs a stronger "d" sound though, don't you think?.

- Elide, Clyde.
- Ah, yes. But I know what you mean.
- Always?
- Sometimes, usually, always.
- That's a lot of time – sounds like more than always if you add 'em up. Looks like I'd better catch up – start talking faster.
- This speed'll do.
- Should I slow down?
- No, no, your talk is wonderful, you know that, and I've told you often.
- But not always. But often is more than sometimes, so, ok. But what do you know what I mean?
- ??
- What you said a minute ago. What were you thinking of? Something made you think of something else.
- I don't know, can't remember. Anyway …
- Clyde!
- Oh, yes – thanks. It was that I know what you mean regarding not being sure whether you've been to a certain place before.
- You mean like déjà-vu?
- No, I mean like your poem.
- You called it a poem – thank you!
- Well, isn't it? What do you call it?
- I call it … now let me see … [holding it away from herself] … I call it … a pyramid! … So, do you think you've been to Barcelona or Monument Valley or the Sea of Tranquility – even though you've never been an astronaut, but maybe you think you have been – though maybe in fact you've never been there? Places seen in movies or photo books, "gee, I feel I know that place" sort of thing?
- Comeon, this isn't a movie.
- But I thought you said it was.
- Well, it is and it isn't.
- But it's like a movie?
- Well yeah, sure.
- Ok, it's like a movie. I mean this is, not your movie-like experiences.
- No – that wasn't my point at all. I didn't mean places like those, I meant places in Tokyo. Like you hearing Clyde in the café, or thinking you have.
- Oh!
- Me too, all the time.
- That's always, just like you said.

- ?
- That you know what I mean. But please, go on.
- ? Uh, ok. Did I really see *Blade Runner* on a rainy afternoon in Shinjuku? Did I really have a good conversation with what seemed like a very nice guy only to find out that he was a *yakuza* at the end – he even showed me part of his tattoo – and to even half-drunkenly remember later that he'd invited me to his home, and then when I never went, wonder if I'd done the right or the wrong thing? And did I really myself experience some sort of bliss in Rikugien and reading Dōgen?
- I don't know, did you?
- I don't know. But like you, I think I may have, I'm not sure, but it all seems rather appropriate regardless.
- Like a movie?
- Like a pyramid.
- You called it a poem – how sweet.

* * *

I'd lost my way entirely. In the middle of my life I was caught between two or three homes – I could have settled on the west coast, in Amsterdam or Paris – and yet I insisted on Tokyo. I was not strong enough. I'd found a home that would take me years to feel completely free in despite those early positive reckonings. The city was free – had no need of me – disburdening would have to begin with me – you have to learn almost everything all over again.

* * *

AUGUST

- We walk all the time, but we never *go* for a walk.
- What do you mean, we go for strolls, don't we, what's the difference?
- They're somehow not the same. We go for a stroll in the neighbor-hoods to get out of the house, to get some vegetables, to "observe the scene," "life's passing parade," and all that. No, going for a walk is different somehow.
- Why, how?
- Oh, on account of because of when you go for a walk … yes, there's a bit of exercise involved; no, there is no particular scene to be ob-served, or at least that is not one of the primary objectives; yes,

nature somehow is involved – the scene is the air, the sound of the cicadas, the cries of children not too nearby …. ah, I've got it – when walking, you don't observe the scene, you take it in! … I suppose too that time is involved. Let me see … strolling is Japanese, the garden and all that, you know, everything unfolding, like Mizoguchi. Walking is Western, ruminating … and then you expect people to break into dance like Fred and Cyd!

* * *

1457: OTA DOKAN

How do we picture him? Dressed in the silks of a court poet, the lacquered armor of the samurai? In the furs of a hunter? (As in the statue of him by Fumio Asakura, now in the Tokyo International Forum.) How did we ever come up with phrases like the "mists of time" and the "echoes of legend"? How did we ever come to think that someone can *found* a city?

People had long lived, of course, on the site of what would become Edo, and later Tokyo. Presumably, there they could fish, live a decent life away from the turmoils of the capitol, the many warring factions that became history and popular drama. That stuff arrived in the twelfth century when a member of the Taira clan settled his family there, renaming it after the site itself, "mouth of the river." That could also be considered a founding moment, all so literally so.

In 1457, Ota Dokan – (or Sukenaga), a "vassal of the Ogigayatsu branch of the Uesugi family, who served the Ashikaga …"; well, the reader perceives how complicated these things can get – built a castle in the town of Edo. The legend has it that Benten, goddess of music and islands, took the form of a fish (a *konoshiro*) and guided Ota to the site where he should build "this castle" (*kono shiro*). In a word, Tokyo was founded on a pun. And immediately it became Tokyo (in character, that is; the name change did not come about, of course, until the 19th century): Ota set to changing water courses, and moving things about – temples especially – east to west. (Though during his time, and even that of the Tokugawa, his west was more to our east. In this regard too, the end really is in the beginning, for it has been a part of this book's contention that the unpaved-over heart of Tokyo – commonly represented by the east, *shitamachi* – thrives today on the west side ((Ota's very far west)), the other side of the Yamanote, similarly downhill and yet still in the plain.)

Further, the facts are almost too good to be true. In a resolution of the Cervantian dilemma, Ota was both a warrior and a poet. The best legend is that of the *yamabuki*. Caught in a rainstorm, Edo's founder approaches a hut and asks the woman there for the loan of a straw raincoat. She returns with a yellow rose (*yamabuki*). Puzzled, he returns to his castle drenched. One of his attendants tells him what any properly bred noble would have immediately recognized: the woman was speaking in the allusive way of the court (and she a peasant too! – what a wonderful *ukiyo-e* the scene would make!); in this case she was referring to a Heian period poem:

> Sad indeed am I
> That I have not one straw raincoat
> Like the seven-petaled, eight-petaled
> Blossom of a yellow rose.

The warrior had received his comeuppance, and resolved to master the poetic arts too; which, apparently he did (though I have been unable to find any of his work).

Ota lived in his castle town for twenty-seven years. The end is all too believable. In an intra-familial conflict, he was assassinated at the command of his own master, after having been falsely accused of disloyalty (recall Sen no Rikkyu's fate). That part of his legacy thrives too today in Tokyo, a place he would not, of course, recognize. In fact, it would probably drive him mad.

* * *

AUGUST

- A double espresso, a story by Dash – you're the best.
- Oh my, choo-choo-ch-boogie.
- Whadda'ya' wanna do today? Revisit the scenes of our youth?
- *These* are the scenes of our youth.
- Invigorated?
- Re-re-re- –
- – turning to the question.
- Stay in? Flop?
- Flop?
- Stay in, do nothing ...
- [Gravely] "We do nothing," quoth the Professor. [End of gravity.]

I don't know. Shop? You said you need a new shirt. No, you always need a new shirt. [Gravely] "How many shirts does one man need?" [End of gravity.] Wear one of your old ones today, eh? That Yohji with the zigzagging stripes, I like that one best, I think.

- Really? Me too. I oughta confess, I bought two, anticipating the day –
- – the first would get too old to wear and you'd miss it so, right?
- Caught.
- Well, I'm glad of it, it wasn't a reckless moment.
- Ok, ok, you're fast.
- Run you around the block?
- More a trapezoid.
- Which one's that? What kind of angles and sides?
- I mean our "block" that isn't one. No, ours is more like a trapezoid.
- So, "I've been around the trapezoid"? No, that doesn't quite sound it.
- Back to the question.
- Ah, the day's itinerary. Well, obviously, we ought to have *zaru-soba* for lunch.
- Oh, I am crazy about you.
- And oh but you are crazy.
- Would you have me any other way? Ordinary?
- Smith. Early ROT. And so, yes, you are ordinary.
- Roberta!
- Oh but you are, Lang. I am too. It's an ordinary world.
- And Tokio's an ordinary city?
- You bet. That's why we're here. Crazy-ordinary, ordinary-crazy.
- Am I supposed to take that as a compliment?
- You'll take it no other way, Pal, and you'll like it.
- Ok, ok, you got me.
- Deed I do.
- What do we do today? Shall we at least get dressed?
- Nakedness is dressed.
- Nakedness is dressing.
- Nakedness is the full serving.
- Servicing?
- It's a term, but not ours. What did Kazuko say? "We're all lucky." If only Gertrud had thought so.
- In the end, I think she did.
- Ya' know, Carole did admit that Irene Bullock is tragic in a way, didn't she? So maybe Carl Theodor is a humorist in some weird – tarpezoidal – way. Maybe.

- Maybe. Are there any films on?
- In this burg? Maybe. ... No, don't get dressed just yet. It's a beautiful day – let's linger.
- "Linger." You've changed. A year or more ago I'd have had to fight to keep you in bed, indoors, doing nothing.
- People change. You have too. A year or more ago you'd already be out – wandering, doing all that stuff you used to do – you know, drinking with VZ and changing the world, sizing it up to your size, all that be modern or be a wallflower stuff ... And me? Yes, I can stay in bed if I want. Home gets closer and closer. Even in Tokyo.
- Serenity?
- Oh, I don't know that I'd call it that. But I'd call it something.
- Call it you.
- You call it.
- Roberta.
- Lang.
-
-
- Let's go out?
- Where? It's a big city.
- Oh, it's not so big.

    [Sounds of kissing, dressing, kissing, door closing, kissing. View of the city.]

* * *

    Weary blues, Kazuko thinks to herself, recalling a song she'd once heard Lang singing to himself. Flophouses, cheap *saké*, weary friendly faces. Why aren't they more hostile, she thought as she gazed at the men and women in Sanya, where she'd come with a friend who wanted to show her a part of Tokyo she'd been missing. They'd made her feel welcome, she did not feel herself the Kyoto lady here, but a part of something more, a part of their scene even here ... and the larger scene that was Tokyo and all of her and their lives in it. She was leaving Kyoto – oh not completely, not forever, it was home, but now and forever, Tokyo would be home too.

- Kazuko?
- Oh, sorry, I was thinking about some friends. Is it time to go, what time is it?

* * *

AUGUST

– Here, look at this.

S
u
n
s
e
t
!

!
e
s
i
r
n
u
S

– Shouldn't they be side by side? Your phallo-vaginal exclamation?
– Hmm, maybe you're right. How about this:

sunr
eyes

– A new kanji maybe.
– Maybe.

[Much later.]

– Amazing.
– What is?
– Oh, that you're still the same –
– but different, and –
– I'm different, but –

- the same.
- Talking in circles? No, spirals from now on. Dizzying –
- – Dazzying. Daffy –
- – Dames. The he and the she of we.
- Grand times.
- Splendors and miseries. But all grand.

[Sound of cicadas, crows.]

- Tofu seller? Knife sharpener?
- Before our time, Lang. You've been reading too much, it's gotten to you.
- You've gotten to me. Never thought I'd like your old city so well. So, is this going to be an American happy ending?
- Oh, you Euros – just because we like one maybe too often enough doesn't mean we believe in 'em. And besides, you could use one. They don't all have to be so somber. Old, suffering world. It's a young and sweet one, too.
- You're probably right. – Ok, you are. But do you really think one can walk and talk too much, or that I do?
- Sometimes – sometimes I think so, that is. That is, if it's at the neglect of … oh, of … of the … oh, you know – everything else, the mix, the hoopla … the craziness at our doorstep, at our bedstep …
- At the all of it.
- At the all of it. Dizzying, spiralling. You know, I never thought I'd come to like your side of the city too – or either. I see your point. … We change sides – same but different. Maybe America's an old world by now too. Maybe. But the new one's here, now, you and me.
- "You and me" – isn't that a clothing line? Or a café? Or a stationery company?
- Or a canned drink, or a magazine? – Or a couple even? You know, I've even picked up one of your habits. I've made a checklist of all the temples in the area – and believe me, there are plenty.
- I've noticed.
- And anyway, I'm trying to visit them all. Some Zen ones, too. Maybe you'd want to do some sitting with me some time. What do you think?
- Sure, I think so. But can couples sit together?
- We wouldn't "sit together." I'm sure there are no rules against it. No, you just sit. Turn off, everything. The all of it. Or try to. And then

the gong clangs. Bang! Back in the world. Old and new, same but for a moment very different. Sitting, that stillness is also dizzying.

- I'm in.
- I thought you would be, I'm glad. So, anyway, what do you think? Want to visit a temple with me?
- Now?
- Why not?
- Yes.

[They kiss.]

[They kiss again.]

- August. August in Japan. What a time.
- August in – as you say it – Tokio.
- There oughta be a song.
- "August in Tokyo" – hmm, the title doesn't really ring. What's it like in Japanese? "*Hachigatsu Tokyo*"? "*Tokyo Hachigatsu*"? Hmm … "August in Japan"
- No, Tokio only.
- We met in August, remember?
- And you left in August.
- You didn't have a plane ticket, remember?
- Negligent of me.
- Right.
- I know – "August, Tokyo" – like a date, a time and place.
- It opens with cicadas …
- No, that's the happy sound.
- Cicadas are happy?
- I'm not sure. But all that energy –
- Beating their wings to death?
- Ok, ok, but they are August. And yes, energy.
- Ok. So what then, at the beginning?
- Crows. "Caw-caw!" It starts out somber –
- – and ends with the cicadas, wistful –
- – filled with promise. The heat burns into you, everything comes out, you just spill, drip –
- – this song's getting a bit too graphic.
- No, you know what I mean.
- I know – I'm joking – I think.
- You know: the Sun! Even in the city, there's only the Sun! You have

to confront something elemental. It seems to attack, but then you realize it's actually life-giving, invigorating. You're down to essentials – and you love it. Memory, the body – the heat is on you.

– It's getting on me. Come here a minute.

[They kiss.]

– Ok, so we have a sad beginning with crows, and at the end a sort of happy ending with cicadas – but are crows seasonal? And once the cicadas fade do we head into cold and darkness?
– No, no, we head into you and me: the heat, both of them, then the cool of Autumn; followed by Winter in Tokio – another great song we ought to write – you were the first to tell me how beautiful Winter is here
– Our "Winter's Tale" – reborn.
– Yes. We'll write that song too. "A Winter's Tokio Tale." But first, "August."
– Well, we have the sound effects for the beginning and end. What about the middle?
– Didn't Buster say that the middle always took care of itself?
– So, we're the middle?
– We're the lyrics. You're my middle.
– And you're my –
– Let me get some paper – where's the next temple?
– ?
– Let's go. We can write the lyrics as we go along.
– Tempura too?
– All of it. Looks like we've got work to do.
– This sounds like fun!
– Rhymes with –

CPSIA information can be obtained
at www.ICGtesting.com
Printed in the USA
LVOW12s1952090916

503916LV00001BA/1/P